WINTER

DANCE

KEVIN KINCHELOE

Printed in the United States of America
Library of Congress Control Number 2016941112

ISBN: 978-1-944887-05-6
eISBN: 978-1-944887-04-9

Present Day *1*
1928 .... *13*
1929 .... *21*
Thomas *81*
1930 .... *250*
1933 .... *362*

I n a forgotten little corner of Seattle is a forgotten little marina
where neglected, forgotten boats molder silently in the still
water. The city bustles all around it. Sparks fly from boatyard
welders and grinders, hammers ring on steel hulls, trucks hurry
around potholes on dusty gravel roads leading to lumberyards and
warehouses. Tugboats and fishing boats churn the water as they pass.
But all is quiet at the little marina, untouched by the pace of the city.
In the shadow of an ancient apple tree, a rusty old crane once used
for haul outs, with broken windows and flat tires, sinks slowly into the
soft ground at the sandy shoreline, dark with spilled diesel and motor
oil. Listing finger docks, with waterlogged floats and uneven planks
beaten by the sun and rain, sag low in the water like the weary boats
moored to them. Lost boats that haven't moved in decades, except to
break their mooring lines and slip silently beneath the water, like the
old Chris-Craft that sank at the dock so many years ago and rests on
the muddy bottom.

There is a rustic charm in the neglect and abandon. An inviting
allure that calls for a closer, more intimate look at the forsaken
vessels rocking gently at the crumbling dock in the wake of passing
boats.

She sat on the sandy beach at the edge of the water all afternoon,
watching the old boats and glancing toward the marina office. It
appeared to be the shack at the end of the dock, but no one knew for
sure. A plastic sign leaning in the windowsill, bent and curled by
years under the summer sun, may have once displayed the marina
name and business hours, but any such message was long since
faded away. No one really knew if it was the marina office or not, but
through the dirty window a desk chair could be seen in the broken
sunlight that streamed through the dusty blinds. And in the corner was
an old desk nearly buried under a pile of paperwork that fell from it
onto the floor. Like everything else there, it looked abandoned.

Nina Van Orton was a beautiful woman, something over forty
years of age, with a unique grace and elegance that was natural

to her. She sat on the sandy beach with her slender arms upon her bent knees and her chin on her hands, patiently looking out over the marina. Ever so often she would glance at her watch, and her eyes would drift again to the office shack. Her long black hair spilled out beneath the straw hat shielding her lovely face from the spring sun. Her gray eyes looked tired, not with the fatigue of a day, but with the weary grief of a precious loss. There was a gentleness about her, a self-possessed calm in the wake of some tragedy.

In the distraction of her pensive thoughts the afternoon wore away without notice. The activity that was present earlier was diminishing; the welding was reduced to occasional flashing sparks, the hammering became a faint intermittent thud, the trucks, too weary to go around the potholes, crawled through them with a bounce and a rattle.

But the slumbering pace was disturbed by the squeak and rumble of an old pickup truck that grew gradually louder as it approached. It lumbered over the decommissioned train tracks that ran through the marina, turned sharply in the gravel, and rocked to a stop near the old crane. A little cloud of smoke and dust washed around it and drifted up into the March sunset, visible through the sailboat masts and spreaders. The throaty, rumbling engine was shut off. A rusty door groaned in protest as it was pushed open, and out lumbered a man looking like he bore as many miles as the truck. The door squeaked each time he slammed it shut, until it finally latched. Slowly, deliberately, with the unhurried pace of long experience, he walked to the back of the vehicle, opened the battered tailgate, and reached into the bed of the truck. He was a big man, several inches over six feet, with a bushy red beard that offered little contrast to his half-century-old sunburned face, and a braided ponytail that fell nearly to his waist. His flannel shirt was stretched tight across his barrel chest. His coveralls were stained by white paint and red lead, and his heavy work boots were well worn.

The chainsaw looked like a toy in his giant hand. At the sight of it a shudder ran through the wooden boats there, like a ripple on a still pond. A gentle breeze blew through the marina at that moment carrying a chill that seemed oddly out of place in the warm evening air, and a whispered dread traveled among the old boats gathered on the still water. He set the saw on the tailgate, took a bandanna from his pocket, tied it around his head with practiced ease, and stood

*stroking his red beard with a meditative frown as his eyes traveled
over the yacht resting in a wooden cradle beside him. Emily C was
the name on her transom. How beautiful she must have been in her
day, but that day was long ago, seventy or eighty years ago. Time had
etched its caustic passage on her lovely prow and little by little stolen
her self-esteem. Her white paint flaking off in the summer sun, littered
the ground beneath her. Long, slender gaps in her hull revealed
where rotting planks had been removed from the decaying frames that
once secured them. But worst of all the stem was soft with dry rot, a
terminal condition for any wooden boat.*

*The man reached into his pocket for a round, slender file, and
sitting on the tailgate of the old truck, applied the file to the blade,
methodically sharpening the teeth of the chainsaw like an executioner
preparing his ax. Death has a way of bringing us closer to ourselves.
Of making us better people. Of closing old wounds, resentments,
grievances, harbored so long in our unforgiving heart. The chill
impartiality of death that whispers or shouts to us all in our turn is a
sobering reminder of mortality. It was death that brought Nina to the
marina, and death that she was about to witness.*

*Hearing the stuttering cough of the chainsaw, she turned. The big
man stood beside the boat, sputtering saw in hand, determining where
to make his incision. She looked away. She had to look away. But as
the snarling echo of the saw carried over the marina, she found that
she must look again and turned back with a grimace.*

*The blade cut deep, and the weary old girl yielded with a dismal
shudder that shook her in the cradle. She seemed almost to welcome
the destructive bite of the chainsaw that would finally end her
pain and save her from further suffering and loneliness. With the
mechanical indifference of cold steel the ripping teeth tore into the
belly of Emily C disemboweling her before the eyes of any who cared
to look, even as the setting sun shined blood red upon her splintered
injury. With her bilge torn open, her wound bled onto the gravel
below. She heaved a melancholy sigh, trembled in the throws of death,
and was still.*

*Nina could bear no more and turned away with the angry
buzz of the saw ringing in her ears. Wishing to be away from the
unpleasantness behind her, she stood and began walking along
the shore of the lake distractedly, watching the boats there rocking
timorously at the crumbling pier. The marina, she mused, was like a*

*care home where one goes to die. Discarded, forsaken, spirit broken,
they wait quietly to pass away, cherishing any visitor, any attention
they may receive in their final days.*

*An impulsive affection for the aged boats drew her to the dock.
The cooler evening air, the sunset on the horizon, the gentle ripple
of the breeze over the lake, all seemed to sympathize with her and
encourage her. She walked along the crooked, uneven planks with
curiosity and interest, growing more intrigued and enamored with
each derelict vessel she happened upon. Poor* Emily C. *Who would be
next, she wondered? The whine of the chainsaw filled the evening air
as it performed its merciful execution.*

*And in the quiet moments before dusk, as the blazing star began
her descent behind the tallest buildings on the orange skyline, and
the waxing moon revealed herself in the darkening sky, she saw the
shadow of a sailboat mast and spreader appear as a cross on a boat
further up the dock. It caught her eye in a mysterious way and coaxed
her along. Drawing closer, she saw an elegantly shaped stern. On
the gray planking of the transom where the letters had long ago worn
away under the harsh sun was the less faded wood once covered by
her name,* Mary Adda. *There was an indefinable uniqueness about
her. Even there, surrounded by festering vessels on all sides that were
dying slow, cancerous deaths, her level of decay was astonishing.
Her grimy waterline was green with slime where the water lapped at
it. Her 1920s vintage hull bled rust from her rotting fasteners. Any
semblance of varnish had long ago vanished, and the wood it once
covered was bare and gray, cracked and dry. An overworked bilge
pump ran almost constantly, pumping a steady stream of dark lake
water from her hull. Nina wondered if stepping aboard might not send
her to the bottom.*

*But there was an unmistakable magic about her. She had poise.
Charm. Allure. There was a proud dignity in the rise of her plum bow.
A majesty in the gentle curve of her hull. Even in her decaying neglect
she was the loveliest thing Nina had ever seen, perhaps even because
of her neglect and decay. Something so proud and noble suffering
such a fate appealed to her gentle, nurturing nature. And there was
the cross, that shadow of a cross that fell upon the withered canvas
deck like the guiding beam of a lighthouse, and drew her to* Mary
Adda.

Footsteps on the dock drew her eye, and she turned to find a man approaching from the shore. He was tall and fit, about her age, wearing threadbare jeans and a gray tee shirt. One hand was in his pants pocket. The other held a leather jacket that was thrown over his shoulder. When he reached Mary Adda he stopped casually, as if reaching his destination, and ran an appreciative eye over the old yacht.

"Quite handsome, isn't she?" he said.

"She's beautiful," Nina replied, in her lovely way. "I was just admiring her."

"I've admired her for quite some time," he answered. "She's a Vic Franck, you know."

"Oh?" she said, intrigued by the man for reasons she couldn't explain. He was handsome, but it was much more than that. It was his quiet confidence, or the way he carried himself. She wasn't sure.

"You can tell by the ports. See how each portlight is smaller as you move forward. It's a Vic Franck trademark."

"I see," she answered. "How old is she?" she asked, then placed a hand on her chin as if in thought. "Or is it considered bad taste to inquire about a lady's age?"

"I don't think she would mind," he said, with a gentle smile. "She's over eighty years old. 1928 vintage."

"So elegant. They don't build them like this anymore."

"No," he said, unable to restrain a sigh, "they build them like that now." And his eyes traveled over the marina where dozens of white-hulled fiberglass boats huddled generically. Nina checked her watch again.

"Do you know the business hours for the office? I've been here all day and haven't seen anyone."

"Are you looking for moorage?"

"I came to see about a boat."

"Buying a boat?"

"No. I inherited one."

"What's her name?"

"I don't know. I was hoping to talk to someone at the marina so I could find out which boat was my father's."

"Good luck. I was told that Mike only comes down a few times each week to grab the mail and see if any more boats have sunk. I've been trying to catch him for weeks so I could find out who owns this *old girl. I'd like to buy her before she sinks, which I expect to be any day now."*

"Oh," she said, "I assumed you were together."

"I do like the older ladies," he replied, smiling, "but I don't have a date with this girl, yet."

"Are there others?" she inquired, curiously. "Other ladies?"

"Three more."

"You sound like quite a playboy," she jested.

"I saved them all from the bite of the chainsaw," he explained. "They were all going to be cut up and thrown away like Emily*, there." He gestured to the dismembered remains of* Emily C, *where the man was still working his chainsaw.*

"Really?" she asked, frowning. "It happens that often?"

"All too often."

"Too bad. These old vessels have so much charm and character," she said, and checked her watch. "I may as well go. It was nice meeting you," she said, and began back along the haggard dock.

"Excuse me," he ventured, after a moment of consideration, and Nina turned. "I've been exploring other ways to locate the owner of Mary Adda. *There's an envelope on the table inside that I can't quite make out. Perhaps your eyes are sharper than mine. It's difficult to catch anyone around here."*

"I don't know that I'll be much help," she said, returning.

"You can just see it through the gap in the curtains right here," he said, indicating a little opening behind the glass. "It's pretty faded, but you can see part of an address and some of the name."

She removed her hat, cupped her tanned hands to shade the setting sun from her face, and pressed them to the glass. A large diamond on her finger caught his eye.

"I see it," she said. "The first name is too faded, but the rest..." She turned her head slightly to see better. "Looks like...it looks like...O'Leary." She pulled back suddenly, surprised, looking Mary Adda *over closely. "O'Leary," she repeated, and her face wore a puzzled frown as she continued studying the boat. "It can't be."*

"What?" he asked, puzzled by her wondering look. "What is it? Do you know the owner?"

"I..." she hesitated, scrutinizing Mary Adda *carefully, "I believe I may be the owner."*

"This is your boat?"

"I don't know. The name on the envelope is my father," she said. Her shear summer dress rustled in the light breeze that whisked over the dock. She ran her long, delicate fingers through her hair.

"I haven't seen the boat since I was a child."

Her hand traveled tenderly over the bare, dry wood. Then, struck with a thought, she reached into her handbag and held up a handful of keys.

"There's one way to know for sure. I grabbed all of the keys in the house that I couldn't identify."

She began trying them one by one in the wheelhouse door. When she reached the third one, it slipped perfectly into the lock. She turned to the man expectantly, breathlessly, and then gave it a turn. The door swung open invitingly, welcoming her aboard. The hesitation was clear on her reluctant face, but after a moment of reflection she took a deep breath and stepped aboard Mary Adda.

Nina stepped from fresh air and fading sunlight to stale, stagnant air as old as the boat and a muted sunset that streamed in through the grimy windows and squeezed through the little gaps in the sun bleached curtains. It smelled strongly of wood. Oiled wood. Old wood. Decaying wood. Remarkably, it looked just as it did when it was launched all those years ago. The bronze bulkhead lamps on each side were original, aged to a beautiful patina. The bronze engine controls and compass, too. Navigation charts, rolled up and stored on slats under the wheelhouse roof, were yellowed by the sun, and their navigational warnings faded away. But more intriguing was the monogrammed hatbox on the helm. It was round, leather, with a brass lock and the monogrammed letters SM near the handle. A little key was in the lock and turned easily in her hand. Opening the lid, she found the case was lined in silk and contained a fashionable woman's hat of 1930s vintage.

The setting sun loitered briefly on the horizon as if reluctant to surrender, then dipped below the broken skyline at last. As if mixed on an artist's palate, a lingering glow of purple-orange filled the night sky and bathed Mary Adda *in a rich, colorful light.*

Slow minutes ticked away. The wheelhouse doors were still open. The boat was quiet and still. The man, who was waiting on the dock for Nina, gave a little rap at the door to announce his presence and then stepped aboard. She was sitting at the galley table when he entered the salon. One hand held the envelope before her distressed eyes; the other wiped them distractedly. At the sound of his entrance, she quickly composed herself.

"Hello again," she said, pleasantly. "I should have asked you aboard. I'm sorry."

"Would you like some privacy?" he asked, observing her condition. "We can talk another time if you prefer."

"No, you're welcome to join me. I wanted to thank you anyway. If not for you I might never have found Grandfather's yacht."

"I was serving my own interest there."

"Have a seat," she said. "I'm Nina."

"An unusual name."

"My mother was American Indian. It's an Indian name."

"And your father?"

"Irish."

He took a seat across from her at the galley table. The lingering sunset poured in through the little portlights, bathing the salon in warm, soft color. He found himself staring, drawn to her gray eyes and striking features. Nina absently fingered the diamond on her finger.

"And you are?" she asked.

"Lauren."

"First name or last?"

"Yes."

"I see," she replied, intrigued by his vague answer. "Would you like something to drink?"

"Thank you, yes."

"I noticed a bottle of Port in the cabinet beside you."

He opened the leaded glass door, grabbed the bottle inside, and glanced at the label as an afterthought. Suddenly intrigued, he held it to the lamplight and studied it closely.

"This is a Quinta do Noval," he said, reverently, "of 1921 vintage. Do you know how rare this is?"

"There's probably a corkscrew in the top drawer," she replied.

Smiling eagerly, he opened the bottle, which yielded the cork without a sound.

Also in the cabinet were ornate wine glasses with silver trim woven into the glass, but they were coated in a thick layer of dust.

"Excuse me," he said, with the glasses in hand, "I refuse to tarnish this experience with a dirty glass. I'll just give these a quick

wash." And he left the boat. A few minutes later he returned, and the glasses were sparkling. "Now then," he said excitedly, and gave them both a generous pour. "To Mary Adda," and their glasses met over the galley table.

"To Mary Adda," she repeated, and they drank. Nina's face was expressionless with the first taste. Her eyes met his as he was in the act of taking a sip. A wry smile formed on her perfect lips, and she delicately spit the wine back into her glass. "Oh God," she said.

"It's awful," he added, spitting his wine into the glass as well, and they both laughed.

"It must be heat damaged," she replied.

"The cork was bone dry, too. Probably been stored upright the entire time."

"I wonder what else there is to drink?"

"She was probably an old rum runner. I bet there are hidden little spaces all over this old girl where one could squirrel away a bottle or two," he said. "There may even be a bottle here." And he knelt down next to the bilge cover, lifted it up, and smiled. "This is where most boat people store wine. It's always dark and cool in the bilge." He held up two bottles of Quinta do Noval. "May I?"

"Of course."

A fresh glass was poured for each. Once again their glasses touched over the table. They drank, tentatively. Nina closed her eyes, savoring the precious sip. She had one leg folded under her and her other foot was on the floor. Her shoes were on the dock, and her high arching, tanned feet were elegant and perfect, like the rest of her.

Darkness fell quickly over the old, ailing marina. A few of the overhead lights illuminating the dock still worked, but most were burned out or flickered intermittently. The wind began to build and the boats rocked gently in their slips. Dark lake water lapped at the finger docks. Rubber fenders squeaked as boats rocked against them. Loose halyards slapped upon aluminum masts with a clatter.

Nina poured another glass from the half-empty bottle and studied the man across from her. There was something about him. Something she couldn't define. Something mysterious and intriguing. Was it the way he carried himself with a quiet, self-assured confidence? In spite of his worn jeans and old tee shirt, she imagined him having good taste in all things.

"Thank you," he said, taking another sip of port. "Someone

somewhere in the history of Mary Adda *has very, very good taste."*

"*I expect it was Grandfather. I doubt that Father ever set foot on* Mary. *He wasn't interested in boats." she said, and took another sip as well.*

"So Nina, shall we talk about Mary Adda*?"*

"I can't sell her," she said. "I'm sorry to disappoint you, but I can't sell her."

"What choice do you have?" he asked, meeting her eyes across the galley table. "The bilge pump is barely keeping up with the water now. One little storm and her seams will open up. She'll be on the bottom of the lake in minutes."

"I could have her restored."

"Do you have any idea what the expense would be?"

"I can't sell her Mr. Lauren. Mary Adda *was a gift to my grandfather. She was a thank you for a favor he did for someone when he was young. I don't know what it was. But he cherished this boat above everything he had. He made my father promise that he would never sell her and that she would always remain in the family."*

"I respect that," he said, grudgingly. "Too many people in the world today have no respect. It's refreshing to meet someone who honors their word." He swirled the port in his glass, and finished it in a gulp. "Even if it is at my expense," he added, and set the glass upon the table. "Thank you for the Quinta do Noval. It was a rare treat. So was meeting you." His eyes lingered on Nina ever so briefly. He ran a hand over the intricate woodwork of the galley table as if saying good-bye to Mary Adda, *and turned to go.*

"What would it take, Mr. Lauren?" Nina asked. "What would it take to restore her?"

"More time and money than anyone will give her."

"Except you?"

"It's not work to me. I enjoy it."

"Would you consider…"

"No," he said, interrupting her, "I wouldn't. There are two shops in Seattle that can do the work. It'll be a bit generic, but the craftsmanship will be good. Too bad," he added, as he ran an eye over the once beautiful woodwork, "she deserves better."

"Generic?" She inquired.

"My theory is that every Boatwright in town went to the same school." He explained. "Their work all looks the same."

"And yours?" She asked. "What does your work look like?"

He smiled with a confidence that bordered on arrogance, and stepped to the door. "I've always been very fond of my grandfather, Mr. Lauren," she said, with a sincerity that caught his ear and gave him pause. "He was a fine man. I need to know that his faith in me was not misplaced. I need to know that grandfather's yacht will not receive a generic restoration."

"His faith in you, did you say?"

"He had to leave Mary to my father. I was only a child when he passed away. But he knew Father had no interest in boats, and he asked that I take good care of her when she became mine."

Lauren threw a last look at Mary Adda in the dim lamplight, then ran a quick eye over Nina. They were both beautiful, he reflected, but one he could own, and one, he knew, he would never possess. Without a word stepped off the boat and into the night.

It was so quiet now that she was alone, but she was accustomed to that. The gusting little wind that blew over the water and lapped musically at the wooden hull provided a comforting cadence in the still night. She picked casually among the things there, going through drawers and cabinets by the dim light of the bulkhead lamps that hadn't been used in decades. Nothing there belonged to her father. The silverware in the drawer was actual silver from the 1930s. So were the serving trays and the teapot. The china in the cabinet, too, was from that time. There was even a seventy year old newspaper on the galley table with a story about Bonnie and Clyde, killed in an ambush. A thick layer of dust covered everything and clung to the tattered, long abandoned cobwebs that fluttered lightly with the breeze gusting through the open seams in the planks. It reminded her of Satis House. She half expected to find a gnawed wedding cake and a wizened Miss Havisham peering at her from the shadows.

Mary Adda rocked with the storm. Her fenders squeaked, her mooring lines jerked tight as the boat rolled away from the dock, the wind whistled in her rigging, but it was a tame storm and contributed to the charm of the old boat so rich in history.

Nina took a sip of port, and her eyes drifted to the bottle on the galley table. What a unique man, she reflected, to recognize the quality of a Quinta do Noval. He must have had a curious past. She imagined him riding a motorcycle and living a rebellious life

*of freedom and solitude. She was thinking about him when she took
another sip of port and, holding the glass in her hand, browsed
among the books on the shelf. They were mostly classic literature,
leather bound, with gold leaf. She trailed her slender finger over the
titles there, coming upon one that read* Mary Adda. *Intrigued, she set
down her glass, picked up the book, and wiped the dust of many years
from its faded cover. The pages were crisp and brittle. The spine was
broken. As she thumbed through, she noticed dated entries made in
a precise flowing manner, as if by the delicate hand of a woman. The
pages were often stained and water damaged, and in some places the
ink had run and blurred, but it appeared legible for the most part.
Was it a journal? A diary? Curious what she might find, she held it to
the lamp and began to read.*

June 11th 1928

I'm so delighted. *Mary Adda* was launched today, among
much fanfare and anticipation. The launch was delayed several
days by Mr. Franck, who wanted the first Sea Queen to be perfect,
and perfect she is. I have never seen a more beautiful vessel. But
I suspect the delay was motivated by more than Mr. Franck's
meticulous nature. By postponing the launch, everyone was so
curious and excited that anticipation has reached a fevered pitch.
Reporters from every newspaper in town were present to interview
Mr. Franck and photograph *Mary* as she slid down the ways into the
water. She made quite a splash. Charles and I are so happy.

Lorelei Dearborn

June 12th 1928

Now that *Mary* is launched we finally have the opportunity
to outfit her, but I find that she has already been so. China, silver,
napkins, hand towels, even bar soap. She is complete in every detail
and even has this beautiful boat journal to document her voyages,
all provided by Mr. Franck. He is quite the gentleman. One thing I
must speak to him about, however, is his inclusion of shot glasses
and decanter. Prohibition is in full swing, and I look forward to this

country at last becoming the Christian nation that it was intended
to be so long ago. We shall be an example to all other nations,
and Seattle has gone a step further toward that goal. We also have
smoking and gambling prohibitions.

Lorelei Dearborn

*Nina skipped ahead, thumbing through the pages of the journal,
skimming over them randomly until something caught her eye.*

…They walked quickly, with purpose, right for us through the
fog that came nearly to their knees. Then the moon slipped behind
the clouds once more, and all was dark. I was too frightened to
speak. I dropped a hand on my husband's arm and tried to mouth a
warning, but nothing came out. He sensed my fear and followed my
stare out the back window but saw nothing in the darkness.
"What is it Lorelei? What's wrong?"

*Her attention was riveted to the page. She wished to continue,
but things were out of context. Who were these men? What were they
doing? Why was Lorelei frightened of them? Curious what she might
find, she returned to the first page and began again where she left off.*

June 16th 1928

I wish I could avoid reading the newspaper, but I am so
hungry for news of our city and nation. Is prohibition working?
Are we becoming better people? It seems it is having the opposite
effect. Crime is on the rise, and stills are cropping up all over the
city. Can't people see it is in their best interest to just stop? Stop
drinking. Stop gambling. Stop smoking. Are they so attached to
their vices?

Lorelei Dearborn

June 24th 1928

Charles and I were driving home from church when I was struck with an idea. Pastor Lomax said that to those who have been given much, much shall be required. We have so much, Charles and I, and we're not doing enough. I asked him if we might not loan *Mary Adda* to the police. They are so understaffed and in need of vessels to patrol the waters of Lake Union and Puget Sound, where rum runners constantly smuggle alcohol into the city from Canada. *Mary Adda* could be a real asset to them. Charles said he would think about it. He is a good man; I know he'll make the right decision.

PS: Amelia Earhart has become the first woman to fly cross the Atlantic. We're all so proud of her.

Lorelei Dearborn

June 28th 1928

I so enjoy coming down to *Mary Adda* and writing in the peace and solitude of this lovely vessel as she rocks gently at the dock. And today I have good news. Charles has agreed to allow the police use of our boat if it will help stem the tide of illegal alcohol entering our city. He was even excited about it. They may use it half-time, he said. We will still have use of it as well. Hooray.

Lorelei Dearborn

July 7th 1928

Melancholy. It's quiet and still on the boat tonight. The city lights are beautiful, reflected on the dark water, but I am pensive. It's silly, really. I have so much to be thankful for, but I needed to get away from Charles for a while, to be alone with my thoughts, and this is the best place for that…I think. Maybe not. I don't know. He could see that I was upset, and kept pressing me to tell him what was wrong, but I could not. How could I? It's *Mary Adda*, you see. Even as I sit here writing by the faint light of the candle, I see him looking at her so adoringly and my heart hurts. I'm not making any sense I know. My thoughts are all a jumble.

It was like this. Charles loves hot chocolate before bed, so I decided to surprise him with some. I made two cups and then went in search of my husband. That he would be in the library I knew; he was always in the library at that hour reading a favorite book, or napping with a newspaper open on his lap. I made my way across the floor to the staircase that led to the library above, but as I passed the corridor leading to the west side of the house, I saw a light at the far end of the dark hallway. The study is in that direction, though he seldom uses it, and the light spilled into the hallway from the study door. Still thinking to surprise him, I carried the hot chocolate quietly along the hallway and came silently to the study door, open ever so slightly. Charles was sitting at his desk. It's across the room on the opposite wall, and he sat at it facing me, his head down slightly, looking at something in his hand by the light of the desk lamp. I nearly went inside, but something held me back. I paused just outside the door watching through the little opening. For several minutes he studied the object in his hand. There was nothing secretive or clandestine in his actions, yet I felt somehow that I was spying or invading his privacy. I was turning to go when he raised it to his lips, gave it a long, tender kiss, and solemnly returned it to the center drawer of his desk. Silently, I retreated back down the hallway and returned to the kitchen. Charles joined me there a short time later. We drank our hot chocolate and talked until late into the night.

I thought no more about the incident until today when I was looking for the letter opener, which he sometimes keeps on his desk. It wasn't there, however, and when I opened the center drawer in search of it, I found something else instead, something that took my breath away like a punch to the stomach. Everything in the drawer was tossed about haphazardly, randomly, without thought or intention, except for a photograph that was carefully placed exactly in the center, with nothing else near it, as if occupying a place of respect and reverence. I had never seen her before, but I recognized her at once. She was beautiful—tall and thin, with long dark hair that fell playfully about her twenty-year-old face, and dark eyes that sparkled timidly. Her head was down slightly, and she looked bashful, embarrassed almost, to be the subject of a photograph. As if she were unworthy of such attention. As if she weren't pretty enough. But she was pretty. She was beautiful. With a demur beauty I had never seen before. And her shyness only added to her natural charm and beauty.

Charles met her one fall day when he was hurrying along the rainy, windblown street, trying to reach his car before he was soaked by the downpour. But as he passed the flower shop on the corner, something caught his eye and he stopped, staring through the window at the girl who was working inside. The wind blew his hat off into the gutter. The rain pelted him unmercifully. But he remained on the sidewalk, looking through the window, oblivious to the storm, until the girl within finally took notice of him. A quick courtship followed, filled with play, and passion, and laughter, and four months later they were engaged. She was French, from the wine country, and each year would return to her family's winery to help with the crush and visit her parents. The last time she went, she had exciting news for them: news of her engagement and approaching marriage. Charles told me the story when we were engaged. He wanted no secrets, he said.

He had gone to New York to meet his fiancée when she returned from France. Her absence was more than he could endure, and he impatiently awaited her return with eagerness and anticipation. Buying fresh flowers that day, he was the first on the dock, waiting to meet the ship when it steamed into port. Throughout the day others arrived, too, to meet their loved ones who had booked passage on the *Valliant* and crossed the Atlantic to America. A sizable crowd had assembled on the pier by afternoon and all eyes peered eagerly across the gray water, looking for a sign of the ship. But no sign came. It was a long passage across the Atlantic, however, and ships were often delayed, so the disappointed crowd simply dispersed at dusk and returned the next day. They were assembled the following morning on the pier, sitting on suitcases, leaning up against pilings, talking together, when a message arrived from the steamship company. It was read aloud to everyone there. The *Valliant* had capsized in a storm, it said, and all hands were lost.

Charles said he wandered around New York City all afternoon in a daze, then stumbled aboard a train and returned to Seattle. He had forgotten all about his luggage until it arrived on his doorstep, compliments of his hotel, later in the week. Five years later, when we were married, he had this yacht built for me as a wedding present. When he was trying to decide on a name for her, I suggested *Mary Adda*, the name of his first love who perished at sea. Charles is a tall man, athletic and handsome, a rough and tumble rugby player who is always smiling after a match, regardless of the beating he may have taken. But when I named the yacht, he took my hand in his, pressed it to his lips, and looked me directly in the eye with a tear in his bold, gentle eyes.

Was I a fool? Was it kindness, or foolishness, that drove me to name the vessel as I did? I had no idea that he loved her so still, or that she occupied such a special place in his heart. When I saw him last night…it's almost as if he sneaked off to his study to be alone with her. When I think now of how he raised her photograph to his lips, and kissed her so tenderly, my heart breaks. How can I compete with a memory? A beautiful, sad, untarnished memory?

Lorelei Dearborn

August 21st 1928

The police have been using the boat for a few weeks now. They have it one week, and we have it the next. I hope it helps, but people seem determined to entertain their vices. Doctors are even writing prescriptions for alcohol now. Incredibly, it's legal with a doctor's prescription. And now organized crime is involved. This whole thing is getting out of control.

PS: I'm better now. I suppose I overreacted before. Charles is always so kind and loving to me that I can never be cross with him for long. He has a silly, boyish smile that disarms me in an instant, no matter how I wish to be angry with him, and lifts me out of my melancholy.

Lorelei Dearborn

September 5th 1928

Charles has left in *Mary Adda* and is riding along with the
police as they patrol the lake. He thought it would be interesting
to see how they work, so I decided to attend a party at the mayor's
house rather than stay home alone. No sooner had I arrived than
I discovered Bertha was serving alcohol. Alcohol! The mayor! I
couldn't believe my eyes. The chief of police was there, and several
circuit court judges as well. All were laughing and drinking as if
it were Mardi Gras. How can we hope to succeed with prohibition
when even our leaders won't participate? I was preparing to leave
when I noticed a sizable crowd gathered near a man by the fireplace,
who was apparently telling some tale that held everyone's interest.
He leaned on the hearth with one hand, while the other held a large
shot of whiskey that he waved about as he spoke in a most animated
fashion. Everyone leaned close, listening intently. I couldn't quite
hear what was being said, but it sounded as if it involved a chase,
and I wondered who the fellow was.

"Excuse me," I said to a passing waiter, "who is that
gentleman?"

"That, ma'am, is Roy Olmstead," he said, with a smile. "I see
you've heard the name before," he added, in response to my look of
shock, and whisked away with his hors d'oeuvre tray.

I had indeed heard the name before. So had everyone in
Washington State. Prohibition had only been in effect for three
months when a young police lieutenant named Roy Olmstead was
arrested by federal agents as he unloaded bootleg Canadian whiskey
on a beach in Edmonds. He was fined and lost his job, but since then
had become the Rum King of Seattle. He now lives in a mansion in
Mount Baker. And there he was at the mayor's house, with a drink
in hand. I felt like my head would explode.

Lorelei Dearborn

November 14th 1928

On and on it goes. The crime rate rises. Violence is everywhere.
All because of this silly prohibition. I have learned an interesting
thing about human nature. Nothing makes an act or deed so

desirable or enticing as prohibiting that act. I see people drinking now who never drank before. It makes them feel just a bit naughty, and they like that. I have always thought that people were good at heart, but my faith in humanity is wavering, and without that anchor I am lost.

Lorelei Dearborn

A stronger gust of wind rocked the yacht, and Nina reached her hand out to the hull of the boat to keep from falling. Standing was difficult in the bouncing, jerking boat, so she took a seat near the circle of light cast by the oil lamp. A moment later the boat returned to the gentle cadence of bobbing and rocking so nicely with the storm. She took a sip of port and returned to the journal.

July 7th 1929

I'm so excited. Charles and I have taken *Mary Adda* so many times on Lake Union and Lake Washington, but rarely do we pass the locks and venture into the saltwater. Today we received an invitation to visit an old school chum on Orcas Island. Charles and I have known Robert Moran for years. They played together as boys and attended the same school. Robert has a summer home on the island and has invited us to visit. I've started provisioning the boat. We leave next week. I'm so excited.

Lorelei Dearborn

The pages were water damaged, and the ink had run and blurred. Some of the words and phrases were not legible.

July 11th 1929

"...later start then expected. It was afternoon by the time we exited the locks and began north, so we decided to moor at Langley and continue the next day...tied *Mary Adda*...dock...to bed... comfortable...

PS: So sad. The silver teapot that has been in my family for generations slid off the galley table and the little round handle broke off of the lid. I must see about getting it repaired when we return.

Nina paused. She looked up from the journal on her lap and, by the sputtering, flickering light of the oil lamp, saw a silver teapot on the galley table. Was it the same teapot? The handle was missing, broken off it seemed. She lifted the lid to find a little round ball inside. Unbelievable. How could it have survived all those years? Shaking her head in disbelief, she picked up the journal and continued.

July 12th 1929

"…early start…beautiful weather…strong current at Deception Pass…waiting for slack tide to slip through the narrow opening… made it through the pass, crossing Rosario Straits with Blakely Island ahead…not far from our destination now…In the distance, high above the shoreline overlooking the water, I see the vague, indistinct shape of…can't wait to see it when we get closer. It must be…"

Later

"…close enough to see it now…spectacular. I've never seen anything like it…sitting high upon the bluff on the northwest side of Orcas Island, with a commanding view that must extend far beyond Vancouver BC. What would the sunset be like from that window, I mused? … giant stone house, no doubt quite old, for it is covered in ivy that scales the towering walls, growing inch by precious inch with each passing season, and extending in all…. In size and appearance, it reminds me of an old university, with stone halls, leaded windows, and many chimneys rising up from the roof. I can see the gray stone walls…gaps of the green ivy leaves, and the traditional roof with its many gables forms a…. I must ask Robert who lives there.

Later

...and arrived at the Moran Mansion shortly after noon. I had
never been to his summer home before and had no idea it was so
grand. A member of his household staff met us at the dock and, once
Mary Adda was properly moored, showed us to the house, a large
structure built in the manner of a colonial home, sitting at the edge
of a low bluff and overlooking Cascade Bay. East Sound is like a
deep, narrow horseshoe, and the Moran Mansion is just inside on
the southeast shore. From the dining room window, I can see down
the opening from which we came and the tree-lined beach across
the way...all is a blur of activity and motion as workers bustle about
in preparation for a formal dinner tonight. I stopped a staff member
as they hurried past and inquired what...said that there was a fund-
raising dinner of two hundred people that night, before she hurried
away to...

Tables were being set with cloths, plates, silver, glasses.
Chandeliers were polished, crystal gleamed. A uniformed gentleman
warmed up on a grand piano in the corner of the room. We went
in search of Robert and found him busily engaged in directing...
events...apologized for not being able to greet us. He had forgotten
about this event, he said, when he invited us to visit. He gave
us a case of his favorite port, Quinta do Noval, then invited...to
attend the dinner that night and said...be busy most of the day and
suggested we take his car for a drive on the island. Charles loves to
drive and warmed up to that idea instantly. I've returned to the boat
to change clothes. We leave in a moment.

Lorelei Dearborn

July 14th 1929

Where do I begin? My hand trembles as I recall the events of the
last few days. It is two days later. So...has happened in two days.
There is...to tell. So much to tell. I must get it down on paper. We
were shown to...garage...picked one of Robert's cars. Then... and
began driving up the long, winding...leads away from the mansion.
At the top...which...most scenic...

..."Right or left?" Charles asked. "It really doesn't matter which way we go, the road just makes a giant loop around the island and comes right back here."

"Okay then, left."

"Left it is."

It was a beautiful drive. The narrow road wound and twisted through thick, dense timber, and sunlight strobed through the tree limbs as we passed. The summer air was warm and lazy, and the gentle rumble of the car on the road was like a sedative that lulled me to sleep. I found myself dozing off and waking with a start, then dozing off again. Charles enjoyed driving and was content to follow the road along the scenic coastline with me sleeping beside him. The last time I woke, I saw the sun setting into the ocean in a fiery blaze of color and noticed little pockets of fog forming beside the road. In the golden-orange twilight before dusk, we approached a young man walking beside the road at a slow, steady pace, footsore and weary, as if he had been walking for quite some time. I caught only a sleepy glimpse of him as we passed.

"Shouldn't we offer him a ride?" I asked, rubbing the sleep from my eyes.

"I thought about it, but it's such a nice drive. Just the two of us enjoying the sunset."

"Very romantic, Charles, but we'll have plenty of time for that. He looks so tired."

"You always were a soft touch," he said with a smile, then pulled the car to the edge of the road and waited for the young man to catch up. He walked on steadily, doggedly, with his eyes on the ground, apparently lost in thought, and would have passed us by if Charles had not called to him.

"Excuse me," Charles said, standing in the half-open car door, "can we help you? Would you like a ride?"

The young man stopped and turned, as if becoming aware of our presence for the first time, then looked at us steadily. He was a handsome man, tall and well-built, with short blond hair bleached by the sun and several days growth of stubble on his tanned, rugged face. His age was difficult to judge. The thick hair and smooth, ruddy cheekbones spoke of youth and vigor, but the defeat in his walk and the fatigue in his weary eyes told of hardship, or age.

There was, too, something in his gait that spoke of hard physical labor, yet his general bearing was that of a gentleman. I guessed him to be twenty-five. He wore new shoes and a new, slightly wrinkled suit, but his shirt was open at the collar, and his tie was knotted loosely about this neck. When he turned to face us, Charles got his first good look at him, and while I couldn't see my husband's face from where I sat, I saw his hand tense suddenly on the car door. The young man saw it, too. I thought he would accept our offer of assistance, but he shook his head with a gentle, almost sad, smile, then turned away and continued walking.

"What was that about?" I asked, puzzled. Still standing at the open car door, Charles leaned down inside the car and spoke quietly.

"I don't know. There's something about him."

"I don't understand, Charles."

"I don't either."

"Have you seen him before?"

"I don't think so."

"Well, then..."

"Maybe it's the clothes."

"The clothes?"

"I don't know. I can't put my finger on it." His face wore a thoughtful frown as he tried to recall. "I think he may be a gangster."

"Like Capone?" I asked, in disbelief. Charles nodded.

"I know I've seen...suit somewhere. It's distinctive. I just don't know...

More water damage. The next half page was a blurry mess. Nina concluded that Charles and Lorelei were debating about whether to stop again for the young man.

"...I don't recall," he said, frustrated.

"Dear, we haven't passed a house or car in miles. If we don't give him a ride, he'll be walking for quite some time in the dark."

"Okay," he shrugged, "but mark my words, there's something familiar about him, and it's sinister. That much I know."

"Okay," I said, smiling. "Now, can we ask this sinister young man one more time if he would like some help?" Charles popped it in gear, and we lurched ahead.

"Whatever you say," he shrugged, "but once he's in the car, we're at his mercy."

"What do you mean by that?"

"I mean this isn't exactly Main Street. We haven't passed another car since we've been on this road. He doesn't look like a hoodlum, but if he is, he could force us to pull over and do pretty much whatever he wants."

"Do you think so?"

"If he's armed, yes. Why's he walking out here in the middle of nowhere?"

"I think we should help him," I said, after considering it.

"Okay, but just for the record, I have a bad feeling about this," Charles said.

"I have a good feeling about him." We pulled up beside the young man, and this time I spoke. I put down the window and called to him. "Please sir, you look tired. May we offer you a ride?"

He looked up the lonely, deserted road that wound along the bluff until it disappeared into the forest, and there was not a car or house in sight. Then he looked past me at the orange sun low on the horizon, hovering over the sea. I read his thought: soon it would be dusk and he would be walking that dark road at night, trying to find his way. Without a word, he stepped to the car, reluctantly opened the door, and climbed into the back. We pulled back onto the road and drove along in silence, an uncomfortable silence that became more so with each moment. Finally, Charles glanced up at the young man in the rear view mirror.

"Where are you headed?"

"The Moore place," he said, quietly, "a few miles up the road I think." He turned back to the window, watching the countryside pass.

"Visiting family?" Charles asked.

"Going home," he answered quietly, still looking out the window.

"Oh, been away long?"

The young man's eyes met Charles in the mirror.

"Perhaps I should walk. If you'll just pull over."

"No, no, I'm sorry. Didn't mean to intrude," Charles added, quickly.

The car bounced along the uneven road that followed the high coastline and sometimes turned inland, winding through patches of old growth timber and passing through small, park-like clearings where deer grazed leisurely in the tall grass. A thin fog hovered over the ground. It was a picturesque drive, made more so by the sunset that painted everything brilliant orange in a last great burst of color before retiring. But there was tension in the air. I could feel it, thick and heavy. The young man continued to look out the window, watching the scenery slide past, absorbed in his own thoughts. Afternoon shadows skipped across his pensive face as the setting sun broke though the tree limbs, but I felt that he saw nothing. His thoughts were elsewhere, somewhere far away.

"Sorry to trouble you," he said, finally, still looking out the window. "Could you pull over a moment? Would you stop, please?"

"Here?" asked Charles, apprehensively.

"Just a moment. I really need you to pull over." Still, he gazed absently out the window, without looking at either of us. Charles looked up the road ahead. It was a lonely place in the wilderness. There were no houses or people in view, and dusk was rapidly approaching. He glanced at me, and I saw apprehension in his eyes.

"How about farther up?"

"No, here. Please." Charles slouched in his seat, annoyed and somewhat apprehensive, but he shifted to a lower gear and his eye fell upon a newspaper on the floor. I saw recognition in his face, and alarm. He sat up straight, and his hands began to tremble with the rush of adrenaline as he pulled the car to the side of the road.

"I'll just be a moment," the young man said, then climbed out of the car, and stepped into the woods. Charles left the engine running. As soon as our passenger was out of sight, he turned to me.

"How would you feel about driving away and leaving him in the woods?" he asked, under his breath.

"What?" was my shocked reply.

In response, he pointed to the newspaper on the floor. The headline read, Four Men Escape from Prison, and below it were mug shots of the men. Each glared menacingly into the camera and held under their chin a prison number. But the photographs were poor, and grainy, and the light by which I studied them was faint, making it difficult to distinguish their features. I couldn't determine if our passenger was among them, or even why Charles thought that he might be. Then I saw the connection. In a separate photograph was a picture of a suit that each of them wore. The same suit worn by our new acquaintance.

"I told you I recognized the clothes. They're state issue," he said, quietly.

"What do you mean?"

"The kind they give you when they release you from prison. They have only one suit. They all look the same." He pointed at the men in the newspaper.

"He's a convict?" I asked, in disbelief.

"An escaped convict," Charles corrected.

"If they escaped, how did they get the suit?"

"I don't recall. It says in the story. You can't very well be walking around in your prison uniform if you want to blend in."

"What do you suppose he's done?"

"I don't know. Robbed a bank. Killed someone. Do you want to wait around and ask him?"

"But we can't leave him out here in the middle of the woods."

"If we hadn't given him a ride he would be walking on this same road," said Charles, exasperated.

"Perhaps so, but it's rude to drive off and leave him stranded here. What would you say if you saw him somewhere later?"

"Rude? You're concerned about being rude? The man's an escaped convict."

"I can't drive away and leave him here, Charles. We don't know that he escaped; he may have been released."

"Well, the timing's a bit peculiar, don't you think?"

"I don't think he's a bad man, Charles. He deserves the benefit of the doubt."

"I'm not concerned about myself, Lori, I'm thinking of you."

"I know you are." I took his hand. "He deserves a chance. What would Pastor Lomax say?"

"Lorelei darling, you're right." He leaned forward with his hands on the steering wheel, and turned to me. "You're absolutely right," Charles chuckled. "If nothing else, we'll have something to talk about over dinner tonight."

Charles glanced in the direction the young man had taken into the woods, and jumped, startled. He was standing next to the car, not two feet away. How long had he been there, I wondered? His face gave away nothing as he climbed into the back, shut the door, and again gazed out the side window.

"Thank you. I couldn't have waited much longer," was all he said. Charles pulled back onto the road, and we bounced along as before. But by then it was quite dark, and the tension was thicker than the night. I couldn't see much of our passenger in the back, just the vague outline of a pant leg poorly illuminated by the dim glow of the instruments, a pant leg that I knew all too well, thanks to the newspaper. Foolishly, my apprehension grew with each silent moment we traveled along the lonely road. I feared every minute to feel his hands reach out of the darkness and wrap around my throat in a violent embrace, and yet I still felt that he was not a threat. Not to us. We had done the right thing in stopping for him. It was the Christian thing to do.

We drove on for about a mile (it seemed like ten) and the car began to steer sluggishly. Charles turned the wheel tentatively back and forth, testing the movement of the vehicle, then pulled to the edge of the road with a sigh.

"I think we have a flat tire," he said, tiredly, and got out of the car to look. A moment later he was back. "Yep. Flat tire." He climbed back in the car, and sat with his hands on the wheel, staring distractedly ahead into the darkness. That he did not know how to change a tire I knew. The question was what to do next. From the darkness of the back seat came a voice:

"Only a flat tire?" Charles nodded. "Do you have a lug wrench and jack?"

"I don't know." Charles turned, looking into the back. "It's not my car." I heard the door handle click behind me, and felt the sudden rush of cool air as the car tipped to one side. Then it clicked shut again. Our passenger was outside rummaging through the trunk. Charles turned, and said very quietly, "Some coincidence. That tire was fine before he got out of the car back there."

"Oh Charles," I answered, equally quiet, "he's stuck, too. What does he have to gain by this?"

Before he could answer, the door opened again and the car tipped as the young man climbed back in.

"There's a gaff, and I found a jack, but no lug wrench. At least I couldn't find one in the dark." He shut the door, and we all sat in silence. It was a dark night. I knew there was a full moon, I had seen it earlier when the clouds scudded past and its silver rays pierced the opening, but all was dark now. I could barely even see the road ahead of us.

"We'll just have to spend the night in the car and figure out something in the morning," I said.

"We'll still have to find a lug wrench somehow, and I haven't seen any houses around here," said Charles. A long silence followed. The clouds parted briefly and I saw the moonlit road was hemmed in by tall timber on both sides until it turned sharply ahead and was lost from view. Then all went dark again, as the clouds swept over the moon. At length, our passenger spoke, and I thought it was with reluctance.

"There's a lug wrench at my house," he said, "or once was."

"We wouldn't want to imposition you," Charles answered, quickly.

"How far do you think it is?" I asked.

"It's hard to tell in the dark. I haven't been on this road in years. I'd guess about three miles."

"Lorelei can't walk three miles in those shoes," Charles said, indicating the high heels I wore. And he was right; I could barely walk three blocks. They were built for style, not comfort, but I sensed he had another agenda, one that didn't involve my shoes. "I'm obviously not going to leave her here alone. Why don't you go on ahead? We'll be alright here."

With the engine off, we sat in silence, in complete darkness, without even the faint glare of the instrument lights or the moon overhead. The seconds ticked away uncomfortably. Finally, our passenger spoke, and I started at the sound of his voice in the stillness.

"I don't like leaving you here alone. It's only Orcas Island, but I don't like leaving you out here alone."

"We'll be fine, really," came Charles's voice in the dark. "We'll just sleep in the car. We can always start the engine if we get cold. We'll be fine."

"Okay." I heard the car door open, felt the car lean, and heard it close again. A moment later the young man was leaning down at my window. I lowered it. "Thank you both for stopping for me," he said, and disappeared into the night.

Charles and I sat silently in the darkness for a moment. He was first to speak.

"Thank God he's gone," he said, quietly.

"Why are you whispering?"

"He could still be out there. Dark as it is, he could be standing right next to the car and we wouldn't know."

"Do you think so?" I peered into the night, searching.

"I wish we had a light. I'd like to read that paper again," he said.

"The part about the escaped convicts?"

"Yes. I didn't pay much attention to it before, but of course, I didn't expect to have one of them in the back seat of the car."

"We don't know that he was an escaped convict."

"We know he was a convict."

"We don't even know that, Charles. It's just a grainy, black and white photograph in the newspaper. His clothes look similar, but they may not be the same. There must be a lot of suits that look like that."

"Lorelei," he said, and though I couldn't see his face in the darkness, I knew it wore an amused smile.

"I just don't think he's a bad man," I explained.

"You see good in everyone." Charles sounded amused. Our conversation was like two disembodied voices speaking in the night, in the absolute darkness. I heard him reach down to the floor, searching with his hand, and heard the crinkle of newspaper.

"Now, let's see just how close we came to having our throats cut."

He struck a match and held it to the newspaper, reading quickly by the sudden flare of light before it burned out. The little flame illuminated his face and fell flickering upon the newspaper.

"Three of them were convicted of killing a man during a robbery, and the fourth was a...ouch." He shook the match out with a flick of the wrist after it burned his finger. "If I had a higher pain threshold we would know what the other one did."

"Just light another match," I suggested.

"That was the last one."

"Then I guess we'll have to wait until morning to see if he was a killer or just your garden-variety bank robber. How are we going to sleep…?"

The next few paragraphs were water damaged, and Nina could make out only random words in the running ink. She skipped ahead once more.

"…more room in the back seat. What do you think?" Charles asked. I turned, looking into the darkness of the back seat, and as I did the moon peeked momentarily between the clouds that slipped rapidly past. Through the back window of the car, I saw in that brief beam of moonlight piercing the night that there were three men walking abreast on the deserted roadway, all wearing the same clothes. They walked quickly, with purpose, right for us, through the fog that came nearly to their knees. Then the moon slipped behind the clouds once more, and all was dark. I was too frightened to speak. I dropped a hand on Charles' arm, and tried to mouth a warning. He sensed my fear and followed my stare out the back window, but saw nothing in the darkness.

"What is it Lorelei? What's wrong?"

"It's…it's them," I muttered breathlessly.

"Who?"

Suddenly, a terrifying face pressed against the car window, grinning through the glass. His teeth were crooked and decayed. His eyes smiled menacingly. I reached to lock the door, but he was quicker. He jerked it open and pulled me out roughly, by the arm. Charles grabbed at me, but the other two men tackled him and pulled him out also. They pushed us up against the car.

"What's this? A couple a socialites out for a drive?" said the man I took to be the leader.

In the darkness, I could distinguish little of his face, but his voice was rough and harsh and his breath smelled of cigarettes and whiskey.

"What's wrong with the car?" he asked.

He got no answer. I heard a thud, and a sharp intake of breath from Charles.

"What's wrong with the car?" he asked, again.

"Flat tire," said Charles, gasping.

"Why didn' ya fix it?"

"There's no lug wrench."

"No lug wrench," the man repeated, thoughtfully.

"Sure be nice to have a car to get around in. We could travel by day without being seen," said one of the others. He was a short, skinny man who had a way of skulking along with his head down and peering up timorously, like a dog that has been beaten. Each time he spoke, he dragged his coat sleeve across his nose, like a period at the end of a sentence. I could just make them out by the light of the moon that shined through a thinner patch of cloud.

"Yeah? Got a lug wench in yer pocket?" asked the leader. "I didn' think so. Check the car fer anythin' we might be able ta use."

One of the men began searching the car.

"I found some kind a key in the back," he said.

"Anythin' else?" asked the leader.

"There's a purse."

"Bring it here."

The purse was delivered to him, and he handed it to me.

"I can't see anythin' in this dark. Git the money out an give it ta me," he said, and added, "Lemme see that key." The key was apparently passed to him, for I thought I saw him hold it up to the night sky trying to make it out.

"What's this ta?"

"I don't know," I stammered, when I finally realized he was addressing me.

"Safe deposit box?"

"I don't know," I repeated.

"Don' lie ta me." He stepped closer, hovering over me, threateningly.

"I don't know what it's to. This isn't our car."

"Leave her alone you thieving reprobate," said Charles.

"Oh," the man answered, stepping over to Charles, "ya got somethin' ta say 'bout it?"

"Here's what I have to say to you." Charles slugged him hard in the stomach, and doubled him over. The other two immediately rushed over and pinned Charles' arms to the car. The leader straightened and appeared unhurt. He slouched lazily, a hand on each hip, regarding my husband with an insolent smile.

"Been boxing all ma life. I can take it in the breadbasket all day long. That's mother's milk ta me. How 'bout you?" And he slugged Charles in the stomach, doubling him over. The other two men released their grip and Charles fell to the ground gasping for air.

"That's what I thought," said the leader, with his hands on his hips, looking down at Charles. "You rich folk just got no gumption a'tall. Take his wallet. And git that jacket off 'im. Looks about my size."

They stripped Charles of his wallet and jacket, then dragged him up, and shoved him against the car beside me.

"Now, what are we gonna do with ya?" he asked, and began pacing back and forth, thinking. "We can't have ya tellin' anyone 'bout us."

"Oh, we won't," I said. "Really we won't."

"I know ya won't." I saw the glint of a knife blade, and he stepped close enough that I could smell the stench of his whiskey, cigarette breath. "Who'll be first?"

"I will," said Charles, unflinching. "Then you can let Lorelei go."

The third man, a tall, handsome fellow with high cheekbones and dark hair, approached the leader and whispered something in his ear. He nodded thoughtfully, and they all stepped a little distance away, where they had a conference while keeping an eye on us.

"When they come back," Charles whispered, "I'll tackle the one with the knife, and you run into the bushes. Run a little ways, then hide in the brush and don't move. They won't be able to find you in the dark. They can't afford to search for you too long, so they'll give up and move on."

"But what about you?" I whispered back. Charles turned his tender eyes upon me and gave me a gentle, lingering kiss.

"Slip off your shoes so you can run," he said. Then the men approached, all three of them, the handsome one removing his necktie as he walked to Charles.

"Put your hands behind your back," he said.

"Why?" Charles asked. In response, he was slapped hard across the face.

"So I won't have to hit you again," the man laughed. Charles spit blood from his lip and then complied; the man used his necktie to bind my husband's hands.

"Let's git off the road. Someone might come along," said the leader, who jerked me away from the car and pulled me along behind him by the hand. I struggled to keep up as he dragged me along in the dark on the narrow, uneven trail carved out of the brush. I could hear Charles being pushed along behind me but couldn't look to see, for fear of tripping. We didn't go far at all before coming to a little clearing in the trail, where they shoved us both down so that we were sitting beside each other in the low fog on the cold, damp grass wet with dew. My eyes were growing accustomed to the darkness. I could see the leader remove some little package from his coat pocket, draw something out of it, and raise it to his mouth. A moment later, I heard a match strike and a flash of light lit his grisly, squinting face as he brought the flame to the cigarette in his mouth. His face was covered in a thick growth of black stubble, his cheeks, sunken and hollow, like someone with no teeth. His cruel eyes were as black as coal. He tilted his head, drawing on the cigarette until the end glowed like a coal, then shook out the match and dropped it on the ground.

"Now then," said the leader, "where ya stayin' on this here island?"

"We're guests of Mr. Moran," said Charles.

"Well, aren't ya a pair of dandies?" He spat. "Ya don't live here, then?"

"No."

"Where ya live?"

"Seattle."

"Got any young un's?"

"No."

"So yer house is empty?"

"We have a house sitter," Charles replied.

"Sure ya do, just a sittin' there in that big ole empty house. How'd ya get ta the island?" Charles paused, stalling for time to think. "How did ya get ta the island?" the man repeated, then slapped Charles hard. Blood was running from my husband's mouth.

"We took a ferry," he answered, angrily.

"Ya ain't a very good liar. How'd ya git ta the island?" Charles was again hesitant, and his interrogator was growing impatient. "Next time I hit her."

"By boat."

"Whose boat?"

"Mine."

"How big a boat?"

Charles hesitated again. The man drew his hand back to strike me.

"Forty feet."

That drew a whistle from all three.

"Forty feet," said the leader, impressed. "That ain't no boat; that's a yacht. Why didn' ya say ya had a yacht? Where is it?"

"At Mr. Moran's home. You can't get to it," he added, firmly. "It's at his private dock."

"We'll figure that out later. Ya probably have clothes, an food, an money, an jewelry, an all sorts a interestin' things on that yacht a yers, don' ya?" Charles didn't answer. He was looking murderously at the man. "Boys our luck's a changin'. Once we git ta that yacht, we're home free."

"It's about time," said the second man, with a timid wipe of his nose. "I ain't eaten in two days."

"You got a shower on that boat?" asked the handsome one. Charles nodded, grudgingly. "I could use a shower and a change a clothes. I've been sweatin' and sleepin' in these prison rags for days now."

With that the leader smiled, displaying a single, decaying tooth, just off center in his foul, fleshy mouth. It was yellowed by nicotine and blackened by decay.

"Well, my friends," said Smyth, turning his coal-black eyes to Charles and then me, "it's time ta do somethin' with ya. I just want ya ta know this here ain't personal, even though you've had everythin' handed ta ya an lived a life a luxury that ya never had ta work for or deserved, while others had ta scrap an fight for every little thing that came their way. I ain't takin' no pleasure in what I got ta do." One hand held the knife. The other hand raised the cigarette to his mouth, and I saw the end glow brightly as he inhaled, dimly illuminating his grizzled face.

"You miserable cretin," said Charles, vehemently. "You poor, downtrodden reprobates always think that society owes you. You had just as much opportunity as anyone else. All of you. No one made you rob and murder that man. You did it because you're lazy and shiftless. Get a job."

"Get a job, eh?" Smyth knelt down so he was eye to eye with Charles. "Ya know why I'm missin' ma teeth?" he asked, and the cigarette glowed in the darkness as he drew on it. "My daddy knocked 'em out, the ones in front anyways, the ones he could hit easy with the back a his hand. He said I wasn't worth makin' a fist for, so he would backhand me. The rest of 'em, well, they was cheaper ta pull than ta fill. He was a mean drunk, was daddy. I quit school when I was fourteen an got a job at the mill pullin' green chain, cause someone had ta put food on the table. Cause daddy was drunk all the time an couldn' keep a job. So don't ya preach ta me 'bout gettin' a job ya silver spoon trust fund..."

Kneeling on the ground, he drew the knife from his belt and raised it high overhead in a rage, as if to stab Charles, but seemed to get control again, and lowered it.

"I was already workin' like a dog, an eatin' worse than yer family pet, while ya was sittin' in yer fancy private school, wearin' yer fancy uniform an wonderin' where ta go fer vacation. An ya tell me ta get a job?"

He stood and looked down at us sitting on the ground at his feet. Then his face glowed once more as he took a drag on the cigarette.

"When I was nine, I stabbed a boy in the belly cause he shoved me down in the dirt. It didn' hurt him much; the knife hit his belt, but he was too scared ta even look at me after that. So years later, when ma daddy knocked a few more teeth outta ma mouth while he was rantin' around the house drunk one night, I showed him ma knife. He just laughed an called me a weak, snivelin' little girl. He was still laughin' when I buried it in his cruel, drunken heart."

I heard Smyth laugh heartily. The clouds moved swiftly past the moon, sometimes offering a brief seam in the billowy mass for the moonlight to squeeze through, and then it was dark again. I listened to each harsh word and every sickening description of Smyth's foul deeds, which seemed amplified in the darkness of the quiet night.

"Get up here," Smyth said. "I can't kill ya properly when yer down there on the ground like that." He bent down and pulled Charles up by his necktie. "Now then." He wedged the cigarette between his lips and ran his thumb over the cutting edge of the knife blade, testing its sharpness. "Guess it'll do," he muttered. "It ain't like I'll be filleting ya." He laughed, harshly, sizing up Charles. "Don't need much of an edge for what I got in mind."

Just then one of the others (the wet nosed one, I think) approached and leaned close, speaking quietly into the boss's ear. Smyth pulled the cigarette from his mouth and answered angrily.

"Ya damned milksop. Go fer a walk then if ya ain't got no stomach fer it. Ya always was weak. Whad'da suggest we do, walk 'em back ta the car an wish 'em a happy even'in?" Then the other man joined them. "Not you, too, Malcom. I know you ain't gettin' cold feet over this here business."

"What I'm thinking is that we might need them for a while yet," Malcom said, quietly. But in the stillness, with my every nerve strained and alert, I heard him distinctly. "If he's telling the truth, we may need them to get to that yacht. But after, when we're out at sea…"

"Huh," said Smyth, thoughtfully. Then he led them farther away where we could no longer hear their discussion. Charles sat back down on the ground beside me and whispered.

"I'm sorry, Lori. This is all my fault. I never should have stopped for that guy. If I hadn't stopped we would be dining with Robert right now."

"I'm the one that wanted to stop, remember? It's not your fault."

"Well, I was driving the car. I should have kept going. Who picks up people walking beside the road?"

"Good people do. Good people living a godly life. We did the right thing."

"Look what it got us."

"I don't want to talk about whose fault it was. I don't care. We're going to die out here, Charles. I'm so scared. We're going to die." I broke down and began to cry.

"You're not going to die, sweetie. I'll see to that." With his hands tied, he scooted closer, and I pressed my head upon his chest. "No one is going to touch you."

"I love you so much, Charles. I know you would sacrifice yourself for me, but what would I do without you?" I said, sobbing.

"You'll carry on," he answered, and kissed me. I felt his lips on the top of my head. "Hell, you can probably find a better man than me at any soup kitchen," he added, with a chuckle.

"How can you joke at a time like this?"

"I don't know. It just seems humorous somehow. Of all the places we could be, we were on just the right road, at just the right time, to happen upon this murderous band of escaped convicts. What are the chances of that? Doesn't it seem funny to you?"

"No. Not in the slightest."

"Okay."

"You like the danger, don't you?" I said, wiping my eyes. "You like the challenge."

"I don't like that you're in danger, but I don't fear these thugs."

"What do you fear?" I asked, with the tears streaming down my face once again. "In all the time we've been married, I've never known you to fear anything. What do you…

Again there was water damage to the journal. Growing more and more frustrated by these interruptions, Nina did her best to discern the intent of the author's hand, but it was impossible. The ink had blurred and run together in a mass of jumbled words. Again, she skipped ahead to portions of the page that were more legible.

"…can't believe we're having this conversation. They're over there talking about whether to kill us now or later, and this is… spend our last moments."

"You're right," he said. "I'm…sorry."

"I love you so much," I said, crying…his shirtfront. "He looked so harmless…alone beside the road."

"That must be why they split up," Charles said, thoughtfully.

"Four…dressed…same draws attention, but one man can get a ride, then…car by force and pick up…others. I wonder where that other guy is. If we get out of this, remember he's out there somewhere."

Smyth had his back to us, and the other two were facing him while they talked and kept an eye on us.

"Lori?"

"Yes."

"You're not tied up. Take off your shoes discreetly, and get ready to run. This trail is quite narrow and the brush is thick on both sides. After you pass, I can position myself in the middle of the trail and keep them from following you for probably a minute or two. You should have plenty of time to get away. Do… said before. Run for a ways then… in the brush and don't move. They can't find you in the dark."

"What about you?"

"If my hands were free, I'd lay even money I could take all three of them."

"But your hands aren't free."

"No, but I can sure slow them down; long enough for you to get away."

"Charles, I love you so much. I can't leave you here like this."

"I'll miss you," he said, with a sad little smile, as his kind eyes searched mine. He leaned forward then, his hands still bound behind him, and tenderly pressed his lips to mine. "Now slip your shoes off and get ready to run. I'm looking forward to knocking that last tooth out of Smyth's head."

There was no other way than to follow Charles' plan, so I slipped off my shoes and waited in the cold, and fog, and darkness, trembling from the chill or the fear of what would follow. The conversation was becoming heated, and when the two men took their eyes off me to argue with their leader, I stood and bolted down the trail. After ten or twelve paces they noticed me and gave chase. Charles was close behind, urging me ahead. When he saw we were pursued he turned and stood his ground, blocking the trail. I had continued on a few tentative paces following the trail around a bend…"

The page became illegible again.

…heard a scream, and the sounds of a scuffle, and stopped… go on and leave Charles like that…turned back to help…him running toward me…"

The writing again became faint and faded, and she could scarcely read it. In her excitement, Nina rose quickly from her seat and held the open page directly under the lamplight as the boat tossed and jerked about in the building storm.

"…grabbed his arm and he led me back down the trail to the car, where we stopped, not knowing where to go from there. We were both out of breath and gasping for air from the exertion and excitement.

"What happen–What happened–back there?" I asked, catching my breath.

"I don't know–I don't know–Lori–They attacked me–I couldn't see–" he answered, panting for air. "Did you hear–that scream?"

"It sent a shiver down–my spine. Who was–it?" I asked.

"I don't know–I don't know what it was. Can you get this off?"

I removed the necktie that bound his wrists and threw my arms around him.

"I thought I lost you," I cried.

"You came back." He smiled down at me in admiration. "Foolish girl. What were you thinking?"

Just then, we heard a movement on the trail and turned to see the vague outline of someone coming toward us from the brush walking at a firm, even stride. The figure passed by us, went to the rear of the car, and in the darkness I heard the trunk open. Something hard was tossed inside, then I heard the trunk close again. Charles and I watched tensely. As the shadowy form approached, Charles raised his hands in fists, prepared for battle. But the man passed by us and continued on to the road before he turned around. I could just see his yellow necktie and white shirt collar against the dark suit that blended with the night.

"Are you coming?" he asked.

It was the voice of our young passenger. We were too surprised for words.

"No? All right," he said.

He began walking away, down the road. My husband's face was puzzlement and awe as a realization of some sort came to him. He dropped his big hands excitedly on my shoulders and looked me in the eyes.

"It was him, Lorelei. It must have been him."

"What do you mean?" I asked. "What did he do?"

"He attached those other convicts."

He paused a moment, recalling the events. "Someone attacked those thugs back there. They all rushed upon me at once, and I was wrestling with the first one, Smyth I think, when I heard the other two scuffling. I heard punches falling, then moaning and screaming. I couldn't tell what was happening. Suddenly Smyth let go, as if he had been struck from behind, and I ran down the trail to find you. It must have been that other convict. The one we had in the car."

"Why would he do that? Why would he help us?"

"I don't know, but there's no other explanation."

"Charles, they may come back for us. They could come back down that trail any minute. We should try to catch up to him."

"You're right. He's a handy man to have on your side," he said.

I put my shoes on and we ran up to the road, following after our young passenger who had not gained much of a lead on us.

"Excuse me," Charles said. "Excuse me." The young man stopped and turned. "I'm Charles Dearborn. This is my wife Lorelei."

"Thomas Moore," he said, and continued walking. We followed.

"Do we need to watch for those other men? Are they coming back?" I asked.

"I don't think they'll be bothering you anymore," he said, quietly, without breaking stride.

"Are you sure?" I asked. On he walked without answering.

"Is your house the first thing we come to on this road?" asked Charles.

"It used to be. I don't know anymore. I haven't been on this road in years."

"Do you have a phone there?"

"Yes," Thomas said, as he walked on. "Why?"

"We need to report this immediately," Charles replied.

Thomas stopped abruptly and whirled around to face us. "I have particular reasons for wishing to avoid contact with the police," he said, his eyes lingering on Charles. Then he turned back, and continued walking. I was struggling to keep up.

"Excuse me," I said. "Can we stop a moment? I can't keep up in these."

Thomas stopped and came back to where I stood rubbing my sore foot.

"Are these terribly important to you, Mrs. Dearborn?" he asked, indicating my shoes.

"Under the circumstances, no."

"Then with your permission, I'll make them into walking shoes." I slipped them off and handed them to Thomas, who ran a quick eye over them by the faint light of the moon. "Salvatore Ferragamo," he said, impressed. "Mother likes to wear these." He snapped the heels off and handed them back. "Sorry," he said.

I slipped them back on, and we continued walking. It was cold and damp as we passed through low-lying pockets of fog that hugged the ground. I was chill without the excitement of earlier to take my mind off the cold. Charles had recovered his jacket from somewhere and draped it over my shoulders, but it did little. We had walked along in silence for about ten minutes.

"Why did you come back?" Charles asked.

"I lost something in your car," Thomas answered.

"A key?" I asked.

"Yes."

"We don't have it. Those men took it," I answered.

"I know."

The clouds had passed for a time, and we walked along the road under the cool light of the full moon. It was a quiet sojourn, each of us lost in our own thoughts as we plodded silently along. The road turned sharply left out of the trees, following the coastline of the island, and we were presented with a remarkable view of the sea.

On any other night I would have been struck by the beauty, but even the full moon shining down like a spotlight on the rippling waves of the gray ocean held little appeal to me. In the distance, a sailboat passed through the moonlight reflected on the water, its canvas sails pushing it silently along. I wondered at the divine destiny that is carved out for each of us when we enter this world. Why would some of us be so blessed, while others, like the licentious leader of that misguided band, are born into a loveless life of misery and suffering? Did he have any choice but to become the evil, forsaken soul that he was? I stumbled along beside Charles distractedly, pondering just how close we had come to death.

"Charles?"

"Yes, love."

"What happened to those three men?"

"I don't know. I suppose they're in the brush back there planning their next move."

"What I mean is," I began, close to tears, "how did they get to be so violent, so thoughtless? They were going to kill us with no more thought than filleting a fish."

"I don't know how people become like that, Lori."

"I do," Thomas said quietly, as if to himself, as he walked along in the darkness ahead of us. It was a chilling response, all the more so because we were alone with him on that deserted road that led… where? What did he do to those men back there? Was he one of them? Who was Thomas Moore? I fell back a few more paces, giving Thomas more distance, and Charles slowed, too.

We continued walking along the shoreline road, bordered on one side by tall timber and open on the other to the gray sea. The yacht sailed picturesquely under the moonlight, unaware that three pensive wanderers watched from the shoreline road thankful to be alive and that somewhere in the darkness, tending their wounds under the pale light of that same moon, three evil men lurked. Was there a chance that any of them would turn away from the godless life they had chosen? Violent and unsympathetic though he was, I felt pity for Smyth. What chance did he have at a normal life, beaten by a drunken father who treated him like rubbish? And what of the others? Did they have similar histories?

Nina took a deep breath and fell into her seat under the bulkhead lamp. The boat journal was proving to be entertaining, and stressful, but the port proved to be a tasty remedy. She took another sip and continued reading.

We continued along the moonlit path in silence. Thomas was in the lead. I followed after him, and Charles after me. The road, turning away from the coastline, entered a dark stand of timber once again.

"What did you put in the car?" I asked, surprised at the sound of my own voice in the stillness.

"Excuse me?" replied Thomas.

"You put something in the car before we started walking. We heard you."

"The gaff."

Along a narrow column carved out of the trees, we walked in a hushed, oppressive darkness. The timber there was tall and thick, and the feeble moonlight low in the sky didn't reach the road. Thomas saw a deeper shade of darkness in the tree-lined column and summoned us over.

"I think this is it. Over here," he said, growing excited.

"When were you here last?" asked Charles.

"It's been years."

"Are you sure of the way?" I ventured.

We turned off the main road, heading west, in the direction of the ocean. After only a few paces, we came upon a tall wrought iron gate that was set in stout brick columns. Each side of the gate was swung open, and woven into the rusty iron bars ivy climbed and twisted wildly. We stepped through, following a long, tree-lined drive that opened into a clearing. Evenly spaced on each side of the path, at intervals of about fifty feet, were ancient, lofty maples with thick, gnarled bark and giant trunks. Their twisting, leafy limbs met over the road, forming a natural canopy. At the end of the drive was the house, the one we had seen from the boat as we passed: that giant, stone home covered in ivy that sat at the edge of the bluff, over-looking the ocean until it was lost to the curve of the earth.

It was everything I imagined it to be. Painted by the silver rays of the moon that briefly pierced the clouds drifting past, I saw that the grounds were vast and rolled on into the distance until they met the dark line of the forest. Little ponds had formed in a few of the depressions among the rolling hills all covered in tall grass. The still, dark water was like a mirror reflecting the moon and stars above. I saw a rose garden near the house, with tall, wild roses that sprang out of a wood framework to curl and twist about where they would.

I was glad to reach our destination at last and yet hesitant too, as I beheld it, with a reluctance that I couldn't define. Perhaps because the house itself was so dark, with no light burning within, and the moonlight pouring through the windows created a peculiar, almost unnerving, effect. The estate was grand, and beautiful, and imposing, but over the grounds, in the little hollows and depressions of the rolling hills, wispy pockets of fog gathered, giving the whole of the place a chill, somewhat ghostly appearance. It was so still. So quiet.

Thomas seemed encouraged by the sight of his home and quickened his pace, hurrying excitedly along the tree-lined drive under the canopy of maple leaves. Charles and I struggled to keep up, but what were we rushing into, I wondered? What awaited us when we reached the house?

"Everyone must be in bed," Thomas said, noting that the house was dark. "They'll all be so surprised to see me."

But as he neared the house, our guide's step faltered and his pace slowed. Finally, he stopped altogether and stood, taking it all in. In his haste, he had gained a considerable distance on us. I could see him at the end of the lane, standing in a circular drive before the massive stone structure. My legs were tired and my feet sore. Even with the heels removed, the shoes were difficult to walk in. Charles had an arm around me, helping me along the path.

"I know you're excited," Charles said, when we finally caught up with Thomas, "but you could have held up a bit. Lorelei is having trouble keeping up."

Leaning heavily on Charles, I turned to see what reaction Thomas might have to that, but his face was blank. I expected to see joy and excitement there, but his face wore no sign of it. By the pale light of the cold moon he stood open-mouthed, staring ahead with disbelieving eyes. Following his gaze, I saw why.

In the distance, with only an intermittent moonlight breaking through the clouds to illuminate it, the estate looked so beautiful and grand, but as we stood before it and saw it in greater detail, it was disheartening. The ivy grew wild and unchecked across the smooth stone, sometimes covering windows and doors as it curled and twisted, spreading itself over the vast surfaces. At our feet were strewn the fallen rubble of stone and mortar that had been dislodged by time and weather, opening little fissures in the stone walls and giving the ivy a foothold to climb. Stooping down, Thomas picked up a handful of the rubble, watching in disbelief as it crumbled through his fingers. High above, a lovely copper gutter aged to an elegant patina hung ungracefully, like a broken limb, clinging to its tether. The roof was covered in creeping moss and scattered bricks fallen from the many chimneys dotting the roofline. Peeking over the mossy shingles, dormers gazed sadly, silently, out over the grounds of the once proud estate, as if depressed by the sight.

We were at the edge of a circular drive set in paving stones that were covered with wild grass and creeping moss. At the center of it was a grand fountain that must have been spectacular in its day. Within a smooth marble bowl stood a life-sized statue in the manner of the ancient Greeks, chiseled from marble. His sage face bore none of the ravages of time, but his muscular form was missing an arm that was broken off above the elbow and lay in the stagnant water at his feet. Within the dark pool, ringed with slime and choked with lily pads, the hand of that arm reached out, as if seeking help.

I felt so sorry for Thomas. Clearly he hadn't expected this. Charles and I shifted uneasily, wondering how we might help or what we might do. In the undisturbed silence of the dark night, I heard the distant roar of the ocean surf and took comfort in it. It felt less lonely, less remote, with that sound filling the night.

"Thomas," I said quietly, though my voice was so clear in the stillness. "Thomas?" No answer came from him. He remained silently staring at the house.

Stepping to the high-arching leaded windows through which the moonlight poured, I pulled the ivy away so that I might peer inside. Within, I saw the ominous, almost eerie outline of furniture covered in white cloths, awaiting the return of the former residents.

What had happened there, I mused, as I stepped away from the window? It looked as if this once beautiful estate had been abandoned suddenly and allowed to fall into neglect, that time and nature were reclaiming it. Except for one quarter. At the north end of the house, taking in perhaps a quarter of an acre, was the family cemetery, surrounded by a low, crumbling brick wall that had an arched wrought iron gate at one end. Curiously, the cemetery was perfectly tended. The grass was trimmed, and in the distance I thought I detected fresh flowers on a few of the graves, where headstones cast their shadows on the ground in the moonlight. It gave me a chill.

"What happened here?" said Thomas quietly, as if to himself. "Where is everyone?" he asked looking quite small and insignificant before the door of the massive house as he gazed upon the ruins of his neglected home.

"When were you here last?" I asked, wondering if he heard me in his shocked state. "Thomas, when were you..."

"Nine years ago."

"Nine years?" I cried. "But you can't be more than twenty-five years old."

He turned then, regarding me with kind, gentle eyes, and answered quietly. "Twenty-six, Mrs. Dearborn."

"But, you were only seventeen when you went away to..." I paused, "to wherever you went."

"Let's go inside where we can be comfortable," he said.

We followed him to the door, a great oak barrier with iron bands securing it to the stone threshold and a proud, rearing stallion carved into the heavy wood. Thomas reached into his pocket.

"Oh, yes, my key." He paused a moment, thinking, then stepped to a large, waist-high urn beside the door, that served as a planter. The bare stem of some plant or flower, long dead, rose up out of the urn; Thomas plunged his fingers into the soil where he felt around searching. I saw him smile. A moment later, he held up a sterling silver skeleton key covered in dirt. He wiped it off and applied it to the keyhole in the door. I saw him turn it forcefully as he jiggled it back and forth and heard the rusty bolt grinding slowly until it shot open with a click. The door groaned in protest when Thomas pushed it, and we stepped inside.

The mildewed air smelled musty and stale, as if the place had been shut up for many years without activity or human presence. I heard the hurried scatter of little paws, and shot a glance ahead to find a small knot of furry balls scurrying away into the darkness; mice probably, disturbed for the first time in years. Thomas stood beside me. I couldn't read his face, but felt certain that he expected a different welcome than this and that he wished to be alone. That every room held cherished memories for him and that he would prefer solitude, for a while at least, to reflect on his past in the house he must have grown up in. He stood unmoving just inside the door, shocked and uncertain, looking over the cloth-covered furnishings by the vague light of the silver moon streaming through the windows. I saw him blink a few times and wipe his eyes. Gently, I pulled the door from his hand and closed it behind us.

"What a lovely home, Thomas," I said, hoping to distract him. "May we see it?"

"Of course," was his hoarse reply. "This way."

He led us to a great room that ran the entire length of the house. Along the wall, high-arching leaded windows carved into the thick stone looked out over the gray ocean, offering a bewitching view. Moonlight streamed through each of the openings, casting a shadow of light upon the stone floor, reminding me of an ancient church I once visited in France. Stepping close to one such opening, I peered out. The sailboat was far beyond the rippling patch of moonlit water and sailing over the gray sea toward the horizon.

"I'm sorry, the tour must be deferred until morning," he said, after trying the light switch. "Apparently the power has been turned off."

He lit a candle and set it on a long stone mantle and then, by the light it cast, built a fire in the fireplace. It too was stone, polished granite if I wasn't mistaken, and massive. I followed it with my eye, but the chimney climbed up until it disappeared into the darkness of the roof high overhead. With a warm fire burning brightly, Thomas took the candle in hand.

"Are you as famished as I am?" he asked. An energetic nod was our answer. "Just a moment. I'll see what wine remains in the cellar, but I can't see how there could be any food about." And with the candlelight guiding him, he disappeared down a dark hallway with his footsteps echoing on the granite floor.

"The phone's dead, too," Charles said, quietly, hanging up a phone that he discovered on a nearby wall.

We stood before the fire, hands extended, warming ourselves.

"Oh, this feels so good," I said, and then turned with my back to the fire, looking into the darkness outside. "I can't shake the feeling that they're out there, Charles, watching us."

"They could have followed us here," he said, "but I doubt it. I think they got pretty beat up back there. Anyway, I was keeping an eye open behind us."

"In the dark?"

"Well, as best I could."

"We really should find a phone and make a report at once."

"Yes, we should."

"They could break into someone's house or stop some car on the road. If they hurt someone it would be our fault. I would never forgive myself."

"You're absolutely right."

"I wonder why Thomas doesn't want us to report this."

"Why do you think?" Charles asked, with a knowing smile.

"But," I lowered my voice to a whisper, "if he escaped from prison he wouldn't return to his own house. That would be the first place they looked. He's not stupid."

"Do you really think this is his house? Look at this place," Charles said, glancing about the room. Even in the darkness, by the faint light of the fire, it was impressive. "It's a mansion. And don't forget, he didn't have a key."

"He lost it in the car."

"Did he? This place has been abandoned for years, Lori. An escaped convict could hide out here for quite some time, maybe years, without anyone discovering him."

"Did you see his face? He has a connection with this home," I said, thoughtfully.

"It could have been a friend's home or relative's house. I think we can assume that he got his clothes the same place those other three got theirs. They were on the same road, at the same time, wearing the same clothes."

"That's true," I grudgingly admitted.

"Four men escaped," Charles added. "We met the other three. And I don't know why he wouldn't want to report this if he didn't escape with them."

"But he's not like them. We've talked to him, Charles. I know he's different."

"You see the best in everyone, Lorelei. I love that about you." He took my hand and looked into my eyes. "You judge others by what you would do in their place, but you can't do that. Those men are escaped convicts. Killers. We don't know anything about Thomas."

"We know we owe him our life," I answered.

"I can't argue with that, but how do we know he wasn't serving his own interests by what he did back there?"

"What do you mean?"

"Why wasn't he with the other three? Maybe they quarreled. Maybe that was his chance to get even with them. Why would he help us?"

"Because he's a good man?" I answered, without much conviction.

"Maybe," Charles smiled, as he nodded his head. "Maybe he is. I can't deny that, if not for him, we would probably be lying in the brush with our throats cut instead of standing here warming ourselves, so even if he did escape from prison, I think our silence should be his due. But Lori," he said, holding my eye, "as a rule, good men don't go to prison." He was right, of course.

"I keep thinking of that awful man with one tooth who had such a miserable childhood. Charles, anyone who grew up like that could turn out the way he did. He didn't have much of a chance at a normal life."

"No, he didn't," he said, thoughtfully, "but it's quite a leap from battered child to remorseless murderer. He has some accountability."

"I pity him, just the same. Even if he was going to cut our throats and leave us beside the road."

"My love, I would have tackled them and fought to the death," he said, looking tenderly into my eyes. "I would cheerfully shed every drop of blood in these veins before I allowed them to touch you."

"I know." I took his hand and pressed it to my cheek. "But there were three of them. And one man against three, even when that one man is you...it's just all so...so sobering. I can't shake the feeling that we should be dead right now. That we would be, if not for Thomas." I saw his eyes fall, and realized what I had said. "It's no reflection on you, Charles, you were tied up."

We heard approaching footsteps from the dark hallway, and Charles added quickly in a hushed voice, "Remember Lori, we know nothing about him. Be careful."

A moment later we saw a flickering light moving along the dark corridor, and Thomas appeared with the candle in one hand and a dusty wine bottle in the other. Glasses were produced, wine poured.

"I don't know that we should be doing this," I said.

"Lori dear, if a doctor were here, he would definitely prescribe a stiff drink or two after what we've been through tonight," Charles replied.

"I suppose you're right," I grudgingly agreed.

Our host removed the cloth covers from several chairs, slapped the dust from them with his hand, and we all settled into comfortable seats before the blazing fire. It popped with a cheerful crackle that filled the quiet room. Thomas reached into his suit jacket and produced a round wheel of cheese that had a rind with a herringbone pattern.

"Manchego," he said, with an eager smile. "From Spain. The longer it ages, the better it is. This one should be spectacular." As he leaned forward in his seat to pass me a piece, he noticed the trace of a tear on my face. "Are you all right, Mrs. Dearborn?" he asked, concerned. "Can I get you anything?"

"I'm fine, thank you." I wiped my face with my hand. "You've done so much already. I just need a moment. It's not every day that I'm threatened with death." Charles took my hand to comfort me.

"Oh, that. Yes. I'm sorry." He was thoughtful a moment. "You'll be safe here. If it's any consolation, you'll be safe here."

The great oak door was stout enough, and the stone walls had an impregnable, castle-like quality. I found comfort in his assertion, but Charles did not. I saw his eye fall upon the suit worn by our host, and linger there. Thomas saw it, too, and the meaning was not lost on him. He took a sip of wine. When he lowered the glass, his eyes assumed a far away, distant expression, as if recalling a painful memory; then his eye, too, fell upon the suit he wore, and he ran a hand over the coat sleeve. Without a word, he slipped off his jacket, wadded it into a ball, and tossed it into the fire. As the flames leapt up engulfing the cloth, I saw a strange, almost exhilarated look in his eyes, as if he were finally released from the last thread of bondage that tied him to a past he wished to forget. I believe he would have tossed his trousers into the fire as well if decorum didn't require that he wear them.

"May I never see such clothing again," he said, and passed Charles a chunk of cheese.

"I don't mean to be indelicate," said Charles, accepting the gift, "especially after your hospitality, but…"

"You would like to know where I've been for the last nine years," Thomas said, quietly. He looked first at Charles, then me, and I felt a sudden chill when I noticed little flecks of blood on his shirt and hands, blood that could have only come from the convicts.

"Only if you want to, Thomas," I said. "We don't wish to open any old wounds."

"The wounds aren't that old," said Charles. "And nine years is a long time. You don't get that kind of sentence for bootlegging."

"I feel no obligation to explain my past to you," Thomas replied, growing angry. "If my actions a short time ago aren't recommendation enough, then perhaps you should find other lodgings for the evening."

Thomas stood and motioned us to the door.

"Thomas," I said, standing suddenly and rushing to him. "What you did for us was very brave and chivalrous. I thank you with all my heart. Please don't undo that by asking us to leave like this."

He softened at once. There was blood on his hands it's true, but I saw kindness in his eyes. He motioned me back to my seat. A moment later he returned to his own, and we remained in an awkward silence that was broken only by the soft crackle of the fire. Eventually he reached for his wine glass, and by the dim light of the flames, glimpsed the blood on his hand. He looked shocked, horrified almost, and it seemed that in that instant he understood the apprehension that we felt for him.

The flames made short work of the jacket and burned low once more. Thomas hadn't moved. He sat with his head down, and his bloody hands folded on his lap. Without looking up, he began in a quiet voice.

"Do you know of the shipyard at Deer Harbor?"

"I saw it years ago, yes," answered Charles, raising his glass for a sip. "It's been abandoned for quite some time. The windows were broken out, the ones that weren't boarded up. There were To Let signs posted as I recall."

"I shouldn't be surprised," he said, sadly. "It was my father's shipyard," he added, with his eyes on the fire. "He was a naval architect. When I was six, he found a meter boat that had grounded and sunk and brought it to the shop. It was rumored to have been raced by the King of Spain in the Olympics, so how it made it over here I don't know. Father wouldn't let anyone else work on that boat. He restored it all himself. A lot of our boatwrights wanted to work on that boat, even volunteered to work on that boat, but he wouldn't let them. He did it all himself, working on it after hours and weekends for two years, and when it was finally ready, he showed it to Mother and I.

"It was the most beautiful thing I had ever seen in my life. If I had been the son of a scholar, perhaps my heroes would have been Nietzsche, Twain, and Aristotle, but as the son of a naval architect, I idolized men like Fife, Herreshoff, and Olin Stephens, some of the greatest naval architects that ever lived. All of them had designed meter boats, but I had never seen one as beautiful as that. She was fifty feet of grace and elegance, with a tiny little wine glass transom, a gently curving shear, and scarcely any freeboard. The mast was nearly seventy feet above the water. When the main was unfurled and she heeled in the wind, it was spectacular to see."

I watched Thomas as he spoke. The former melancholy expression had vanished, and his eyes sparkled in the firelight as he recalled the memory of his father's yacht. Charles, I noticed, was already enamored with the tale. He loved boats and sat on the edge of his seat listening alertly.

"Father was performing sea trials, making sure everything worked properly on *Diva*, and fine-tuning the rig. Sometimes he would take me with him. I would take the tiller and maintain course while he went forward and made adjustments to the rigging. I was so proud to be out there sailing with him on that beautiful yacht.

"It was a sunny day in mid-October, and we were to go sailing that afternoon. Mother made a sack lunch, and I was sitting in the window watching for Father's car to come up the drive. For several hours I fidgeted impatiently, watching the trees bend and sway in the wind as the sky grew dark and a gale blew over the island. I was disappointed, but not surprised, when I heard the phone ring and Mother told me we wouldn't be sailing that day. It was too stormy, she said. I fell asleep at the window to the music of the rain drumming on the windowpanes and the unwelcome sight of whitecaps building on the gray sea. Mother must have carried me upstairs to bed.

"When I woke the next day, the rain was still beating upon the window as I lay in bed. Thinking I had overslept, I jumped up and ran downstairs, intending to catch Father before he left for work and ask if we could sail that day. But I saw no one. The house was quiet, disturbingly so for that hour when everyone was usually bustling about preparing for the day. I wandered hesitantly to the dining room and saw that breakfast had been made and a place set for Mother, Father, and I, but the food was cold. Someone had poured tea and food had been served, but everything was cold, as if everyone had left suddenly. With a growing sense of uneasiness, I wandered through the quiet house searching for my parents."

Thomas paused, staring into the fire with a knit brow as he recalled the memory. He took a sip of wine and continued.

"Only eight years old then. I remember how very cold the stone floor felt on my bare feet as I walked through the house in my pajamas. Already it was becoming cold. Faint and far away, a sound caught my ear, and I followed it to find my mother. She sat there."

He indicated a high back armchair, placed at one of the leaded windows overlooking the moonlit ocean.

"It was a favored vantage point for her. She sat there that day with her face in her hands and her head hung, crying softly. Our nanny, Elsie, stood behind her chair gently stroking her hair.

'What's wrong, Mother?' I asked, hesitantly, as I approached.

'Oh, Thomas,' she said, wiping her eyes with her hand, 'come here child.'

"I walked over beside her and she lifted me up onto her lap. Mother looked me directly in the eye as she spoke slowly and deliberately.

'I assumed your father worked late last night and spent the night at the boatyard,' she said, struggling with her emotions. '*Diva* was discovered a short time ago, grounded on a beach in Mud Bay.

'What?' I asked, in disbelief.

'He changed his mind at the last minute and took the boat out yesterday in the storm. He's missing.'

"She held me close, and I felt her chest heave as she sobbed quietly. But I was too stunned to think or do anything for her. I simply clung to her like a silly, nursing child drawing comfort from his mother. Later that day, *Diva* was lifted off the beach by the high tide and towed back to the boat yard. They searched for Father day after day but never found him, or any trace of him, and a void was opened in my life that day that could never be filled. I was so young when he left us that I never really got to know him well. I'm sure he had faults and flaws and imperfections, like anyone, but I never came to know any of them, and so in my eyes he was always perfect. The perfect father. The perfect man.

"Everything changed after that day," said Thomas, turning to look at his mother's vacant chair in the window. "The warmth and serenity of our home was gone. All of the comfort and harmony vanished that October morning with Father. For months afterward, I would see Mother crying. She would just break down and cry suddenly as she walked along through the house or sat reading a book or saw a sailboat passing in the distance from the window, and I knew she was thinking of Father and feeling the sting of a void in her own life. To the wild imagination of a child, the house had always seemed large and intriguing, with the promise of hidden passages, and secret doors, and concealed chambers, that compelled me to roam about for hours and explore, tapping on walls, lifting carpets. The stone walls were often cool to the touch, even on the warmest summer day, and there always seemed to be a bit of a draft, but there was an emotional warmth and spiritual comfort with Mother, and Father, and Elsie, that drove away the chill and soothed the soul. It was home. But with Father gone, the house became so cold. The tolerable little draft grew to an insufferable chill in this mirthless house without laughter or cheer to combat it. Grand spaces that invited mystery and intrigue to a playful boy became nothing more than cold, cheerless rooms to an anguished youngster. Mother would sit at the window for hours looking out over the sea, as if waiting for Father to return. As if he would come sailing back to her over that vast expanse of ocean and all would be as before. She loved him so much. It was almost as if time had stopped for her that day.

"But the clocks had not stopped at the hour of Mother's discovery. Slowly, by degrees, she became herself again and ordered a headstone, which she added to the family cemetery on the grounds. The largest of the headstones there belonged to my grandfather, who founded the shipyard and built the house. His was a towering monolith that dominated the little cemetery, and the others were gathered around it like disciples. I remember for years afterward we would sit by the fire on stormy winter nights, Mother and I, and through the rain spattered window, would see Father's headstone there under the trees as the rain fell and the storm beat upon it. We were snug and warm before the crackling fire, and it seemed as if the doors and windows of the house had been almost cruelly closed upon him there in the rain, shutting him out of our lives, excluding him from our company.

"One rainy winter night, Mother sat beside the fire reading, and I sat next to her, contemplating Father's headstone through the window as I had done so many times."

'Mother?' I inquired.

'Yes, Thomas,' she answered, without looking up from her book.

'Do you miss Father?'

"She looked at me then, and I saw such pain in her eyes. The book slipped from her grasp, falling to the floor. She covered her face with her delicate hand, and the tears welled up suddenly. But just as suddenly, she stopped herself and put on a brave face. Retrieving the book from the floor, she sat up straight in the chair, again becoming the self-possessed, poised mother I had always known. She forced a smile and regarded me with loving eyes.

'I miss your father very much,' she said. 'I don't know what I would do if I didn't have you.'

"She was so beautiful there in the firelight, with her cheeks aglow and the fire dancing in her sea-green eyes. Her long blonde hair fell so gracefully about her shoulders. She was always so poised, even in defeat."

Thomas wore an affectionate smile as he stared into the flames, recalling the memory. Then he finished his wine with a gulp, cast a glance at our empty glasses, and stood.

"Sorry I'm such a poor host; I'm a bit out of practice. I'll return in a moment with a fresh bottle."

As before, he took the candle from the mantle, and the feeble light preceded him through the dark hallway. Sitting before the crackling fire I turned in my seat, looking though the window into the night, unable to shake the feeling that we were being watched in the darkness. Could the convicts have followed us? Might they be outside watching, waiting for an opportunity to act?

We saw the light before we saw our host. It went before him, casting flickering shadows upon the hallway walls, as the darkness yielded before him. He returned with another bottle of wine, wiped the dust off, and sat down as before.

"How do you feel about Château Neuf De Pape? It's difficult to find anything in that dusty old cellar, and it's rather cold down there just now."

"The Chateau Neuf is one of our favorites, thank you." Charles answered.

Thomas refilled our glasses, set the bottle on the floor between us, and made himself comfortable in the chair once again.

"Now then, I don't wish to burden you with an epic narrative of the Moore family history. Perhaps you would prefer to speak of other things," he said.

"What were you in prison for?" Charles inquired, to my surprise and embarrassment. It wasn't asked in a hostile or threatening way, but Thomas frowned as if put off by the abrupt manner of my husband. He swirled his glass, allowing the wine to breath, then took a sip. Again my eye was drawn to the bloodstains on his shirt. What was he in prison for? I was intensely curious and yet feared to know. Thomas lowered his glass, paused a moment, then opened his mouth as if to answer.

"Please continue your tale," I blurted, before he could speak. He was surprised by my sudden interruption. "Please continue your tale, Thomas. You've aroused my curiosity." I avoided looking beside me, knowing that Charles was glaring in my direction.

"Very well," he said. "You may have noticed that there are few homes on the island, and none close to ours. Father's death haunted me for quite some time. All of the pleasant pastimes that I formerly engaged in held no interest for me. There were no children to play with, and I wasn't in the mood for play anyway. I was bored and restless and sad. I missed Father. But youth is resilient, and the memory of a child can be all too brief. Eventually, I returned to my former ways.

"The property is just over fifty acres, so there is room for a youngster to roam and explore. That's just what I was doing one summer day a few years after Father's disappearance. I had wandered far from the house and was walking along the edge of the bluff where I wasn't allowed to go. But I was in pursuit of imaginary pirates who had raided my ship and stolen my treasure, and I calculated that, given the circumstances, Mother's mandate should not apply that day. Armed with a tree limb that served as a sword, I was in hot pursuit of the villains, who I intended to capture single-handedly where my crew had failed. I charged around a tree, my sword drawn, prepared to do battle, and came face-to-face with a girl the same age as myself who was as surprised to see me as I was to see her.

'Hold.' I said, when I had gathered my wits. 'Who goes there?' I challenged, with my tree limb directed at her.

'Who are you?' she asked, undaunted.

'Captain Moore. My ship is at anchor in the bay, and I am pursuing pirates.'

'Oh, is that all?'

"I was a little dismayed that my rank and weapon commanded so little respect, and tried a different approach.

'This is my property.'

'Really? Ya look a little young ta be a property owner.'

"Still more dismayed, I lowered my weapon and studied her. She was easily as tall as I, and her short black hair framed her face perfectly. Her blue eyes were irreverent and inquisitive, and her features elegant and refined—or would have been with the application of soap and water. Her cheeks were smudged with dirt, and so were her trousers, which I had never seen a girl wear before. Girls wore dresses, of course. She wore a flannel shirt, which was too large for her, with the sleeves rolled up. I was puzzled.

'Are you a girl?' I asked.

'What? Are you some kind of idiot?' she mocked.

'But…you're dressed like a boy,' I ventured.

'And you sound like a silly little girl,' she said, with a blush, 'but I didn't ask if ya was one.'

'Hold your tongue, wench,' I said, lifting my imaginary sword, 'or I'll take you prisoner and hold you for ransom.'

'Maybe I'll take you prisoner and hold ya for ransom,' she retorted.

'Ha, you don't even have a ship,' I laughed. 'Anyway, a girl take Captain Moore prisoner? That I would like to see.'

'Would ya?'

"She lowered her head and charged at me, hitting me in the stomach and knocking me to the ground. I was surprised at the strength and suddenness of her assault, and was taken off guard. When I came to my senses, I was on my back and she was on top of me, smiling down with a smug grin. But I was stronger. I pushed her off and rolled over so that I was on top, smiling down at her.

'Give?'

'No,' she answered, obstinately.

'Give,' I demanded, pinning her arms to the ground.

'No,' she insisted.

'Give,' I repeated.

'Never.' She struggled, trying to get up, but I held firm.

'Give.'

'Never, never, never.'

"She struggled furiously in one last great effort, then gave up, and started to cry. I felt that I had gone too far and climbed off, then stood looking down at her timidly. Still crying, she stood slowly, rubbing her elbow, which I had apparently hurt. She seemed embarrassed. Her eyes were on the ground.

'I hate you,' she said, and ran away suddenly, disappearing into the forest.

"It was a long, melancholy walk home. I thought about her all night as I lay awake in bed, unable to sleep. That I made her cry was too much for my boyhood ego. Boys were supposed to protect girls, not make them cry, and she hated me. I wanted to help her, to show her that I was a gentleman. Her eyes were so blue and her face so pretty, even smudged with dirt, that I thought of her constantly. I returned to the same place at the bluff for the next six days but didn't see her. On the seventh day, I found her sitting back against a little boat in the shade of the tree, reading a book. It was an old dugout canoe nearly grown over by grass and vine maples that crawled over it. The bow was broken off, and missing.

'Hi,' I said, timidly.

'Hello,' she answered, without looking up from her book.

'What are you reading?' I ventured.

'Scarlet Pimpernel,' she answered, turning a page.

'Oh, I like that one.' I sat beside her on the ground, and she didn't move away. 'Have you got to the part where he disguises himself as a captain of the guard—'

'And rides past the barricade with all the aristos dressed as his soldiers,' she said, enthusiastically. 'I love that part.'

"An awkward silence followed as I searched for something to say. In my shyness, I looked everywhere but at her. My eye fell upon the boat.

'I like your canoe.'

'It ain't mine,' she replied.

'Want to get in it and play?' I asked, shyly.

'Oh, no,' she answered, seriously, 'ya can't play in this canoe.'

'Why not?'

'Cause it's magic.'

'Really?' I asked, intrigued by the broken old boat. She nodded solemnly.

'Indians use it ta catch yer soul.'

'How does it work?' I inquired, somewhat frightened by the power of the little boat.

'Ya have two souls, ya see.'

'You do?'

'Uh ha. A life soul, and a heart soul, and if yer bad, one of 'em leaves and ya have ta get it back.'

'Oh.'

'Ya take the canoe out ta sea at night with a shaman and have a ceremony and if yer good, ya get yer soul back.'

'Oh,' I answered, reverently.

'It's called a night dance…no wait…it's a winter dance.'

'I'm Thomas.'

'I'm Sophia.'

'Do you live around here?'

'A few miles away. I'm not supposed ta come here; my mom's afraid I'll fall over the edge.'

'Mine too,' I replied, sagely. 'What about your father?' I inquired.

'He's dead.'

'Oh. My father's dead, too.'

'Really? Do ya miss him?'

"I nodded. 'We used to go sailing together out there.' I pointed out over the ocean. 'He had a sailboat that was owned by the King of Spain.'

'I never knew my dad.'

'Why not?'

'He died when I was four. I don't remember him.'

'Oh. My father built boats. What did your father do?'

'I don't know.'

'Would you like to play a game?'

'No. Not right now anyways.'

'I'm sorry,' I said, shyly. 'I'm sorry I made you cry.'

"She closed her book, and, holding it in her lap, turned, looking me in the eye. For a very long time, or so it seemed, she sat beside me there on the ground looking directly into my eyes as if searching my soul. It made me uneasy.

'I like ya, Thomas, yer sweet,' she said, at last.

'I like you, too.'

'There's no one ta play with out here. Wanna be my friend?' she asked excitedly. 'We can play together. We'll have so much fun.'

'Sure.'

'Let's make a pact.'

'Okay.'

'Friends forever.' She spit on her hand.

'Friends forever,' I repeated, and spit on my hand.

'Now we shake.' We shook hands warmly, confident that our contract was binding, and that we would be best of friends forever. 'I need ta go now. I have ta go home. Race ya ta that tree.'

'Okay.'

'Ready, go.'

"And Sophia sprinted toward a tree about fifty yards distant on her path home. She was fast, but I caught up and passed her just before we reached the tree. She stood bent over, with a hand on each knee, catching her breath.

'That was fun,' she said, between breaths. 'Bye Thomas.'

'Good-bye Sophia,' I answered, and then she started walking home.

"My way home was the opposite direction, and I reluctantly parted with her as I began walking away. When she reached the trees, she turned to wave then was gone.

'Good-bye Sophia,' I said, under my breath, and continued home happily.

"She was true to her oath. We became best friends and spent nearly every day together that summer. We would meet in the forest and walk in the woods, or comb the beach for driftwood or seashells, or swim in the creek or ocean. I would always have Elsie make a sack lunch for both of us, and we would picnic in the warm sun.

"One day, we were lying on the sandy beach drying in the sun after a swim.

'I'm hungry, Thomas.'

'Me too. I forgot to bring lunch. I could go back home and get it. I saw Elsie make our lunch and set it on the table.'

'Who's Elsie?'

'She's the nanny.'

'What's a nanny?'

'I don't know,' I replied, thoughtfully. 'Someone who helps around the house.' I was suddenly struck with an idea. 'Hey, why don't you come home with me? We can have lunch at my house.'

'Is it far?'

'Not too far.'

'Will your mom make ya stay home if we go back?'

'No.'

'We can still come back out an play?' she asked, eagerly.

'Sure,' I answered.

"But as if struck with a sudden thought, she looked at the ground and shuffled her feet shyly.

'What if she don't like me?'

'Why would she not like you?'

"Her embarrassed eyes, so demure and blue, fell to her flannel shirt and trousers.

'Because I'm a tomboy,' she said, quietly.

'Well,' I thought for a moment, 'if she doesn't like you, then she must not like me either.'

'Why?'

'Because I'm a Tom-boy, too,' I said with a laugh, feeling very smart.

'Oh, Thomas, yer so clever,' she said, smiling. It was the sweetest smile I had ever seen. 'Tom-boy,' she repeated, with a laugh.

"We began toward my house, walking through a field of tall grass and daises that swayed easily in the warm summer breeze. With my eyes on the ground, picking my way through the grass, I started suddenly at the sight of a snake and jumped back, afraid. Sophia walked over to see what had startled me and quickly stooped down, scooping up the snake before it could escape.

'It's just a garter snake. Would ya like ta hold 'im?' she asked, as she held him by the tail.

'No.' I backed away. 'I don't like snakes.'

'He won't hurt ya.' She held him toward me.

'Put him on the ground and I'll stomp on him?'

'Why would ya do that?' she asked, shocked.

'To kill him.'

'No, Thomas,' she said, sternly. 'Every life's precious. You mustn't kill somethin' because ya fear it or don't understand it. Everything wishes ta live. Do ya hear me?'

'Yes.'

'Then say it.'

'You shouldn't kill something because you fear it or don't understand it.'

'He's just a little baby. All he wants ta do is catch a few tiny insects so he can eat. He doesn't want ta harm us.'

"She returned it to the ground, and the little snake disappeared into the grass with a wiggle. We skipped merrily along the field to my house. Sophia was chattering and carrying on about this and that, but when we came out of the woods and she saw the house she stopped suddenly and was quiet as she looked it over. Her eye traveled over the entire length of the structure, and her jaw dropped. Then she turned her attention to the grounds. She looked out over the trees, and lawns, and ponds, and seemed puzzled, astonished, and dismayed all at once.

'Come on. I'm hungry,' I said, and continued on.

'This is yer house?' she asked in disbelief. I nodded.

'There's a turkey sandwich and a ham sandwich. I'm calling dibs on the turkey.'

'I get the turkey,' she said, running past me for the door.

'Why you?' I asked, chasing after her.

'Cause I'm a girl. And I'm yer guest.'

'You're only half girl, because you're a tomboy.'

'Yer a Tom-boy, too, so we're even,' she said, giggling. We were winded when we reached the door and stood outside a moment, catching our breath.

'You can have the turkey,' I said.

'No, you take it.'

'But I would like for you to have it.'

'I'll have half, an you have half, cause that's what friends do,' she said.

'Okay.'

"Rested then, I applied my shoulder to the heavy oak door. Creaking on its heavy iron hinges, it opened slowly, reluctantly, until Sophia added her shoulder as well. Inside, we were met by Elsie who had a sack lunch in each hand.

'I thought you might be returning for these. I've been keeping my eyes open for you.'

'Thank you, Elsie,' I said, taking the lunches from her.

'And you must be the friend I've been making an extra lunch for all this time.'

'Yes, ma'am. Thank you,' Sophia said, and then dropped into an awkward curtsy.

"Elsie knelt down with an amused smile and took Sophia by the hand, studying her. I wondered what she was thinking as her eyes traveled over Sophia's black work pants and up to her flannel shirt with rolled up sleeves.

'Aren't you a pretty thing? And such a lady, too,' she said, kindly. 'My name is Elsie.'

'My name is Sophia. I'm pleased ta meet ya, Elsie.'

'I'm pleased to meet you, Sophia.' Elsie studied her, shrewdly. 'Do you have a brother, child?'

'No ma'am.'

'Well, I expect you're both hungry,' she said, as she stood. 'I was baking a short time ago, so there's a little something extra in your lunch today. Run along now.'

"We shrieked with delight as we ran for the door. I knew what that little something would be and loved Elsie's peanut butter cookies.

"Minutes later, Sophia and I were seated on a big mossy log in the shade of a giant cedar tree that leaned out over a fast running little creek. We had finished our lunch and were feasting on fresh cookies as we watched little baby trout meandering around the shallow water.

'Thomas?'

'Yes.'

'Do ya know where babies come from?'

'No," I answered, thoughtfully, 'do you?'

'They come from here,' she placed a hand on her tummy, while munching a cookie, 'but how do they get there, and how do they get out again?'

'I've never really thought about it. What's that?' I asked, pointing at the water. Sophia leaned forward, looking down into the stream, and I tapped her on the shoulder and ran.

'Tag, you're it.'

"She jumped up and ran after me.

"Our dining table was quite large, and since it was only Mother and I now and she never entertained, we would often use the little kitchen table for meals. We were seated at the kitchen table that night, and I was absently picking at my dinner.

'Mother?'

64 | *Kevin Kincheloe*

'Yes, Thomas.'

'Where do babies come from?'

"She choked ever so slightly, and raised an elegant hand to her mouth as she cleared her throat.

'Why do you ask?' she inquired, amused.

'Well, Sophia asked if I knew while we were eating our cookies by the creek today.'

'Yes, Elsie mentioned that she had met your friend. Sophia made quite an impression.'

'She liked her, then?' I asked, eagerly.

'She liked her very much.' Mother studied me, thoughtfully. 'Growing up so quickly,' she said, under her breath. 'Maria said you need to spend time with children your own age. That's difficult to do on the island, especially out here. Will you be seeing Sophia tomorrow?'

'I see her every day.'

'Are you fond of her?'

'She's my best friend.'

'Would you like to have lessons with her?'

'Would I ever?' I answered with glee.

'Give her this note tomorrow,' Mother said, as she wrote on a little notepad and tore out the sheet, 'and ask her to give it to her father.'

'Her father's dead.'

'Oh,' she said, surprised, 'when did he pass away?'

'When she was four.'

'Poor dear. Is she all alone with her mother?'

'Yes. She doesn't have a nanny.'

'Have her give this note to her mother, then. If she says it's all right, you can study together.'

'Okay. May I be excused?'

'Yes.'

"I arose earlier than usual the next day, so eager was I to tell Sophia about Mother's idea. I dressed quickly, grabbed a piece of toast from the plate in Elsie's hand, and darted out the door before she could protest. Note in hand, I ran happily through the meadow, across the fallen log that served as a footbridge over the creek, and then followed the trail that wound through the woods to our rendezvous at the bluff. Sophia was already there when I arrived. Out of breath, I handed her the note and waited eagerly. She seemed intrigued and a little apprehensive as she unfolded it slowly and held it in her tentative hand. Her brows came together in a puzzled frown as she read. At last, she raised her eyes from the page and appeared uncertain.

'Well?' I asked, brimming with impatience.

'I don't know what to say,' was her tentative response.

'Do you think your mother will let you?'

'I…I don't know,' she answered, fidgeting with the note in her hand.

'We have a little schoolroom set up in the house with a desk and a chalkboard and textbooks. All we need to do is get another desk for you. We can share the book.'

'It sounds wonderful,' she said, hopefully, but with a hint of apprehension.

'Do you think your mother will allow it?'

'We'll see,' she said, happily, and shoved the note into her pocket. 'Come on, I found a dead seal on the beach. I'll show ya.' She ran down the trail that skirted the bluff, and I ran after her.

'It'll be so fun to have you in class with me. I'm in the fourth grade. What grade are you?'

'Fourth,' she said, running along ahead.

'Mrs. Stowe is my teacher. You'll like her. Who was your teacher?'

'We just moved here at the beginnin' a summer.'

'Oh, where did you move from?' I said, jumping over a tree root as I ran along.

'Coos Bay.'

'Where's that?'

'Oregon. We weren't there very long. Mom likes ta move around.'

'Oh.'

"It was a chill September morning. From high atop the bluff we were in the warm sunshine, looking down upon a thick white fog that hovered over the water like a fluffy cloud, but as we followed the descending trail we entered the damp mist. I could hear the ocean lapping the shoreline rhythmically but couldn't see the water through the fog. The trail ended abruptly at a limestone bank three or four feet high, beyond which was the beach. Sophia hit it at full speed and leaped off the bank, landing perfectly in the soft sand eight feet distant. Determined to beat her mark, I sprinted to the edge and jumped as far as I could, flying through the air and touching down a foot beyond her, but my momentum carried me forward and I tumbled over and over until I hit the surf. A little dazed, I sat in the wet sand nursing my wounded pride as the tidewater washed in around me. Sophia approached laughing, and helped me up.

'Nicely done, Tom-boy,' she said and led me through the fog along the shoreline, just beyond the reach of the incoming tide. Perched on the body of the dead seal, a seagull squawked in protest and took flight as we approached. Sophia knelt down beside the lifeless little body that was circled by flies.

'He's just a pup,' she said. 'Poor thing.'

"He looked like a puppy, with his short little snout, black nose, and gray whiskers. Three deep, parallel gouges along his side spoke of his fate. He had escaped attack by a shark, but eventually succumbed to his wounds. Sophia was petting the lifeless body compassionately.

'So, Thomas, when ya start school,' she said, distractedly, 'you'll be in class all day, and I won't see ya anymore.'

'But you'll be in class with me,' I said, cheerfully.

'Oh, yeah.' She stood, and took my hand. 'It's so cold and dreary down here; let's go back up ta the bluff where the sun's shinin'.' She was trying to be a good sport, but I could tell by the way her arms hung listlessly at her side that something troubled her. We began back up the trail.

"The next day, Sophia reported that her mother gave permission to study with me. The news was delivered rather off-handedly, without enthusiasm, and I wondered at the source of her indifference. I passed it on to Mother, who scheduled a meeting with Mrs. Stowe and Sophia two days hence so that they could determine Sophia's grade level.

"At the appointed hour, I heard a timid little wrap at the great oak door and rushed ahead of Elsie to get it. Sophia stood on the doorstep fidgeting nervously, looking very small, timorous, and frightened in her black pants and a white down jacket that was too big for her. She had washed her face and hands and was so pretty.

'Hello, Sophia.' I threw my arm around her excitedly and led her inside to where Mother and Mrs. Stowe waited. She stood looking shyly at the floor, her little face nearly lost in the fluffy down jacket. I could see that Mother was enamored with her at once. Smiling gently, she knelt down before her and brushed back the hair that had fallen around Sophia's shy face.

'Hello Sophia. I'm Carolyn Moore, Thomas' mother.'

'Hello Mrs. Moore,' she said, timidly, her eyes on the floor.

'What a pretty little girl,' Mother said, running her fingers tenderly through Sophia's hair. 'This is Mrs. Stowe; she'll be your teacher.'

'Hello Mrs. Stowe,' she said, quietly, as before, with her eyes on the floor.

'Hello sweetie. Come along, let's get started.'

"She took Sophia's little hand and led her away. When they reached the hallway that led to the classroom, Sophia turned and her downcast eyes met mine for a brief instant, but if that moment had been an afternoon, those doleful eyes could not have said more. A condemned man climbing the gallows to meet his fate would not have shared a greater sense of sorrow and farewell than I saw in those troubled blue eyes that day. It puzzled me, but I attributed it to her sometimes-shy nature. With a gentle tug, Mrs. Stowe led her away.

"I expected half a day of tests, so I was prepared to occupy myself all morning. I had recently acquired a copy of The Three Musketeers, which I was taking great delight in, and wished to show to Sophia at the first opportunity. Mother sat beside the fire thumbing through a magazine, and I was settling into a chair at the window to read, when Mrs. Stowe appeared. She had been away only a few minutes.

'Have you forgotten something?' Mother asked, looking up from her magazine.

'I'm finished.'

'So soon?' Mother frowned.

"Something passed between them in the silence that followed—

some adult communication that was beyond my boyhood interpretation.

'Thomas, be a good host and keep Sophia company,' she said, with her eyes on Maria. 'She's all alone in the classroom.'

'Okay.' I dashed off down the hallway with all possible speed, and then remembered the book. I wanted to show it to Sophia, so I made my way back. I could hear Mother and Mrs. Stowe talking and approached quietly so I wouldn't disturb them, but there was something in their confidential tone that caught my attention, and I paused at the door to listen. They spoke quietly, in a sort of hushed, conspiratorial voice.

'...have to start from the beginning. She's had no education at all,' Mrs. Stowe said.

'Excuse me?'

'She knows nothing of arithmetic, and she can't read, so of course she can't write. She knows a little of the alphabet. That's all.'

'But Thomas said she was reading The Scarlet Pimpernel when they first met.'

'It's a common ruse, Carolyn. They see other children their age reading, and know they should be able to, so they fake it to avoid ridicule and scorn. They often have low self-esteem because they feel stupid. I'm not surprised she was pretending to read a book. She didn't want Thomas to think poorly of her.'

'Is she,' Mother paused, searching for the right word, 'slow, Maria?'

'Slow?'

'Is she simple? Can she learn?'

'It's difficult to say. I don't know how to test her since she can't read. My sense, though, is that she may be quite bright.'

'Bright?' I could hear the emotion in Mother's voice. 'And she can't read. How does something like this happen?'

'I don't know. She lives alone with her mother, who she said moves around quite a bit. It's easy to get behind, and difficult to catch up.'

'What do you propose, Maria?'

'Well, Thomas won't start class for another three weeks. I can work intensively with Sophia over that time, and perhaps bring her up to a level where she can sit in classes with him and be able to follow along. If she really is bright, and she's willing to work hard, I think she can do it.'

'I know that's a lot more work than you were expecting. I'll bear the expense. It seems clear that her mother doesn't care about her education.'

'Carolyn, this borders on criminal. No child should experience this. I'll cheerfully donate my time to this cause.'

"I slipped away quietly while they were planning a curriculum and made my silent way along the hallway. At the door of the classroom I paused. What would I say to Sophia? Everything was different than I expected, and I didn't know what to think of her then. When I entered, I found her sitting at my little study desk staring dejectedly at the floor. Looking so small and wounded in her black work pants and down jacket, she was crying quietly, demurely, as if her tears would be a nuisance to us.

'Hi Sophia,' I said, trying to sound cheerful.

'Hello, Thomas,' she sniffled, meekly, without looking up. It took a moment for her to summon her courage. 'Do ya…still like me?' she asked, in a little voice that I could scarcely hear.

'Best friends forever, right?' was my cheerful response.

'Really?' In her shame, she still had not looked at me, but kept her guilty eyes on the floor. She dragged her coat sleeve across her wet nose. 'Did Mrs. Stowe tell ya…about me?'

'No,' I said, softly, 'but I overheard.'

'Ya don't care that I'm stupid?' Tears sprang forth again from her downcast eyes.

'You're not stupid, Sophia. Mrs. Stowe thinks you're quite bright,' I said, reassuringly.

'Really?' She peeked up at me timidly, the beginning of a little smile on her lips.

'Really. That's what she said, I promise.'

'But I…I can't read, ya know? I was only pretendin' before. So ya wouldn' think I was dumb. So ya would like me.' Blushing in her embarrassment, her eyes fell to the floor again.

'I do like you. You're my best friend in the whole world,' I said, passionately. Encouraged perhaps by the passion in my voice, she peered up at me from her fluffy down jacket where she had shrunk, like a turtle seeking refuge in his shell.

'Oh Thomas,' she said, trembling with emotion, 'how can ya like me? I'm just...I'm just...nothing.'

"And she burst into tears again. More than anything in the world, I wanted to comfort her, to sooth her. I wrapped her in my ten-year-old arms and held her to me. She was crying into my shirt.

'I never really had a friend before,' she sniffled. 'We move around all the time. Just when I start ta make friends we move.'

'Why?'

'I don't know. Mom just gets restless, I think,' she said, wiping her eyes with the sleeve of her jacket.

'Have you ever been to school?'

'Just part a the first grade.'

'What part?'

'The middle. I started three months late, then we moved a month or two before the end a the school year.'

'Why didn't you go to the second grade?'

'I think the teachers were mad at mom about somethin', so she just said I wouldn' be goin' anymore.'

"Sophia sat with her head down and her eyes fixed on the floor, as if ashamed. Her little girl voice was so soft that I strained to hear it. I felt so sorry for her. We heard voices in the hallway, and a moment later Mother entered the classroom followed by Mrs. Stowe.

'Well Sophia, I have good news,' Mother said. 'School starts tomorrow. Are you ready?'

'Really? You're gonna teach me?' she asked, surprised.

'That's right. Be here at seven o'clock tomorrow, and we'll begin,' said Mrs. Stowe. 'I have a lot of prep work to do, Carolyn. I should get started.'

'Thank you, Maria.'

'You're quite welcome. And you,' Mrs. Stowe said, stooping down eye-to-eye with Sophia, 'are going to be my star pupil. Do you know how special you are?'

'No,' said Sophia, timidly.

'Of course you don't,' answered Mrs. Stowe, laughing, but I could see tears in her sympathetic eyes, too. 'Good-bye everyone,' she said, and left the room.

'Unless my nose deceives me,' Mother said, 'Elsie is making peanut butter cookies, and I'm certain she would give some nice hot ones fresh from the oven to anyone who asked nicely.'

"I took Sophia by the hand and we raced to the kitchen. She seemed delighted that her secret was out and that everyone accepted her. With the burden of her deception removed, she looked wise, sage almost, as she bit into a fresh peanut butter cookie and pondered her future."

Thomas took a sip of wine, then turned, looking first at Charles, then me, as if gauging our interest in his tale. He needn't have been concerned. We were sitting forward in our seats, eagerly waiting for him to continue. Smiling, he began again.

"Not far from the main house is a little redbrick building that Father had made into a home shop. It has a low shingle roof and a white garage door, which, set against the red of the brick, has a charming appearance, like a little cottage. There are windows with painted white frames all around, allowing plenty of light. Brown paving stones extend from the circular drive across the green grass to the garage door. Father and I had started building a little lap strake sailing dinghy in the shop before he passed away. The stem and keel were laid up, and the frames were steam bent into place. It was Father's own design and had beautiful lines.

"Sophia arrived every morning at six thirty and joined us for breakfast. It was unusual for us to eat at that hour, but Mother felt that our new student needed a hearty breakfast for her long day and believed it would not be provided unless she did it herself. She also felt that our neglected little guest should have company, so we all joined her. At seven o'clock, her lessons began. There were no breaks until noon, when they paused for a half hour lunch, then lessons again until four o'clock. It was an ideal time for me to work on the dinghy. The September mornings were crisp and clear; I could see my breath before me as I walked to the shop. As the day warmed, I would open the garage door and work on the boat in the bright sun, in the broken shadow of a giant maple tree at the corner of the garage, with turning leaves that were becoming golden brown in anticipation of the new season.

"At noon each day, I walked across the yard and joined Sophia for lunch. She was always focused on her lessons and between bites talked excitedly of what she learned. She would have preferred a shorter lunch period so she could return to her studies, but Mother insisted that the break remain half an hour. Each afternoon, when class was over, she would hastily gather up her homework, thank Mrs. Stowe, and rush home before the sun set, which was getting earlier each night. I had not been to her house, but knew that the nearest home was two or three miles distant and that the journey would be a frightening one through the winding trails and dark woods at night.

"In this way, the three weeks passed in a whirl. I had planked and painted the dinghy and was applying the final coat of varnish to the fir gunwale on Sophia's last day of class. Preparations were being made for a little surprise party in her honor as she took her final exam. When I entered the kitchen that Friday afternoon, it was a bustle of activity.

'Get the plates from the cupboard and set the table, please, Thomas,' said Mother, hurriedly, as she spread the tablecloth on the kitchen table.

"Elsie rushed to the oven to remove a freshly baked cake. Taken by surprise by the bustle, I didn't move fast enough.

'Thomas,' Mother said, sharply.

"I sprang into action, setting the table as Mrs. Stowe entered the kitchen.

'She'll just be a moment,' she said. 'She's nearly finished. Carolyn, I've never seen a more devoted pupil. In twenty years teaching, I've never seen anyone work as hard or learn as quickly as this dear girl.' She shook her head in wonder, and her face became suddenly serious. 'I don't think she's ever had a compliment or kind word, either. With the slightest praise her little face just lights up, and she tries even harder.'

"We could hear Sophia coming then. Her soft footsteps rang in the hallway as she ran, and moments later she burst into the kitchen victorious.

'Finished!' she said.

"Everyone stopped what they were doing, and applauded. Sophia blushed. I'm certain that she had never had a party in her honor before and simply beamed as she gorged herself on cookies, cake, and ice cream, all the while looking about her in wonder, as if in a dream. I believe it was the best day of her young life, and I know I saw her pinch herself several times to confirm it was real." Thomas shook his head, smiling as he thought back to that day, and then continued.

"It was early autumn and the maple leaves were beautiful to look upon. In the stillness of the country, without the clamor of machines or the murmur of voices or constant bustle of city life, they could be heard breaking lose from the tree limbs before dropping to the soft ground. Our tree lined drive was covered in fall leaves, red, golden, brown, and alive with motion as squirrels darted among them with short, quick movements, searching the ground for their winter store.

"The Monday following Sophia's triumphant graduation our lessons began, and she sat beside me at her own little desk. Compelled to attend, school had always been rather dull and prosaic for me, a duty of sorts. But for Sophia, from whom it had been withheld, it was of tremendous joy and interest. My attempts to distract her with pokes, doodles, and other boyhood gestures were met with polite but firm rejection. I soon resigned myself to the fact that this was going to be all business and settled in to study. Mrs. Stowe was correct; she was an apt pupil. She had, in a very short time, made up for her lack of instruction and by year's end had quite caught up with me. Summer gave way to fall, and with the new season came an unwelcome change in the weather, one that spread its cold, wet embrace over the island and wore heavily upon Sophia, who had to brave it each day in her journey to and from our little schoolroom. As the days waned and the sun sank into the distant ocean earlier each evening, I saw her watch the setting sun through the window of our school room with melancholy resignation, knowing that her period of daylight travel was diminishing and she would eventually be walking home in the dark on a foreboding little trail through the woods.

"That day came late in November. Mrs. Stowe had excused us and left for home, but instead of gathering her things and rushing away, Sophia remained at her desk with her eyes on the sunset. It was already too late; the trip home would be a dark one. Her face, bathed in the orange glow that poured through the leaded window, was a picture of wonder and awe as she witnessed the spectacular close of that fall day through the turning maple leaves that clung near the window frame. But there was something else there, too, in that pretty face and glowing eyes. For all her wits and maturity, she was still a little girl, and the thought of walking that gloomy trail after sunset was terrifying. In minutes, the fiery sun half submerged in the ocean would vanish altogether. Already the shadows were deepening and darkness was gathering around us. Sophia simply closed her book and, as she had done all of her young life, made the best of the situation.

'Do you think your mother will invite me to stay for dinner tonight, Thomas?' she asked, demurely.

"I smiled, and then ran down the hall to find Mother and ask if Sophia might not join us for dinner. She had issued the invitation many times, but always it had been politely and reluctantly refused. That Sophia wanted to join us, longed to join us even, was clear to me, but that would have meant a dark walk home through the dreaded woods. She had never mentioned her fear, and I alone had perceived it, perhaps because only I knew her route, or something of her route, and had imagined making that lonely nighttime journey myself. I never mentioned it to Mother. I was certain that she thought Sophia's house was quite close—just over the hill—or she would not have allowed her to walk such a distance through the woods at night. Mother rarely ventured out upon the grounds, and when she did, it was nearly always to visit Father's grave. There she would sit, hour after hour, pensively observing his headstone or talking quietly to his grave, upon which she would place fresh flowers. She didn't know of the path that Sophia took and I didn't tell her. If she had known, she would have forbidden the long, dangerous walk, and I feared that would mean no more school for Sophia.

"I found Mother in her usual place, sitting at the window, reading a novel by the fading light of the sunset. She granted my request with a silent nod, and I dashed away to tell Sophia.

"Since we had a dinner guest, we were officially entertaining, which meant employing the formal dining room. Sophia was always observant and precocious. Our home, our dinner table, our very lives were a classroom to her. She watched everything and learned like a sponge, soaking up knowledge. By the end of the first dinner, she had learned proper table manners.

"After that day, it was dark at the conclusion of each class and Sophia became a regular dinner guest. Out of a sense of etiquette, Mother continued to invite her each evening, but it was understood that she would be joining us, and Elsie took it for granted and prepared the meals accordingly, making extra. She was always so pleasant and thankful. Everyone loved her and enjoyed having her at the table. The cold draft and quiet emptiness that had settled upon the house with Father's passing was giving way to Sophia's exuberance and good cheer. Her inquisitive, playful young soul was a torch that drove away the shadows of gloom and despair, and lifted us all. It felt like home again, and everyone sensed the change.

"At the beginning, she would always leave shortly after dinner, and I sensed that she was careful not to overstay her welcome, but with time, as she became more comfortable with us, she stayed a little longer each night. Elsie would attend to the dishes, Mother would retire to another room, and Sophia and I would remain at the dinner table talking or move to the fire, which was always burning brightly in the evening. She loved the fire. It seemed to comfort and sooth her. She was always so cheerful and animated, but at the fire she would just relax and stare thoughtfully into the flickering flames.

'Penny for your thoughts,' I said, one evening. We had been sitting before the fire after dinner, and she had been silently watching the flames for quite some time.

'I was just thinking how sweet you were,' she said, smiling.

'No you weren't. Your face was too serious for that.'

'How do you know that?' she inquired, curiously.

'I've been reading Sherlock Holmes. I was deducing.'

'Does it really teach you how to do things like that?' she asked, inquisitively.

'Sort of. It makes you more observant.'

'You're always so clever,' she said, with a warm smile, then her face became sober. 'All right then, I was thinking about that awful walk home. It frightens me, Thomas, especially on a night like this.'

"For the last half hour we had been listening to a storm blow outside. From nowhere a tremendous gale had blown in over the island. Thunder, rolling and cracking throughout the valley, announced the arrival of the storm, then the rain came, and the windows shook with the gusting wind. Sophia had not brought a raincoat or a light. It would be a wet, miserable walk home on the dark trail through the woods.

"I saw Mother approaching from the shadow of an unlit corner of the house. She walked quietly, almost like a spirit, along the wall past the windows that looked out over the sea, but her eyes were on the floor. She must have been thinking about something; she didn't see Sophia and I until the firelight caught her attention, and she glanced in our direction.

'Oh, you're still here,' she said, surprised, and looked apprehensively into the stormy darkness. 'What a foul evening. Would you like to stay here tonight, Sophia?'

'I wouldn't want to impose, Mrs. Moore,' she answered, demurely.

'It's no imposition dear, but what will your mother say if you don't come home tonight?'

'Nothing,' she said, quietly.

'Really?' Mother asked, frowning. Sophia nodded meekly. 'All right then. I'll have Elsie show you to one of the guest rooms.'

'Thank you, Mrs. Moore.'

"Mother continued on, and a few minutes later Elsie led her away, up the long staircase that connected to the bedrooms upstairs. She returned a short time later wearing a crisp, white dress shirt from my closet and a clean pair of white socks from my drawer.

'Elsie said it would be all right,' she explained, apologetically.

"I liked her wearing my clothes. She was so pretty the way her black hair fell over the shirt collar and her thin arms extended beyond the rolled up shirt sleeves. I had never seen her in anything but her tomboy clothes, and she was quite cute. We sat together just the two of us on the floor in the small circle of light before the fire, which by then had burned low. She was quiet as she looked into the dying embers, and I couldn't read her face.

'Are you worried about your mother?' I asked. 'Will you get in trouble for not coming home?'

'I'll be surprised if she even notices,' Sophia mumbled.

'What did you say?'

'We're best friends forever, right?' She looked at me earnestly.

'Course.'

'Come over here and sit behind me.'

"I did so.

'Now put your arms around me, and hold me.'

"I held her, and she leaned back, snuggling into me.

'Oh, I feel so safe here,' she said.

"We stayed like that, sitting in the darkness, looking into the dying fire without speaking, until we fell asleep. Sometime later I stirred, half awake, as someone lifted me up and carried me to bed.

"I awoke the next day to the sound of rain drumming on my window, and remembered that Sophia had slept over. Happily, I jumped out of bed and raced to her room. The door was slightly ajar and I paused, not wishing to wake her if she still slept. I peeked in. She had pulled the blankets up close to her face and was rubbing the sheets upon her cheeks, delighting in the texture. She wiggled and squirmed and twisted delightedly under the heavy covers, smiling all the while, cozy and warm.

'Hello, Sophia.'

'Oh Thomas, this bed is so warm and yummy,' she said, holding the covers up under her chin.

'Are you hungry?' I smiled. 'Let's have breakfast.'

'Okay,' she answered, eagerly, then threw back the covers, jumped to the floor, and raced to the door. She would have brushed right past me, but as an afterthought paused, and kissed me on the cheek. 'Thank you, Thomas,' she said, and we raced down the hallway.

"The little kitchen table was set for breakfast, and Elsie was dishing up the food. Mother was already seated when Sophia and I stumbled into the kitchen laughing. I took my usual seat, and Sophia sat across from me at the place that was set for her.

'Good morning, Sophia,' said Mother.

'Good morning, Mrs. Moore.'

'Did you sleep well?'

'Gosh yes. I felt like a princess in that huge bed with all those beautiful covers.'

'Really?' Mother smiled, gently. 'What is your bed like at home?' "Sophia's eyes fell, and she began picking at her food. Mother studied her a moment. 'Sophia?'

'It's okay.'

'Where is your house?'

'Just down the trail a little ways. May I have some orange juice please?'

"Elsie poured orange juice into her glass. Later that day when we had taken a break from our lessons to eat lunch, we sat in the grass beside the fishpond throwing little pieces of bread into the water and watching the fish rise to the surface to snatch them. Sophia seemed distracted and thoughtful.

'Are you sad?' I asked.

'Of course not.' She smiled, sweetly. 'Why would you ask that?'

'You just don't seem very happy. I thought I may have done something wrong.'

'Oh Thomas, you could never make me unhappy,' she said, earnestly. 'I was just thinking.'

'About what?'

'Well,' she said, framing her words carefully, 'this place. Your home.'

'Oh. What about it?'

'I've never been to a place like this before.'

'Like what?' I asked, innocently.

'It's...it's...like a park, Thomas. A park that you get to live in.'

"I was puzzled by her remark.

'Have you ever been to a park?' she asked.

'No.'

'Have you ever been...' she paused, thinking, 'have you ever been beyond these gates?'

'I've been to Father's shipyard. He kept his boat there, and we would go sailing.'

'Anywhere else?'

'I've been to town with Mother a few times.'

'Anywhere else?'

'All the places you and I went when we were exploring.'

'Is that all?'

"I nodded.

'Thomas, this place is different than anyplace I've ever been before. It's like...well, some magical place where nothing bad ever happens. Evil can't enter here, you see? Nothing bad ever happens here.'

"She moved closer and held my eye intently.

'There are no bad people. No one will ever hurt you. Do you know what I mean?'

"I didn't know what she meant. But she seemed so earnest, like she really wanted me to see, to understand what she was trying to tell me; so I said I did, but I didn't know what she meant. It was years later that I finally understood, and Sophia was no longer around for me to tell. She was gone.

"A raven had been watching us closely from a nearby fir tree, intent on our lunch.

'Yes, that's it,' Sophia said. 'Let's call it...' she paused, thinking, and spied the Raven, 'let's call it Ravenswood, like some English castle. It'll be our own little magical world,' she said, excitedly. 'When I'm on my little footpath through the woods, I'm always so frightened that I start at every little sound along the way. I hear birds fluttering away in the darkness and crickets chirping and twigs snapping, and I never know if I'm being followed or if someone is going to jump out and snatch me. But it's safe here. Your mother is so pretty, and so thoughtful, and Elsie is so kind, and you're my best friend. You've all made me feel so welcome. When I get home, the house is dark and empty, and I feel so alone and frightened.'

'But where's your mother?'

'At work. She doesn't get home until very late.'

'You're alone in your house all night? I don't think I would like that.'

'I make my own dinner, then wait up for Mother to come home.'

'Why don't you go to bed?'

'Oh no. I can't sleep until she gets home. I hear tree limbs scratching against the house or animals outside the window. It's all so frightening.'

'I'm sorry, Sophia. I can walk home with you.'

'No,' she said, quickly. 'I didn't tell you this so you would feel sorry for me. I just want you to know that I appreciate it here.'

"Sophia was dining with us nearly every evening then, and it was impossible for me to not feel sorry for her walking home in the dark each night. She would slip on her coat, kiss Mother and Elsie good-bye at the door, and disappear into the darkness with a brave face. I alone knew that she was terrified, and it tore at my boyhood chivalry. How could I allow this sweet girl to brave that dark, perilous path each night, while I remained at home warm and safe? I asked if I might accompany her many times, but the answer was always a firm no. It would do little to ease her fear, but I could follow at a distance to make sure nothing happened to her. To at least see what her journey was like.

"The next time she left our house after joining us for dinner, I quickly slipped out and followed. I had worn a black shirt and trousers that night and slipped on a dark coat before leaving. I would be invisible in the dark. I was quick, but nearly too late. All I could see was her white coat in the distance, and I hurried after it before it disappeared into the woods. It was a dark, moonless night, and I could see nothing but Sophia's coat, which seemed to float along ahead. The trail was just a little footpath worn into the woods, which turned and meandered and doubled back and crossed a rotting log that had fallen across it, and descended to a quickening little stream that one could step across, and climbed back up again. I was soon quite lost. When the jacket disappeared at a bend in the trail, I had nothing to guide me and nearly panicked. Several times I nearly turned back, but I would be hopelessly lost without the jacket to light the way. I thought about calling out to Sophia to wait up, but my presence would be difficult to explain. So I tried to keep her in sight, to stay close, but not so close that she would hear me trailing along behind. She was right: it was a terrifying journey in the darkness. I wondered that she kept doing it. A few times I heard noises in the bushes and saw the jacket pause. She had stopped to listen, then hurried along again. The trail seemed to go on and on. I had no idea how I would find my way back.

"Eventually, it felt like the trees had fallen away before me, and I was at the edge of a clearing. In the darkness, I thought I could just see the faint outline of a house ahead. The jacket made a straight, rapid approach to it, and I heard a door creak open and closed. Moments later a light came on, and I saw Sophia inside. The dim light illuminated little, but it was enough to see perfectly into the house, and some spilled out through the window, allowing me to see the outside. It was tiny. Just a little shed. If it had been painted once, there was no evidence of it then. The weathered siding was bleached gray by sun and rain and looked like the faded bark of a tree. The door hung crookedly by broken hinges, and the whole of the little shack seemed to have settled ungracefully on its foundation (if it ever had one) and sagged in the middle as if it preferred to fall in and tumble over. It could only have been a hastily constructed fisherman's shack that had been long abandoned before being occupied by the current tenants.

"It was then that I realized I had been born with an insensitivity that I did not, until that moment, perceive. To a child, the world is small, but they are small. The little world in which they live is built upon all that their innocent, inquisitive eyes find around them. They grow as their perception of the world around them grows, and in their growth they gain knowledge and experience. I grew, but my world did not, and so I did not. In my sequestered existence, I learned only what could be experienced within the confines of Ravenswood. In all my young life, it had not occurred to me that other people lived by a different standard. I had not considered that another yardstick existed. In my world, everyone had a sprawling estate, with a nanny and a team of gardeners to maintain it.

"Watching in the darkness through the limbs of an old fir tree that swayed with the breeze, I saw Sophia so clearly in the little shack as she took off her jacket and hung it from a peg on the door, and then removed her shoes. It was just one square little room. The kitchen, if it could be called such, was on the far wall; it was nothing more than a countertop, with a sink and oven. There was a sofa in the middle of the room, at the end of which was a little table and lamp. On the wall to the left, I saw the corner of a bed.

"Sophia brushed her teeth at the kitchen sink and then removed her trousers, folded them, and placed them on the sofa back. Her flannel shirt hung to her knees, serving as pajamas, and she knelt down at the sofa with her arms on the cushions, praying. But closing her eyes for prayer was beyond her frightened capacity. Wide-eyed, she searched the shadows of the little room constantly, as if expecting something to jump out at her. The prayer was said quickly, with eyes wide open, and she jumped up.

"Sheets had been tucked neatly into the cushions of the sofa, and blankets pulled up over them. Sophia crawled between the sheets and pulled the blankets up close under her chin, whether from cold or fear I could not tell. On a short table at the end of the sofa, behind her head, was the lamp that lit the room, and the small circle of light fell upon her frightened, pretty face. She remained in her little makeshift bed, wide-awake, starting at every little noise. I could see her eyes darting back and forth as she listened to the night sounds. The wind blew through the trees, not strongly, but evenly, with little gusts that sounded like the distant roar of the ocean surf. There was a crippled old apple tree beside the house with bare, skinny limbs that extended haphazardly in all directions. It leaned heavily upon the little shack, and the shack leaned heavily upon it, like two drunks supporting each other. One of the limbs high above the ground scratched upon the side of the house with an eerie screech as the wind pushed it, and Sophia's eyes frequently turned in that direction.

"I pitied her with all my young heart and wished to rush to her, to comfort her. But that could not be. It was getting late, and I must go before my absence was detected. But how? My guide would not be returning with me, and I was lost without her. I remembered that the trail was narrow, barely wide enough for one to pass, and that the trees and brush were thick enough to form a sort of wall on either side. I wouldn't be able to see where I was going, but I wouldn't be able to stray from the path. I would just need to go slow.

'Goodnight Sophia,' I said, under my breath, and began home.

"Several weeks had passed since my twilight vigil to Sophia's house, and nothing had changed. She arrived early each morning a little flush from the walk and the chill, and we had class together. By then it was mid-December, and the temperatures often fell below freezing. She would sit before the fire with her hands extended toward the flames, warming herself before our lessons began."

A gentle smile spread across our host's face, as he recalled a warm memory.

"But one morning there was a spring in her step when she arrived and skipped past the fire to pass a note to Mother. Sophia waited eagerly, expectantly, while Mother read.

'I'm guessing by your expression,' said Mother, with a smile, 'that you are aware of the contents of this note.'

"Sophia nodded, energetically.

'And that you have no objection.'

"Sophia shook her head as enthusiastically as before.

'Very well. Did you bring your things?'

"In response, she produced a little bundle the size of a bread loaf and held it before her.

'That's all? Okay. You may have the room that you were in before. Put your things away and come down to begin your studies.'

"I had watched all this with eager anticipation, wondering what it could mean, and Mother saw the look on my bewildered face.

'Sophia's mother is going to Seattle for a week and has asked if she may stay here with us during the time she is away.'

"I was delighted and ran through the house with unbound happiness. We studied by day and played by night. Mother would always find us in some part of the house playing a game or talking, and it was with reluctance that we parted long enough to sleep each evening. The week whirled past, and each day we expected a visit from Sophia's mother, a visit I was not looking forward to. If Sophia was, she didn't say. One week became two, and Mother was growing concerned. On the weekend of the second week, she found Sophia and I playing chess in front of the fire.

'Sophia, dear.'

'Yes, Mrs. Moore.'

'Would you run home and see if your mother has returned? Perhaps she's ill and hasn't been able to leave or send word.'

'Okay.'

"Sophia slipped on her white jacket and struck off at once. I knew it to be little more than a twenty-minute journey each way, so I waited for her return with the thought of finishing our chess game. The December morning had started cold and clear with the sun shining on my face when I awoke, but the weather had become rough and tumultuous. Dark clouds heavily laden with moisture had blown in over the ocean, bringing wind and rain. Trees swayed in the breeze, and the few leaves that remained on the old maples lining our drive flew up and away. The leaded windows shook in their frames; even the heavy oak door rattled with the gusts. I stood at the window watching a few fishing boats hurry back to port as they pitched and rolled, buffeted by white-capped breakers building with the wind.

"Sophia was gone for well over an hour, and I was growing

concerned. With each rage of wind and gust of rain I heard her timid little tapping at the door and rushed to it, but she was not there. I formed an opinion that her mother was home and prevented her from returning, so I put the chessboard away and was climbing the stairs to my room. On a whim I decided to check the door one last time. I had only just turned the latch when the wind caught the door like a sail and flung it open, pinning me against the wall. Elsie was passing at that moment and rushed to my aid.

'Careful child,' she said, 'you could be killed.'

"I could offer little help as she pulled the door away from me to latch it shut. But just before it closed, she glimpsed something through the gap and shrieked.

'Good lord.'

"The door was forgotten and she rushed through the opening. Had I not darted out of the way, I would have been crushed as the wind caught the heavy oak and slammed it into the wall with such force that it shook in the frame. Unfettered, it continued to strike the wall randomly as the wind tossed it about. Puzzled by Elsie's actions, I stepped to the doorway to see what had drawn her attention and saw Sophia. She sat on the edge of the fountain, shivering from the cold and staring absently at the ground. The wind had blown her white jacket into the bare tree limbs far down the drive. Her flannel shirt and black trousers, heavy from the drenching rain, hung from her slender limbs, which trembled violently from the chill wind that whipped her.

"What had happened? Why was she so distraught? Her wet hair clung to her delicate face, trailing raindrops from the tips as tears streamed from her vacant blue eyes, running freely down her cheeks to mingle with the rain. She was stooped forward staring at the ground, rejected, forsaken, defeated, while the wind tugged and pulled at her wet clothing and the rain beat down upon her.

"Elsie knelt down at her feet, then reached out with a gentle hand to pull the wet hair away from Sophia's face.

'What's happened, child? What's wrong?' she asked. 'Are you all right? Sophia?'

"But Sophia only stared at the ground, crying, trembling, as if unaware of her presence.

'Can you hear me? Are you hurt? Sophia? Let's get you inside.'

"Still kneeling before her, she lifted Sophia's arms and draped them over her shoulders, then threw her arms around Sophia's middle, and lifted her up. Her sad face rested against Elsie's chest like an infant. As the wind gusted through the open doorway, the heavy door continued to beat upon the wall with tremendous force. Neglecting it in my haste, I rushed to follow Elsie and her passenger.

"She knelt down, setting Sophia on the hearth before the blazing fire in the main room, but Sophia had locked arms around Elsie's neck and refused to let go. Crying, trembling, staring vacantly ahead with her cheek pressed to Elsie's chest, she held tight.

'Sophia? Sophia, sweetie, can you let go?'

"It seemed as if Sophia could hear nothing. Elsie lifted her again, holding her close, then sat down on the hearth herself, with Sophia still in her arms.

'What's happening?' I heard Mother say from another room. 'Why is the door open?'

"I felt the wind stop, and Mother appeared a moment later.

'Oh,' she said, when she saw us. She looked affectionately at rain-soaked little Sophia trembling in Elsie's arms.

'What happened Elsie?'

'I don't know, ma'am. We found her like this, sitting outside in the rain.'

'Poor dear,' said Mother, tenderly. 'We need to get her out of those wet clothes. I'll get a towel. Thomas, get some of your clothes for her. You're about the same size.'

"My path and Mother's were in the same direction, so I tagged along. When we were out of earshot I ventured a question.

'What's wrong with her, Mother?'

'I don't know, but I can guess,' she said, gravely. 'We can dry her and wipe away her tears, but some wounds never heal, Thomas, they're just too deep. She needs to feel loved right now.'

'I don't understand.'

'She's a tough little girl, but she may not be the same after this.'

"Then Mother rushed away to get the towel. I went through my closet and selected clothes for Sophia. Mother was waiting for me on the stairs when I returned.

'I'll take them. Go back to your room please.'

'But I want to help.'

'You can help best by being absent. This is just between us girls.'

"Reluctantly, I returned to my room. I tried to read, but that was impossible; my thoughts kept returning to dear little Sophia sitting on the fountain with tears streaming down her cheeks. I lingered near the window, I lingered near the bed, I lingered at the door. Did I dare? Mother was quite clear. Heaving a frustrated sigh, I paced up and down the room. I sat down. I stood up. I paced some more. I had to know what was happening downstairs, but couldn't leave the room.

"Eventually, I fell into the chair to think and drifted off to sleep in nervous exhaustion. When I awoke, I was in the dark and Elsie was tapping at my door.

'You can come down now, Thomas. Thomas? You can come down now if you like.'

'Okay.'

"I rushed to the door. Elsie caught me by the arm before I passed.

'Be gentle. Don't ask her what happened, okay?'

'Okay,' I answered, uneasily.

"Mother's words rang in my ears. Would she be the same? I found Sophia sitting on the hearth before a warm, quiet fire, her face glowing in the amber light of the coals and the trail of a tear still glistening on her young cheek. With her hands folded on her lap, she looked down at the fire beside her with a melancholy smile that did little to hide the sadness in her heart. Taking a seat beside her, I said nothing. It was quite late by then and quite dark, but for the faint firelight that flickered in the tears falling silently from her blue eyes. In those tears I saw the weight of rejection and the burden of a pain that would not mend. Thinking I had not seen them, she did her best to master them and turned her face away from me for a moment to wipe her eyes with her shirtsleeve. Dress pants from my closet were held up by a belt that was too long and was tied around her slender waist in a knot. The shirt was rolled up to the elbows and hung to her knees.

'Hi,' I said, tentatively, after a long period of silence.

'Hi,' she answered, softly, without taking her eyes from the fire.

A long silence followed while I searched for safe ground.

'Some weather we're having,' I added, lightheartedly, and she laughed.

'You can always make me laugh, Thomas.'

'You're sweet, Sophia. I like making you laugh.'

'I know you do,' she said. Then her face became grave. 'You probably wonder what's going on.'

'Nope,' I said, nonchalantly.

'Is that so?' she said, with a little smile. Then she became serious again. 'Remember when I said my father was dead?'

"I nodded."

'Well, that's what Mother told me, but I don't think it's true. I think he left. I think he ran away because of me.'

"She looked so hurt, so dejected, so frail and small sitting there in the firelight wearing borrowed clothes that were too big for her in a hurtful world that was too big for a frightened little girl who only wanted a normal life.

"I took her hand.

'We may not be able to see each other anymore,' she said, softly.

'What?' I asked, alarmed. 'Why?'

'I may have to go away,' she added, quietly, looking into the fire.

'Why?'

'I may have to leave Ravenswood forever.'

'Why?'

'I just...I may have to go.'

'But why?' I persisted.

'I don't want to think about it. Let's just try to enjoy the time we have left together. Okay?'

'Does it have something to do with that piece of paper?'

"When I first saw her sitting on the fountain shivering in the rain, I noticed one little hand was clenched tightly in a fist. As she clung to Elsie on the hearth, that same hand was closed in an unyielding fist around Elsie's neck. And now I could see she still held that hand in a fist and within was a piece of paper. She took the scrap and shoved it into her pants pocket, then took my face in her two cold hands and pressed her head to mine.

'You're my best friend in the whole world, Thomas.'

'You're my best friend in the whole world, Sophia,' I said,

earnestly. 'Why must you go?'

'I didn't say I had to go. I said I may have to go.'

'But why?'

'Things don't always work out the way you want them to,' she answered, quietly.

'Maybe I can help. Maybe Mother can help.'

'You can't help.'

'How do you know?'

'You can't help.'

'How do you know?'

'Oh Thomas, you're incorrigible.'

'Tell me what's happened,' I said, desperately.

'I have to...' she choked back a sob, 'I have to go to an orphanage.'

"She stood suddenly, looking down at my puzzled face, then ran sobbing across the dark room and up the stairs. In the quiet house, I distinctly heard her footsteps dashing along the hallway and, a moment later, the close of her bedroom door. She was gone. An orphanage? I wanted to ask Mother what this was all about and why we couldn't help, but she was in bed. So was Elsie.

"Had she lost her mother? Sitting all alone on the hearth, I turned to the window that looked out over the graveyard and saw Father's headstone through the rain-spattered pane that I had peered through so many times before. It looked so lonely, so neglected. The wind was gone and the rain fell steadily, quietly. I felt a tinge of shame that I hadn't been thinking about him as much since Sophia came into our lives.

"In stunned silence I crossed the floor and climbed the stairs to my room. Sophia's was across from mine, and as I passed I thought I heard ever so quietly the muffled sound of a lonely girl's cries. My bed provided little comfort. I lay awake and alert, staring at the shadows overhead hour after hour, my mind racing, my ears tuned to the cries across the hall, until I fell into a fitful, dreamless sleep.

"The next day brought no relief. I woke to the sound of thunder rolling through the hills and valleys and echoing over the island like the beat of a giant drum. The sky was dark and threatening. A gentle rain fell steadily, drearily I thought. I turned my head on the pillow, looking blandly over the grounds, feeling a vague uneasiness without knowing why. Then it came to me. The orphanage. I sat bolt upright in bed. Sophia was going to an orphanage. I jumped out of bed and rushed to find Mother, taking the stairs two at a time. Elsie was passing at the foot of the staircase carrying an armful of clean towels.

'Good lord, Thomas, what happened, did you see a ghost?'

'Where's Mother?'

'She's gone to town.'

'To town? But she hardly ever goes to town.'

'Well, she's gone today.'

'But why?'

'I don't know.'

'When will she return?'

'She didn't say.'

'But I must speak to her.'

"In response she simply shrugged, and continued on her way.

'Where is Sophia?'

'She went for a walk.'

'Which way?'

'Thomas.' She stopped, looking me directly in the eye. 'She needs to be alone right now. I know you want to help, but she needs to be alone.'

'But…'

'You upset her last night, didn't you? After I asked you to be gentle with her, you upset her didn't you?'

"My silence was answer enough.

'You see, she just needs to be alone right now.'

"I spent a slow, restless morning roaming about the house. It felt like a prison. The two people I wanted to speak to, Mother and Sophia, were away, and I knew not when they would return. With childlike impatience, I sat at the window fidgeting, watching for Mother's arrival. The hours dragged past, and still Mother had not returned. It was dusk, and the sun was setting into the ocean, in that tiny space between the clouds and the sea, when I heard her car and saw the headlamps streaming between the maples along the tree-lined drive. Waiting for her to enter the house was out of the question. I ran through the door and was standing near the fountain when she pulled up beside me and parked the car. The back seat, I noticed, was nearly full of shopping bags and gift-wrapped boxes that smelled sweetly of Christmas. I opened the car door for her.

'Such a gentleman,' she said, impressed. 'Hello Thomas.'

'Hello,' I said, and closed the car door after her.

"Taking her hand then, I led her up the path toward the house, while she smiled wryly at my sudden show of courtesy.

'Mother,' I said, attempting to sound very grown up, 'what's this I hear about Sophia going away to an orphanage?'

'Ah. So this is the source of your newly acquired manners. Shame on you,' she said, amused.

'But why must she go to an orphanage?'

'So she told you, did she?'

'Yes, but she didn't say why.'

'It's not my place to tell you. If she wants you to know she'll tell you herself.'

'Did her mother...' I paused, not knowing how to ask, 'well, did she, did she, die?'

'That would be so much easier to bear,' she said, under her breath.

'Excuse me?' I asked.

'Nothing. I can't tell you any more than you already know.'

'But why can't she stay with us? Why can't she stay here?' I pleaded.

'She's not a stray dog that you've brought home as a pet, Thomas. There are considerations. Things you're not aware of. Things you wouldn't understand.'

"By this time we had reached the house, and Elsie was waiting at the door.

'There are some things in the car, Elsie, would you get them please?'

'Of coarse, ma'am,' she said, and hurried to the car.

'But Mother...'

'Thomas,' she said, abruptly, 'I will do what I can for her. You'll just have to accept that.'

"It was stated with such an air of finality that nothing more was to be said on the subject; that was clear. I threw myself unhappily into a chair and watched Elsie carrying the packages from the car. There were a number of fancy sacks filled with boxes and white tissue paper, some smelling feminine and sweet. Sophia returned at that moment and followed Elsie through the door as she made her last trip from the car.

'Hello, Sophia,' Mother said.

'Hello Mrs. Moore.'

'Are you just returning? Have you been away all day?'

'Yes,' she answered, pensively, 'I went home to get my things.'

'Where are they?'

'Here,' she said, holding before her a book and a few articles of clothing.

'Is that all child? Have you no toys or trinkets or other possessions?'

"Sophia shook her head, embarrassed, and seemed on the verge of tears again.

'Come here.'

"Sophia rushed to her, burying her face in the folds of Mother's dress, and burst into tears.

'There, there,' she said, hugging Sophia close, and rocking gently from side to side to sooth her. 'I did a little Christmas shopping today, but we don't need to wait three weeks to open a few of these.'

"She led Sophia to the next room where Elsie had stacked all of the boxes and sacks.

'Some of these are for you, Sophia. Sit over here before the fire and open a few of your gifts.'

"Returning to her tomboy roots, Sophia dragged a shirtsleeve across her nose in a most unladylike manner (she was still wearing my shirt) and regarded Mother with timid, almost suspicious, eyes. Even then, after all of the time she had spent with us, her suffering young soul felt unworthy, and she couldn't help but regard kindness with some measure of suspicion. I don't know that anyone outside of my family had ever treated her kindly, and she was unsure of how to react. Mother's expression was sincere and unmistakable, though, and Sophia gradually succumbed to it. Her face was a picture of tentative surprise and uncertainty as she sat obediently on the hearth, watching Mother arrange the gifts around her, growing more and more animated as the number increased.

'Okay,' Mother said, 'you may open two today.'

"We all watched closely as Sophia looked around her in wonder.

'I...I don't know where to begin,' she said, timidly, conflicted between laughter and tears, and again dragged her shirtsleeve across her nose.

'Here,' Mother said, 'start with this.'

"She handed Sophia a small box. Carefully pulling off the lid, she reached inside, and proudly held up a teddy bear.

'How pretty,' she said, overjoyed, hugging it close. 'Thank you Mrs. Moore.'

'You're welcome,' she said, and passed her another box.

"Sophia received the gift, looked at each of us in turn, and took a deep breath before removing the pink ribbon and tearing away the paper. She removed the lid and looked inside.

'It's beautiful,' she said, breathlessly, holding up a little sundress as she sat on the hearth wearing my baggy trousers and a dress shirt from my closet that hung from her little arms. 'I've never had a dress before.'

"It was said so matter-of-factly, so offhandedly, that she didn't give it a thought. But I saw Mother lift a hand to her chest to still her breaking heart.

'Thank you, Mrs. Moore,' Sophia said.

'You're welcome, Sophia,' Mother answered, tenderly.

"Our tomboy guest stayed with us that night and the next and the night after that. It was supposed to be temporary, until something more permanent could be arranged, until she went to the orphanage, but we all loved her so. The days just ran on together, one after the next, and Sophia remained. Mother bought her more clothes and things for her room. She was happy to be with us, I knew, but there was a sadness in those lovely blue eyes too, a pensiveness at times that seemed to haunt her lovely smile. I would see her sometimes when she thought she was alone, standing at the window, looking out over the ocean as Mother had done, wearing the same melancholy yearning as if searching for someone she had no hope of finding. I never asked Mother how long Sophia would be staying with us. Each day, I feared that she would be asked to pack her things and Mother would drive her to the orphanage. In my fear, I relived a troubling vision of Sophia leaning her arms on her portmanteau, peering sadly at me from the back window of our car as Mother drove away along the tree-lined lane. I made a point of not asking how long Sophia would stay, as if Mother might forget that she was only visiting, and things would simply continue on.

"We studied together by day under the instruction of Mrs. Stowe, and in the evening did our homework or played together. Sophia rarely wore her tomboy clothes after that day. Regardless of how cold or damp or chill or miserable the day was, she wore her sundress. Only when we were heading out into the woods to explore the island would she slip on her flannel shirt and trousers, grab her pocketknife, and drop an old straw hat on her head that she had found somewhere. She looked like a pretty Tom Sawyer.

"And then it was Christmas. Like every other day of the year, that day had changed for us too, since Father's passing. I think we all hoped that the spirit of the holiday would move us to good cheer and remove for a time that feeling of loss that always seemed present in the house, and in our heart, since his death. His headstone was just beyond, in plain view of the window, always in view of the window, as a gentle reminder that he was not with us. We hung stockings, decorated the tree, made hot buttered rum, and did a hundred other things that had always been pleasant Christmas pastimes, but try as we would we could not summon good cheer. We felt the sting of Father's absence even greater on that day than any other and began to dread it.

"But there was Sophia. We had not spoken of it, but I believe we all wanted to make Christmas special for her, and in making it special for her, it became special for us once again. Our little orphan houseguest was always so playful and inquisitive, so eager to learn and do whatever was asked of her, that her good-natured presence seeped into the very fabric of our lives, lifting us all and replacing the silent mantle of grief that we all wore with Father's passing. I know that we all felt she had never experienced a proper Christmas before. I know too that we all wished to give her something special as a sort of gift for all she had given us.

"I had hardly slept the night before, thinking about all of the presents under the tree in their beautiful gift wrapping and which I would open first. So at the first light of dawn, I sprang out of bed in my pajamas and rushed to Sophia's room. She had marked the approach of Christmas with excitement and apprehension. I had often seen her examine the decorations on the Christmas tree with great interest, and when she saw a present under the tree with her name on it, she would kneel down and trace her hand along the ornate wrapping paper, as if it were the most precious thing in the world. I knew she couldn't wait to open her gifts, but I sensed apprehensiveness, too, and I think it was because she had no presents to give.

"When I ran into her room that Christmas morning, I found her wide awake in bed with the covers pulled up under her chin, waiting for me. Without a word, she dashed out of bed and raced down the hall with me, laughing. We took the stairs two at a time, and when we hit the bottom, sprinted across the floor and slid to a stop in our socks, nearly knocking over the tree. Mother and Elsie were seated near the Christmas tree, patiently awaiting our arrival.

'Well, Merry Christmas,' Mother said.

'Merry Christmas,' Sophia and I answered, in unison and out of breath.

'Would you like breakfast first?'

"We shook our heads vigorously.

'What a surprise,' Mother said, smiling. 'Okay, everything is clearly marked.'

"Sophia and I distributed all of the gifts under the tree and then sat down to open our presents. While we were all excited to see what we had received, Mother, Elsie, and I were more interested in watching Sophia. With childlike wonder and intrigue, she would open each gift and shriek with delight when she saw what was inside. It brought a smile to everyone's face.

"Soon, the room was littered with wrapping paper, boxes, discarded ribbons, and empty sacks. Sophia received an elegant evening dress and matching shoes, with a dainty hat and watch. Mother also gave her several skirts and blouses for every day use, and curiously separate from the other gifts was a box wrapped simply in newspaper. Sophia tentatively opened it to find a pair of trousers with a flannel shirt, a pocket knife, and a leather bound copy of Tom Sawyer, for when she felt like being a tomboy, Mother said.

"'I'm not trying to make you into something you don't want to be, Sophia. You can be a lady or a tomboy, or both,' she said.

"Sophia was overwhelmed.

"Only one gift remained. It was a large box, beautifully wrapped, with a big red bow and a little card bearing Sophia's name, written in Mother's flowing hand. Everyone stopped what they were doing and all eyes were on our intrigued little houseguest as she approached the gift. She stretched out her little arm toward the box, turned suddenly to Mother, who nodded her encouragement, and then carefully peeled the wrapping paper away. Sophia turned the box on its side, opened the end, and, reaching inside, pulled out a beautiful leather portmanteau. She looked at it in childlike surprise and wonder, running her hand over the lovely, smooth leather and breathing the pleasant smell. Then her face changed suddenly with the significance of the gift. She lifted a hand to her mouth in shock. Her eyes began to well up. Mother rushed to her at once and wrapped her arms around her.

'No, no, dear. It's not like that. I'm not sending you away,' Mother said, kindly. Sophia was unsure at first, but gradually became at ease once again.

'I'm so silly. You've all been so wonderful to me,' she said, once she recovered from the shock. 'I don't deserve any of it.'

'Yes you do, you dear, sweet girl,' Mother said, as she gently wiped a tear from Sophia's cheek. 'Yes you do. I hope you'll always remember that. What you don't deserve is all this other nonsense that's happened to you.'

'I made something for each of you,' Sophia said, and handed an envelope to each of us.

"Elsie opened hers first. She removed a handmade card from the envelope, admired the artwork on the cover, and then read the inside. We all watched expectantly, awaiting her reaction. Slowly, her trembling hand lowered the card to her lap, and her body shook as she struggled to maintain her composure. It was a struggle she ultimately lost. Without a word, she bolted from her seat and rushed out of the room in tears. Sophia looked concerned. Mother frowned inquisitively and opened her own card. As she read, her features relaxed and she wiped her eyes.

'You're most welcome, Sophia,' Mother said lovingly, and kissed her on the cheek. 'I had better check on Elsie; she always did wear her heart on her sleeve, bless her soul.'

"And Mother left the room. Curious at the content of the other cards, I then opened my envelope."

Here, Thomas reached into his shirt pocket and produced an envelope. The surface was worn smooth and shiny from constant contact. The corners were tattered, the fold missing. It seemed clear that he had been carrying it with him for years. He carefully, reverently, removed the card from the tattered envelope and passed it to me. On the cover, two figures were drawn. One was a boy of ten or twelve, wearing an eighteenth-century captain's uniform, and brandishing a sword. Huddled close behind him, seeking his protection, was a lovely girl the same age who was wearing a dress also of that period. The drawing was done in pencil, and the skill was remarkable.

"Is this you and Sophia?" I asked. Thomas nodded.

"It's an exact likeness," he added.

"What talent. May I read the message?"

"By all means," said he, and I read aloud:

'Thomas,

Little did I know how dramatically my life would change when I met Captain Moore pursuing pirates along the bluff one fine day last summer. You have shown me a life that I never thought, or feared to dream, possible. I have nothing to give you this holiday season but my unfailing love, devotion, and thanks. You are my hero.

Best Friends Forever,

Sophia'

It was the most beautiful thing I had ever read, and I found myself wiping my eyes. Thomas had probably read the card a thousand times but was still moved by it. He sat back in his chair, gazing into the fire with a tender smile. Even Charles was blinking and rubbing his eyes nonchalantly. A long period of silence followed as we all watched the fire burn. It cracked and popped, sometimes throwing embers on the hearth. But I wanted to know the rest of the story. I was certain Charles did, too.

"And this was written by a ten-year-old?" I asked.

"Who three months earlier could neither read or write, yes,"

Thomas said, with pride. "She was quite precocious."

"Go on, Thomas," I said.

"Yes, please," added Charles.

"All right." He smiled.

"Mother returned with Elsie in tow. She was always such a sweet girl, that Elsie. She grew up on a farm milking cows, feeding chickens, cooking and cleaning and ironing. She was a cute little Dutch girl with blonde hair and blue eyes. I think she had a good cry in the kitchen and returned refreshed.

'Try a few things on, Sophia,' said Elsie, excitedly. 'Let's see how they look on you.'

"Sophia searched our eyes, tentatively, unaccustomed to so much attention. Even then it was difficult for her to believe that anyone would care for her as we did or find joy in her happiness.

'Yes, do,' Mother added.

'All right,' she said, and hesitantly began gathering up the clothing.

'I'll make some hot buttered rum,' said Mother.

'I'll do it, Mrs. Moore,' Elsie said, and rushed off to the kitchen.

'Where shall I change?' Sophia asked demurely, and I saw a shy eagerness in her face.

'You can use the bathroom around the corner,' Mother answered.

"Sophia took her new clothes and stepped around the corner, leaving Mother and I alone.

'She's a very sweet girl, Thomas. It takes strength and character to rise above the circumstances she has been bound by all of her young life.'

'What circumstances, Mother?' I asked, as we sat together on the hearth.

"Mother reached over and tenderly brushed the hair back from my face, as I had seen her do to Sophia so many times.

'You'll see one day. You won't always be here at Ravenswood.'

'How do you know about that?'

'Oh, we had quite a little talk, Sophia and I. She's a very insightful girl. Very deep. Very bright.'

"Mother frowned, then, as if something suddenly occurred to her.

'You don't mind all the attention she's been getting, do you?'

'Of course not,' I said, sincerely.

'I don't want you to feel neglected,' she added, running her fingers through my hair.

'She's my best friend, Mother. I want to help her.'

'You're a fine young man, Thomas. I'm very proud of you.'

"Elsie returned with hot buttered rum for everyone and set them on the coffee table near the fire.

'I made some for the children, too,' she said, 'with just a splash of rum.'

"A moment later, Sophia stepped shyly, bashfully, from around the corner, wearing a new plaid skirt and white blouse with little white socks. She performed a timid twirl before the fire and blushed bright red. She was so adorable.

'Oh, Sophia, you're so beautiful,' Elsie said.

"Blushing even deeper, Sophia rushed away. When she returned, she was wearing the black evening dress with matching shoes and her new watch. She was stunning. She would have turned heads at any ball. We stared open-mouthed, all of us. Suddenly self-conscious, she turned away embarrassed and tried to cover herself. Even as we sat in our places at the fire looking upon her with admiration and wonder, Sophia saw herself as nothing more than an unwanted, dirty-faced tomboy.

'No, no,' Mother said, reassuringly, 'you're beautiful. So very beautiful.'

'Oh, Sophia,' said Elsie, at a loss for words.

"Blushing again, Sophia turned to go change.

'No,' Mother said. 'Leave it on. It's beautiful on you. Come over here and sit with us.'

"We sat together on the sofa, all of us, drinking hot buttered rum before the fire, talking and laughing until late in the night. For Mother, Elsie, and I, it was the most enjoyable evening we had experienced since the death of Father. It was like we were a family again. The house felt warm and joyous.

"The fire had burned low, and the evening had drawn to a close. Elsie collected the boxes, sacks, and wrapping paper that had been discarded in our haste. When everything was cleared away, a tiny little box, so small it been overlooked, was found under the tree. Sophia picked it up.

'There's no name on it,' she said.

'It's for you,' Mother replied. Everyone stopped what they were doing and watched. With all eyes upon her once more, Sophia bashfully opened the little box and held up an elegantly shaped bottle of perfume that I would ever after associate with her. It had an intoxicating smell that I could never get enough of, and she wore it often, but sparingly, so I always wanted more.

'Thank you so much Mrs. Moore,' she said. 'Thank you all.'

"We helped Elsie clean away the last traces of Christmas from around the tree, then gathered up our gifts and carried them up to our rooms. Among the clothing in my arms were the pajamas that Sophia had worn that morning, something that Mother had given her weeks earlier. I heard the crackle of paper in the pocket and reached inside to find a note. It was the one she held so relentlessly in her hand the day we found her at the fountain."

Thomas grew emotional and agitated. He stood abruptly, tossed more wood on the already blazing fire, and sat again. Then he lifted his wine glass and toyed with it absently.

"It was a note from her mother," he said, at last, "that read: 'You are better off without me, and I am better off...' His voice broke. He took a sip of wine, and continued. 'I am better off without you.'

We sat in silence watching the flickering flames, in the same seats before the same fire as they had that night. Thomas took a moment to collect his thoughts, and continued.

"How could anyone be so cruel? No wonder Sophia was so crushed. Her mother had left her—simply moved away without telling her where she was going—and her father had left her, too. Both parents had abandoned her, and she thought it was her fault. That no one wanted her. All she had to remember her mother by was that deplorable note, and she carried it with her as a constant reminder.

"If there had been any question of our houseguest remaining with us, it was removed that Christmas night. She had resided with us for only three short weeks, but already it was difficult to imagine her not staying with us always. Sophia's indomitable spirit was like a torch driving away the gloom and despair that had seeped into the house with Father's death.

"Motivated perhaps by the obvious talent displayed on the cards she drew for us, Mother bought a sketchpad and pencils and later an easel, canvas, paint, and brushes for Sophia. I would see her sitting in different places around the house, sketching, or find her in her room, painting at the easel. It came so naturally to her that I don't think she ever realized how talented she was. Her paintings hang all over the house. You can see them tomorrow, by the light of day. But her artistic talent extended beyond that medium. We were once passing the grand piano there in the corner…"

Thomas gestured to a flawless old Steinway near the window.

'Do you think your mother would mind if I played a little bit?' she asked.

'I didn't know you could play?' I answered.

'Only a little bit.'

'I'm sure she wouldn't mind.'

"I found some pillows to put on the piano bench so she could reach the keys and she sat down. Her feet dangled a considerable distance from the floor, as she studied the keys intently.

'I've never played a grand before,' she said, and began. Beethoven's "Für Elise" was the only composition she knew, but she played it flawlessly; her little artist fingers danced on the keys, while her face was fixed in a concentrated frown. As the last note dissolved to silence, I stood looking at her in wonder once again.

'Where did you learn to play like that?'

'My mother lived with a musician for a few months. I used to play on his piano when I was home alone.'

'What kind of musician was he?'

'He played in a jazz band at the bar she worked at. She was a bartender.'

"Everything came easily to Sophia.

"That summer we launched the sailing dinghy. I had built spars for it in the spring—a mast and boom fashioned from a single piece of fir. Elsie showed us how to sew new sails out of canvas cloth, and we toiled for days at the sewing machine. With a new mainsail, jib, and Genoa all folded nicely in their new sail bags, we launched the dinghy at the boat yard and rigged her. It was too late that day to go, so the next day we returned. Under the bright sun of the new summer day, we left the dock, headed up into a gentle north wind, and raised the sails. The main filled and the little boat heeled to port, then shot forward effortlessly. With Sophia at the helm, I raised the headsail and cleated off the sheet. When the sails were trimmed, the boat balanced perfectly and we glided quietly along with the water lapping the hull. Sailing along the coastline of the island, we passed sandy beaches, tree-lined shores, and quiet coves, giddy with our newfound freedom. Elsie would make a lunch in an old wicker picnic basket with iced tea and sandwiches, and we would sail each day, exploring the islands. Sometimes we would fish, sometimes catch crab, and sometimes bring sleeping bags and camp overnight on one of the little islands, but always we would sail.

"And so the years passed at Ravenswood. We had our studies with Mrs. Stowe. Sophia had her art and music when we weren't studying together, and I had my shop near the house where I would build boats and hone my boatwright skills. It was expected that I would follow in Father's footsteps and become a naval architect like he and grandfather and great grandfather before him, and I was eager to continue the family legacy. I loved building boats. My only hesitancy in pursuing that course of action was Sophia. The illiterate little tomboy was gone, and in her place was a beautiful young girl with all the poise and charm and dignity of Mother. We had been inseparable since she arrived seven years earlier. I couldn't imagine not seeing her every day, and was reluctant to leave home in pursuit of a higher education. What would the house be like if she were to leave, I wondered? Her cheerful, exuberant nature had lifted us all out of the melancholy shadow that we had dwelt in and made us whole again. Mother, especially, seemed happy and healed of her pain.

"The tomboy never left Sophia, and we all delighted to see her in her Tom Sawyer clothes. As she outgrew them each year, Mother would replace them with a new flannel shirt and trousers. Her original clothes, the ones she wore when she came to live with us, were folded neatly on the corner of her dresser where she set them the day she took them off. Elsie asked if she might discard them one day.

'No,' Sophia answered. 'I need to keep them.'

"I think we all knew why. She wanted to remember. Not to dwell in the past, but to acknowledge how far she had risen.

"It was the summer of our sixteenth year. Sophia and I had been taking the dinghy out nearly every day, sailing around the island to all the places we had visited so many times before. As we approached the boat yard where the dinghy was moored, we passed *Diva* as we had done so often. With the eye of an artist, Sophia had the fondest appreciation for the grace and beauty of that vessel, and admired it tremendously.

"She slowed as we passed the elegant yacht and ran a gentle, admiring hand over the flawlessly varnished mahogany.

'You know, Thomas, hasn't moved from her slip in eight years, except to get fresh varnish and bottom paint.'

'Thank you for a summary of her maintenance,' I answered, jesting. 'You have a gift for stating the obvious.'

'What I'm getting at should be obvious even to you, smarty pants,' she jested. 'We've been walking past this beautiful, unused yacht for years on our way to the little sailing dinghy beyond. Does that give you any ideas?' she said, and added quickly, 'unless that's forbidden. I know *Diva* is sacred to the memory of your father.'

'No,' I answered, thoughtfully, 'you're right. I don't know why I didn't think of it before. I'll just tell Mr. Johnson that we're taking her out today, and be right back.'

"Mr. Johnson was the shop foreman and was delighted at the news.

'She's been at rest too long, Mr. Moore,' he said. 'A yacht like that needs exercise. We've kept her tiptop for ya. The fellas and I hoped to see ya at the helm one day.'

"When I returned to the dock, Sophia was waiting breathlessly, which I thought funny. I didn't expect any suspense.

'Well?' she asked, hopefully.

'He said no.'

'Oh.' Her face fell.

'I'm jesting silly. I don't need to ask permission. I was just telling him I would be taking the boat out.'

'For that you'll pay, you young reprobate,' she said, with a smile.

"The sails were all folded in the sail bags, and placed in the forepeak. We hanked them on and raised the mainsail, leaving the mainsheet loose in the wind.

'Okay Sophia, I'll get the stern line, you get the bow.'

"While I released the stern, she ran up on the deck and tossed the bow line to the dock. I returned to the cockpit and sheeted in the main. The giant sail filled with wind; the yacht heeled to port and began moving gracefully forward. Sophia returned to the cockpit. Even with only the mainsail flying, the yacht gained speed and raced along splendidly. When Sophia raised the jenny and trimmed the sheet, it verily flew with the additional sail. She shrieked in delight and joined me on the high side of the cockpit. With the morning sun on our faces, we raced along the shoreline in twelve knots of north wind, smiling wildly, giddy from the speed and performance, as the yacht sliced through the water like a knife. It was like riding a thoroughbred horse that needed only the slightest guidance. The little sailing dinghy provided us with a sense of freedom and independence that we coveted, but *Diva* spirited us along swiftly, elegantly, majestically.

"In the early afternoon we anchored at a quiet little bay on Jones Island for lunch. We had made the journey in just over half an hour, a journey that would take three hours in the little dinghy. We set the anchor and then adjourned to the comfort of the cockpit where the picnic basket awaited. With the bay serving as a natural barrier to the wind and waves, the yacht rocked ever so slightly with the diminutive swells, providing a comforting sense of motion. The breeze, barely a whisper, rustled Sophia's hair gently as her delicate hands searched through the dainties in the picnic basket. She never wore her tomboy clothes sailing, and that day she was dressed in linen pants and a white shirt that accented her figure beautifully. She paused, lifting a slender hand to brush her hair back behind her ear, then frowned as she peered into the basket.

'Elsie has provided one turkey and one ham sandwich again. I wonder why she does that? She knows we both prefer the turkey.'

'She wishes to provide me with an opportunity to exercise my chivalrous nature. I'll take the ham,' I said, halfheartedly.

'It would have been much more chivalrous if your offer had not been accompanied by the heavy sigh of sacrifice.'

'Well, is it not enough that I would sacrifice for you; must I also do it cheerfully?'

'That is the nature of chivalry,' she said, smiling. 'It is hardly noble to sacrifice yourself for the one you love, only to be dragged kicking and screaming to the gallows. You must go quietly, with dignity, smiling as the noose is dropped over your head.'

'Well, then,' I said, smiling as big as I could, 'would you please pass me the ham sandwich?'

'I cannot allow my handsome protector to make such a sacrifice. We shall divide it evenly, as before. One moiety for you and one for me.'

"She had never called me handsome before, and the appellation had a peculiar effect on me. My heart skipped a beat, my pulse quickened, my hand trembled ever so slightly. I watched her poised, graceful movement as she sliced our lunch into equal parts. The way she sat, the way she held her head, the playful, focused way she sliced the bread, all struck me as special and unique. Was there ever anyone like her, I mused? So beautiful and pleasant? So kind and good-natured? I realized at that moment that I cared for her with tender, unguarded passion."

Thomas paused a moment to reflect.

"Unguarded, did I say? Her beauty and manner gave her an air that rendered her inaccessible, or so I thought in my childlike naivety, and sealed my lips, guarding my heart from the rejection that I feared would follow if I revealed my feelings.

'Thomas? Thomas?' she said.

"My reverie was broken. Sophia was handing me a sandwich, regarding me with a curious smile from under the brim of her big picnic hat.

'Penny for your thoughts.'

'I was just…um…thinking…' I shifted, uncomfortably.

'Yes, thinking what?' she asked, with an inquisitive smile.

'Well, how pretty you are.'

'Oh Thomas, you're so sweet.' She kissed me on the cheek. 'Was that so very hard to say?'

'I suppose not,' I answered, blushing.

"Amused by my reply, she grinned as she poured iced tea for each of us. We relaxed in the cockpit of that beautiful yacht, eating our lunch in the warm summer sun, as it rose and fell ever so gently with the rolling swells. I have a fondness for that little cove still, formed by the impressionable nature of inexperienced youth and the soft touch of her lips upon my blushing, boyish cheek. I had never been so happy as when Sophia took my hand and looked across the blue water to the island nearby.

'It's so beautiful, Thomas, I just love it here. We should do this every day. Can we take *Diva* sailing every day? Maybe we could take her overnight. Maybe we could take her for several nights,' she added, growing excited. 'Maybe we could take her on a journey. We could go to Vancouver Island or someplace distant. Does that sound exciting? Just the two of us?'

'I would love to do that,' I answered, growing excited myself.

'Do you think your mother would allow it?'

'I don't see why not. We have no demands on our time. We would spend every day sailing around here, anyway.'

'Oh, I'm so excited. Let's ask as soon as we get home.'

'Okay.'

"We spent the afternoon sailing through the islands with *Diva* gliding along effortlessly, responding to the slightest touch. People we saw on the shore waved enthusiastically when we passed, impressed by her flawless form and unequalled beauty. It was late afternoon by the time we sailed back to the boatyard. Sophia stepped off the deck with the bow line, and secured it to the dock.

"Shortly after dusk, we reached home. We had ridden our bicycles to the boatyard with joy and enthusiasm that morning, eagerly anticipating a pleasant day on the water. The return journey was a leisurely one. Tiredly, we pedaled along the country road, passing through green fields and pastures in the quiet moments before dusk, when nature draws a deep breath and relaxes at the end of the long day. As the last sliver of sun dipped below the horizon and the stars began to shine and the crickets to chirp, we turned down the familiar driveway to home, pedaling under the canopy of maples that lined the way. We left our bicycles at the door and, retaining the youthful resiliency of teenagers, neglected our fatigue, stepping lightly into the house in search of Mother and her blessing. That she would give it was a certainty, a formality really. Armed with that confidence, we proceeded through the house without the usual chatter, each imagining our self at the helm of our thoroughbred, racing north through unexplored bays and passages, investigating secluded coves and sandy beaches, surrounded by blue skies and blue water.

"Following the hallway to the west side of the house, we found Mother in her usual place at the window. She was not sitting with a book, as was her habit, but rather standing with her hands on the chair back, looking out over the orange sunset that was rapidly yielding to darkness. There was in her eyes such an expression of weary fatigue, of loneliness, of loss and yearning, that our feet failed us. Sophia took my hand and, raising a finger to her lips ushering quiet, led me softly away, back the way we had come. Outside once again, in the shadow of the great oak door, she turned to me in the fading light of the sunset.

'I can't do it, Thomas. I can't leave her all alone. We're all she has.'

"I nodded in agreement.

'It wouldn't be fair after all she has done for me.'

'I didn't know she was so lonely,' I answered.

'I didn't either,' she said, thoughtfully. 'Come on.'

"I followed Sophia back to the house. This time we shut the door with gusto and made plenty of noise when we entered. Mother greeted us with a smile, without the faintest hint of the loneliness we witnessed only moments ago. We were home again and she was happy."

Thomas refilled our glasses, then walked over to the window, his mother's favorite, and stood restlessly watching the glowing moon over the rippling ocean. Clouds had gathered around it, and some streaks of moonlight streamed through picturesquely. The minutes passed. I thought he would continue, but he stood motionless, looking out the window as if recalling a memory or wrestling with a decision. Charles and I waited, sipping our wine. He turned to me after some time and shrugged his shoulders inquisitively, as if to ask what was happening, but I knew no more than he. I stood up from my chair and walked to the window, standing beside Thomas.

"Are you all right, Thomas?" I inquired.

He took a large gulp of wine and ran his hand tenderly over the chair that his mother used to sit in.

"Mother remarried," he said, and the words seemed to leave a sour taste in his mouth that he sought to wash away with the wine in his glass. He took another sip.

"She…she what?" I asked, wondering if I had heard him correctly.

"She met him at church. She went there on Sundays when Sophia and I were out sailing. I think it gave her comfort to be around people. She was always home, you see, in this big house, with little to do. He was tall and handsome, with dark hair and thick sideburns, charming and worldly. They were married that spring in a quiet service at the church, with only Sophia and Elsie and I in attendance. He moved into the house shortly after they were wed, and Mother was so happy. I hadn't seen her so happy in years. We all liked him, if only for the happiness that he brought to Mother's face."

Thomas returned to his seat at the fire and stared into his wineglass. I resumed my seat as well and waited for him to continue.

"We all liked him…at first, but as he settled into the house and became more comfortable with his new home, he began to change, or more accurately, he dropped his facade and became himself. It was a slow, gradual process, and the alteration was subtle, but I saw it so clearly. Mother did not. He was careful to maintain his pleasant persona in her presence, but I began to see that it was not his nature to be so, and it began to wear on him. He was cruel and malicious by nature. I'm sure he was capable of kindness and generosity, but he was mean-spirited and spiteful at heart. He could tame his malice and collar his wickedness for just so long, but it wasn't his nature to keep them in check, and it was building inside him. His anger became more and more difficult for him to control as the months passed, and it would slip out unexpectedly at times, but never around Mother. Around Mother, or when we had guests at the house, he was always so courteous and charming that I found myself making excuses for his ill temper, as if it wasn't his fault."

Thomas finished his wine with a gulp and then pondered the empty glass in his hand by the flickering firelight.

"But it was his fault," he said, thoughtfully. "William was a wicked man." Thomas turned to me then and smiled sardonically. "That is to say, the Honorable William Thomson was a wicked man.

He was a circuit court judge, you see." Thomas shook his head. "How that man could sit in judgment of others is beyond me. I always called him William, but he took that as a sign of disrespect and asked that I call him Father. That, of course, I would not do, and while he seemed all right with it at first, it became a growing annoyance to him. He became more insistent, but I was firm. Sophia reluctantly agreed to call him Father, but I would not, and it was becoming intolerable to him. He had been in the house only three months when he asked me to join him in the study one afternoon. I followed him inside.

'Close the door,' he said, as I entered after him.

"I did as requested and took a seat across from him at the desk where he sat.

'You'll remain standing for this.'

"I wasn't certain I heard him correctly, and didn't move.

'Stand,' he demanded, harshly.

"I stood before him like a felon waiting to be sentenced.

'I'll have respect in my house,' he said, arranging a few little items precisely on the desk—my father's desk.

"This was something that was becoming an issue for me. He was making himself too familiar with the house, especially Father's things. I know that it was his right, but I didn't care for him and didn't like him assuming Father's role and possessing his things.

'Your house?' I answered, barely disguising my contempt.

'Yes,' he said, holding my eye with a malicious one of his own, 'my house. And in my house you'll address me as Father.'

'I will not,' I replied, firmly.

"I saw his eyes flash angrily and his fists clench, but just as quickly he was smiling.

'How are your studies coming along, Thomas?' he asked, almost pleasantly.

'My studies?'

'With Sophia and Mrs. Stowe. Quite a pleasant little circle of education, you three.'

'My studies are going well.'

'Rather a sheltered education though, really, all of you gathering here at the house for school. You're missing out on so much. Sports. School dances. Girls. All of those social elements of school that are lacking here.'

"I was taken off guard by the sudden change and simply stood quietly before the desk watching him.

'I wonder...' he said. Then he stood and walked to the window, looking out over the grounds. 'You don't have many friends, do you, Thomas?' he asked. 'Being isolated out here like this, you don't meet many people do you?'

'No.'

'You know, I have a wide circle of friends. Other circuit court judges, parole board members, prison wardens, a senator or two, boarding school superintendent. I've sent a few young men there: troubled youths mostly, but not all. Some were simply insolent and needed a change, the sort of change that only a boy's school in Vermont could provide. Such a shame to break up a family like that, don't you think?'

'I'm sure it upset you tremendously,' I said, dryly.

'It did. It surely did.' He turned from the window, facing me. 'I like to stay in touch with my friend there, sort of monitor how the boys are doing. I take a professional interest in their welfare.'

'Are you always successful in placing young men there? I should think that their parents would sometimes object.'

'Yes, but parents always want what's best for their child. Sometimes you simply need to convince them that it is in their son's best interest to go away, to acquire discipline and learning and social skills. I can be very convincing.'

'What if the young man doesn't care to go?'

'Ah,' he laughed, 'one doesn't ask the lamb if it wishes to be slaughtered.'

'An interesting analogy.'

'An apropos one.'

'Is this school a harsh environment?'

'Some would say so, but there are always the coddling parents who think any type of discipline is harsh.'

"While he didn't say so, I knew that he uttered those final words with someone in mind, someone close to me, someone like Mother. His lips formed the faintest suggestion of a smile, and his eyes wore a look of triumph as he studied me. I felt that he was measuring me for a train ticket to Vermont. I felt a sudden chill, too, which he seemed to sense. William had passed judgment on a great many individuals who had trembled before him and could read them like a newspaper. My discomfort brought him pleasure.

'You may go now,' he said, with a satisfied smile, and turned back to the window.

"Two or three weeks later, school was out for the summer. Sophia and I resumed our summer routine of sailing each day. We returned one afternoon after a day of sailing through the islands in the summer sun and, as we walked up the path to the house, heard a voice that we didn't recognize. We turned to each other, puzzled, and followed the sound to the back yard. A young man, perhaps a year or two older than us, stood near the small fish pond in the back, encouraging a chipmunk to come closer and take the morsel of bread that he had placed on the ground near his foot. The chipmunk was well known to us. Sophia had rescued him when the tree that his nest was in blew down in a storm the previous winter; all the other chipmunks in the nest were killed. She raised him as a baby and then released him to the wild so he could live a normal life. His name was Oscar.

"The young man calling to him was unknown to us. He had blond hair, blue eyes, and ruddy cheeks. Sophia and I watched as he called Oscar closer. The little chipmunk darted forward in short, jerky movements, as chipmunks do, and sat up nibbling the little morsel that he held in his two front paws as his tail curled straight up behind. As we watched, the boy slowly drew his foot back behind him, paused a moment, then swiftly brought it forward, catching Oscar under his paws and lifting him high in the air until he slammed into a distant tree and fell to the ground in a crumpled heap. At the first contact, Sophia shrieked and ran to the tree trunk to her little companion. The boy was bent over, holding his sides in laughter.

'Oh that's rich. The best one yet,' he said, as he laughed. 'I wonder if there are any more of those rodents around?'

"Sophia was on her knees at the tree, cradling Oscar in her delicate hands. I walked over to the boy.

'Why did you do that?' I demanded. He paused in his laughter to look at me.

'Who are you?' he asked, with disdain.

'Thomas Moore. I live here.'

'Do you have any more of those little rodents? I think I can better my mark.'

'That was a pet.'

'Well, you do have funny ways out here in the country,' he said, laughing.

"Turning my back on the boy, I rushed over to Sophia who still knelt beside the tree with Oscar in her blood-stained hands. He was on his back with his head twisted unnaturally to the side and blood trailing from his mouth, forming a little puddle in her palm.

'He's dead Thomas. He's dead,' she cried. 'Why would anyone do such a thing?'

'I'm sorry, Sophia. We'll find a nice little spot to bury him.'

"Still crying, she stood and, with Oscar in her hands, began walking toward the house. As she passed the boy, he got his first look at her, and his laughter trailed off as he ran an appraising eye over her slender figure.

'Well, what is this?' he said under his breath and made to follow her, but I stepped in front of him.

'What are you doing? Get out of my way.'

"He tried to step around me and follow Sophia, but I moved in front of him again.

'I think you're the last person in the world she would like to see right now.'

'I don't care what you think. Get out of my way.' He attempted to step around me again, but I moved into his path once more.

'Leave her alone,' I said.

"He glanced past me and saw that Sophia was reaching the house, then pushed me aside impatiently and began after her. But he had taken only a few steps when I grabbed his arm and spun him around. Growing angry, he pushed me hard, and I fell back a few steps, but when I got my feet under me again, I rushed at him and slugged him hard. He fell to the ground holding his belly and looked up at me with hatred in his malicious blue eyes.

'I'll get you for that,' he spat.

'Get up. We'll finish it right now,' I said.

'That's not my way.' He glared up at me. 'You'll see.'

"Having no idea who he was, I left him on the lawn and rushed after Sophia. Her gentle spirit had received quite a shock and she sat in a chair under an umbrella on the rear deck of the house, quietly mourning the loss of her little pet.

'I'm sorry about Oscar,' I said, taking a seat beside her.

'I just don't understand,' she said, looking down at the broken little body in her hand as the tears ran freely over her lovely cheeks. 'I just don't understand how anyone can find sport in snuffing out a harmless little life.'

'I'm so sorry Sophia.' I held her close, with her head on my chest. 'I've been making a little jewelry box for you in the shop. It was going to be a gift. It would make a nice coffin for Oscar.'

'That's so sweet Thomas. Thank you.'

"I took her hand, and we walked together to the shop. Oscar was placed in the Coco Bolo jewelry box and we buried him in the shade of the maple tree at the corner of the building. Sophia was quiet and pensive.

"When we reached the house, it was time for dinner. I could smell it long before we arrived, and the scent was delicious. Mother always insisted that everyone be present and dressed for dinner, so we went directly to the table where everyone was taking their seats. When Mother saw us she turned, and smiled happily.

'Thomas, Sophia, where have you been? I've been looking all over for you. We have a surprise guest,' she said, motioning to the insolent boy who was standing next to William at the head of the table. His smile was cool and gave away nothing, as he looked us over. 'This is William's son, Rockwell. He's home from school and will be with us for the summer.'

"Absolute silence followed. My surprise was swallowed up by an impending sense of doom that weighed heavily upon me with my first sight of him at our table. That he could be William's son made perfect sense. They were cut from the same bolt of malicious cloth that never should have been, but that he should be sharing our house, that another member of that degenerate family should be sharing our house, was alarming. I turned to look at Sophia and saw shock and fear in her face.

'Pleased to meet you, Rockwell,' I said, and stepped over to him to shake his hand. 'I hope you enjoy your stay here.'

'I'm sure I will,' he said, smiling wickedly as he shook my hand.

"I've had occasion to think many times since that day—of the blow that fate delivered that seemingly ordinary afternoon—and to contemplate what I may have done to provoke it. In hindsight, I see so clearly that the seed of my destruction was planted that day with the arrival of Rockwell Thomson, who watered, nourished, and coaxed it along, until it bore fruit three months later. Our house, our family, our life, would never be the same again."

Thomas took his empty wine glass and returned to his seat at the fire. His tale, which had mostly been a lighthearted account of his association with Sophia, was beginning to take a painful turn, and while I wished to spare him the discomfort of reliving it, I was intensely curious. How did he find himself in prison, and why was the house empty? Where was everyone?

"William had an ally in Rockwell and was quick to use it," he said, with his eyes on the floor. "I don't know what their intention was, but I suspect that they wanted to get Sophia and I out of the house so they would be free to plunder it somehow. I would sometimes find them talking quietly together in some out-of-the-way corner or see them walking through the house with an appraising eye, like an auctioneer determining the value of his wares. And I learned an interesting thing about Rockwell. He was a big boy, much bigger than me, but he was a coward. He would never face anyone in a fair fight. The odds had to be in his favor. He was cunning and manipulative, malicious and mean. Striking from ambush was his style.

"He tried to charm Sophia, but there he met his match. Always he watched her and looked for an opportunity to get her alone. He found it one afternoon when I left her in the back yard to get a book from the library upstairs. She had fallen asleep in a lounge chair under the warm rays of the summer sun, and I was reluctant to wake her. I had seen how Rockwell looked at her and would not leave her alone while he was in the house. There was an agreement between us. We never spoke of it, but Sophia knew that I would not leave her unprotected while that cunning reprobate was around. But I would be away only a few minutes. I hadn't seen Rockwell all day, and she looked so peaceful sleeping there in the sun. So I slipped away, and hurried through the house to the library upstairs, at the opposite end of the house. The book was quickly found, tucked under my arm, and back I began. Little more than five minutes had passed, so I was confident that Sophia would be fine, but as I exited the house I heard laughter and approached quietly. A large maple tree hid me from their view, and I kept it between us. I could see that Rockwell was in my seat, and that Sophia was still reclining on the lounge chair. He was seated facing her, smiling and smooth, and she was laughing—actually laughing playfully. In the same way that a professional athlete makes their sport look easy in their fluid, graceful movement, refined through years of practice, Rockwell's seduction of Sophia was conducted with a practiced ease that astonished me. He had gained her confidence, and even had her laughing, where only minutes ago she loathed and despised him. Using the tree as cover, I listened.

'Walk with me, Sophia,' he said, with a tender, endearing smile. 'I found a trail that leads down the bluff to the beach. It's a beautiful walk.'

'Oh, Rockwell,' she said with her lovely blue eyes smiling, and her head titled shyly, 'I can't walk with you.'

'But why not?' he asked, with the injured air of a lover.

'Because your smiling face,' she said, smiling sweetly, 'doesn't change the fact that you're still the same cruel, mean-spirited monster that killed my little Oscar only a few weeks ago.'

"His smile became a malicious sneer, and he stood suddenly, looming over her as if to strike.

'Does it, Thomas?' she added, looking past him to me as I approached.

"He smiled again, this time with no pretense of kindness, and studied her with a newfound respect.

'You're much more cunning than I gave you credit for. That sort of thinking isn't native to this backward little island. You must have had an interesting life before you came here. I'll destroy you both before I return to school, though,' he added, casually. 'It'll be great sport.'

"And with his threat still ringing in our ears, he turned and walked back to the house whistling. When he was inside, out of earshot, Sophia dropped her mask of confidence and turned her troubled eyes to me.

'He makes me so uneasy, Thomas,' she said.

'Don't worry about Rockwell, Sophia. I'll see that he doesn't bother you.' She smiled kindly, and took my hand.

'I know you will,' she said, 'but your kindness and generosity are no match for his cunning and cruelty. You can't think like him. You'll never understand the wickedness that drives him. It's not in you.'

'But...how do you know?' I asked.

'I know you quiet well, Thomas, that's why I lov...' she corrected herself, 'that's why I'm so fond of you.'

'How do you know him so well?'

'Oh, that.' Her eyes wore a far away expression. 'My mother had friends that she would bring home from the bar where she worked. I've seen my share of Rockwell Thomsons.'

'Well, don't underestimate me. I'm not a country bumpkin.' I said. Sophia smiled kindly.

'I wasn't asleep when you left to get your book, Thomas. I was only feigning sleep.'

'Okay,' I said, puzzled by that bit of news. 'Why?'

'I wanted to test a theory.'

'What theory?'

'Let's just say I was right.'

"My face must have expressed the confusion that I felt just then, because Sophia continued.

'You're too good-natured to play this game, Thomas. You've never had to think this way, growing up out here on the island where things are what they appear to be. Be very careful. Rockwell only wants to seduce me, but he wants to hurt you for what you did to him. He'll do something. We need to be careful.'

"But Rockwell did nothing. We saw him around the house, of course, but he seemed indifferent to us. When Mother or Elsie were present, he was always warm and kind to us, but if not, he was simply indifferent, as if we were beneath his notice. I thought that Sophia overestimated his vengeful spirit, that she was mistaken about him.

"It was a Sunday morning about three weeks later that Elsie went to town to buy groceries, as she did every Sunday, and William took Mother for a drive. Sophia and I were left alone with Rockwell, but he soon left as well. We saw him walk across the grounds at the back of the house and begin along the trail that led down the bluff to the beach. He had a fishing pole in his hand and a krill over his shoulder, which I thought odd. I had not seen him fish before, or show any interest in such outdoor activities.

"I entered the kitchen looking to see if Elsie had made breakfast before leaving and found a bowl of porridge at my seat and Sophia's. Since William arrived we had resumed our former routine of eating in the dining room, and only when he was away did we eat at the kitchen table. I sat down at my seat and tasted the porridge, but it was bland. Elsie knew that I liked chopped walnuts and dates in mine, but this had none. Perhaps she was getting some when she went to town, I mused. In any case, I wasn't eating it as it was, and took it outside where I had seen Tolstoy sleeping in the back. He was an old Samoyed that came limping down the driveway years earlier with a broken leg. We tended to his wound, and he stayed with us. He always liked porridge and raised himself up on his arthritic old legs, then limped over, following his nose to the bowl I had placed on the ground. When I returned to the kitchen I found Sophia sitting at the table eating her porridge. I read the newspaper while she finished her breakfast, and we talked about how we would spend the day. It was decided that we would go for a bike ride in the morning, and when the wind picked up in the afternoon, we would go sailing.

"It was a beautiful day for a bike ride. The sun was shining in the clear blue sky unbroken by clouds, but it was early enough that the air was still cool, and not a breath of wind disturbed the morning peace. We stopped a few times to rest in the grass beside the road and looked out over the rippling water reflecting the sunlight. It was so peaceful and serene, unlike home where there always seemed to be a shadow of tension in the air with William and Rockwell there. I looked beside me where Sophia lay in the grass, propped up on her elbows, looking out over the water. The morning sun glistened in her blue eyes, bluer than the sky, deeper than the ocean.

'You're staring Thomas,' she said, still looking out over the water.

'Sorry,' I stammered.

'It's okay,' she smiled, turning to me. 'I like it.'

'You do?' I asked. She nodded.

"The house was still empty when we returned. We put our

bicycles away and went to the kitchen to make a lunch for sailing. The wind was starting to build. I could see little ripples on the water. It would be a perfect day for sailing. Sophia got out the bread, and began making sandwiches.

'I'll make lunch Thomas,' she said. 'You made breakfast.'

'I didn't make breakfast. When have I ever made breakfast?'

'Then who did?'

'Elsie.'

'It couldn't have been Elsie. There was nothing on the table when she left this morning for town. Breakfast was put there after she left.'

"I was puzzled by this, but Sophia was not. She was suddenly tense and alarmed.

'Did you eat yours, Thomas? Did you eat it?'

'No,' I answered, puzzled by her alarm, 'it didn't have any walnuts or dates. I didn't like it.'

'What did you do with it?' she asked, in a panic.

'I gave it to Tolstoy.'

'Oh, no.'

"She rushed outside. I followed.

'What's the matter? What's wrong, Sophia?'

"We found Tolstoy in the grass where I had left him, lying on his side, asleep. The empty porridge bowl was a few feet away. We breathed a sigh of relief. Sophia bent down and stroked his face affectionately. Tolstoy didn't move. She moved up behind him, hugging him in her arms. A moment later her face changed, and I saw a tear in her eye.

'Oh Thomas,' she said, 'he's not breathing. He's not breathing.'

"It was the most peculiar thing. There was a ringing in my ears, and it was as if time stopped for a moment or moved very slowly. When I realized what happened, I was sitting on the grass next to Sophia, and her head was pressed to my chest. I stared dumbly for a moment, then absently wrapped my arms around her and held her as she cried.

'I never thought he would go this far. Poor Tolstoy.' She looked up at me. 'That could have been you Thomas. That could have been you.'

'He was old, Sophia. He could have just passed away.'

'No.' She shook her head adamantly.

'You ate the porridge. You're all right.'

'He didn't want to hurt me. He wanted to hurt you. Oh my God, he's so evil.'

"Rockwell returned a few hours later, whistling happily with the fishing pole over his shoulder. I watched silently from an upstairs window of the house as he cheerfully made his way across the backyard toward home. With curious intensity, his eyes quickly darted over the house, searching for movement or activity, as if he expected to find something different there than when he left. He seemed slightly puzzled by the quiet. I left the window and made my way downstairs. When he entered the house, I was standing just inside the door to greet him. I wanted to see his face, his reaction, when he saw me alive and well. I was not disappointed. When the door opened and he looked up to see me standing before him with a blank face that gave away nothing, he was shocked and his step faltered. Only for an instant, but in that instant I knew that Sophia was right.

"Rockwell expected to find me dead when he returned. He expected to open the door to a great bustle of doctors and police and detectives, all milling about the house as they attempted to ascertain what had happened to his poor stepbrother. His step faltered, it's true, but only for an instant. Rockwell Thomson was far too practiced, far too sophisticated in his malice and cunning to betray himself for more than a fleeting instant. A second later, he was whistling again, and resumed his step with a, 'Hello Thomas,' as he passed.

"I don't believe I had ever hated before that moment," Thomas said, as his eyes left the fire and fell on mine. I saw a confused sort of sadness in them as I searched his face, as if he had lost something that he didn't understand or found something that he didn't want. He turned back to the fire, looking into the flames.

"I don't recall ever being angry before William and Rockwell came to live with us. But I thought of Tolstoy lying dead in the backyard and the whistling, smiling face of Rockwell Thomson as he passed me without a care in the world, and a consuming hatred was born that instant. It was so foreign and new to me that I didn't know what to do with it at first. Sophia was right. I was too kind and good-natured to think like Rockwell, or contend with him, until that moment. But as the days passed and my hatred of Rockwell bloomed, it bore fruit, and one of the flowers on that poisoned tree was cunning.

"Sophia saw it. She saw it on my face so clearly. I built a coffin for Tolstoy in the woodshop, and we buried him under his favorite apple tree in a service that included Mother and Elsie. When it was over, and they were gone, Sophia took my hand and led me away to the path that followed the bluff down to the beach. It was always a favorite walk of ours. We took off our shoes and walked along the sand with the surf washing over our feet.

'Thomas?' she inquired, as we walked along hand in hand. I scarcely heard her. My thoughts were elsewhere. In a dark place. 'Thomas?' she repeated, and stopped, turning to face me. 'Thomas?' She studied my face a long, searching moment. 'Don't do it.'

'Don't do what?'

'Whatever it is you're thinking. Don't do it.'

"I turned away so she couldn't see my face.

'I've seen the change in you. Don't become like him. You'll lose everything.' I felt her hand on my cheek as she gently turned my face to her. 'Do you understand?' she said, peering into my eyes. 'Everything.'

"I couldn't endure the sight of Rockwell after the Tolstoy incident. His presence was an unwanted distraction that we had to suffer, and even though his snare had failed to catch me, he took pleasure in the fact that he had caused me pain. Sophia and I avoided him when possible and counted the days until his return to school. But he would not go quietly. It was not in him. His two goals, hurting me and seducing Sophia, had failed, and he couldn't live with that. I saw him roaming the house and knew that he was hatching some new plot, but the day was drawing near that he would soon be departing for school. It looked as if Sophia and I might escape his malicious design. We were together all of the time and gave him no opportunity to strike, or so I thought.

"With only one day remaining before he left for school, Sophia and I said goodnight in the hallway outside our bedrooms and breathed a sigh of relief. When I climbed into bed that night it was with a light heart, confident that Rockwell would be leaving the next day and we would have our house back in some measure. Smiling in my misguided security, I drifted off to sleep."

Throughout most of his narrative, Thomas had been staring into the flames of the fire, absently cradling a glass of wine in his hand as he recalled the events that he shared with us. But the fire had burned low again, and he rose from his seat, tossed more wood on the dying embers, and then returned to his chair deep in thought. As he stooped down to pick up his wine glass, he saw Charles and I waiting expectantly on the edge of our seat. Suddenly startled, he looked as if he had forgotten we were there.

"Oh," he said, his eyes moving from Charles to me. "Would you like to hear more?"

"Yes," we quickly answered.

"Well," he said, with a heavy sigh, "all right." And his eyes fell again to his blood stained hands. "Excuse me." He said, scowling, and left the room. Thomas returned a moment later wiping his hands with a damp cloth and dropped into his seat once more.

"Did you get your wish?" He asked, looking up at Charles while he worked the cloth over his hands. "Did you knock his tooth out?"

"Excuse me?" Charles asked.

"Smyth. You said you would like to knock the last tooth out of his head."

"How could you have heard that?" Charles asked. "I barely spoke above a whisper."

"I was quite close," he said. "I heard many things." I shuddered at the memory of Smyth and his nearly toothless smile as he ran his thumb over the blade of his knife, testing the edge. "You're very lucky, Mrs. Dearborn. Your husband is a very brave man."

"I know," I said, taking my husband's hand.

"You're no slouch yourself, Mr. Moore," Charles replied.

"I knew you were a good man the moment I saw you, Thomas," I said. "Whatever else you've done, you're a good man."

Thomas seemed amused by my words. I thought I detected a faint little amused sort of smile on his lips as he wiped the last of the blood from his hands, and tossed the cloth on the hearth.

"So, Mr. Moore," said Charles, "what else have you done?"

I got the sense that Charles would not spend the night in the Moore house without an answer to that question. I think that

Thomas sensed that, too, and was not put off by it. He seemed to enjoy our company. I could only imagine how lonely and quiet that big empty house would be if one were all alone there. He refilled his wine glass, studied us a moment by the dim light of the fire, and continued.

"I woke suddenly to some sound in the night which I could no longer hear," he said. "In the darkness, I lay awake listening and heard what sounded like crying outside my door. Suddenly alert, I climbed out of bed and tentatively opened the door to find Sophia on her knees in the dark hallway, beside a body on the floor.

'I'm so sorry. I'm so sorry. I didn't mean to do it,' she kept repeating.

'Sophia. What happened?' I asked, unable to see much in the dark hallway.

'Oh, Thomas,' she said, rushing to my arms, pressing her head to my chest, her whole slender frame trembling. 'I've done something terrible. It was an accident. I didn't mean it.'

"With one arm around her, I stroked her hair with my free hand, while looking down at the lifeless body of Rockwell Thomson.

'What happened? Tell me exactly what happened.'

'I got up for a drink of water," she said, sobbing into my shirtfront. "On my way back, I saw the sewing scissors that I've been looking for. I was walking along the dark hallway, thinking about all those nights that I walked home on the dark trail through the woods and how frightened I used to get and how scared I was when I was lying on the sofa all alone waiting for Mother to come home at night." Sophia looked up at me then with frightened, tearful eyes. "I stepped into my bedroom, and before I could turn on the light something jumped out and grabbed me. I struck out at it without thinking. I forgot I had scissors in my hand. Oh, what will I do?' she cried. 'I'm so sorry.'

"Only a saint like Sophia could be sorry about the death of this young tyrant, I thought. But what would we do? Before I could give it much thought, I heard footsteps approaching rapidly on the stairs. Heavy footsteps.

'Go,' I said, urgently. 'Quickly. Downstairs. To the other end of the house. That way.' I pointed to the opposite staircase. 'Hurry.'

'But what about you?'

'I'll be all right. Go.' I pushed her toward the staircase. 'And promise me you'll tell no one what happened here.'

'What?' She hesitated.

'Promise,' I said, firmly.

'O...okay,' she answered, reluctantly.

'Now go,' I said, and Sophia took a few tentative steps. If I had known then what a cruel turn fate would deliver, I would have been kinder. I would have held her a bit longer. She hesitated briefly, but upon hearing the angry footsteps climbing the stairs, Sophia hurried away fearfully. Reaching the top of the stairs, William spotted his son's body lying in the dark hallway, with me standing over it, and rushed forward like a charging bull. The vacant, lifeless eyes staring blindly confirmed his fear, and he turned upon me in a rage.

"I saw the fury in his eyes when he struck me. I felt my nose break with that first punch and dropped to my knees. The room began to spin before my eyes. Before I lost consciousness, I felt him kicking me again and again, lifting me off the floor with the force of each blow.

"I awoke in a hospital bed some time later. There are no hospitals on the islands. I still don't know exactly where I was. My broken ribs were taped. There was a bandage on my nose. My jaw felt as though it were broken as well and throbbed with a constant pain that nothing would alleviate. I couldn't move or even breathe beyond a shallow breath without excruciating pain to ribs. As my eyes fluttered open and I gradually became aware of my surroundings, I saw a dark shape move toward me and lean down close to my face.

'So you're awake,' he hissed, quietly, and pressed firmly on my bandaged ribs, causing me to cry out through clenched teeth. 'Shh, not too loudly now. I have a few things to say to you in private,' he whispered like a snake. 'It wouldn't do to be interrupted, oh no, that wouldn't do at all. You're going to pay for killing my Rockwell, you see. This is only the beginning.'

"He pressed again on my bandaged ribs, and I fought back a cry.

'I'm going to use all of my considerable influence to have you sent to a maximum security prison far away from here where no one will ever be able to visit you. You'll see no one but filthy criminals for the rest of your natural life, which will be spent in a dark little cockroach-infested hole. Well, except for the days when you're bound to your fellow sufferers, working on a chain gang in the hot, lone star sun. How does Texas sound? They know how to treat an inmate down there.' He chuckled at his own malicious thought. 'You can always take comfort in the fact that I'll be comfortable in your house, sharing your mother's bed, with your pretty little girlfriend just down the hall.'

"I was possessed with a blind, seething hatred so great that I would have killed him on the spot, if I could but move my arms. He saw my impotent fury, and laughed.

'If you oppose me on any of this, the women will suffer, and I know something about making people suffer. Enter a guilty plea and accept the maximum sentence, or …' and he smiled, cruelly.

"Hearing footsteps in the corridor, he quietly slipped back to his seat beside my bed and feigned sleep. A moment later, Mother entered the room drinking a fresh cup of tea. When she saw I was awake, she rushed quickly to my side.

"'Oh Thomas, Thomas darling, are you all right? How do you feel?' She pressed her lovely hand to my cheek, and nearly cried for joy. 'No, don't try to answer; it was foolish of me to ask. I'm just so glad you're awake. Sophia was here until a moment ago; she just left to get some fresh air. William is so sorry he beat you like this. In the darkness, with you standing over Rockwell's body, he thought you were an intruder.'

'Sorry folks, visiting hours are over,' a doctor said, appearing in the doorway.

'But he just woke up,' Mother answered.

'Sorry, you need to leave now. There's always tomorrow.' He replied, and remained in the doorway to ensure their departure.

'Sophia and I will return first thing in the morning, Thomas,' she said, and kissed my cheek.

"With his arm around her waist, William escorted Mother from the room. At the doorway, she turned around, giving me a smile and a wave before continuing, but it was the malicious sneer of William that I was left with as he triumphantly strode away. There was something in that sneer that chilled my blood, something he knew that I didn't. I was to find out that night, or more accurately, the next day.

"I remained in my hospital bed, nearly immobilized by my injuries, unable to find a position that was comfortable or didn't cause me pain. My head throbbed with a constant pulse that coincided with my beating heart, and I was sometimes dizzy, sometimes nauseous. Anything more than a shallow breath delivered insufferable pain from my frail, broken ribs. I drifted in and out of sleep, vaguely aware of the steady tread of footsteps in the busy corridor outside my open door and nurses sometimes popping in and out of my room. It had no window, so day and night were indistinguishable, but the hospital seemed quieter. I sensed less traffic in the corridor and speculated that evening had arrived.

"I awoke suddenly to sharp pain in my arm and turned to see a syringe piercing my vein. Holding it was a nurse, and behind her were two uniformed officers. Before I could speculate or utter a word of protest, my eyes closed in sleep and I had fitful dreams of voices, footsteps, and clanging doors."

Thomas paused in the narration of his history and finished his wine in a gulp. He appeared reluctant to continue and seemed absorbed in his own thoughts as he pondered the empty glass in his hand. I wondered if the story was reaching a painful turn, if perhaps we were about to open the door to an event he wished to forget. I longed to hear the rest of the tale but sensed reluctance from our host.

"I trust I haven't taxed your patience too heavily with my dry tales and family history," he said at last, with a yawn. "It's quite late, and you must be terribly fatigued after your stressful day. Shall I show you to your room?"

Charles was about to protest that he would like to hear more, but I stopped him with the touch of my hand on his arm.

"Thank you," I answered, reassuringly. "We would like to turn in for the evening."

"This way."

He took the candle from the mantle, which by then had burned down to a little stub, and guided us across the dark room to a long, sweeping staircase that ascended gradually to the second floor high above. The feeble candlelight climbed the stairs before us, casting its glow in a small circle that fell unevenly upon the steps and throwing our shadows upon the walls. At the summit of the stairs a wide hallway stretched before us until it was lost to darkness at the far end, and in this hallway were intricately carved doors on both sides. Thomas led us past several, and at a particular one near the far end of the hallway, stopped.

"This was Sophia's room. I think you'll be comfortable here." He led us inside and, using his candle, lit another on a table beside the bed. The room was slowly revealed as the flame gained purchase, and I found it to be quite charming and comfortable. On one wall was a large canopy bed and, opposite it, a chest of drawers with a matching wardrobe of some dark wood. In the corner was an artist's easel, beside which curtains were drawn open displaying a leaded window that looked out over the moonlit ocean.

The history recently shared with us invited imagination in this poorly lit room, once occupied by the lovely orphan girl who squirmed under the covers and rubbed the soft sheets upon her cheek. I pictured little Sophia in the giant bed, with the covers pulled up under chin, smiling contently, warm and safe.

"Thank you, Thomas," I said.

"My room is across the hall if you need anything," he answered, and followed the candle out of the room. Within minutes we were in bed. Any apprehension Charles may have had about spending the night in that house must have vanished. He was fast asleep in no time, while I lay awake, listening to the steady rhythm of his breathing, looking restlessly about the room still lit by the candle beside the bed; or to be more precise, the darkness was troubled only slightly by its feeble light. With my back propped up on the pillows, I could see the easel that Mrs. Moore had given to Sophia and, upon it, an unfinished painting that seemed to beckon to me from the shadows. There was a face on that canvas in the darkness, a face that I could just see by the flickering candlelight, and eyes that watched me.

Careful not to wake Charles, I slipped out of bed and, taking the candle with me, moved to the painting for a closer look. By the imperfect light of the wavering flame, I saw the portrait of a beautiful teenage girl with black hair and blue eyes, which I took to be the artist herself. She regarded me with an expression of optimistic melancholy, as if sad, but hopeful, and I imagined her standing at the easel, working the paint brush with her delicate fingers while she thought distractedly of Thomas, recently taken from her. How sad she must have been with her dear friend gone, I mused. How frightened she must have felt in that big house with William just down the hall. The self-portrait was unfinished. The face was complete, and skillfully rendered, yet the rest of the composition was vacant and blank. Why had she not finished, I wondered? What had become of Sophia? Why was the house empty? Where was everyone?

So much had happened that day that my thoughts were still racing, and I had no mind for sleep. I would dress and walk about the house, I decided.

The door opened noiselessly. With Charles sleeping soundly in the big canopy bed, I crept into the hall, leaving the unsnuffed candle behind. The way to Thomas's room was closed and I didn't wish to wake him. Making my way quietly along the carpeted hallway, I trailed my hand along the wall as a guide in the darkness until I reached the stairs. The room below was lit by the moonlight pouring through the many windows and the red glow of the dying fire that illuminated a little arc beyond the hearth. In the stillness, it looked so warm and inviting. But I had already seen that part of the house; I wished to see more, to wander about and explore in my restlessness. I wanted to see the places that Thomas had mentioned as he told his tale: the kitchen table where they had their meals, the window that looked out upon the cemetery. I wanted to imagine everyone there as he had said.

The pale light of the glowing moon streamed in through the towering windows that looked out over the gray sea. I stepped quietly, descending the dark staircase, then past the dying embers of the fire, and picked my way among the dusty, cloth-covered furnishings on the main floor, growing slightly uneasy by the sight of it all. There was an unnerving quality in the quiet, the solitude, the late hour, the furtive scurry of little feet retreating before me in the darkness, that gave me pause. But the windows overlooking the graveyard were just ahead, and my errand intrigued me.

Stepping close to the glass, I peered out at the cemetery marked by the low brick wall, which had crumbled and fallen in several places. The moon had by then climbed high in the night sky, and the moon-cast shadows were short and close. At one end of the cemetery stood several gnarled old maple trees with trained boughs that hung gracefully over the headstones gathered in their shadow. Not a breath of wind stirred the leafy boughs of the silent guardians. All was as still and picturesque as a photograph.

Which belonged to Thomas' father, I wondered? I moved still closer to the glass, studying the dark headstones, checking off each as my eye traveled over the polished granite reflecting the broken moonlight that streamed through the maple leaves. The graveyard had been recently mowed, and the grass trimmed neatly from the headstones. Two still wore fresh flowers—red roses I believe— though it was difficult to tell in the silver light, but I could see that they had been placed with care on two graves that were slightly apart from the others, in the corner of the cemetery. And something strange. There was a shape near one of those headstones that caught my eye; a dark, indistinct figure in the broken shadow of moonlight filtered through the maple leaves. Even as I moved closer to the glass, straining to see it in the darkness, it moved. It stood up.

I jumped back from the window, startled, my heart pounding suddenly like a drum. Had the convicts found us? Were they going to force their way into the house? Where were the other two? Instantly alert, I stepped back to the glass, watching. The figure was kneeling on the ground then, with his arms on a grave and his head on his arms. He remained so for quite some time, long enough that I thought I may have imagined the movement from before and that maybe this was a stone figure of some sort added to the cemetery, something that I simply hadn't noticed before. But if so, then where was the thing that I saw move a moment ago?

The house was so very quiet. The soft pop of the distant fire would sometimes reach my ears in the stillness as I continued watching from the window. I felt a sudden chill then, as if someone was watching me, and whirled around, peering into the dark corners of the house. No one was there, of course, but in the stillness of the room and the heavier air of the darker corners, I wondered if something unwholesome were not dwelling there. I chided myself for being silly and turned back to the window. The dark figure was moving among the headstones, directing his steps toward the house where I stood at the glass. The moon at his back cast a menacing shadow over his face, disguising his features, but I recognized the pants; I had seen them earlier, and the memory made me shudder. Where were the other two, I wondered? Should I run for Charles and Thomas? I was riveted to the spot and felt helpless to move as I watched him approach. Closer and closer he came, and still I was too frightened to stir. He was only a few paces away from the window where I stood when he paused suddenly and turned to look back at the cemetery. For just a moment, the moonlight fell upon his face as he turned, and I saw that it was our host. It was Thomas.

Breathing a sigh of relief, I moved away from the window and took a moment to collect my thoughts. Thomas had given me quite a scare. That he wished to visit his father's grave after an absence of nine years was not unusual. I was touched by his devotion. But surely he had visited it before. Wouldn't it wait until morning? Perhaps there were other graves there that he wished to visit, graves that were added while he was away. Where was his mother, and where was Sophia? If well, then why were they not at the house? I had grown quite fond of them through his narrative and fostered hope for their well-being.

My innocent notion of exploring the house had taken an unexpected turn and seemed improper, with the possibility of being discovered by Thomas. I suddenly felt as though I were snooping or spying and feared that I would offend our generous host if I were discovered in that part of the house. Hurrying back through the moonlit room, I picked my way through the melancholy furniture hidden away by the dusty, moth-eaten cloths as I attempted to gain the staircase and return to bed before my presence was revealed. As I passed before the fire, I heard the soft click of a latch and glanced up to see Thomas closing the door after entering the house. With his eyes on the floor, he crossed the room distractedly and walked to the windows through which the clear moonlight streamed. There, he fell with a heavy sigh into his mother's seat, hung his head in his hands, and wept quietly.

More than ever I wanted to disappear, to slip away quietly, unnoticed, to leave him alone with his grief and give him privacy in his own house, but that was not possible. I would surely be seen. So, I dropped quietly into a high back chair before the fire that nearly swallowed me up and hid me from view. The fire had already burned low, but produced a soothing warmth that encouraged slumber. I found myself nodding off as the minutes ticked away. I was beginning to wonder how long this might go on when I heard a soft rustle behind me, then footsteps on the stone floor.

"Oh, Mrs. Dearborn," Thomas said, somewhat embarrassed as he quickly wiped his eyes, "what a pleasant surprise." He took a seat next to me before the fire. I wasn't sure that the surprise was such a pleasant one. He had enjoyed precious little solitude since arriving at his home, and I suspected that he sought it.

"I couldn't sleep. I'm sorry. I'll return to bed."

"No, no, you're welcome to remain," he said, distractedly.

No doubt his thoughts were still in the cemetery. And while I sensed that he would like to be alone, I also sensed that he took comfort in my company.

"Where is Mr. Dearborn?"

"Charles can sleep anywhere, at any time," I said, smiling. "He's in bed."

"He impressed me as a pioneering sort, none too faint of heart. They usually sleep well."

"You're very observant; that's him exactly. I'm always the one lying awake, unable to sleep. Thinking about what transpired that day."

"This day was unlike most," he added, gravely. "We all have much to think about."

"But my thoughts were not what I expected. I was thinking instead about you and Sophia, and about Elsie and your mother. Where are they?" I glanced to the window, beyond which lay the cemetery. "Not there I hope?"

His eyes fell, and he nodded.

"All?" I asked, horrified.

"Not all, thankfully," he added, and the pain was clear on his grief-stricken face, "unless I missed their headstones in the darkness."

"Thomas," I said, taking his hand, "I trust you will never again have such persistent and troublesome houseguest as this, but I...I..."

"What is it, Mrs. Dearborn?" He said, sensing my hesitancy.

"Would you," I paused, "would you please finish your tale. I won't get a wink of sleep until I learn what became of everyone."

"Only that?" he replied, quietly, attempting to muster a smile.

"There is an unfinished painting of Sophia on the artists easel in her room. She's beautiful, Thomas."

"Yes," he said, with a gentle smile. "I haven't seen the painting. She must have started it after I went away."

"Do you know what became of her? Why is the painting unfinished? Did she leave suddenly?"

"I don't know," he answered, sadly. "I don't know what became of her. I don't know what became of anyone. I didn't expect to find the house abandoned when I returned. I thought everyone would be here."

"Will you tell me the rest?" I pleaded. "Will you tell me what you know?"

"Mrs. Dearborn…" he began, and I saw weary reluctance in his grieving eyes that were drawn to the cemetery.

"I'm sorry Thomas. I didn't mean to impose. You have other things to think about, I'm sure."

"I suppose I could use a distraction," he said. "Where did I stop?" He paused, thinking.

"You were in the hospital and had been given a shot after William threatened you."

"Oh yes," he said, with a shudder, recalling the memory.

Thomas rose from his seat, tossed more wood on the dying fire, then dropped back into his chair. He thought for a moment, and then began.

"I drifted slowly out of sleep as the effects of the drug dissipated and lay with my eyes closed on a cold, hard surface. The smell of cigarettes and urine pervaded the foul air. That struck me as odd, and I wondered where I was. When I opened my eyes, I found I was flat on my back, and a square light recessed in the ceiling glared down at me. It took quite a little time for the effects of the drug to dissipate entirely. I felt groggy and nauseous, unable to move or avoid the persistent glare of that annoying light. I rolled my head aside so that my cheek was flat on the thin mattress and studied the room. It was yellow painted cinderblock, with a stainless steel sink-toilet in the corner and bars on one wall. Slowly, painfully, I pushed myself up into a sitting position on the bed and studied the little chamber in disbelief. I was in jail. The bed was a flat piece of steel bolted to the wall, with a thin mattress on top and two threadbare blankets folded at one end. In the bars of the door an opening had been cut for the passage of food, and a metal tray rested in the opening. As I hadn't eaten in quite some time and was terribly hungry, I rose painfully and made my slow way to the tray to investigate. I found two pieces of white bread with something resembling butter in between and a cup of water in a stained, dirty glass.

"I hobbled back to the bed and sat down. How did I get there? Did anyone know? Did Mother? Without so much as a book to pass the time, I sat alone and helpless on the bed, listening to the jail sounds. In the concrete and steel of the building, every noise was amplified and carried along the cells and hallways. I heard the distant sound of buzzers and the heavy clang of steel doors slamming shut. Voices. Laughing. The jingle of keys. I hugged my legs up under my chin and lowered my head. I was glad it was not Sophia in the cell. With my eyes closed, I mused about Ravenswood. It seemed so very far away. Would I ever see it again, I wondered? Suddenly I realized that a jingle of keys was approaching, and attempted to stand, to move to the door.

"'Excuse me,' I intimated timidly, pulling myself up by the bars at the end of the bed, as a man passed. My nose and jaw throbbed painfully. My ribs were still taped and stabbed at me if I moved wrong. 'Excuse me,' I said, finally making it to the door, but he passed by without so much as a glance in my direction. The footsteps continued to the end of the hall. I heard the keys jingle again and then the rumble of a heavy steel door sliding in a steel track, until it clanged at the end. Moments later, the jailer passed again, leading an inmate who shuffled along with his hands cuffed before him. 'Excuse me,' I uttered again, louder this time, but again he passed without a glance in my direction. Gingerly, I returned to bed and contemplated my fate. Never had I felt so alone, so forsaken, so depressed. I buried my face in the tattered blankets at the end of the bed and began to cry."

Thomas reached for the open wine bottle on the coffee table.

"Would you like a bit more?" he asked. Our glasses remained on the table where we had left them from earlier.

"Maybe just a little."

He poured a splash into my glass, and then his own, and took a sip.

"A routine soon developed—a dull, monotonous, never varying routine under the glare of the ever-present light. On a steel tray each morning, a thin, watery porridge was left in the opening of my cell door. At lunch, the same steel tray held two pieces of bread covering a meat-like paste of some sort. And at dinnertime, the steel tray bore some mysterious combination of gravy that had bread or meat mixed in with it. As my windowless cell admitted no light and the incessant glare of the lamp overhead never changed, it was impossible to tell daylight from darkness or the passage of one day to the next. But the introduction of the meal trays each day allowed for a rough estimate of the time and the slow, gradual passage of the day. If only the light could have been extinguished at the close of each day served. What a little treat that would have been. To sleep in the muted light of that barren cage would have made it so much more palatable. Waking in the morning to a new light on a new day. But that was not to be. The light remained on always. It was like one long terrible day that would never end. Responding to the exigency of the moment, I slept as much and as often as possible, waiting for I knew not what. There had been no trial. No charges had been leveled against me that I knew of, and my presence there was a mystery so far as I was concerned.

"I had just borne witness to the delivery on my tenth breakfast tray when I heard the approaching jingle of keys and the heavy tread of the jailer. He stopped at my cell door.

'You there, Moore, get up,' he demanded. I rose from the bed and stood tentatively, wondering what was next. 'Well, put your shoes on, you have court.'

"Quickly, I slipped on my shoes, eager to leave the little cell. In the courtroom would be people who could provide answers. I may be released, or at least discover why I was in jail, what the charges were, how severe the penalty was. The jailer, who I later learned answered to the name of Bob, opened my door, cuffed my hands, and led me through a maze of buzzers and locked doors. The courthouse, he said, was across the street. For security reasons, a tunnel had been constructed under the street and led, by various turns and twists, to it. With a plodding, monotonous gait that equaled the plodding, monotonous routine of everything within the jail, Bob took my arm and escorted me through a dank tunnel. Lit by grimy, naked bulbs hanging from ceiling timbers by a cord, the tunnel had the appearance of having been constructed hastily, as if for escape rather than regular use or agency. I found that I was constantly wiping my face free of dirty cobwebs that I plunged headlong into, unable to perceive them in the dim light. In the dirt walls, I saw the scalloped bite of the shovel that carved them and, just as often, a thin trail of water meandering along. There was the constant sound of dripping water that I never saw the source of.

"Bob, it seemed, had been employed in the capacity of jailer to the extent that the vocation had removed any possibility of individual thought, any suggestion of joy or happiness from his personal life, and any desire to change any of those things. Simply put, he went about his job mechanically, without emotion or concern, never troubled by the fate or outcome of those in his charge; his sole concern was the faithful discharge of his duty. He delivered me to the courtroom, where I expected to see Mother and Sophia but discovered, to my alarm, that I knew no one present. I was motioned to a seat on a long pew-like bench in the first row of the courtroom, next to several others who, like me, had their hands cuffed before them. Apprehensively, I sat. Bob shuffled to the rear of the room, where he stood leaning back upon the wall, repressing a yawn. I turned in my seat, searching the audience for a familiar face, but saw only judgment and suspicion in the eyes of the strangers present. The air in the courtroom was heavy and somber, smelling of fear, hopelessness, and dread.

'Hello. Hello there, Mr. Moore.'

"Before the first row of pews was a polished mahogany table and two chairs. A man had taken a seat there and was quickly, efficiently, organizing papers from his briefcase. He was young and handsome, with a smile that came easily to his practiced face, but my impression of him was not a favorable one, for reasons I could not explain. He summoned me to a seat next to his when I turned to face him.

'But, he said to sit over…' I began.

'No, no, it's all right. We're first,' he said, patting the seat beside him.

"I moved to the seat indicated.

'I'm Jim Scavera, your attorney. William hired me to represent you.'

"I was not comforted by that knowledge, but before I could give it, or him, much thought, I heard movement and saw Mr. Scavera look past me and frowned as he nodded a greeting. Following his frowning eyes, I saw a man taking a seat at a table like ours on the other side of the courtroom. He checked his watch, opened his briefcase, and rapidly sorted through the papers within.

'All rise. The Honorable Judge Barron presiding.'

"I heard the rush of people standing suddenly and stood as well. Behind a high, ornate bench at the front of the room entered a man in a black robe who walked quickly and took a seat at the bench. He was a tallish man, with long limbs and a pale complexion, which, contrasting with the black robe, looked sickly. His thin, bloodless lips seemed to be pursed in a constant sneer.

'Be seated,' he said, with an expression of boredom.

"Everyone sat.

'What do we have today?' he asked. The court reporter handed him a document.

'People versus Moore, your honor.'

'Are the people prepared to proceed?'

'Yes, your honor,' came the response from the man at the table next to us.

'Is the defense ready?'

'Yes, your honor,' answered Mr. Scavera.

'Mr. Moore, the grand jury has returned an indictment against you for murder in the first degree. How do you plead?' said the judge routinely, without looking up at me.

"Mr. Scavera stood and motioned for me to do the same. Puzzled, I stood as instructed, and turned to him for guidance.

'Guilty,' he whispered into my ear. 'Say guilty.'

'Guilty,' I answered, weakly, to the judge.

'Your honor,' Mr. Scavera added, in a whisper. 'Guilty, your honor.'

'Your honor,' I added.

'Very well. A guilty plea has been entered,' said the judge, consulting a document in his hand. 'I see a plea agreement has been reached, so we'll proceed to sentencing.'

'Sentencing, your honor?' asked the man at the other table, who I learned was the assistant district attorney.

'Yes, sentencing Mr. Leason. It's what we do after a verdict.'

'"There isn't even a pre-sentence report.'

'I don't need one. We have a plea agreement.'

'I don't have a copy of the plea agreement, your honor.'

'Where is Mr. Burgett?' asked the judge, impatiently.

'He had a family emergency, your honor,' said Mr. Leason. 'I'm filling in for him.'

'Well be prepared next time.'

'I was told this would be a simple arraignment, your honor. This is the defendant's first court appearance.'

'A plea agreement has already been reached. There's no need to postpone sentencing. Will someone please give Mr. Leason a copy of the plea agreement so we can proceed?' said the judge, annoyed.

"My attorney walked to his counterpart and handed him several pages of documents, then returned and waited patiently while the other attorney read.

"I watched his face closely; I believe everyone in the courtroom watched his face closely, since we were all waiting for him to finish. He scanned the document with the bored routine of familiarity, as he had probably done many times before, then his brows came together in a puzzled scowl, which only deepened as he continued. When finished, he stood with his hand on the document lying on the table and turned to me, studying me with a mystified frown while everyone in the room watched and waited.

'Well, Mr. Leason?' asked the judge.

'There must be some mistake.'

"I noted that he forgot to add, 'Your honor.'

'There's no mistake, Mr. Leason. You'll notice Mr. Burgett's signature on the plea agreement.'

'Yes, your honor. But I'll want to confirm with him before I accept this.'

'Oh, you'd like to waste tax payer money and drag everyone back in here a second time so you can satisfy a whim?' the judge asked, glaring at Mr. Leason, who held his eye without flinching.

'The people are not prepared to proceed on this matter,' said Mr. Leason firmly, still holding the judge's eye.

'Very well,' answered the judge, livid with anger, 'sentencing will be rescheduled, per Mr. Leason's whim, for October twenty-third. What's next on the docket?'

"I pitied the next defendant to come before the Honorable Judge Barron but had little time for such reflections. Bob had taken me by the arm and was leading me away. When I turned, halfway to the door, I saw Mr. Scavera gathering up his documents and returning them to his briefcase. It was Mr. Leason who was watching me with a curious eye as I departed.

"We took the same route back to the jail, with Bob leading me along under the dirty, naked bulbs of the tunnel that struggled, in a losing effort, to light the way. His normally expressionless face bore the first signs of a frown. His lips were pursed ever so slightly, and one brow was raised in an inquisitive fashion, denoting thought, a condition he had probably not experienced in quite some time. We passed through all of the buzzers and steel doors as before and reached my little cell at last. He ushered me in, closed the door behind me with a heavy clang, and remained looking through the bars at me, as if seeing me for the first time. He opened his mouth to speak, thought better of it, and turned away. His clumsy tread and jingle of keys grew fainter and disappeared altogether after the clang of the steel door at the end of the corridor.

"I kicked off my shoes and then sat down on the bed to think. What was in that plea agreement that had caused Mr. Leason so much ire? My confinement had left me weak, and the little exercise of walking to court and back had taken its toll. Within minutes my head fell to my chest, and I drifted off to sleep.

"Two dinner trays later, I was seated on my bed, as always, when I heard the all too familiar jingle of approaching keys. They stopped at my door, were applied to the lock, and the door swung open to admit a new tenant, who entered readily, almost enthusiastically, carrying a mattress and blankets, which he tossed upon the bed above mine. The jailer, who I didn't recognize (it wasn't Bob's shift yet), shut the door without a word and departed.

'How ya doin'?' he said. 'Herbert Mayer.'

"I stood and shook the offered hand.

'Thomas Moore,' I answered.

"He was a large fellow, a head taller than me and three times my age, possessed with a warm, genuine smile that seemed never to leave his face. Even then, arriving in jail, he smiled and seemed in good spirits. There was about him a simple sort of casualness that I found endearing. His lazy gray eyes took in the little cell as he spread his mattress out on the bed and unfolded his blankets.

'Guess I'll be spendin' the night. They don't make these things any too comfortable, do they?'

'No,' I answered.

'Well, I can handle one night,' he said, tucking the blankets in where they fell over the edge of the bed. 'How long are you gonna be here?'

'I don't know.'

'What's the charge?' he asked, jovially.

'Murder in the first degree.'

"He whistled long and peeked down at me curiously. I had resumed my seat on the bed by then, and had been speaking to his knees while he stood making the bunk above.

'Ya don't say? You?'

"He sat down on my bed beside me, which I thought a little presumptuous, and looked me over closely from behind bushy gray brows.

'Ya don't look like you'd hurt a fly. Who'd ya kill? Or I should say,' he added with a grin, 'who'd ya allegedly kill?'

'My stepbrother.'

'Ah, family quarrel, eh?' he said, and added in response to my stifled frown. 'Sorry about the smell. It's been with me all day, so I don't notice so much anymore. Is it the fuel or the salt air?'

'Both.' I answered, as politely as I could.

'Well, I'm sorry,' he replied, affably. 'I didn't get a chance to change outta my work clothes.'

'Oh. What type of work do you do?'

'Importer,' he said, with a wide grin.

'What do you import?'

'Gin, Scotch, rum. Whatever ya fancy.'

'Alcohol?' I repeated, surprised.

'Yeah, that's why I'm sharing a room with ya tonight. I'll be out first thing in the morning, though, my attorney'll see to that. He's always good about gettin' me out quick.'

'This isn't you first time here?'

'Oh, no. I don't make a habit of it, ya understand, but I get pinched now and then. It goes with the turf.'

'How did you get caught?' I asked, enjoying our conversation. Mr. Mayer was proving to be as entertaining as a good book.

'Well, this time they was waitin' for me when I arrived in my boat. Someone tipped 'em off. I think I know who, too.'

'You're not going to harm them, are you?'

'Harm them? Lord no. What put that idea inta yer head? I'll put 'em on the payroll.'

"Sitting together on my bed, we spoke together until late into the night, Mr. Mayer and I. It was so refreshing to have someone there, a companion with whom to converse, that the time passed so quickly. Mr. Mayer was a shrewd man whose company I took pleasure in, partly because he was older than I and knew so many things about a world I had never imagined before and partly because he possessed such an endearing, jovial manner that he set me at ease. He had been laid off, he said, shortly after the death of the business owner who had kept him on more out of goodwill than necessity. Business had fallen off and they didn't need him, but jobs were difficult to come by and the owner was sensitive to that.

'They was pleased well enough with my work, ya understand, but they didn't need me so much anymore. When the owner died, the shop foreman, who was a much more practical fella, let me go, ya see.'

"That was when he started his import business. He spoke quite freely and enthusiastically about it, as if it were an adventure. He enjoyed the danger and intrigue, he said. It was like a high stakes game of chess. Sneaking past the patrols in his boat at night, heavily laden with illegal cargo. Ducking into secret coves and harbors known only to smugglers. Outwitting the police. Transporting his cargo in storms when the police boats wouldn't go out. He no longer needed the money, he said, and did it for the sheer pleasure of the thing. It was great sport. I imagined myself skippering a smuggled cargo past the police fleet and hiding in some secret cove under the cloak of darkness.

'But, how did you get caught?' I asked, intrigued by his tale.

'This last time, you mean?' He laughed. 'Well, there was only one way to catch me, ya see. I can buy all the booze I like in Canada, legal like, so they can't catch me on that end. And I don't tell my boys where I'll be offloading on this end until the last minute, so the police can't organize a trap for me if anyone's indiscreet. But this time around, my boat wasn't fueled up like she was supposed to be, and there was only one place I could stop for fuel on the way back. So I pulls up there all pretty as ya please, never suspectin' a thing, and the old boy at the fuel dock comes hobblin' out of his shack, leanin' on a cane, his white hair pourin' out under his cap, barely able ta grip the pump handle with his arthritic hands. Well, I step off the boat to help him, and the next thing I know those arthritic old hands have nimbly slipped a pair a cuffs on me ever so quick.' He laughed merrily at his own misfortune. 'They got me fair an square. The whole thing had been a trap, ya see? The police came out of the woodwork then, dozens of 'em hiding here and there on the dock. They'd been a waitin' for me. Well, the only way they could know I would be stoppen' there is know I didn't have fuel enough to make it all the way back. And that leads right to the man who fueled up the boat.'

'It all sounds so exciting,' I said.

"For hours I had listened spellbound to my companion's adventures.

'So, what about you,' he asked. 'What's yer story?'

'I don't know that I'm old enough to have much of a story,' I answered. 'I haven't had many adventures like you.'

'Well, you're in jail on a murder charge,' he said, good-naturedly. 'There must be some story behind that.'

'Oh, that. Yes, I suppose so.'

'Well, let's have some a the details. Ya really don't look like the murderous type, so there must be somethin' ta tell. Come on, I've got the time.'

"It was so pleasant to finally have some company in my dreary little cell. Starting with Father's death, I told him everything. I told him about Elsie and Mother and how I had met Sophia, and how she had come to live with us. Then about William and his son, Rockwell. He listened quietly, with great interest, as the hours passed. Finally, I related how Rockwell had been killed and how I had been beaten by William and found myself there.

'Well, that's some story, make no mistake,' he said, scratching his chin thoughtfully. 'So you ain't the fella that killed that scoundrel, Rockwell? Can ya prove it?'

'William is capable of tremendous violence. If I don't admit to it, I fear for the safety of Mother and Sophia. He's said he'll harm them. Anyway,' I reflected pensively, 'If I don't go to jail, Sophia will.'

'You're an honorable man, Mr. Moore, I respect that,' he said, shaking my hand. 'A man has ta protect his family.' He held my eye a moment. 'I've heard lots a tall tales in this jailhouse; everyone's innocent as a lamb. Yours is the first one I've believed.'

'Thank you.'

'This William Thomson, now. There's a circuit court judge by that name. I don't suppose it's the same man?'

'Yes, that's him.'

'Huh,' he snorted, contemptuously. 'It's a well known fact among those in my profession that ya get as much justice as ya can afford with the Honorable Judge Thomson.'

'What does that mean?' I asked, innocently.

'It means that with the proper bribe ya can walk out of his courtroom free as a bird on any charge.'

"I told him then about my experience in the courtroom. He thought about it a moment, but before he could answer, we heard the clang of the steel door at the end of the corridor and the approach of keys. I recognized the heavy, clumsy tread of Bob at once and waited. He glanced into the cell in passing, clipboard in hand, then stopped abruptly and peered inside, his eyes wide.

'What are you doing here?' he asked, alarmed, looking at Herbert in his slow way.

'What's that supposed ta mean?' Herbert answered, confused.

'It means that Moore ain't supposed ta have a cellmate. He's ta be isolated. It's in his paperwork. It's in his paperwork, I tell ya.'

"Bob hastily opened the cell door and motioned for Herbert to step out.

'Come along,' he said.

"We were both taken off guard by the suddenness of the thing. Herbert rose slowly.

'Come along, now,' Bob insisted, impatiently.

"Herbert turned to me and shrugged, reluctantly.

'Sorry, Thomas,' he said, and stepped out into the corridor.

"The door was quickly closed after him and Bob hustled him away with Herbert looking back at me apologetically. I heard the jingle of keys and their muffled voices growing distant until they were lost after the clang of the door at the end of the corridor. I was alone again. It had all happened so rapidly. The sting of my solitude was felt even more keenly with the absence of my new acquaintance. Left alone in the stillness of the bare little cell, under the glare of the never changing light, I felt so lonely. Why was I not to have a companion in my solitude, I wondered, as sleep finally took me?

"Counting my meal trays, I judge it was four or five days after the departure of Herbert Mayer. I was lying on my bed staring absently at nothing in particular when I heard the door at the end of the corridor open and close and the approaching tread of Bob. I knew his gait so well by then. He would enter every two hours, on the hour, carrying a clipboard that he used to confirm the count was accurate. I assumed it was count time, but he stopped at my cell.

'Attorney visit, Moore,' he said, opening my cell door. I sprang up and slipped on my shoes. He led me through the same maze of buzzers and clanging steel doors as before, but this time he directed me to a steel door that had a little window in it, through which I saw a man sitting at a table shuffling papers in a briefcase.

'Here?' I asked, confused.

'Yeah, here.'

'But…that's not my attorney.'

'Well, he says he is.'

"He opened the door, shoved me inside, and locked it after me.

'Just a moment,' the man said, without looking up from the paper in his hand, as he read intently.

"When finished, he set it on the table frowning, and stood to introduce himself.

'I'm Howard Goodfriend, attorney at law. I've been asked to look into a few things regarding your case.' He shook my hand. 'I assume I have the pleasure of addressing Mr. Thomas Moore.'

'Yes. I'm sorry,' I said, a little confused. 'I'm just a little overwhelmed by all of this. I don't really know why you're here, Mr. Goodfriend.'

'You can call me Howard. Have a seat Thomas.'

"I took a seat at the table across from him and watched while he quickly shuffled through papers in his briefcase. Mr. Goodfriend was a slightly built man in his late-thirties, with dark red hair cut short and freckles on his boyish looking face. His fashionable suit fit his slender, confident frame perfectly. Looking up from his briefcase, he studied me with keen, friendly eyes, but not for long. I got the impression that every moment was precious to him, that he had far too few moments available, and that he made the best use of all that he had. I liked him at once.

'I haven't had much time to investigate, but I see a number of irregularities,' he said, consulting a paper in his hand. 'You've had no visitation?'

"I shook my head.

'No mail?'

"Again I shook my head.

'And you have a two-man cell to yourself in a crowed jail.'

"I nodded a confirmation.

'Very odd. They can only deny visitation for disciplinary action. In other words, if you were to assault an officer, throw food, or some such thing. You haven't, have you?'

'Of course not.'

'And they can only withhold mail for security reasons. You're not planning a jailbreak, are you?'

'No.'

'Isolation is a security or disciplinary action as well, which we've already covered. This is all very peculiar. Would your family write and visit if given the opportunity?'

'Yes, constantly.'

'Well, someone is preventing them from doing so for some reason. I'll look into it. But these are all trifles. We need to look at your case. I see you've pleaded guilty. What was the substance of the plea agreement?'

'I don't know.'

'You agreed to it without seeing it?' he asked, surprised.

'I never spoke to my attorney. I was just standing before a

hostile looking judge and my attorney told me to plead guilty. I didn't know there was a plea agreement.'

'Amazing,' he said, shaking his head. 'So you had never talked to Mr. Scavera before your court appearance?'

'No.'

'Who hired him to represent you?'

'He said my stepfather hired him.'

'That would be the father of the young man you allegedly killed?'

'Yes.'

'I think that explains a lot. Jerry Leason, the ADA in this case, is a close friend of mine. I'll talk to him when I leave here and find out what's going on in this Alice in Wonderland case. Would you like for me to represent you?'

'Yes,' I answered, after a moment of reflection, 'but I think you should know I'm not going to change my guilty plea. And I won't contest whatever sentence they recommend.'

"His piercing eyes bored into me, searching. 'Then we'll need to persuade them to recommend a light sentence.'

'I don't know how this works exactly, Mr. Goodfriend. I can't pay you.'

'Don't worry about that. It's been taken care of.'

"He rose suddenly and wrapped on the little window in the door.

'I'm sorry Thomas, but I have much to do in a short period of time. I'll be in touch.'

"The door was opened. He quickly stepped past me into the hallway, paused, then turned, and came back.

'I'll have clothes waiting for you for the next court appearance. Get a haircut and shave. And don't worry,' he said reassuringly, ' I'm in your corner.'

"And he was gone.

"I returned to my cell with a light heart. Howard Goodfriend was in my corner, and he seemed like a formidable force. But I had no illusions. I would still have to plead guilty and accept whatever judgment the court handed down, so what could Howard Goodfriend do? I waited. The days of dull, unvarying monotony dragged slowly past under the constant glare above. Still there were no visits. Still no mail. And still I had no one to share my cell with.

"I was picking over the porridge in my breakfast tray when Bob appeared at my cell. I heard him coming, but failed to register his arrival.

'All right Moore, you have court today.' He opened my cell door and passed in a suit of clothes. 'Make it quick,' he added.

"Clean clothes. What a wonderful surprise. Quickly, I changed out of the dirty clothes I had been wearing and sleeping in for perhaps a month (I didn't know how long) and slipped into a new suit. The jacket hung on me like a scarecrow and the pants would have fallen to my knees if not for the belt, but they were clean and I was delighted.

"Through the maze of buzzers and doors, under the naked lights of the tunnel, and back into the courtroom, Bob led me. This time it was Howard Goodfriend at the table, and I sat next to him.

'I'm sorry I didn't get to visit you and apprise you of my progress,' he said, arranging papers in his briefcase. 'I've been working virtually every moment since I left you. I made the last motion only this morning. Are you ready?'

"I nodded.

'Good. I've managed to recuse every judge that is friends with Judge Thomson. It took some time. Now we'll at least have a fighting chance. The fix was in. The judge, district attorney, and defense attorney were all conspiring to send you away. If you had been sentenced at your last court appearance, you would be spending the rest of your life in prison.'

"I turned pale, and felt faint. Howard saw my face, and smiled.

'It's okay. That's not going to happen now. Are you all right? Have some water.'

"He poured water from an ewer on the table and passed me a glass.

"The court reporter stood at her little table beside the bench.

'All rise. The Honorable Judge Gillespie presiding,' she said. That black robe again. I trembled with the memory of the last black robe hanging on that anemic frame with the thin, bloodless lips. But this judge was old, with gray hair and intelligent eyes. He looked like someone's grandfather. Howard leaned over and spoke quietly as he opened his briefcase.

'Ah, Gillespie, good. We'll at least get a fair shake with this fellow.'

'Be seated,' the judge said.

"Everyone returned to their seats.

'What do we have today?'

'People versus Moore, your honor,' answered the bailiff.

'Are the people prepared to proceed?'

'Yes your honor,' answered the district attorney.

"At the sound of his voice, I looked over at the table beside me, and beheld a new person there. He was a handsome man, about thirty-five, impeccably dressed, well-groomed, in whom I could find no fault. I imagined the serpent assuming the same smooth, flawless appearance as he persuaded Eve to take the apple.

'Defense?'

'Yes, your honor,' answered Howard.

'I have before me a plea agreement that I find rather puzzling. Perhaps you can enlighten me, Mr. Burgett.'

'Yes, your honor,' answered the district attorney.

'Well?'

'What part, your honor?'

'The whole thing Mr. Burgett. It makes no sense to me. In a plea bargain, there is generally a bargain for the defendant. They enter a guilty plea in exchange for a reduced sentence. In this case, I find a guilty plea and a recommendation for a maximum sentence. Where's the bargain?'

'Well…'

'Let me put it another way. I've been on the bench thirty-three years, and I've never seen this situation before. It makes me suspicious.'

'The people feel that there were aggravating circumstances which merit the maximum sentence in this case your honor.'

'Aggravating circumstances? I'm reading the pre-sentence report. It says that Mr. Moore comes from a well-respected family and has no prior criminal record or history of violence. Not so much as a jaywalking violation. The investigator who wrote the report recommends the minimum sentence for this first time offender, who should probably be tried in juvenile court rather than here in circuit court. And you say there are aggravating circumstances.'

'There is a dead teenager, your honor. Stabbed in the heart.'

'That's why Mr. Moore is charged with murder. That in itself is not an aggravating circumstance.'

'The aggravating circumstances are complex, your honor. Mr. Moore planned this murder for months and executed it in cold blood because his lover, who was residing in the house, left him for the deceased.'

'That's a lie,' said a voice at the back of the courtroom.

"Everyone in the courtroom turned. Sophia had just stepped through the door when Mr. Burgett uttered those words, and was appalled.

'That's a lie, sir,' she said. 'I have never been anyone's lover, certainly not Rockwell Thomson's. And Thomas didn't kill him, I did. He attacked me.'

'Take a seat miss. And hold your tongue,' said the judge, tiredly. 'Approach the bench.'

"Mr. Burgett and Howard approached. Howard motioned for me to follow. We all stood before the bench looking up at the stern face of Judge Gillespie, who appeared to be growing angrier with each passing second.

'Is this Rockwell Thomson the son of Judge William Thomson?' he asked, looking directly at Mr. Burgett.

'It's possible, your honor,' Mr. Burgett answered, reluctantly.

'It's possible?' the judge asked, through clenched teeth.

'I believe he is the son of Judge Thomson, your honor,' Mr. Burgett answered, growing visibly uncomfortable.

'I have here a summary of Mr. Rockwell Thomson's performance while at boarding school, compliments of the defense,' the judge said, holding a document in his hand. 'He was expelled from two institutions for unbecoming conduct and in one case narrowly avoided criminal charges, which I assume his father was instrumental in dismissing. There's quite a litany of his indiscretions. A picture is beginning to form, Mr. Burgett. I see a young miscreant forcing himself upon a pretty young girl and getting a knife in the chest as a reward. How long did she reside with your family, Mr. Moore?'

'They were scissors, your honor,' Howard interrupted.

'Excuse me?' the judge asked.

'Not a knife, but scissors,' added Howard.

'Premeditated, did you say Mr. Burgett?' The judge scowled. 'How long did she reside with you son?'

'Since she was ten, your honor,' I answered.

'That doesn't sound like a live in lover to me, Mr. Burgett,' the judge said, glaring.

'Well, your hon…' Burgett replied.

'And you've always protected her?' the judge asked, addressing me.

'There was never a need until recently,' I replied.

'Do you still intend to plead guilty?'

'Yes, your honor,' I said. Judge Gillespie was an emotional man. He looked at me kindly and swallowed hard, impressed by my gesture. Then he scanned the courtroom for Sophia and found her sitting near the front row, with her hands clasped before her and concern in her beautiful eyes. The judge was moved by the tense, worrying way she observed everything that happened in the courtroom.

'That's very noble of you, young man,' he said, 'but with this charge, in terms of sentencing, my hands are tied. I can do only so much. Do you understand?'

"I nodded.

"He lifted a hand to his forehead, rubbing his brow indecisively, hating what he had to do. A moment later he turned to Mr. Burgett and all the compassion that he felt for me was transformed into wrath for the District Attorney. I witnessed Mr. Burgett take a step back out of fear when he saw the fury in Judge Gillespie's face.

'So you got together with Judge Thomson and the defense attorney, this Mr. Scavera, and conspired to send young Mr. Moore to prison for the rest of his life. Is that it? The judge thinks Mr. Moore killed his son and wants revenge?'

"Mr. Burgett was mute.

'Your only hope of saving yourself, Mr. Burgett, is to be totally frank and honest with me. If you lie or withhold anything, I swear I'll see you disbarred and in irons.'

'Yes, your honor.' Mr. Burgett answered, like a scolded school child.

'Yes, what?'

'There was a...' he paused, searching for the correct words, 'meeting of the minds.'

"Judge Gillespie leaned back in his chair and exhaled a long, deep breath. The next moment, he was leaning his arms on the bench and peering into Mr. Burgett's eyes wrathfully.

'I'm not given to profanity, Mr. Burgett, but at this moment I'm so angry I could swear. When you return to your office this afternoon, you'll resign your post as District Attorney, and no, there is no appeal,' he added, in response to Mr. Burgett's upraised hand as he prepared to protest.

'Do it today and you'll still be able to practice law. If not, I'll have you disbarred, and your legal career will be over. This Mr. Scavera will be reported to the bar association and will undoubtedly be disbarred. As for the Honorable Judge Barron and his cohort, Judge Thomson...well, we'll see about them. And now Mr. Moore,' he said, turning to me, 'I have the unpleasant task of sentencing you. Thanks to some politician who was attempting to glean votes with a get-tough-on-crime rhetoric, I have no choice but to impose a mandatory minimum. I am truly sorry.'

"He motioned for us to return to our places. When we had resumed our former position at the table, he continued.

'A guilty plea has been entered. Mr. Moore, do you have anything to say before sentence is imposed?'

'No, your honor.'

'Very well, in accordance with state law, this court imposes the mandatory minimum of twenty-five years in prison. You are remanded to the custody of the Washington State Department of Corrections.'

"Upon hearing the pronouncement, Sophia could remain seated no longer. Leaping from her seat, she rushed along the pew, up the walkway in the center, and threw her arms around me.

'Twenty-five years? Twenty-five years. Oh, Thomas, I'll never forgive myself,' she cried. 'I must speak to the judge.'

"He was making his way to the door behind the bench, which led to his chambers. Her eyes marked his progress and that of Bob, who had begun toward me with the delivery of the sentence. I would be led away momentarily. The indecision was plain in her face. Did she run after the judge and plead with him on my behalf or remain in my arms and cherish a last moment together? I held her close, not letting her go, and witnessed panic in her eyes as the chambers door closed after Judge Gillespie. With her hope gone, I felt her relax then; the die had been cast. She pressed her head to mine and looked into my eyes.

'Noble to the end,' she said, her voice aquiver.

"With a blush on her delicate cheek and a tear in her lovely eyes, my poised Sophia was more radiantly beautiful than I had ever seen her before. There were none in the courtroom who were not moved by her. Even the stoic face of Bob registered compassion for her distress.

'I'm sorry miss,' said he, timorously. 'Mr. Moore and I must go.'

"Sophia remained with her head pressed to mine and her eyes closed. I reveled in her touch, her smell, as I ran my fingers through her lovely hair. Bob waited patiently.

'You've become so very thin,' she said, and forced a weak smile to her trembling lips. 'Good-bye Captain Moore.'

"Taking my arm, Bob reluctantly led me away. Sophia remained at the front of the courtroom, her hands clasped before her, watching as I was taken from her. At the doorway, I turned for one last look. Never had I seen such anguish on a human face. I was relieved when Bob gave me a gentle tug and we disappeared around the corner.

"The walk back to jail was a somber and familiar one. When we were in the hallway, beyond the sight of Sophia, Bob stopped me and reached for the handcuffs that he always kept in a leather sort of holster on his belt.

'It's the rules,' he said, apologetically.

"I brought my hands together at my waist to facilitate the procedure, but he hesitated. The cuffs were in his hands; all he had to do was drop them over my wrists and click them closed. Instead, he peered down the hallway in his simple way, first one direction and then the other, and finding it clear, replaced the handcuffs in his holster.

'Just this once,' he said, and led me away once again.

"We continued down two flights of stairs, then into the dark tunnel strewn with wispy cobwebs that always smelled of dank soil, and along under the feeble glow of the naked bulbs. The image of

Sophia standing in the courtroom watching me leave in anguish was one I could not shake, but where was Mother? Why was she not there?

'Your mother was ill and couldn't make it ta court today,' Bob said, as if in answer to my silent thought.

'Excuse me?'

'The pretty girl asked me ta tell ya,' he said, as he lumbered along. 'I almost forgot.'

'When?'

'When ya was talking ta the judge, up at the bench. She was afraid she wouldn't get ta talk ta ya, so she asked me ta tell ya that.'

'Oh. Thank you.'

"There was no mistaking the expression on Bob's face. Something in the courtroom had moved him out of his lethargy and compelled him to thought. Could it be Sophia? Was her beauty and disposition great enough to pierce the fog of indifference that had enveloped his soul? We were near the end of the dank, foul-smelling tunnel when Bob stopped under the dim light of a dirty bulb, and turned."

'Was that true what she said back there in the courtroom,' he asked, 'about killing that boy?'

'I confessed to it, Bob.'

'I know. I was there. But was it her?'

"He held my eye a long moment, searching for the truth there, and apparently finding it.

'There's precious little justice in the justice system. If that boy was killed by that angel, then he richly deserved killin'. That's all I got ta say.'

"Alone in my windowless cell once more, I thought about Judge Gillespie's words. Twenty-five years. Was that to be my life? I looked around me at the depressing little box, so harsh and utilitarian. A lifetime spent there? Like that? When would I see the sun or stars again? Would I ever again stand at the helm of *Diva*? Would I ever sleep in my own bed, in my own house? Or see Mother and Sophia? I sat on the edge of the bed staring blankly at the floor.

'Are you all right?'

"I turned to find Bob watching me through the bars.

'I'm going to spend the rest of my life in a prison cell, Bob.'

'Twenty-five years is a very long time. I'm sorry about that, Mr. Moore,' he said, and looked like he meant it.

'Thank you,' I answered, sincerely.

"Bob shuffled away, keys dangling on his belt.

"The jail was usually quiet. Bob was often the only guard in that part of the building. Over the next few days, he lingered longer and longer at my cell, talking. I believe he was as lonely as I. We got to know each other pretty well he and I—two suffering souls on opposite sides of the same wall. He would often bring a folding chair with him, set it outside my cell door, and we would talk until his shift was over.

"Bob had taken to saving for me the daily newspaper, and like a fine wine, I savored each delicious page. It was a pleasant distraction that lifted me for a short while out of the dreary confines of my bleak little cell and offered a glimpse into the workings of the world outside the glaring light and cold brick.

"With my back against the cold wall, I sat cross-legged on the bed one quiet afternoon, immersed in the exploits of Benito Mussolini, who was marching on Rome after being sworn in as prime minister. Hearing a little sound, I glanced up from the newspaper to see Bob standing outside the bars of my cell. I was shocked. Never before had I seen him without first hearing the heavy tread of his boots thudding on the concrete floor or the ever present jingle of the giant key ring that always seemed to announce his approach. He peered up and down the hallway, secretively, and then stepped close to the bars.

'You've got a visitor, Thomas,' he whispered, excitedly.

'What? Now?' I answered, perplexed.

"Visiting hours were long over, and I had never enjoyed one in any case.

'You'll need ta be quiet,' he said, and motioned me to the bars.

"I slid off the bed and stepped close, growing more surprised and intrigued all the time.

'I don't understa…'

'Shh. Just stay right there.'

"Bob glanced back down the hallway from which he came and motioned to someone. He smiled to me then and hurried away.

I waited with intense interest, imagining all sorts of wild things and speculating on the identity of my secret visitor, trembling in anticipation. I smelled her lovely scent an instant before she stepped to the bars of my cell.

'Oh Thomas,' she cried, and her quick eye traveled over my bleak little cell.

'Sophia,' I stammered, excitedly. 'How did you...'

'Oh, Bob is a sweetheart. Since they're not allowing you visitors, he contrived to smuggle me back here.'

"Her voice was like music. I reveled in it.

'I've missed you so much,' I said.

'I've missed you, too. Not a day passes that I don't think of you, and how I should be in this cell in your place. I'm so wicked, Thomas.'

'No you're not, Sophia. I don't want you to experience this. I'm sorry you had to even come here.'

'I had to of course. I tried many times, but they wouldn't let me see you.' She began to cry then. 'It's all my fault. I'm so sorry.'

'It's not your fault that Rockwell attacked you. If I hadn't beaten him, perhaps he would have left you alone.'

'Always so noble and chivalrous,' she said, and wiped her eyes. 'Remember the card I gave you that first Christmas?'

'Of course.' I smiled at the memory.

"She held it in her hand for me to see.

'See how I drew you, protecting me with your sword against unseen foes. Captain Thomas Moore protecting his lady. I suppose that's how I always thought of you. You're protecting me still. This time your sword is sacrifice and deception.'

'I would do anything for you, Sophia,' I said, earnestly.

'I know. And I would do anything for you. Best friends forever?' She searched my face.

'Best friends forever.'

'Some friend I am.' Her eyes fell in shame. 'I met with the judge in his chambers. I told him the truth.'

'What?' I asked, concerned. 'What did he say?'

'He wasn't surprised, but he couldn't do anything about the sentence. He's going to write to the parole board on your behalf, though.' She glanced down the corridor in the direction Bob had taken. 'Bob is saying I have to go already.'

"The tears began to stream down her cheeks, again. I took her hand, and caressed it tenderly.

'I'm being sent away,' she said, wiping the tears from her blue eyes.

'What do you mean? Where?'

'A boarding school. I leave by train tonight. That's why I'm here. I couldn't leave without seeing you first. I told Bob I must see you. He turned me away so many times that he felt guilty and relented.'

'Who is sending you away?' My heart sank.

'William has been trying to send me away for quite some time, but your mother wouldn't allow it. Without you in the house, she capitulated. I think she was concerned for my safety.'

'For how long?' I asked, fearing that I would never see her again.

'I don't know,' she said, growing distraught. 'What else can I do Thomas? He's such a brute. Tell me what else I can do?'

'Nothing,' I answered, trying to appear cheerful for Sophia. 'It's good that you're going to school.'

'I'll write every day, I promise,' she said, earnestly.

'That'll be nice,' I replied, knowing that I would receive none of her letters.

'Okay,' she whispered to Bob, as she again glanced down the hallway in his direction. 'Bob is saying I have to go.' She burst into tears. 'Oh, I love you so much. I'm so sorry about all of this Thomas. You probably regret the day you met me.'

'Not at all.' I smiled. 'You're the best thing that's every happened to me, Sophia.'

'I love you.'

"Through the bars, she kissed me on the lips, pressed the card into my hand, and ran away crying. She was gone.

"With my eyes closed, I sat on the edge of my bed replaying every precious word of my conversation with Sophia long after she had gone. I recalled her every word, her every gesture, even the lovely path her tears took as they trailed over her divine cheeks. I reveled in the memory of her visit. Somewhere in the distance, I heard, but failed to register, the clang of the steel door at the end of the hall. I was still pondering Sophia's face when Bob appeared at my cell door. Immediately, I slid off the bed and stepped to the door to greet him.

'Thank you Bob. That was very kind of you.'

'You're welcome, Thomas,' he answered, sincerely.

'I hope you don't get into any trouble over it.'

'Ah, let 'em make an issue of it if they want. It ain't right that you're not allowed ta visit like everyone else.' He stepped closer and looked me in the eye, confidentially. 'I'm a simple man, Thomas. I know it. I know my limitations. I know quality when I see it, too: that girl now, and you, too. You're a proper gentleman, and she's a lady. Ain't many folks like that around no more. I heard what was said. I know the sacrifice ya would make for each other. That's a fine thing. Very gallant. All I ever see here is thieves and murderers who'd sell their own mother or sister for a way out of a situation they put themselves in. Makes your heart kinda sick after a while. Just takes all the spirit outta ya.'

'I can see how it could have that effect.'

'I been here too long, Thomas. I need a change,' he said. 'That girl a yers now,' he stroked his chin thoughtfully, 'she's in love with ya. She'll wait for ya ta get out. Don't ya worry about that none.'

'We're dear friends, Bob. We grew up together.'

'Mr. Moore,' he smiled in his simple way, 'I know yer a lot smarter than I am, and I know ya talk good and have a education and all, but ya can't see what's as plain as the nose on yer face. That girl is crazy in love with ya. Even old Bob can see that.' He checked his watch then. 'I need ta finish count. Goodnight Thomas.'

"And he continued on with his clipboard in hand. I returned to my bunk and sat down. Was Bob right? Did Sophia really love me?

"Several days passed after her visit. I sat on my bed one afternoon, eagerly awaiting the arrival of the newspaper that Bob had delivered faithfully for weeks now. I heard the familiar clang of the steel door sliding open and closed again, which always echoed throughout the concrete corridors, followed by the steady tread of Bob's boots and the jingle of keys. But there was no newspaper in Bob's hand, and his face wore a dismal frown.

'Roll it up, Thomas,' he said.

"My pulse raced. This was it. I was going to prison.

'Am I leaving?' I asked.

"Bob nodded apologetically.

"I had longed to leave the depressing little cell and yearned to escape the never failing light since I arrived, but now I was apprehensive. What would prison be like? It was with a hesitant, nervous hand that I rolled up my mattress and shoved it under my arm, while Bob stood watching uncomfortably. I stepped through the cell door into the corridor and held his eye a long, searching moment.

'I asked to drive ya. That's something anyway,' he said.

'Thank you,' I answered.

"With the mattress under my arm, he led me once again through the harsh, glaring corridor I had come to know so well, past the other cells that I glanced into in passing. I saw men sleeping or sitting on the edge of their bed staring listlessly at the floor. One man was kneeling at his bedside in prayer. On we went through the series of buzzers and doors to a little room with a window where an officer sat typing.

'You can set the mattress down here,' Bob said.

"I did. He motioned to the other officer who pressed a button under his desk, and the door buzzed and popped open. I don't recall much of that journey; my thoughts were elsewhere. Bob led me along. I know that somewhere I changed out of my dirty, tattered clothes into my court suit. I was handcuffed, then led through some dark tunnels. Eventually, we arrived at a police car parked underground. Bob opened the rear door and helped me in. I felt like a condemned man being taken to his execution. In the back I sat, as if in a daze, oblivious to all around me. Suddenly, we moved from darkness to blinding light. We had traveled up to the street and the sun glared brightly on my face. I hadn't seen the sun or sky in months. There were people on the sidewalks and cars on the streets and buildings and shops and blue sky. And color. Everywhere, color. It all seemed so fresh and bright and wonderful. With my face pressed to the window, I drank it all in like a simpleton seeing it for the first time.

"Bob drove for a few blocks, then pulled to the side of the busy road, got out, and opened my door. In response to my questioning frown, he motioned for me to get out. With my hands cuffed before me, I scooted along the seat and made my slow way to the open door. He helped me out, and stood me up beside the car. My cuffs were removed and returned to the holster on his belt. My thoughts whirled. Was he letting me go? But where would I go? I had nowhere to go.

"He dispelled my fantasy.

'It's against the rules. You can ride with me in the front. Just don't tell anyone,' he said.

"I climbed into the front seat and we resumed our journey. We both wanted to talk, but neither of us knew what to say, so we drove along in silence. I looked out the window, feasting on the sight of simple things that we all take for granted. Somewhere out there in that world where people are free to do as they please, to love and marry and pursue life, was Sophia. Where was she? What was she doing at that exact moment? And what about Mother?

"The miles slid past. We had been driving for about an hour when Bob pulled off the interstate onto a gravel road that led to a little diner beside the freeway. He pulled up outside and shut off the engine, then turned to me.

'It's against the rules. Come on, my treat,' he said.

"We were seated at booth with a view of the freeway and ordered lunch—a greasy, grilled cheese sandwich. The best I'd ever had. Knowing the fate that awaited me, I felt like a condemned man enjoying his last meal."

Thomas appeared to be getting restless again. Deep in thought, he lifted his wine glass, took a drink, and returned it to the table. A heavy sigh escaped his lips. Standing then, he walked to the dying fire, upon which he tossed more wood; satisfied with the result, he returned to his place and fell back heavily into his chair. I heard a sound outside the window and whirled, startled.

"Sorry," I said, "I jump at every sound. I keep thinking it's those convicts."

"It's not them, Mrs. Dearborn."

"But how do you know? How can you be sure?"

"I'm quite sure."

"You don't know them, do you?" I asked, apprehensively.

"It's been quite a long night, Mrs. Dearborn," he said, tiredly. "Shall we try to get some sleep?"

Taking his hint, I nodded.

"Thank you, Thomas. Charles and I are very appreciative. You may rely on our discretion."

I saw a weak, or perhaps tired, smile cross his lips. At the top of the stairs, I looked back and saw that he remained slouched in his chair, staring into the flickering flames of the fire, wine glass in hand. With Thomas awake and the rich tenor of my husband's snore reaching my ears from the distant bedroom, there was little need for quiet, so I proceeded casually along the dark hallway to the bed, undressed, and slipped under the covers. Thomas was correct; it had been quite a long night. I had scarcely drawn the covers over myself before I was sleeping soundly. Our host had eased my mind, or fatigue had supplanted my curiosity.

The next day, I awoke to blue sky and blue water. I turned my head on the big, fluffy pillow, looking through the window beside the bed, and was treated to the soothing sight of a cloudless blue sky and a vast expanse of blue water broken only by the tiny speck of a white-hulled fishing boat that motored slowly across. The bed had only one occupant. Charles must have awakened before me and gone downstairs. I pulled the heavy bedcovers up under my chin and smiled, writhing and squirming in the bed as Sophia would have done. I knew just how she felt; it was so luxurious. How cute she must have been.

I sat up suddenly, peering at her self-portrait across the room. In the full light of day, without the impure cast of the flickering candle, she was so very beautiful. Nearly flawless. The morning light revealed only one defect, only one blemish in her lovely face, one that was easily corrected. But I may overstep myself here. Not so easily corrected perhaps, and yet perhaps so. If only the mood of the artist were amended so that her melancholy smile and sad eyes were of good cheer.

Pondering that, I dressed and made my way downstairs. Following the voices of Charles and Thomas, I found them in the kitchen.

"Good morning love," Charles said, cheerfully.

"Good morning, Mrs. Dearborn," added Thomas.

"Good morning," I answered with a curious smile as I looked

about. "What are you doing?"

"Well, we were attempting to make breakfast, but as you see, we are hopelessly out of our element," Charles answered.

That they were uninitiated concerning the working of a kitchen was quite obvious, but what they had intended was quite beyond me. They had assembled a number of fruit baskets and a few vegetables and were apparently attempting to form some sort of breakfast from them.

"Haven't either of you ever prepared a meal for yourself?" I asked.

They shuffled their feet and looked sheepishly at the floor.

"Dear Lord, really?" I asked, surprised.

"There's no food in the house. We picked the fruit from the trees and found some vegetables in the garden," Thomas explained.

There were baskets of apples, pears, cherries, and plums, along with a few potatoes and carrots that must have been from a past garden.

"I can make some pan fried potatoes, but other than that I don't know what I can do. I can't make bricks without clay," I said.

"I must apologize, Mrs. Dearborn. The hospitality of the Moore house has suffered of late. It is not our custom for guests to prepare their own meals," Thomas said.

"I'll forgive you this once," I jested.

While the potatoes were cooking on the fire, which Thomas had rekindled, I visited the garden myself and found some rosemary and garlic, which I added to the dish to make a tolerable breakfast. For Thomas, who had presumably eaten only prison food for quite some time, it was a culinary delight. Charles and I found it to be quite good as well, but none of us had eaten recently and we were ravenous.

Pleasantly refreshed after a nice hot meal, I washed dishes (there was no hot water) while Thomas and Charles struck off to find a lug wrench. The fireside tale had been told in such vivid detail that I had little trouble picturing Elsie working here in this kitchen and the others seated at the table eating and chatting. She was someone from his past who could return and perhaps restore some semblance of family. Would he seek her out, I wondered?

The men returned successful, with Charles bearing an odd

looking tool that Thomas said was the lug wrench. A curious bond had developed between them, I noticed. They had been laughing and jesting together all morning, as if old friends, in spite of the fact that Charles was ten years his senior and suspected him of being an escaped convict. We had known Thomas little more than half a day, but so much had transpired in that short time that I almost felt like he was a part of our life and that we had carved a page in the history of the Moore Estate.

We began along the maple drive, walking under the broad leaves of the giant trees that hung over the road. A short distance away, I paused and looked back. Such a lovely old home. Little did I think when I saw it from our boat in passing (was that only yesterday?) that I would find myself in a bed within the grand estate and that there had been so much happiness and suffering there.

"What are you doing Lori? Come on," said Charles.

He and Thomas had walked on a few paces before noticing that I had stopped. I ran to catch up (wearing shoes from Sophia's closet, given to me by Thomas) and we had a pleasant walk back along the shoreline road under the warm summer sun. Thomas could be quite animated when the mood was upon him, and the ease of his manner freed us from restraint.

We reached the car. The tire was changed, with Charles assisting Thomas, and we were ready to return. Charles climbed behind the wheel. I got in on the other side. The car was started. But Thomas remained standing beside the vehicle, frowning thoughtfully.

"Jump in Thomas, we'll give you a ride back to your house," Charles said, through the open window.

Still, Thomas remained beside the car, peering down the trail the convicts had forced us to take.

"Will you excuse me a moment?" he asked.

"Of course," Charles answered.

When Thomas trotted off down the trail, he turned to me with a curious frown. "What would he be doing down there?" he asked.

I shrugged, equally curious, and not without trepidation. I don't know what we expected, or rather, what we feared. We were certain that Thomas was not in league with the other convicts, but what purpose drew him into the woods? We waited together in silence, with the engine running, peering down the trail that Thomas had taken. It seemed quite some time, but I'm certain that it was no more than a minute or two before he came trotting back and climbed into the back seat.

"Again, thank you," he said.

Charles shifted into gear and pulled back onto the road. We rumbled along a few minutes until I broke the silence.

"May I have a word with you, Thomas?" I asked.

"Certainly, Mrs. Dearborn."

"I'm concerned about those other men. They're desperate, and I fear for the safety of anyone else they happen upon. I would like to report our incident to the police when we return."

"I understand your concern Mrs. Dearborn, but really, I prefer to avoid further contact with the police. Is it enough that you have my assurance they'll not be harming anyone again?"

"I don't know how you can say that. They nearly killed us. They're going to hurt whoever they…"

"They won't be hurting anyone again," he interrupted. "Ever again," he added, holding my eye in a firm stare that gave me a chill.

I turned back in my seat, looking straight ahead at the road. When I glanced over at Charles, he simply shrugged and smiled. The rest of the drive was a quiet one. I at least, and I'm certain Charles too, was pondering the meaning of our passenger's words.

We turned down that majestic tree lined drive. Charles drove up next to the broken fountain in front of the house and stopped at the door. With the engine running, we remained in the car, Charles with his hands on the wheel, looking silently ahead, I with my eyes on the floor of the car, fidgeting uncomfortably, Thomas quietly in the back. This was the end, and no one wished to be the first to break up our little company. An intimacy had grown between us. We were friends. Closer in so many ways than any friend I had ever known before. Charles turned the key at last, and all was quiet. Still, no one moved. Eventually, I heard Thomas sigh. He pushed the door open and stepped out and we followed, gathering together beside the car.

"Ever again?" Charles asked, significantly, looking Thomas directly in the eye.

A little nod was his answer.

"You're a good man, Mr. Moore," he said, shaking his hand

respectfully. "We're in your debt."

"Oh, you silly men are always so proud and formal," I said, throwing my arms around Thomas. "We owe you so much. Thank you, Thomas, with all my heart."

I held him close with my cheek pressed upon his chest. When I released him he took my hand in his own.

"And to you, Mrs. Dearborn, I must apologize. I fear your inquisitive ear grew weary of my epic tale. May God bless you both."

"I hope you find Sophia, Thomas," I answered.

"Good day my friends," he said, and turned away.

Charles opened the car door and slid behind the wheel, but I remained, reluctant to go for reasons I couldn't really explain. There was something special and unique about Thomas. Something noble and pure and honorable. Something rarely found in the world. Watching him walk away from us that day, I knew we would not see him again, and it left me with a heavy heart.

"Lori, it's time we were on our way," Charles said. "Lori." I stepped around to the passenger side and returned to my seat. Charles started the engine, took one last look at the ivy-covered estate, and shifted into gear. We drove around the fountain then and began back up the tree-lined path. I turned round in my seat and looked out the back window before the road turned and the estate was lost from view and my last memory of Thomas was a snapshot of him kneeling at a grave in the cemetery.

"That Thomas Moore is quite a man," Charles said, turning back on to the main road, continuing our circuit around the island.

"What do you suppose he meant when he said they wouldn't be hurting anyone ever again?"

"That can only be interpreted one way, you know."

"But he wouldn't have killed them, would he?"

"Darling, that murderous rabble would have faired no better at my hand. It doesn't make him a bad person."

"I just can't get used to all this violence. It makes no sense to me."

"It's the world we live in." We drove on. The road exited the timber suddenly, hugging the bluff that plunged sharply to the sea just below my door. There was the blue ocean sparkling in the sun.

"I never found out what happened to any of them."

"Who?" Charles asked.

"Sophia or Carolyn or Elsie. Or even that degenerate William. Where is everyone? Why is the house empty?"

"Maybe Robert can tell us something. He seems to know of all the doings on this island."

"That's an excellent idea, Charles," I answered, excitedly. "Let's ask as soon as we return."

When we arrived at the Moran Mansion, we went directly to the house and asked to speak to Robert.

"He'll be down in a moment, sir," said an elderly butler. "Would you like to wait in the library?"

We sipped tea while awaiting our host, and a moment later he appeared, bustling into the library, freshly dressed for lunch.

"Hello my friends, did you enjoy the drive?"

"It was interesting," answered Charles.

"Very interesting," I added.

"I didn't see you at dinner last night. Were you fatigued after the long day?"

"We spent the night elsewhere," Charles said.

"Really?" replied Moran, puzzled and somewhat offended. "I wasn't aware that you had other friends on the island."

"We made a new friend only yesterday," I answered. Now he was offended.

"And who was that?" he asked, stiffly.

"A young man who was returning home after nine years in prison."

"Thomas?" he inquired, with a shocked frown. "Thomas Moore has returned?"

"You know him, then?" asked Charles.

Robert seemed not to hear as he walked across the library and stood at the window, looking out over the water. "Thomas Moore," he said under his breath, then glanced back over his shoulder at Charles and I. "His parents were two of my dearest friends. I didn't know of his release. He had a twenty-five year sentence. Where is he now?"

"He's at home," answered Charles.

"It must have been quite a blow to see the place like that."

"He told us the story," I added.

"Did he tell you he confessed to killing his stepbrother?" Robert's eyes flashed. "Stabbed him in the heart. You should be more discriminating in who you befriend."

"Robert," I said calmly, ignoring his remark, "can you tell us what became of Carolyn? Is she all right?"

"How did you happen upon Thomas Moore?" he asked, sternly. "Where did you see him?"

"He was walking home from the ferry," Charles answered. "It was nearly dark, so we gave him a ride."

"We had a flat tire near his house," I added, hoping to appease Robert, "so we spent the night there. He was a perfect host, Robert."

He turned back to the window and stood with his hands on the sill, looking out.

"Can you tell us what became of Carolyn and Sophia and Elsie?" I asked, moved by a strong emotion that I couldn't explain. "Are they well?"

Robert sensed the concern in my voice and turned away from the window, looking at me.

"That was a bad business," he answered, gravely. "Come with me."

He led us to a veranda at the rear of the mansion that overlooked Cascade Bay. We could see our boat at the dock, resting peacefully in the blue water. Under an umbrella a little table had been set with appetizers and iced tea. We took a seat there, and he began.

"Caroline Moore was beauty, poise, and elegance," Robert said, reverently, as he gazed out over the bay. "Everyone on the island loved and adored her. How she ended up with that William Thomson is anyone's guess. He was attractive and charming, I'll give him that, but there was a dark side to him as well, and he was able to keep that well hidden. I didn't see much of her after Daniel's death. She kept to herself and rarely left the estate. But after Thomas went away, I began to see her more often. I think she wanted to get away from William. She would sometimes come here for little events I had, dinner parties or book club meetings or the like. But her smile wasn't as I remembered it when Daniel was here. I suspect she was thinking about Thomas...."

The next six pages of the journal were missing. Puzzled that there was a gap in the narrative, Nina held the book up to the lamp as the boat continued to rock and toss about in the storm and discovered the slender remnants of the missing pages that had been torn roughly, hastily it seemed, from the journal. She thumbed quickly through the rest of the volume in the hope that someone had replaced them somewhere within, but found nothing. With a frustrated sigh, she fell back into her seat. The journal continued with the following entry.

July 15th 1929

It is morning. I wrote all afternoon and late into the night. I'm not sure what possessed me, but it felt good to pen my thoughts and clear my mind of so many troubling images, as if committing them to paper opened the door for their escape, so I labored tirelessly while Charles explored the grounds of the estate. He would return to the boat from time to time to check on me and invite me to join in his latest adventure, and then depart. At some point, he discovered a lake above the bay where we are moored (as told by someone on the household staff), so he has struck off, hiking up the hill to find it. He busied himself all day yesterday, so that I might write undisturbed. After breakfast this morning, we shall go in search of Robert and press him to tell us more. Poor Carolyn. I didn't even know her, but like everyone on the island I miss her too. Such a woman.

PS: It must have been her grave that Thomas discovered in the cemetery on the night of his return. I'm so sorry I didn't give him privacy that night. He must have wished to be alone.

Lorelei Dearborn

Later

We took the little footpath that wound through the manicured grounds, passing brightly colored geraniums, rhododendrons, and roses in full bloom, their sweet scent filling the warm air as birds sang happily and the deer grazed unconcerned on the apples fallen from the trees. It was difficult to believe there was so much death and intrigue on this beautiful island. The path wound across the lawn through the gardens to the door of the stately mansion. It was larger than the Moore house, I reflected, but not nearly as grand or imposing. The Moore estate, with its ivy skin and stone halls, its many chimneys and leaded windows set deep in the stone, sitting high above the bluff, had an impregnable, almost castle-like quality. I recalled seeing a coat of arms over the fireplace in the main room and almost expected to find a suit of armor standing in the corner somewhere, holding a sword. The Moran mansion was painted white, and splendidly so, like an old plantation house, but it lacked the sophistication of the Moore home. Where Thomas's house contained only one inhabitant, however, Robert's was filled with the bustle of household staff constantly dashing about for some event or another.

At length, we found Robert at an open window in one of the libraries of the house. It was on the top floor of the mansion, secluded at the far end, and he stood with his hands on the sill, looking out meditatively over the bay. Upon hearing us enter, he turned, and though he smiled when he saw us, it was with the practiced ease of a man who meets many people and not the welcome warmth of a dear friend. His proud eyes bore the faintest suggestion of melancholy, and I knew at once that he was still thinking of Carolyn and wished to be alone with his thoughts. Charles sensed it, too, and we were both uncomfortably aware of our intrusion. We had never seen Robert pensive. He was a strong man who had built his fortune with his own hands, and I had never seen sorrow or sadness in his proud eyes. But Carolyn had a peculiar effect on people. They all adored her, admired her, respected her. Everyone seemed to feel that something special, unique, and precious had been lost forever with her passing and that the world was a little plainer and dimmer without her. Robert was thinking about her, I was certain.

"What a beautiful room, Robert," I said, hoping to lighten the mood.

And it was a beautiful room. He had several libraries in the mansion, each devoted to a specific topic. We were in the nautical library; tattered boat journals from famous old ships were displayed under glass, leather bound boat books lined the shelves, drawings and photographs of yachts and ships hung on the walls, and antiquated boat hardware was arranged about the room like a museum.

"Thank you," he replied, with a quiet smile. "It's my favorite room in the house. I come up here when I wish to get away."

Charles and I mumbled an embarrassed good-bye and departed. We descended as far as the second floor and were walking along the hallway when I noticed how many doors there were there. It looked as though there were ten or twelve bedrooms on that floor alone and a uniformed maid was cleaning the rooms.

"I'm never going to find out what happened to Elsie or Sophia," I said, tiredly.

I saw the maid pause when she heard me and then continue on into the room she was cleaning.

"Just ask someone else," Charles suggested. "It can't be that difficult to find someone who knows what happened. Everyone seems to know everyone else on this island."

"I suppose you're right," I said, and followed the maid into the room.

"Excuse me," I began, as she fluffed the pillows on the bed.

She was a slender young girl, no more than twenty-five or twenty-six, with long dark hair pulled back in a braid and big, dark eyes.

"May I ask you something? Do you know anything about the Moore family? Do you know what became of Elsie or Sophia?"

She finished fluffing the pillows on the bed as if she hadn't heard a thing I said, then turned and looked first at me, then Charles. With her hand on her chin she considered us for a moment and then returned to cleaning the room.

"Elsie came here," she said, smoothing out the duvet on the bed with her hand.

"Here?" I replied.

"Well, she wasn't about to stay in the house with William."

"No, of course not," I agreed.

"She packed her things and came here at once."

"How long did she stay?"

"Just until Carolyn's funeral. Then she left to work on her parent's farm."

"Is she still there?"

The girl simply shrugged as she moved about the room, cleaning and straightening things up.

"I haven't seen her," she added.

"Do you know anything about Sophia?"

The girl was reaching to her cart for fresh towels, but at the mention of Sophia's name, I saw her start suddenly. It was only for a second. The next minute, she was pulling a towel from the cart and hanging it on the bathroom towel bar.

"I don't know anything about her," she answered, carelessly.

"Please," I pleaded, "it's important to me."

She was cleaning the bathroom sink at that moment and I saw the rag in her hand pause as she thought it over.

"No one really knew her, ma'am. I don't think anyone had ever even seen her. She stayed out there at the Moore place all the time. There's only a few people who even knew what she looked like."

"Can you tell me anything about her at all? Did she go to boarding school?" I asked. "Maybe we can find her, Charles," I said, turning to my husband who had been quietly watching from the doorway. "Maybe we can find Sophia and bring her back here to Thomas. Wouldn't that be wonderful?"

The maid had been watching me with a knit brow. I thanked her for her time and began walking away, while prattling on to Charles about how we would hire a man to find Sophia.

"Ma'am," she said, "excuse me, ma'am."

I turned back and found her pulling the rag tensely through her hands while she bit her lip.

"I think you'd be wasting your time," she said, hesitantly.

"What do you mean?"

"I just think you would be wasting your time, that's all."

"Why?" I asked, fearful of the answer.

"Well...it's just a rumor you understand. A few years ago... eight or ten I think, I don't remember exactly, they had the trial for Thomas Moore. Some people from the island were there that day and heard Sophia confess to killing the judge's son."

"Yes?"

"Well, some think she said that just to save Thomas. I don't know. The judge heard about it though. Judge Thomson. He heard about it. The rumor was that he… well…that he…"

"That he what?" I asked, impatiently.

"Well," she said, fidgeting with the rag in her hand, "that he killed her," she added, quietly.

"But…she went to boarding school. She was sent away to a boarding school," I replied, desperately.

Our young maid shrugged sympathetically, moved by the desperation in my eyes.

"It's just a rumor," she added, apologetically. "People love to gossip on the island."

"But why would they think that? There must be some reason for it."

"Well, everyone knows how cruel Judge Thomson was. He beat Thomas nearly to death, and then, well, what he did to Carolyn. Why wouldn't he kill Sophia if he thought she killed his son? If she were alive she would have been at Carolyn Moore's funeral. She would have moved back into the house after William disappeared. It's been empty for years."

Everything she said made perfect sense. I hadn't thought about it in those terms. Staring at the floor in stunned silence, the reality washed over me, bringing a lump to my throat.

"I need to get out of here, Charles," I said, feeling dizzy.

"Of course love," he answered, gently, taking my hand and leading me away. "Where shall we go?"

"Home."

"Home?" he asked, surprised. "Now?"

"Yes. Right now. I can't stand the sight of this island anymore," I answered through my tears. "I've never seen such wickedness and violence. I want out of here. I want to be home, in my own house, in my own bed."

"But Lori, we have an appointment with Marcus in an hour, remember? It's one of the reasons we came up here."

"There are other attorneys. We'll see one in Seattle when we get back."

"But Marcus is an old Rugby friend. We went to school together. I thought you liked him."

"I do like him. I just…I just need off this island. I want to be home."

"Okay. Okay. We can leave today."

We wound our way through the mansion past all of the staff and guests, through the gardens, and across the lawn to the boat. Charles went forward to get the bow-line.

"I'll just call Robert when we get home and explain that we needed to leave. I think he'll understand."

I suddenly felt selfish and foolish. For days, Charles had been talking excitedly about seeing his old friend again, and I knew that Robert would take offense if we left without a word of good-bye.

"Charles," I said, "I'm being foolish. I'm sorry. Go meet Marcus. We can leave in the morning."

"Really? You're certain?" he asked, smiling eagerly.

"Go."

"I love you," he said, with a hasty kiss on my lips. "We'll leave first thing in the morning," he added, and rushed back up to the mansion to get Robert's car.

"Remember Thomas," I shouted after him. "When you see Marcus, remember Thomas."

"I will," he shouted back as he ran.

I'm quite alone now, and quite melancholy. It's so peaceful and serene on the boat. The warm summer sun sparkles on the blue water all around me. From my window seat, I see Robert's mansion glistening white on the hill, surrounded by trees and flowers. But I am pensive. Without ever meeting Carolyn or Sophia, I have developed a fond affection for them and feel such a sense of loss at their passing. But what troubles me most in all of this is the growing sense of animosity that I feel for their tormentor. Never in my life have I hated. Never have I felt the hostility that I harbor for William, and it troubles me. I pray that God will give me strength to forgive.

Lorelei Dearborn

July 15th 1929

It is the next day. A heavy fog has swept in over the water, covering everything in an impenetrable mist. I can see the ghostly silhouette of boats anchored in the bay, but beyond everything fades to white. It is so still and quiet. From somewhere in the fog comes the sound of voices, laughter, the click of a cabinet door closing, all so clear and distinct, floating over the water. We have been in such fog before. It is often localized in little patches, easily navigated, and on the other side is blue sky. We wait for it to clear, but I am impatient to depart. I'm pressing Charles to disembark, and he is uncharacteristically reluctant. Odd. He possesses a daring, almost reckless, sense of adventure, but doesn't like this fog. Now that we have decided to go, I wish to depart and keep pressing him to leave. I want to be away from here. I want to be home. The beauty of this island, which I once thought so lovely, is tarnished. I want to be home.

Later

I have finally prevailed upon him to begin. It was under protest, but the fog has shown no sign of lifting anytime soon, and Charles has reluctantly agreed to start for home. He said we could give it a try. If we don't clear the fog soon, we'll return to the dock. I'm certain we will soon leave it behind us and have blue sky all the way home. He has started the engine. I am off to throw the lines.

Later

We picked our slow way though the boats anchored in the bay and turned south, following the compass. The fog, which was quite dense at the bay, only thickened as we progressed. Charles continued on apprehensively, unwilling to venture too far into the cloud for fear that we would be unable to find our way back. I was beginning to question the wisdom of my impetuous decision when suddenly we passed through to the other side. It was like stepping through a curtain. One moment it was dense, misty white fog, and the next, blue sky and sunshine. It's so beautiful. I see other patches of thick fog ahead, like billowy clouds from the sky hovering over the blue water.

Later

We have just passed Blakely Island on our port side and begin into another fog bank. This one seems much larger than the last. On and on we go, picking our slow way through the haze, but it is unyielding. It is the most peculiar thing. There is no sensation of movement in this all-encompassing whiteness. We could be racing wildly along or we could be stalled and unmoving, but it is impossible to tell without some sort of landmark or sensation. Even the sea is perfectly flat and calm, disturbingly so. There are islands everywhere, and we must find the narrow passages between them to get home, but it is impossible in this thick mist of fog. I wish we had remained at the dock. I'm so frightened.

Later

Now we are quite lost. We have a vague idea of our direction with the compass but can see nothing beyond fifteen or twenty feet of the boat. The fog goes on and on. It is not a little patch, as I supposed. Charles has stopped the boat. Who knows if we have actually stopped or not? With the engines running we could at least guess at our speed based on the engine rpm, but that may be horribly flawed, too. If we were traveling at six knots against a six-knot current, we would be gaining nothing.

We cannot go forward, and we cannot go back. Charles fears that we may ground the boat. There are many rocks and hazards here which are shown on our charts, but the charts are useless to us without knowing our position. The safest thing to do is anchor and wait for the fog to lift, but that is not without danger, too. We may be in a shipping lane and may be struck by another boat unable to see us in this dense cloud. Charles thought he heard one pass close by only a moment ago, but this fog is so deceptive. It may have been near, or it may have been a hundred yards away. Sound carries so over the water. I'm so scared.

Later

We have anchored. It is so eerie to be enveloped in this white mist. All is breathlessly still and silent. I hear the click, click, click of an anchor windlass and the sound of muffled voices from another boat, but where are they? I am apprehensive and fear being run down by another vessel traveling in this soup. I start at every sound, searching the fog for an image that I expect to see bearing down on us. Someone else is out there. I can hear them....

The rest of the journal was missing. It looked as though a large chunk, nearly half, had fallen out of the cover. The spine of the book was cracked and broken, and even the portion that Nina read hung precariously by only a few tattered threads and a bit of glue. Curious to learn what became of Lorelei and Charles, she searched the cabinets, rummaged through drawers, peeked under seat cushions, and examined every place she could think of for the missing pages, but found nothing. Suddenly the boat felt quiet, unnervingly quiet, and she realized that the storm had passed and with it, the gusting breeze and bouncing swells. The soft wind and rocking little waves allowed for a pleasant, lulling symphony to read by. Without it, there was an almost eerie quiet at that late hour. Apprehensively, she glanced about the salon by the faint light of the flickering lamp and her eye fell upon the galley table. Was Lorelei sitting at that very table when she wrote those words? Were they her last? How frightened she must have been.

Nina closed the journal distractedly and held it forgotten on her lap as she thought about Charles and Lorelei. But her musing reflection was interrupted by the struggling whine of the bilge pump that clicked on suddenly, and seemed so loud in the stillness. She tucked the journal under her arm and blew out the lamp. At the doorway, she paused for an uneasy glance behind. The weak glow of the dock lamps streaked through the grimy skylight in Mary Adda's *deck, throwing peculiar shadows about the salon, while the bilge pump fought to keep her alive.*

Morning sunlight was peeking over the older, shorter buildings on the space needle horizon when Mary Adda's *mooring lines were tossed on the dock for the first time in decades. She trailed Lauren through the water like a dog swimming after her master. It was a beautiful spring morning, cool and crisp, with a pleasant chill in the brisk, dawn air. Through the quiet marina he led her, past the sailboats, and powerboats, and fishing boats, all suffering the slow decay of time. A murmured fright ran through the marina when* Mary *reached the clear space at the shore reserved for haul outs; there was a rumored anxiety that she would suffer the same fate as poor* Emily. *The old crane was temporarily revived. Her tires were inflated and her engine was coaxed along by virtue of jumper cables and starting fluid. An ungraceful belch of black diesel smoke rose in a puff from her stack. The next few belches were white smoke that drifted over the marina in little clouds. The engine coughed and shuddered and coughed, then settled down into a misfiring rumble.* Mary Adda *was lifted from the water and set in the wooden cradle exactly where* Emily C *had been, but she seemed to know what awaited her and met her fate bravely, eagerly.*

Each morning, as the dark sky grew brighter and the rising sun climbed over the Seattle skyscrapers to the east, it found Lauren wearing faded blue jeans, a white tee shirt, and a Fedora hat, already at work on her elegant hull. In the shadow of an apple tree that had for over a hundred years provided shade to marina residents and a canvas upon which young lovers would sometimes carve their tender affection, a Harley Davidson was parked. At precisely noon, Lauren would stop what he was doing and walk to the Harley, where he would reach into a saddlebag for a picnic basket and a bottle of wine. Sitting near the rusty crane with his bare toes in the lake, he dined each day and poured himself a single glass of Chardonnay from the bottle. An hour later he returned to work.

Nina was pleasantly surprised when she arrived at lunchtime one day to find him sitting in the sand with his toes in the water, drinking wine as though on vacation. He was so unusual. So intriguing. There was a sophisticated, yet rebellious quality about him that she admired, and the fact that she knew so little about him only added to the mystique.

The forgotten little marina, so quietly tucked away in a lonely little corner of the city, was not overlooked or forgotten by everyone. It was sometimes observed by passing vagabonds who strayed away from the busy streets in search of a quiet quarter. For them the solitude and neglect proved advantageous. These bleary eyed wanderers who carried in one hand a brown-bagged bottle and in the other a cardboard sign, found refuge in the seclusion. The festering boats, lying so lonely and quiet at the rotting dock, had an unscrupulous appeal to an opportunistic eye. There was an inviting temptation in the privacy and isolation. It was not uncommon to see shadowy figures moving along the poorly lit dock in the early evening hours, or find shaded lights burning in the deserted old vessels, or jimmied doors, or even the smell of cooking that escaped from their vents.

On a chill, foggy morning near the end of October, the old crane was persuaded to awaken once more. Prepared to spend a quiet winter under the blanket of maple leaves that covered it, the crane was reluctant to stir. It cried egregiously at the inconvenience, and the rusty, old, graffiti tagged panels shook in chorus to the rumbling engine, but Mary was lifted from the wooden cradle and gently returned to the water. The lake welcomed her, and a watchful, silent audience observed as she made her quiet way back through the dewy morning fog to her previous place at the dock. Drunken, unwashed hands furtively drew back boat curtains to watch her pass.

The doorway to fall was well open, and through the opening rushed the chill season. Lauren sat in his twenty-year-old Range Rover one morning, peering through the rain-splashed window at the marina before him, waiting for a break in the downpour. Except for the boats rocking with the blustering wind and the seagulls in the gray sky that were struggling against it, there was no movement at all. The marina, he reflected, was like an old barn owl. It slept by day and awakened slowly each evening under the cover of nightfall. He was sometimes there at night and saw the timid creatures that came quietly to dock in the darkness. They didn't belong there it was true, but they bothered no one. He understood them, and shared with them a reclusive bond.

The rain only grew in intensity as he watched. He pulled his coat collar up, dropped the fedora on his head, and prepared to make a dash for Mary Adda just as a car appeared in the marina parking lot.

At any other marina, a Mercedes would not draw attention, but this was not any other marina. The car, black and sleek, moved slowly along the gravel road, past the rusty old crane, through the fallen leaves of the bare apple tree. There was something ominous and threatening in the cautious, wary pace. Under the cover of the drenching rain it moved quietly, as if hunting or stalking, almost like a predator. And like prey, Lauren instinctively paused with his hand on the car door.

The black car parked in the back row of the gravel lot, in view of the marina ahead, and remained. For quite some time, or so it seemed to Lauren, there was no movement. Then the door opened and a man stepped out.

Lauren couldn't see him well through the rain that fell heavily and the condensation that collected on the cold windshield, but he appeared to be tall. He was wearing a black overcoat and held a black umbrella over his head. He walked first to the little office shack at the edge of the shore and peered through the window. Finding no one inside, he continued on to the dock. Undeterred by the rain, he went methodically to each boat, knocking on the hull, glancing inside, and moving on to the next when there was no answer. The tapping rose above the sound of the rain drumming on the boats and carried over the marina. Lauren saw curtains drawn back in several vessels as occupants investigated the disturbance, but they were quickly pulled closed again. The man covered three docks before he received a response to his rapping. It was an elderly woman living aboard an old Chris Craft of 1940's vintage. Stella was her name. She was a slender woman with white hair and kind eyes.

In these forgotten little corners of the world where discarded souls gather, a code exists. It is never spoken of, but is instinctual among them. There is an understanding that is borne of necessity and lends itself to the solitude that is their life. It is a code of silence. Lauren rarely saw these exiles and was never close enough to speak to them. He tried once when he attempted to find the owner of Mary Adda, but the man lowered his head and hurried away before he could get close. But he found that he liked these simple people and their simple ways. There was no pretense with them. No deception. They kept to themselves and asked no questions. They offered no answers.

They were unsure of Lauren when they saw him arrive on his Harley that first day. It spoke of affluence and prestige, which often lead to judgment and reprisal. But it was also a symbol of freedom and rebellion, traits they knew well. As they came to know him through distant observation, they understood that he was like them. He bothered no one. He kept to himself. They understood each other.

Holding the umbrella in one hand, the man reached into the pocket of his overcoat and showed something to Stella. She stooped forward, looking it over closely, then straightened, and her eyes went to Mary Adda at the other side of the marina. Her gaze lingered briefly, then travelled over the parking lot, stopping at Lauren's Range Rover. He knew she couldn't see him at that distance through the rain-spattered windshield, but she seemed to be looking directly at him. Stella looked again at the object in the man's hand and shook her head. He asked her something, and she nodded that she was sure. He tucked it back in his pocket, and continued on to the next boat.

When Stella stepped off her boat the following day, she found a bouquet of flowers and a bottle of wine. There was no card, but she was pretty certain who placed the gift there.

On a wet, windy November afternoon, Nina was raking fallen leaves from the many cherry trees in her yard when a car turned into her driveway. She propped the rake on the nearest tree and walked over.

"Did you have a problem finding the place?" she inquired, glancing at her watch.

"Finding it? No," he answered, climbing out of the old Range Rover. "Getting in was another matter however."

"Why?"

"There's an over zealous cop at the end of the street."

"Goodman," she answered, nodding her head. "I forgot he was working."

"I think he wanted to waterboard me."

Nina laughed.

"I'm serious," Lauren continued. "He was getting pretty hostile."

Nina ran a quick eye over him as the clouds passed swiftly overhead, and the winter wind tugged at their clothes. He was wearing faded jeans, a sweatshirt, and four days stubble.

"Looking like that, I'm surprised he didn't arrest you."

"In this neighborhood that's probably a capital offense."

"The first time is only a fine," she answered, walking to the garage and opening the door. "Not until the second or third offense do they shoot."

"I'll keep that in mind," he replied, dryly, and walked to the garage. "So you're a masochist, too."

"Am I?"

In response, he pointed to a Range Rover in the garage, even older than his.

"Oh that," she answered. "I suppose so. She's in the shop more than she's ever on the road."

"Join the club."

Lauren's vehicle was filled with boxes and crates overflowing with possessions from Mary Adda. Dishes, silver, clothing, photographs, *books; everything that was stored on the boat was moved into the garage. To Lauren's surprise, Nina helped to moved it all.*

"If you'll come in I'll get you check," she said, when they were finished.

The home was different than others on that street with a rustic charm that he found attractive. It was a timber frame structure with large, roughhewn timbers that fit together perfectly in an intricate system of notched joints that required no fasteners. The timbers formed a skeleton of sorts upon which the house was built. It looked like a ski lodge with its high roofline, tall windows, and huge beams. They passed a beautiful totem pole near the path that led to the house, and reached the door, which bore the carved image of an Orca whale.

Nina led him inside to the dining table; a five foot wide slab of fir, twelve feet long, cut from the heart of a giant tree. It was positioned in a vaulted space where the windows reached from the hardwood floor to the cedar ceiling high overhead; windows that offered an enchanting view of Lake Washington, and the still, cozy, cove below. The water was already dark with the anticipation of night, and little dock lights just switching on were reflected in it. They stood side by side at the window enjoying the tranquility of the sunset. It was almost as if they were a couple, she mused, standing together at the window like she and her husband would do. That brought a quiet blush to her check, and she moved away from him ever so slightly, without his notice.

"Nice plane," he said, indicating the float plane moored at the dock down the hill from the house.

"Nicholas got that years ago."

"No Boat?"

"I'm hoping to put Mary Adda *there when she's finished."*

"Is that a Chagall?" Lauren asked, as his eye traveled around the room and fell upon a painting near the fireplace.

"It's one of his lesser known works," she replied, much impressed. "I'm surprised you're familiar with it."

"I had an interest in art once,' he answered, casually. "Where did you get it?"

"At a gallery in Chicago," she replied, and her thoughts traveled to that night. Nina's interest in art had taken her to many galleries, but the Chicago experience was one that was etched in her mind. She went there to see the Chagall, but the people there were the real

*show. The gallery owner had a special invitation only event for a
select group. It was a catered affair with caviar and Champaign.
Limousines were dropping guests at the door; high society guests,
who all seemed to know each other. Nina preferred to avoid such
events, but she wanted a look at the Chagall, and feared it would sell
that night. What was so unusual about that evening was the whispered
gossip she heard as she went about the gallery. In hushed little groups
of two or three she would find these well dressed society folks eagerly
gossiping about someone from their circle. They were always careful
that Nina should hear very little of their conversation, and lowered
their voice when she approached, but as she moved about the gallery
she overheard little pieces of the tale from each group she passed.
They were all talking about the same thing, and over the course of the
evening she was able to piece together the story. It seemed that one of
their own had defected. Shortly after the death of his father he flew to
Seattle on business, and never returned. He was to be away for only a
few days, but something transpired during his absence, and he never
came back. It was speculated by the eager, gossiping circles, that he
finally discovered the liaison between his closest friend (someone
he knew from childhood) and his fiancé. Everyone in that high
society circle seemed to know about the indiscretion except for him.
He learned of it when he called his fiancé's home from Seattle one
morning, and it was his best friend's sleepy voice that answered.*

*Nina marveled at the callus smiles on the smirking, Botox faces.
Those faces, she mused, were as artificial and lifeless as the heart that
supported them. Their tongue, sharper than Sweeney Todd's razor,
was just as lethal, but provided a slower, more intimate demise. But it
wasn't the kill they sought, it was the sport.*

*Small wonder he never returned, she reflected. How could he
face this group? How could anyone? As the story continued, she
learned that this man owned an investment firm in New York City,
and that the firm had hired a private investigator to locate him. It
was rumored among the smirking, gossiping circles, that he was too
embarrassed to show his face, and that he had renounced his former
life of affluence. He was said to be leading a simple life somewhere in
Seattle, and that he was living aboard a sailboat.*

*The gallery memory flashed through Nina's thoughts in an instant
as she stood before the Chagall. When she turned to Lauren, she
found that she regarded him with even more interest than before.*

"Would you like a little bite before you go," she asked. "I was just going to open a bottle of wine." Her invitation took him slightly off guard. He expected to finally meet her husband, that mysterious figure that she seldom talked about, but seemed so dedicated to. There were a pair of men's shoes at the door, he noticed, and a leather jacket belonging to a man, hanging on a coat hook near the door. But where was Mr. Van Orton?

Nina sensed his hesitancy and added, "It's a '95 Chateau Margaux."

The sun set quickly, bringing a comfortable warmth to the timberframe home. As the sunlight failed, the flickering light of the fireplace spread its cozy, soothing glow over the timbers and stones. There were animal skins about the room; a bearskin on the floor before a large river rock fireplace, and a mountain lion skin on the wall.

They sat across from each other at the dining table sipping wine and eating cheese by the light of two candles on the table. Nina lit them out of habit. It wasn't until after she did so that she realized how intimate and romantic it was, but it was too late then to extinguish them. The light of those candles fell softly upon her perfect face, and danced in her gray eyes with an almost hypnotic effect that drew Lauren in. He found it difficult to look away. Where was her husband, he wondered? Lauren noted that she seldom spoke of him, but when she did it was always with tender affection and unmistakable devotion. Devotion? He smiled sardonically at the thought. What did the wealthy know about devotion? He finished his wine in a gulp, grabbed his check from the table, and managed a polite "thank you" on his way out.

Nina was still pondering the abrupt departure when she took her wine she stepped over to the fireplace where she had a brief conversation with her husband. Curious what she might find, she went into the garage and glanced casually among the boxes recently placed there. Everything was so dusty and old, and smelled as if it had been locked away in a chest for a century. There was a photograph of her handsome grandfather accepting an Olympic bronze medal. That brought a tear to her eye. She was returning the photograph to the box when she noticed some weathered, crumpled, pages, shoved in like packing material around a collection of antique wine glasses. But Nina recognized the handwriting on one of those *pages, and her heart leaped. She took the box inside, set it on the hearth before the warm fire, and began removing the wadded pages from between the glasses. Excitedly, she smoothed each page with her hand, arranged them in order, and began to read.*

...are they anchored, too? Are they steaming along on a collision course? Tense and alert I listen with every nerve strained.

There is another option. Charles thought he heard water lapping the beach on our port side. An island may be close by; Blakely Island most likely. We could launch the dinghy and row to the safety of the island, and there wait for the fog to clear. I vote for that. I want off the boat.

Lorelei Dearborn

Later

We are launching the dinghy. We'll row to the island, and wait for the fog to lift.

Lorelei Dearborn

Those were the last words by Lorelei Dearborn in the journal of Mary Adda. Her flowing, precise hand ended, and was replaced by an unsteady, masculine hand that followed.

October 14th 1929

With a heavy heart I take up my pen to conclude the narrative begun by Lorelei Dearborn. Some account should be entered here to explain what happened that final day, or speculate what happened that day, and bring closure to the life of my two friends. I have only just come into possession of this journal, and as yet have read only the last few unsettling pages. I should begin by saying... No. I'm sorry. I've stared at the page for half an hour. I cannot begin. The journal must wait. Forgive me my friends. I miss you more than I could have imagined.

Thomas Moore

Nina was stunned, and a chill ran through her in spite of the warm fire. She pulled a light blanket around her shoulders. With misgivings she picked up the pages and continued.

October 21st 1929

Another wet October morning. I miss my friends, Charles and Lorelei, the only friends left to me in the world. I never knew a place could be so cold, so empty, so quiet, all the more so because it is home. The image of Mother seated in her favorite place at the window haunts me day and night. I sit there now, looking out at the gray sky, the gray sea, the depressing drizzle. That there would ever be a time when she would not be here was beyond my childhood imagination. I find that she is often in my thoughts of late; called to mind as I pass the places she used to frequent. I hear her light step in the stillness of the quiet house, or see her reflection in the window, or fancy I hear her knock at the door. There are ghosts in this place. Not the wispy apparitions of fireside tales, but fading memories of people and times past, that haunt my thoughts. Father's grave has been joined by Mother's. I see her headstone from the window, dripping in the cold rain. Should there not be one for Sophia, too, I wonder? And Elsie? Where are they?

Hope is the best of things. I had it in my lonely cell, and it sustained me. It kept me going in the long days and long years that I was away. The hope that I would return home one day and see everyone again, but there is no hope of that now. They are all gone.

I am out of sorts, and cannot get used to this place, cannot get used to the house I grew up in. Even with the fire blazing brightly there is a chill in this hushed, empty house that draws a shudder, and cannot be extinguished. Is it the fall weather that has seeped in beneath the doors, and bled in around the unshuttered windows, filling the house with its unwelcome season? I sense that there is a chill which no fire, spark, or flame, will drive away; a chill that resides here, engendered by the hushed emptiness and cheerless rooms, not the cold. In the full light of a bright summer day, with the windows open and the warm air filling the house, it may seem less so, but I know in my heart it will not. The warmth that is lacking is the sound of laughter, the touch of a hand, the smell of coffee from the kitchen. Such as this would warm the house on the coldest day, but that will never again be. What have I come home to? I never imagined that I would be alone here, or that my footsteps would ring upon the stone floor with such a lonely echo.

After nine years I returned to my room to find that it was just as I left it, and furnished with childhood remembrances that came rushing back, warming my cheek with an embarrassed blush. Nearly a decade of dust and silence had settled upon everything there like a blanket and a lonely spider web, long abandoned, clung to the windowpane over my bed, but all was just as I left it, preserved as if a shrine. How often had the room been visited, I wondered? How often had Mother gone there and taken comfort in my room, among my things, as she thought of me in my absence? Or Sophia? Had she sneaked in against William's wishes? I was certain he would prohibit that. I imaged her sitting at my desk, wearing one of my shirts as she wrote long, heartfelt letters that I would never receive.

On the writing desk beside the bed, in precisely the same place, was the sailboat model that I had made as a child, and also on that desk lay the unfinished book that I was reading at the time, open to the same page. The window behind the bed, through which the morning sun sometimes streamed, was still open half an inch, as I always left it, and the cobweb fluttered delicately with the breeze. I opened the closet door to find my hats organized on the shelf, my shoes arranged on the floor, and my clothes suspended by the hangers, just as I left them. Nothing was out of place. Nothing had been moved or altered. But my moth-eaten clothes were in ragged tatters, my hats too, and my leather shoes had been gnawed by mice. I could see the trail of their scurrying footprints in the dust on the floor. And covering everything in the closet like a forgotten veil, cobwebs and dust, cobwebs and dust, cobwebs and dust. It was an unsettling sight, as if a century had passed, rather than a decade. How much more at ease I might have been if everything had been changed, if all my things were gone, and the room empty? Seeing it as it was took me back to that day. A day I wished to forget.

I removed my prison trousers one last time, tossed them on the bed, and slipped into a musty pair from my closet. But the clothes no longer fit me. Or to be more precise, I no longer fit them. That person was gone, as surely and irrevocably as Mother and Father buried in the cemetery beside the house. The clothes no longer fit me. What would I give to wear them again with the same optimistic naivety and childlike enthusiasm that is assigned to youth and inexperience? With a pensive sigh I reached for my prison clothes once again.

And then it struck me as I left the room and descended the staircase, dragging my hand along the rail, making my way to the floor below. The house no longer fit me, either. Or, like my clothes, I no longer fit it.

Thomas Moore

October 24th 1929

My apologies. My intention was to explain what had become of Charles and Lorelei, and shed some light on how I came into possession of this journal, not carry on about myself and the empty house. It happened like this:

There is no hot water or electricity in the house. As I had just emerged from a very cold shower, and my thoughts were bent on toweling off and placing myself in front of the warm fire, I did not hear the approach of the vehicle that turned down the lane. Rather, I heard it retreat, and thinking that it may be Elsie or Sophia, rushed downstairs and threw open the door in time to glimpse a mail truck through the bare, craggy limbs of the maples along the drive. At my feet lay a letter addressed to me. Who knew I was here I wondered? Wearing only a towel, I picked it up and examined it as I stepped back into the house and shut the door thoughtfully. There was no return address.

Dressed, and seated on the hearth before the blazing fire, I opened the letter and read. It was only a request from Robert Moran, an old family friend, that I join him at his home the following day on an urgent matter of business. The appointed time was two o'clock.

I could not imagine what sort of business Mr. Moran might have with me, but more than that, I could not imagine how to accept his simple request. The Moran estate was nearly ten miles away, and I had no satisfactory means of traveling such a distance. The car, which had not been started in years, was locked in the garage to which I could find no key, and I was confident that it would not start in any case. What I needed was a bicycle.

Next to the trees, not far from the main house, is a little red brick building that is reached by a paved footpath leading across the grass. It was originally constructed as a caretaker's cottage, but as no one beyond my great-grandfather, who built the house, had use for a caretaker, it had gradually assumed other uses, and was employed by Father as a woodshop. It has a low, gabled roof that was nearly buried under the brown maple leaves recently fallen from the sprawling old tree at the corner, and rising up from the mass of decaying leaves a little dormer peeks out. There were splashes of white against the brick; the painted garage door for example, and the entry door, and window frame, but the paint had peeled and curled back upon its self in large strips, and ivy had begun to scale the brick walls, sending its creeping tendrils along the mortared seams. There was a rustic charm about it that often drew Sophia and I to the bare little attic above, a charm that had increased in my absence, aided by the addition of decaying leaves and sprawling ivy and peeling paint.

Diverging from the path that led to it I picked my way through wild grass and soggy ground, coming finally to the window, where I pulled the ivy away from the glass and peeked inside. With my face pressed to the pane, and my hands cupped on either side as a shade, I peered through the grimy glass that was nearly opaque from the dirt and cobwebs clinging to it. Little could be seen through the dingy glass in the poor morning light, but I perceived the vague shape of a ladder in the center of the room that rose up through the trap door to the attic above. It was the perfect hideout for two playful children seeking intrigue and privacy, and held a blushing secret; it was there that I first kissed Sophia. I smiled, recalling the memory....

Pouring through the attic window, the summer sun illuminated the tiny dust motes that twirled slowly in the still air. Sophia and I sat cross-legged in the square shaft of light on the dusty fir floor, telling ghost stories. Mine was a retelling of an obsessed doctor who raided cemeteries for body parts and attached them to a cadaver in his basement laboratory. Sophia's blue eyes were open wide and she leaned close, listening breathlessly as I spoke in a frightening whisper. When I concluded my tale with the vengeful doctor tracking the reanimated being to the frigid Arctic, she sat quiet and unmoving, watching me intently. In the stillness, I heard the buzz of a persistent fly hitting the attic window again and again in an effort to escape.

"Did he kill the doctor?" she asked, in a hushed whisper, as if afraid the walls would hear. "He was so much bigger and stronger. He could easily kill the poor doctor."

"The poor doctor, did you say? That poor doctor first tried to kill him, his own creation."

"Yes, but the doctor was trying to rid the world of his monster."

"But he wasn't a monster at first. He was kind until everyone rejected him."

"That's true," she said, thoughtfully, with thumb and finger on her chin.

"Now it's your turn," I said, and waited for her to begin. Sophia leaned back on her elbows with a concentrated frown as she thought of a story. The minutes passed. The fly buzzed angrily at the window. She nodded her head with a far away look in her eyes, then sat up again, and rolled first one, then other of her flannel sleeves up to her elbows before beginning. Leaning forward, with her face close to mine, she began her whispered tale. It was a story about a frightened little girl making her home through the dark woods late at night. On and on she picked her way through the trees and brush, fearing she had lost the trail, hearing footsteps following behind, and jumping at the sound of night creatures rustling in the darkness. When she emerged at last in the open space she knew to be her home, she rushed across the yard and into the house, shutting the door quickly behind her, then stood inside the dark room out of breath, listening. But home was no refuge. She lit a candle and peered into the shadows, searching for an intruder that might jump out and grab her at any moment. In her terror she saw him in every dark corner, behind every door, skulking under the bed, hiding even in the cupboards, waiting to jump out and seize her. She had retreated to a corner of the room and sunk to the floor with her candle held before her scanning the darkness, when she heard a scratching noise at the window over her head...

"Then what?" I asked eagerly, waiting for her to continue. But Sophia had a wild, almost terrified expression on her young face, and seemed not to hear as she stared straight through me. I reached out touching her shoulder, and she sprang back like a wild animal, scrambling across the floor until she struck the wall. There she was suddenly herself again, and forced an embarrassed laugh.

"Oh Thomas, you gave me such a fright," she said, with a hand to her chest.

"You were so funny," I laughed. "You were more frightened by your own story then I was."

Little thought did I give to the narrative at the time beyond the belief that it was an adlib fiction conceived for the entertainment of two adolescent souls one playful summer afternoon. It was many years later that the story returned to mind, and I was then standing over the dead body of Rockwell Thomson in the dark hallway outside my bedroom door.

It was time to leave our little attic hideout. I stepped through the opening in the floor, taking a few steps down the ladder.

"Have you ever kissed a girl, Thomas?" Sophia asked, suddenly, on her hands and knees, watching me.

"No." I paused on the ladder, with my arms resting on the floor on either side. Crawling closer, she closed her lovely blue eyes and leaned forward in a silent invitation. With a flutter of excitement that my young heart had never before felt I leaned forward, closing my eyes, bashfully touching my lips to hers. Her touch was electric. A thrill ran through me. Pulling back, I opened my eyes to see that she was still on her hands and knees, eyes closed, lips puckered, but now her face was relaxed, almost serene. She opened her eyes with a big smile.

"Race ya to the house," she said.

But that was long ago. Sophia and I were only children then, and she was here with me. We were a family.

I walked back to the path, following the grass-covered paving stones to the shop door. Expecting it to be locked, I was pleasantly surprised to find the handle turning easily in my hand and the door creaking open to admit me. The air was stagnant and heavy, smelling of paint thinner and wood. I closed the door behind me and stood just inside, looking over the tools and tarps and boxes in the dim winter light. Everything was still and quiet and undisturbed, just as I had left it. There on the work bench under the window were boat winches, belaying pins, wood blocks, chocks, handrails and a host of other boat hardware covered in a layer of cobwebs and dust. My bicycle, which I had outgrown, was propped up against a pile of lumber looking quite melancholy. Many years accumulation of dust clung heavily to the intricate network of cobwebs sagging under the weight, and the multitude of bloodless flies trapped there bore witness to the industry of the bloated spiders that watched me lazily. But cobwebs, spiders, and dust, are easily brushed away. It was the limp, deflated tires that rendered it useless.

My footsteps fell softly, cushioned by thick dust on the concrete floor as I searched the shop for a tire pump. I discovered the outline of a bicycle under a canvas tarp in the corner, and taking the tarp in hand, pulled it back to find Sophia's bike, looking as clean and unblemished as the day Mother brought it home for her. She always took particular care of her things. Where could she be? While I heard Mother's light footsteps in the night when all was still, or saw her sitting at the window in her favorite place, I knew they were only fading memories of a time past, a time that would never again be. But I also saw Sophia painting at her easel or seated by the fire with a book, and entertained the hope that she would again do so. Would I ever see her again? At the close of each day I toasted her empty place at the table, and the love I felt for her was slowly, gradually, turning to bitterness. I had sacrificed so much for her, and where was she? Did she make any effort to find me? Had she found someone else? Was she married and happy now?

There was something else to consider if I intended to meet Mr. Moran. None of my old clothes fit me. To my embarrassment I found that I had no choice but to wear the clothes I returned home in. The jacket I had consigned to the flames the first night, but the shirt and trousers I wore daily, and they chafed my spirit like a scarlet letter upon my chest. The longer I was home the further away that wretched experience seemed, and the more acutely I felt the sting of my scarlet reminder. At home with only my own conscience to witness my indiscretion I could bear the sting, but how could I leave the grounds and subject myself to the scrutiny and judgment of others? I thought about it all night but could see no other way, so the next day, feeling the sting of my offense even greater than the day my sentence was pronounced, I reluctantly pulled on my prison suit of clothes (as I had done every day), and swallowed my pride. Encouraged by the hope that few people would recognize my attire, I threw a grudging leg over Sophia's bicycle and began along the tree lined lane under the naked maple boughs as the sky, which had been threatening rain all morning, began to pour down upon me.

It was at times a heavy rain. Twice the wind blew my hat from my head and I stopped to pick it up out of the road. As if the embarrassment of my clothes wasn't enough, I stood at the door of the Moran house, soaking wet and trembling, and rang the bell feeling like a beggar from the street. I was regarded as such by the stiff looking old man in a butler uniform who opened the door. When I apprised him of my errand he raised a bushy gray eyebrow in doubtful disdain, and resentfully stepped aside, allowing me to enter. Saying he would tell Mr. Moran of my arrival, he indicated with a careless gesture and suspicious eye that I should remain where I was, then turned his proud back upon me and struck off in no great hurry. If the foul weather did little to improve my humor, the haughty attitude of the servant only aggravated it. After waiting for a quarter of an hour in the entryway, cold, wet, and neglected, I went in search of Robert myself, and found him at his desk in the study, hastily drying his hands with a towel. Hearing me enter, he glanced up, and finding me in the doorway dripping water on his hardwood floor, quickly tossed the towel under his desk as if he had been caught in some surreptitious act.

"I was told of your arrival," he said, testily. "Weren't you asked to wait?"

"Asked? No. I was told to wait by your surly butler."

"Then it seems your amended prison term did little to teach you patience," he answered, sternly.

"Prison isn't intended to teach patience," I replied, growing angry. "Its sole purpose seems to be to remove whatever faith one has in humanity, and plant in the heart of its residents the seeds of vengeance, animosity, and spite."

"Then it seems to have succeeded wonderfully," he said, with a false smile. "Have a seat. We'll conclude our business, and you can return to your pursuit of vengeance, spite, and animosity." He took a folder from a drawer in the desk, and opened it on the desktop.

"I wouldn't want to stain your precious chair," I said, and remained standing. Robert shrugged indifferently, and then slipped on his glasses and began to read.

"You may have noticed that the Moore cemetery has been well cared for in your absence. I've had my gardener tend to it while you were away," he said, carelessly as he read.

"And you did this out of the kindness of your black heart, I suppose? Or will I be presented with a bill?" His hands clenched into fists as he struggled to keep calm. He lifted his eyes, peering at me over the glasses with a look of mistrust and enmity.

"Apparently you learned more in prison than spite and animosity. You seemed to have developed a gift for obfuscation as well, if this file is any indication. Or perhaps you had more in common with your step-father then I gave you credit for," he said, grinning smugly. I took a step toward the desk, and holding his eye, spoke in a soft, calm voice that brought a chill to him.

"If you ever again mention me in the same breath as that godless degenerate, you'll find yourself occupying a hospital bed." I stood over him, holding his eye with cold, unflinching malice, until he leaned back in his chair from fear. Then I took a seat in the chair before the desk, and waited patiently while my rain soaked clothes formed puddles on the floor. At length, Robert recovered from his momentary shock, and began again.

"I was hoping in the course of this interview to learn that my suspicions about you were false, but I see I entertained a charitable faith in the Moore family name that was regrettably misplaced. Sometimes the apple falls far from the tree." I listened passively, with my arms crossed as he spoke. "When I was asked by my friends to be their executor I didn't know the contents of their will, or I would have attempted to dissuade them from this course of action. As it is, I have no choice but to honor their wishes." He removed a form from the folder, and slid it across the desk to me. "Just sign in the bottom left hand corner, and I'll transfer ownership of *Mary Adda* to you."

"What do you mean? Who are your clients, and who, or what, is

Mary Adda?" He studied me shrewdly over the top of his glasses.

"You knew nothing of this?" he asked, suspiciously.

"Nothing of what? If you'll dispense with the cryptic dialogue we can conclude this business, whatever it may be, and I can bicycle back home in the rain."

"You bicycled here?" he asked, incredulous. "Ten miles in the rain?"

"Robert," I said, tiredly. "I'm leaving here in five minutes. That's how long you have to finish whatever this is about."

"I'm the executor of a will in which you are named as a beneficiary. In the event of the death of Charles and Lorelei Dearborn," he said, reading from the folder on his desk, "ownership of the yacht *Mary Adda* and the boat journal accompanying the yacht are to be transferred to Thomas Moore." He peered up at me over his glasses. "The yacht is at the Harbor Patrol dock on the other side of the island. The journal is there." With a nod of his head he indicated a leather-bound volume on the corner of his desk. "It's for your eyes only," he added somewhat uncomfortably, as he watched for a reaction.

"They're dead?" I asked, in disbelief. "But how?" I'm sure Robert could see the grief in my troubled face. His stiff bearing relaxed, and he sat back in his chair tiredly. "I saw them only a few months ago. What happened to them? How did they die?" I asked, anxiously.

"That hasn't yet been determined," he said, in a more gentle tone. "The Harbor Patrol found their boat anchored a few hundred yards south of Blakely Island, near Spencer Spit. The tender was missing. They're presumed lost at sea." He studied me astutely over his glasses. "What happened between the three of you? How did you coax them into leaving you their yacht? They knew you less then twenty-four hours."

"Is that what you think?" I bellowed, contemptuously. "You can keep your yacht, and your precious journal," I said, rising from the chair. "You insufferable lout," I snorted, as I made for the door. I saw Robert rise from his seat, as if to follow. "Stay away from me," I said, firmly, and left the study.

With the bite of his words stinging my ears, I strode out of the office, and, making my way back down the hallway, heard him calling after me to come back. The butler heard it too. He appeared in the hallway wearing a haughty, inquisitive frown, and, seeing me, positioned himself in the middle of the hall with his arms crossed to arrest my retreat. I carelessly brushed him aside with the sweep of my arm and continued on to the door where I paused. I was already trembling from the cold, and now had to step back into the rain and bicycle all the way home again.

How could Robert think such a thing of me? He knew my parents. He had known my family for years. How could he entertain such an unflattering opinion of me? Was this the attitude I could expect from everyone on the island now that I had returned from prison? Wishing to be far away from the Moran Mansion I flung the door open and was greeted by a downpour. It was raining lightly in the morning with heavy gusting wind, but it was pouring down as I stood in the doorway looking out. The sky was growing darker, and the wind was building. I saw the trees bending to the breeze that blew in over the water.

Winter days were so short. It would be dark soon, before I reached home probably. I should start immediately, but I thought about Charles and Lorelei. The first time I saw them. Charles stood at the open car door in the middle of the road, tall and handsome, with a crooked, boyish smile that made him look younger than he was. And Lorelei, pretty Lorelei, with a big, white, plantation hat, watching from the open car window. They were both so affable and full of life. I did not know them long. I will not say that I did not know them well, because I believe I did know them well. There was between us a bond that had grown out of a shared experience the night we met. A bond of respect and honor. An unspoken admiration and attachment that did not require a lengthy courtship to germinate. I did not know them long, that was true, but I knew them well and I missed them. They were my friends.

Standing in the open doorway with the wind rushing in around me and the rain coursing down outside, I took a deep breath and prepared to step into the downpour when a hand fell upon my shoulder. Whirling around, I saw Robert.

"I'm sorry Thomas. I haven't been very professional," he said, apologetically, then handed me the journal and paperwork. "At least take these with you. It'll save you a trip back here."

"Thank you," I said, receiving the items from him. An awkward silence followed. I did not wish to remain, but was hesitant to step into the storm. The rain fell heavily, and my parcels were sure to get wet. Robert must have followed my thought.

"Come back inside. Can I give you a ride home?" I looked out into the rain once more, as if it had somehow changed. It hadn't of course, but I was reluctant to accept. "I'll have someone bring a car around. Just wait a moment, if you will." And he began away to find the driver. But after a few paces he paused, and remained with his back to me a moment, before turning finally.

"I was very close to them, you understand. They were very dear to me. I don't understand why they would leave so much to someone they barely knew. Given your past, I feared that you had..." he paused, searching for the proper word.

"Swindled them?" I said, finishing his thought.

"Or worse. A lot of men learn to be proper criminals when they go to prison," he replied.

"I'm as surprised by this as you are."

"There's nothing you'd like to tell me?" I thought about it in the silence that followed. I knew quite well what they were thinking when they left me their boat, but Robert didn't need to know that.

"No," I said.

The return trip was uneventful. I had been wearing wet clothes for over an hour, and sat in the back of the car shivering from the cold as the driver made his slow way along the winding, twilight road that followed the bluff along the coastline. I vaguely noted the whine of the car engine and the mechanical squeak of the wipers as I looked out the window, thinking about my friends, Charles and Lorelei. Still, the rain fell. It had fallen all day. It seemed a fitting consequence of my mood and errand. I glimpsed my transparent reflection in the car glass and failed to recognize the image looking back at me. It was old and tired, angry, ill-tempered, and pessimistic. The driver pulled up at the house, opened the door for me, and then removed my bicycle from the trunk before climbing back into the car and driving away.

Again the rain fell upon me. I stood in the dark near the choked, decrepit fountain with my hand on the bicycle and the journal under my arm, watching the retreating taillights through the maple trees.

My friends were gone. Perhaps the only friends I had left in the world. How very cold and dark the house looked. How I dreaded to enter.

Thomas Moore

October 27th 1929

It is one thing to be sequestered and confined to a drab, barren little cell year after long year, surviving on the tiny hope that one day, though it may be in the distant future, I would be returned to my family, my home, and all the comfort it affords. It is one thing to be sustained by such a hope. It is quite another to realize that desire and come to understand that it was an empty fantasy. I returned from my meeting with Robert Moran last night and straight away built a fire. Even that simple pleasure was a luxury that I could ill afford. There was precious little firewood remaining, and no possibility of more, but I was pensive and cold and needed the warmth and cheer of a fire. Candles too are in short supply. Only two remain. Without them there will be no light but the fire, for as long as that lasts. I find that I am growing depressed. I sit with my back to the fire looking out at the empty darkness, feeling the hush of the cold, vacant house. There is no electricity. There is no heat. There is no money. There is no food. There is no Sophia, or Mother, or Elsie. Where can they all be? Why is the estate abandoned? Mother will never return, I know. It's all so sad.

My spirit is lifted by the kind gesture from the Dearborns. That they would remember me in their will touches me deeply. It is the one spark of hope in an otherwise bleak and hopeless existence. Several days ago I finished the last of the canned meat and canned vegetables that I found in the cellar. Tomorrow I go to claim *Mary Adda* if I can find the strength. I haven't eaten in days and feel weak and ill, so much more so after riding in the rain. If only I could...

The crumpled pages ended with that unfinished remark. Nina placed the last page with the others on the hearth, moved by the suffering of poor Thomas. She pictured him famished and alone in that cold, cold, house, growing weaker and lonelier each day.

What became of him, she wondered? And what of Charles and Lorelei? She considered searching through the boxes for more of the journal, but it was late and the pages recently read left her pensive and dispirited. She said goodnight to her husband and went to bed, but her sleep was fitful and restless, troubled by dreams of swirling fog and ghostly images of a boat passing through it.

It was in the spring of the following year that Lauren returned. The day was beautiful, all the more so after the dreadfully long, wet winter. The Harley rumbled along the perfectly tailored, tree-lined street, announcing his presence to the residents there. He drove through the open gate following the paving stones that led to the timberframe home. Nina heard his approach well in advance, and was waiting outside the door.

"Hello Mr. Lauren," she said, greeting him.

"Nina," he replied, and shut down the engine.

"You know, I can mail these to you if you'll just give me an address," she said, handing him a check.

"I don't mind," he replied, slipping the check into his shirt pocket without looking at it. "It's a nice day for a ride," he added, still sitting on the bike.

"It's been six months since your last check."

"Yeah, well," he smirked, "they always keep a spot open for me at the shelter."

"Do they?" she smiled. It was almost as if he didn't like receiving money from her. As if he didn't want to be her employee.

He saw her looking at the Harley with an intrigued, curious eye, and asked smugly, confident that she would refuse, if she might like to go for a ride. But Nina sensed his prejudice. She felt it in their first meeting when his defiant, rebellious eyes traveled over her judgmentally as they sat together in the salon of Mary Adda.

Lauren was mildly surprised when she accepted his invitation, and dropped a long, shapely leg over the seat. He shrugged smiling, started the Harley, and they began down the driveway. It was the first time in their association of nearly a year, that she touched him. She had her bare arms around him, and he remarked to himself that her touch was both warm and cold at the same time, like the rest of her.

They went east, to the country. The warm sun of early spring was on their face as they wound and twisted along the curving country road passing farms with old barns faded by the sun and rain, rusty tractors entangled in briars and weeds, and fields of golden hay and budding corn. Cattle turned to stare dumbly as they passed. They crossed the valley, following the twisting road at a leisurely pace as it climbed into the hills and thick timber. Afternoon sunlight streamed through the tree limbs, flashing on Nina's relaxed, smiling face. Lauren expected her to tap his shoulder any time, indicating that they should turn back, but on and on they rode.

Turning a corner, a quaint little general store cropped up in a clearing beside the road. There was a small field next to it with large, ancient fruit trees bearing the assurance of summer fruit. An old picnic table carved with the names of young lovers was painted cherry red by the fruit tree hanging over it. The little store was white with a plank porch in front, worn smooth by the tread of many feet over many years. Daisies sprang up in the unmoved field, and in the open windows little curtains rustled in the breeze.

The big Harley rumbled up to an old gas pump in front of the store. The pump was faded and dented, and hadn't worked in twenty years. There was a metal sign on top that read "Mobilgas." under a winged horse that was flying away. Lauren shut the engine down, and climbed off. He and Nina grinned at the sight of the charming little store, half expecting to find an apple pie cooling in the open window. They stepped up onto the porch, and through the open door. Just inside was an old cooler with glass bottles of Coke inside. With a smile and a shake of the head they each grabbed a bottle and moved to the counter.

Outside in the sunshine they drank their soda while sitting at the picnic table.

"There are little country stores like this in the San Juans," Nina said. "I used to see them when I visited grandfather. You could buy one of these for a nickel." The weariness that seemed habitual to her in the solitude of her home was gone, and she felt young and alive again. The country air seemed to suit her.

"Are you a country girl?" he asked, noting her relaxed smile.

"I love the country. I would go to Orcas Island every summer and spend weeks with grandfather, riding horses on his property, and exploring the island. We sometimes took his boat and visited the other islands."

"Mary Adda?"

"I don't know. It was so long ago I don't remember the boat."

She tipped the Coke to her beautiful lips, and finished it in gulp. Little beads of sweat trickled down her neck and chest. "It's so hot."

"Let's go for a swim," Lauren taunted.

"What will we wear?" Nina asked.

"I have some extra clothes in the saddlebags."

Her playful eyes were smiling as she considered.

The Harley was parked in a turnout beside the mountain road. A short distance beyond it a swift little stream followed a meandering path through the tall, green, timber. On a sandy beach near the creek Nina shimmied out of her snug pants while Lauren stood in his swim trunks with his back turned, giving her privacy.

"Why do you carry swim trunks with you?" she asked.

"I swim after working on the boat to clean up," he answered, still looking away. "The shower at the marina looks like it hasn't been cleaned in a few decades."

"Why do you have two pair?" She pulled a pair of his trunks over her long, tanned legs, then removed her shirt and slipped into one of his tee shirts.

"So one pair is always dry."

"Okay," she said. Lauren turned to see. She was beautiful, as always, and looked charming in his clothes, like a teenage girl wearing her boyfriend's clothing. He smiled appreciatively when she did a little twirl, showing off her figure. But he was careful not to give her too much praise.

"Ready?" he asked. Nina nodded. Lauren stood on a sandy beach at the edge of the water. "It's a bit cold," he said.

"Good," she answered, joining him there. "The colder the better." She was taken completely off guard when he pushed her suddenly, and she flew forward into the cold, clear, stream. Nina surfaced spitting water, and her playful eyes meet his.

"I'll get you for that," she said.

Lauren was laughing when he climbed up onto a boulder next to the creek, and dove deep into a sparkling pool. When he surfaced a moment later his eyes were wide.

"Holy Mother of God. It's even colder than I thought."

"Wimp," she jested.

The stream, a melting ice pack from high in the mountains, was just too cold for swimming. They crawled up onto the sandy beach shivering, feeling like teenagers, and rested in the warm sun. Lying on her back in the sand, Nina reveled in the warm sun upon her face. The wet tee shirt borrowed from Lauren clung to her lovely figure revealing every beautiful curve. He tried not to stare at the stunning vision beside him. The water beading on her shapely legs and gracious neck, the wet hair falling casually about her radiant face, the blissful look on her closed eyes, the thin material revealing her perfect breasts, was more than he could suffer. Irresistibly drawn to her he leaned forward, closer and closer to her flawless, inviting lips, parted ever so slightly. And in that moment a flash of sunlight struck him in the eyes like a searchlight upon his soul. The pure, glaring light of a life long oath gleaming on her ring finger drew his eye and gave him pause. When he looked back down at Nina, her eyes were open, and she was looking up at him.

"We should probably start back," she said, and closed her eyes once more enjoying the warm sun on her face. Lauren fell back into the sand beside her, and closed his eyes, too. But he couldn't keep them closed long. He turned his head, watching her breasts rise and fall with each relaxed, slumbering breath.

He awoke sometime later to Nina gently shaking him. The sun, he noticed, was below the trees, and they were in the cooler shade where evening shadows were beginning to form.

"We should head back," Nina said. "It'll be dark soon." He took a moment to wipe his eyes and get his bearings. It was already getting cold with the sun setting over the hills.

"Maybe we should spend the night here," he answered, after a moment of thought. "Neither of us brought a coat. It'll be a very cold ride back at night."

"Where would we sleep?" Nina asked, rubbing her arms to get warm.

"I have a sleeping bag in the saddle bag."

"You have a sleeping bag in the saddle bag?" she asked, smiling. "What else do you have in there? A kitchen stove?"

"They're very handy, those saddle bags."

"I should say so. How big is this sleeping bag in the saddle bag?"

"It's built for two." He replied, with a demure smile.

"Really?" She smiled, skeptically. "Because you usually just buy two sleeping bags. I've never seen a sleeping bag built for two."

"The girl who sold it to me said you can fit two in it. I tested it."

"With the girl who sold it to you?" Lauren nodded. "Was that before or after you bought it?"

"No comment."

"We don't have anything to eat," Nina said.

"The store is only a mile or two away. I could ride back there and see if they're still open." The air was rapidly cooling, and Nina was feeling the chill on her bare arms.

"I'll build a fire while you get dinner," she said.

"Really? You can do that?"

"I'm half Indian, remember? I've spent more time sleeping under the stars than in a bed."

"Okay. I'll be right back."

The swiftly flowing little stream sounded unusually loud in the darkness. In a little circle of light cast by the crackling fire, Lauren sat in the sand rotating a hot dog on the end of an alder limb so that the flame would cook it just right. With the eye of a connoisseur he turned it over and over, watching it carefully from under the brim of his Fedora hat. Nina sat across from him with her own hot dog in the fire. In her other hand was a beer bottle, which she tipped to her lips in a long, refreshing drink. The shirt she wore to swim in was drying on a tree limb, and she was wearing her own clothes again.

"This is so good. I don't even remember the last time I had a beer."

"You need to get out more," he said.

"Like you?"

"I get out a bit."

"It occurs to me," she said, "that I don't know anything about you. Where did you grow up?"

"That's a hotly debated issue. Some people believe I never did."

"Never did grow up?" She smiled. "There is a youthful playfulness about you."

"Yeah, they call that immaturity."

"Youthful playfulness has a better ring to it."

"I think so too."

"So where did you grow up?"

"Would you like another beer?" he asked, still turning the hot dog.

"You don't like talking about yourself, do you?" she asked,

watching him closely in the firelight. His eyes met hers over the fire. Nina sat in the sand with her jeans rolled up to her calves, and her arms on her knees. Holding a hot dog in one hand and a beer in the other, she was simply lovely. There was such a grace and elegance about her that she was simply lovely in all she did.

"So, how about this grandfather of yours?" he asked, changing the subject. "He sounds like quite a man." Nina watched Lauren by the light of the crackling fire. He was quite a man, too, she thought. Well built. Handsome. Charming. If only he would grow up.

"Grandfather was great. Everyone on the island loved him. He was in the Olympics when he was young," she added. "On the crew team. He won a bronze medal. I could go anywhere I wanted on Orcas Island when I was a little girl, and every shopkeeper I passed would give me something. When they heard that I was Patrick's granddaughter they would just open their shop to me and give me anything. I got candy and soda pop and sandwiches, and a hundred other things." She took another drink of beer, and continued turning the hot dog. "Grandfather did something for them. I never found out what it was. I heard them whisper together, and saw the looks that were exchanged. They were grateful to him for something, but no one would ever tell me what it was."

"The whole island?"

"Yeah. I know it sounds crazy."

"Did you ever ask him?"

"Of course."

"Well?"

"He pretended like he didn't know what I was talking about," she said, and finished her beer. "I asked my father one night, and he looked like he swallowed a lemon. He just tucked me into bed and shut off the light without answering."

"Maybe he didn't know," Lauren said. Nina lifted a hand to cover her mouth as fatigue brought a weary yawn to her lips. Taking that as a sign, Lauren walked to the Harley and dug through his saddlebags. "So, how are we going to do this?" he asked, walking back to the fire with the sleeping bag under his arm.

"You're going to offer the sleeping bag to me, like a gentleman. Then you'll sleep on the ground next to the fire," she said, with her pleasant smile, and bit the end off the hot dog on the stick.

"That's exactly right," he answered, with a sour smile of his own.

Then he rolled the bag out on the ground near the fire. "That's just what I intend to do."

"I just love old fashioned, chivalrous men," she said, and took another bite. "But I can't accept that without feeling like a helpless little girl. We need to decide it in a more democratic way."

"Like what?"

"How about Rochambeau?" she suggested.

"Rock, paper, scissors? Okay"

"Ready?"

"Go," Lauren said, and they hit their hand twice, and made the symbol. Nina made the sign of rock. Lauren had scissors. "Damn," he muttered.

"Oh, this looks so cozy," she said, as she slipped off her shoes, and climbed into the warm sleeping bag next to the fire. Taking the loss well, Lauren simply rolled up a towel for a pillow then lay down on the sandy beach near the quietly burning fire. When he looked over at Nina he found her squirming in the sleeping bag.

"What are you doing?" he asked.

"I can't sleep in my clothes. They get all bunched up around me," she said, and set her pants on the sand next to her. Then she shimmied out of her shirt, and set it on the beach, too.

"Comfortable?" he asked, factiously.

"Very. Thank you."

The rushing creek murmured in the darkness. Stars twinkled in the clear night sky. Flickering firelight cast dancing shadows over the sandy beach. It all seemed so natural and charming. With the sleeping bag pulled up under her chin, Nina was warm and comfortable. She could see her breath in the cool night air. When she looked over at Lauren lying on his back with his hat pulled down over his face and his eyes closed, she saw him shivering from the cold.

"Lauren?" she ventured.

"What now?" he answered, without opening his eyes. "Is your head cold? Do you want my hat, too?" Nina laughed.

"Come over here," she said, unzipping the sleeping bag to allow him in. "This thing is supposedly built for two."

He lifted the hat off his face and turned his head. Nina was propped up on one arm holding the sleeping bag open for him invitingly. Her white bra against her tanned skin in the flickering firelight was a stunning sight. Rising quickly to his feet he stepped over to Nina and began unbuttoning his shirt.

"What are you doing?" she asked.

"I can't sleep in my clothes, either," he said, and tossed his shirt on the ground, then took off his pants, and climbed into the sleeping bag. Using his pants as a pillow, he nestled in, getting comfortable, and turned over on his side, with his back to her.

"Lauren?" she asked, studying him with a curious eye.

"Yeah," he muttered, sleepily.

"Why did you change your mind about working on Mary Adda*?"*

Filling the silence that followed was the melodic murmur of the rushing creek and the persistent chirp of Crickets. Lauren didn't move at all. It was as if he hadn't heard her. Eventually he turned back, facing her. They were nearly nose-to-nose, and he was peering into her beautiful gray eyes while she waited expectantly.

"Thank you," he said, at last, with a playful smile, "for sharing my sleeping bag with me." Then he turned back on his side, facing away.

"Well, it is your sleeping bag," she said. "And it is cold."

"Yep," he answered, with his eyes closed, and a broad smile on his face. "The shivering was a nice touch, don't you think?"

There was a moment of surprise in her disbelieving eyes. Then she broke into a broad grin, rolled over with her back to him, and closed her eyes with a smile on her lips.

Early morning sunshine bloomed on Nina's smiling face. She awoke softly, slowly, still smiling from the memory of a pleasant dream. As the sound of the creek wove its way into her thoughts, she became slowly aware of where she was, and looked about her. Lauren was still lying on his side sleeping soundly, and Nina was draped over him. Her head was on his shoulder, her arm hung over his chest, and her leg was wrapped over his. She was more than a little surprised, and embarrassed, to find herself in that compromising position. Careful not to wake him, she disengaged herself from Lauren, who stirred slightly, and continued to sleep. She slipped out of the sleeping bag, then dressed quickly before he awoke. When she was dressed she went to the fire, which was completely burned out, and found a few hot coals at the bottom of the ashes. She blew on them patiently, an added wood, eventually coaxing it into a flame. When Lauren awoke a short time later she had a proper fire burning, and was making breakfast for them; little sausage links on the end of a tree limb turning in the fire. It was the best sausage they ever had. They took another quick dip in the icy creek, dressed, and climbed on the Harley pleasantly relaxed. But Lauren was thinking about what to expect when they reached her house. Where was her husband? What kind of man was he? The return trip was as warm and pleasant as the day before, but Lauren sensed a change in Nina. They didn't speak as they traveled along the country road on their way back, but he could feel a tension in the lovely arms around his waist as they approached the city; a strain that seemed to increase as they grew closer to Nina's home. She rode quietly, with her cheek upon Lauren's shoulder, staring listlessly at the passing countryside.

When they finally reached the timberframe house and Lauren pulled up before the tall, carved door, and shut off the engine, Nina was a different person. She climbed off the Harley languidly, with a quiet reserve that Lauren sometimes noticed in her, thanked him for the ride, and went into the house. When the door closed behind her, Lauren was stunned. He remained on the bike, staring after her, wondering what just happened. And where was her husband? Lauren noticed each time he visited that there was a different pair of shoes near the front door, and a different jacket hanging on the coat hook, but where was the man?

October 28th 1929

The car battery was dead, of course. It hasn't been started in many years. It's just as well. If I had driven it to claim *Mary Adda*, I would have had to leave it at the dock and somehow return for it later. I rode the bicycle instead, though I was ill and weak, and brought it back with me on the boat.

Nina read by the early light of the summer sun that poured through her bedroom window. She awoke that morning relaxed and refreshed, thinking about the impromptu motorcycle ride months ago, and wondering about that curious mixture of gentleman and rebel. Lying in her comfortable bed with the warm sun of a new day on her face she wondered what he was doing at that exact moment.

Working on Mary Adda, *no doubt. It was that thought that recalled to mind the journal. She jumped happily from her bed, grabbed her robe, and hurried to the garage where she rummaged through the boxes. There were a number of letters inside wearing postmarks from the 1940s. They were neatly bundled, and tied together by a string. Under them was a thin hardback book that appeared to be an accounting ledger. There were dated entries indicating shipments and deliveries of something. It didn't indicate what. Why would it be so vague, she wondered? And last of all, on the very bottom of the box, was the remaining portion of Lorelei's journal. Giddy with her find, she quickly made a cup of tea and hurried back to bed with the journal in hand. Nina fluffed the pillows, pulled the covers up under chin, and settled in to read.*

The morning sky was dark and overcast, threatening rain, but the ride was a cool, pleasant one. I knew where the harbor patrol was. I had bicycled past it before as a child. It is little more than a phone booth sized shack with a dock nearby that the police used to moor their patrol boat, or other boats that they had seized, or confiscated.

I walked to the run-down little office and told the officer there that I was claiming the yacht *Mary Adda*, then produced paperwork supporting my claim. He glanced up from the newspaper in his hand long enough to run a lethargic eye over my documents, at a distance from which he couldn't possibly read them, then reached into a drawer of the desk where he sat and produced a key, which he tossed in my direction. I caught it, somewhat surprised by his lazy indifference, and turned to go. Without having uttered a single word, he returned to his newspaper.

There was only one vessel on the harbor patrol dock, and even at a distance I could see that she was stunning and unique. Vic Franck was an excellent boat builder. Father had designed boats for him, and they were good friends. As I studied *Mary Adda*, I I could see the trace of Father's influence in her design. She is a beautiful yacht. A splendid vessel. Normally I would take a moment to familiarize myself with the controls of a new boat, but I glimpsed the lazy officer scrutinizing me from the window of the shack and wished to avoid further contact with him. So I walked my bicycle into the wheelhouse, started the engine, tossed the lines on the dock, and got underway. It felt so good to be back on the water again, to feel the gentle sway of the ocean beneath my feet, and to watch the sandy coastline slipping past as the boat rocked with the swells. I smiled, the first real smile since I had been home, and reflected. My happiness has been purchased at a high price. My friends have perished. They must have known that I would entertain a particular fondness for such a beautiful vessel. Bless them. I resolved to read the journal as soon as I got back.

I eased *Mary* up next to the dock behind *Diva* (who was looking rather abandoned after nine years of neglect) and tied her bow-out on a port tie so the swells would break harmlessly on her plum bow. The October days were short, the nights long. With this day nearly at an end I performed a quick search of the yacht for anything I might be able to use before leaving. To my surprise and delight I found the galley well stocked. There were two or three bags of groceries that I could take with me. Pasta, canned food, all sorts of things. Charles had a hanging closet full of clothes that were my size, and last of all I discovered a wooden cigar box with nearly a hundred dollars in it. I couldn't believe my good fortune. That would last me for months. I loaded one large sack with food, tossed some clothes on top, added the cigar box, and peddled for home with a light heart in the last light of the day.

Thomas Moore

October 30th 1929

I have had my last cold shower (October mornings are cold enough without beginning the day under the brisk spray of cold water) and my first real meal. It was only a can of soup, but it was delicious. I slipped into the clothes found on *Mary Adda*, which fit perfectly, and with a light heart rode Sophia's bicycle into town where I stopped first to have the electricity turned on again, then to buy a battery for the car. I had been to town only rarely, and that hadn't been in years, but it looked just as I remembered it. No one gave me undue notice dressed as I was in Charles' clothes, but I felt self-conscious as I walked before the storefronts and imagined the shopkeepers who glanced up as I passed, looking at me judgmentally as if I still bore my scarlet reminder. It was all in my head of course, and will take time to get out. But something was different. I could feel it. Everyone seemed to go about their business in a sort of subdued silence, as if preoccupied by some weighty matter. No one looked at me at all.

I rode home, replaced the car battery, and then drove the car into town to buy groceries, something I had never done before. I'm certain I looked quite foolish as I walked through the store with a silly grin and perplexed frown, unsure of what to buy. I have never cooked before either, and had no notion of where to begin. But there was a young girl nearby stocking shelves, and she watched me pacing back and forth indecisively, while she worked. I saw her raise an eyebrow curiously as I paced, and as I continued along my well-worn path with no end in sight, she finally asked if she might help.

I was putting the groceries into the car when gold leaf font on a glass door across the street caught my eye. The door belonged to an old Victorian style home, lovingly restored to its former grandeur. The distance was too great to make out the writing on the glass door, but I had the vague feeling that there was something familiar about it, something that called for a closer look. Without thinking, I began across the street and took only a few steps when a car horn rang out and I jumped back, nearly run down. I was still shaking from it, and had forgotten my errand, when I reached the other side. But glimpsing the little house recalled it to mind and I glanced at the door to see the name of "Howard Goodfriend, Attorney at Law."

Anticipating a pleasant reunion, I stepped lightly to the door, and let myself in. It was a square room with a little reception desk just inside, but no one was present. Three Victorian style armchairs were placed on one wall for visitors.

"Is that you, Martha?" Came a voice from an open doorway across the way. A moment later a head peeked out, and I recognized it at once. It recognized me as well. "Thomas Moore," he said, delighted, and stepped quickly across the floor to shake my hand. "How are you doing son? My, how you've grown. Come in, come in." He led me into his office, which must have at one time been a bedroom of the little house, and took a seat at his desk, then motioned me into one as well. There was always a directness about Howard which suggested time was short. In his presence I always felt that he wished to come to the point quickly and move on. I imagined him with a stopwatch in hand at all times, and his office reflected his precise nature. There was everything an attorney would need; law books neatly arranged on shelves within easy reach of the desk, two chairs for clients, a telephone, a letter opener, and a notepad. Nothing else. It wasn't so much spartan as it was functional. No extra movement was required. No need to look for anything. I took a seat.

"What can I do for you today?" he inquired, peering at me alertly as was his way.

"Oh, I was just passing by and saw your name on the door."

"Yes, but you have a question or two no doubt." His manner always felt rushed, as if short of time, and it always made me hurry. I did have a question, though. There was something I wished to know.

"About my release," I said.

"Yes?"

"Did the judge write a letter on my behalf?"

"No."

"No?"

"He wrote three letters on your behalf."

"Oh, three?"

"He was determined to secure your release, and was quite frustrated by the delay."

"No more so than I."

"Undoubtedly. Next."

"Do you know the details of Mother's death?" He took a deep breath and studied me over the desk.

"That would require more time than I have at present."

"Of William's disappearance then?"

"About that I may say only that he is presumed dead. His body was never recovered, but suspicion has fallen on a certain individual."

"Do you know what has become of Sophia?" I asked hopefully.

"No. Now, may I put a question to you?"

"Of course."

"How are you getting on out there?"

"Not so well."

"You're all alone?"

"Yes."

"You have no means?"

"None."

"No expectations?"

"None at all," I added. Howard darted a glance at the clock behind me.

"I have no more time today, Thomas. I'm sorry." I stood to leave.

"One more thing if I may," I asked.

"Yes."

"There could be a question concerning my ownership of the family estate. Did Mother mention anything about a will?"

"I never spoke to your mother."

"How did she hire you to represent me?"

"She didn't."

"Not William?" I asked. Howard merely raised an eyebrow. "Sophia couldn't have done it." He shook his head. "Elsie?"

"Who is she?"

"Who hired you then?" I inquired, quite puzzled.

"I am not at liberty to say. I'm sorry Thomas, but I really must go now. I have court." With a hand on my back he ushered me to the door and pulled it open. As a sort of afterthought he asked, "How long have you been home?"

"Three and a half months."

"And you're all alone out there? Have you seen a newspaper recently? Do you know what's happened?"

"What do you mean? What's happened?" I asked.

"Here," he said, whisking a newspaper off the reception desk, and passing it to me. "Come back when you like, and we'll finish our conversation," he added, and a moment later I was on the porch, in the cold October air, blinking in the bright sun, wondering who my unknown benefactor could be. Who would pay Howard to represent me? It is a matter that has caused me no little concern, and try as I might, I can't imagine who would intercede on my behalf.

Thomas Moore

November 2nd 1929

I was passing the window a short time ago and looked out at
the lush, green grass between the old fir trees nearby. It reminded
me of Sophia's first year here. It was a spring day, warm and wet,
sometimes raining, sometimes sunny, depending on nature's fickle
whim. A little gray cloud passed by, bringing rain with it, and
Sophia sat down on the wet grass in the path of the rainfall. She lay
back, looking at the cloud overhead, then closed her eyes and rolled
her shirt and pants up so she could feel the raindrops striking her
skin. The cloud was small and the sunlight also poured down upon
her.

"Come here, Thomas," she said, with her eyes closed, and
a smile on her face. "It feels wonderful. Nature's massage."
She looked so content, lying there on the grass, smiling sweetly
as the rain fell all about her and the sun warmed her skin. I
grinned, watching her. She was always so cheerful and eager to
try something new. "Thomas," she asked, with her eyes closed,
reaching out beside her, "are you lying next to me? Doesn't this feel
wonderful?"

I should have joined her immediately, but hesitated, and in that
brief moment of indecision the rain cloud rolled away, and the
moment was lost. But little Sophia had left her mark on my soul
that day, and this afternoon when I saw the approach of a little gray
cloud heavy with rain in an otherwise blue sky, I rushed outside,
shedding my clothes as I ran. Warmed by the winter sun, I lay down
upon the cool grass waiting for the rain. It fell free and unfettered
from a pure place in the blue sky overhead, pelting my face with a
welcome sting that cleansed my soul, washing away the shame and
guilt and stench of incarceration. I was clean at last. And home. And
free. With the freedom that only a caged man can know. I cherished
it. I coveted it.

When the rain cloud passed at last, I rose from the wet grass
refreshed and returned to the house. Even in her absence I have
shared something special with Sophia today. As I sat on the hearth
drying before the warm fire I wondered where she might be, and if I
would ever see my dear friend again. The house is so empty without
her.

Thomas Moore

November 6th 1929

Walking through the house this afternoon, I glimpsed the newspaper that Howard thrust into my hand. It was lying forgotten on the piano where I tossed it several days ago and was dated October 30th 1929. "Black Tuesday" was the headline dominating the front page. There was something so ominous and threatening in that bold font, that Howard's words came to mind. "You don't know what's happened?" he asked that day. I spread the page out upon the polished wood of the piano and stood in stunned silence reading. Stock prices fell fifty percent in one day, it said. Businesses were going bankrupt, and shutting down. Banks were closing. People had lost their entire life savings and were throwing themselves off of buildings. The economy was collapsing all around me, and I had no idea. I'm so isolated here, and so removed from people and activity, that anything could happen and I wouldn't know.

Years ago, Father returned with an AM radio after one of his Seattle visits, but it sits unused in the corner, collecting dust. There were no radio stations close enough for us to receive a signal. We were all gathered excitedly (Mother, Elsie, and I) around the radio when Father switched it on, but alas, only static.

I must try to stay more in touch somehow. It's disconcerting to learn that the world may be crumbling around me while I go ignorantly about my business.

Thomas Moore

November 7th 1929

Though I've penned my own entries and made my own observations here, I've been reluctant to read what has been written before me in Lorelei's hand. Were her thoughts and reflections private to herself? Did she expect for this to be seen by eyes other than her own? It's only a boat journal, and not a diary, and yet I can't shake the feeling that I would be prying by reading her entries. I don't wish to violate Lorelei's trust in me. But after giving it some thought, as I lay in bed unable to sleep last night, I concluded that she wouldn't have left the journal to me simply for safe keeping. She must have expected me to read it at some time, so I have resolved to do so soon.

Since I have returned to my home and the responsibility of its care now rests with me, Robert's men have not been tending to the family cemetery. Without their constant attention, it has quickly begun to look neglected and unkempt. I spent the day, therefore, mowing and trimming grass away from the headstones while the rain fell with a dreary, monotonous regularity that seemed fitting to the occasion. Often my eye would return to Mother's headstone there beside Father's, and I could not look upon it without a sob rising in my throat. How did she come to be there? What happened to her? I was not notified of her passing. Never during my absence did I receive any news from home. There were no letters or cards of any sort, William saw to that, so I expected to find things much as I had left them when I returned. By then Mother would have seen William for the degenerate that he was and divorced him. Sophia would have returned from boarding school, and Elsie would have remained in her original capacity, so that when I strolled casually to the fire that first night home, everyone would look at me with wonder and surprise and a tearful reunion would follow. What had happened here while I was away? My eye was drawn again to Mother's grave and the tears ran freely.

I was not equal to the task I had chosen, but neither could I endure the thought of the cemetery, which held so many souls precious to me, suffering another day of neglect. So I labored on, and as my eye drifted from grave to grave while I cut and trimmed pensively, the headstones spoke to me in their silent, practical way, telling when each family member interred there had entered the world and departed from it. I watched the gentle raindrops break upon the firm, obstinate granite with the knowledge that the patient, eroding shower, spread over decades and centuries, would win in the end and the withering stone would wear away and vanish under its gradual persistence.

Where was William, I wondered? There was no stone in the family graveyard that spoke of his fate. Why was he presumed dead? I could scarcely think of him with any emotion resembling kindness, and yet I recalled how very happy Mother was when they first wed. Could I feel a pang of regret for him without that kindness of emotion? As I worked distractedly in the cemetery I thought of the times when he had been harsh or cruel to me. They were few, since our association was brief, and how quickly, how vividly, they returned. But they did so with a softer edge to them, that had been frayed by the wear of time perhaps, or a decade of insight and forgiveness. For even then, in the music of the rain splashing upon the cold headstones, there was a whispered message that said a stone would one day mark my place there, and in that day would I not wish that the memory of others walking in the rain were softer toward me?

Thomas Moore

November 8th 1929

I spent a fitful, sleepless night staring at the shadows on the walls while thinking of her. Restlessly, I lay on her bed with my eyes on the dark window, awaiting the approach of dawn so that I could make a journey. When it came at last, I rose tiredly and dressed by the first faint light of the cold, gray morning. Through the misty morning fog I found the little trail. It was difficult to find and even more so to follow. It hadn't been taken since her tearful discovery, and that was so many years ago. The trees and brush had grown together covering the path and barring the way, but I pressed on, simply bulling my way through the tearing limbs and damp branches, wet with the morning dew, that pulled at my clothes. With my head down, I threw myself into the tangle of biting, scratching, tearing brush, feeling the anger building inside me with each cut or jab I suffered. I pressed on with fierce determination, clearing the way with my arms, sweating and panting, until I was nearly exhausted from the effort. At last I tumbled forward with a final, great push, and fell out of the snarl onto the cold, wet grass. I was cut, bleeding, sweating, and panting in the chill fog. My shirt was torn in a dozen places, and stained with my blood. My arms were bruised, and bleeding. But I laughed. Sitting on the ground, knowing that I had to face the same malicious trail on my way home, I laughed. Too long had I been wandering restlessly about the house, brooding helplessly over my fate, longing for something to do. It felt good to be doing something, anything, which may help to find Sophia or distract me for a time.

The yard has become a field, with broken tree limbs rotting

in the wild grass that grew nearly to the windows of the dismal little shack. It had collapsed upon itself, but remained in a fashion, leaning in heavily on all sides. The roof, sagging terribly under the weight of the moss that flourished upon the decaying shingles, had finally capitulated, and fallen in at the center, dragging the walls with it. But they still stood, all four of them, leaning heavily inward. Still they stand, somehow. Where is my Sophia? I had not expected to find her there of course, but as I stood looking at the crumbling remains of her former home by the pale light of the morning fog, I wondered if her troubled soul were not being comforted by its gradual destruction.

Most of the windows were cracked. One was broken out entirely, and from it issued the splintered stub of a limb from the crippled apple tree. It had fallen some years earlier under the attack of boring insects that devoured it in time and lies rotting in the tall grass. At the broken window a tattered, sun-bleached curtain rustled lightly in the breeze, as if signaling surrender.

I tried the door, and found it to be locked. I'm sure it hadn't been visited since she went there to gather her few things the day she came to live with us. How long ago that was. I put my shoulder to the door and it yielded easily, taking the rotting jab with it. Dry rot, wet rot, mildew, dung, and every other form of decay and mischief that nature could muster was at play and introduced to my nose. Directly under the gaping hole in the roof, through which the morning light poured, was the faded, rain soaked sofa that she once slept on. Rat droppings were thick on the kitchen counter, but they were not fresh. Even they had abandoned the dilapidated hovel. It was a depressing sight, but also the only connection I had with her. It was my hope that I might find something in this place of hers that would lead me to her, some clue of her family history perhaps. Some indication of where she might go. But there was nothing. It was depressing and foul, and I wished to be far away from there.

I turned to go and spotted something on the mantle of the fireplace, which held the fallen bricks of the crumbling chimney. It was a book. One I had seen in Sophia's hands. How did it come to be there? With an excited, trembling hand, I reached out and took hold of The Scarlet Pimpernel. It was Sophia's favorite. Only a few days ago when I was in her room, I noticed there was a book missing from her collection. Could this be it? Why was it here? My hands shook from excitement as my thoughts raced. I opened it to find a note within. It was written in Sophia's flowing hand long ago, for the paper was yellowed from time and the ink faded.

"Dear Thomas,

I have little hope that you will ever find this, and so I hide it away like so many other things that I never shared. You never knew that I once resided here in this little fisherman's shack, and I, out of fear or embarrassment, could never tell you. If you did know, would you ever come here seeking news of me? It will be so very long before you have the opportunity. My heart nearly failed me when I heard your sentence uttered in court that day. I'm so sorry.

If not you, then I hope that someone will find this note and know something of my fate. You see, William now knows or suspects that it was I, and not you. It may be that one of the attorneys told him of my courtroom confession; I don't know. But I saw it in his face a few weeks ago when he turned his cold, vengeful eyes upon me after returning from town one afternoon. I could see the malice there. The hatred. A few days later I saw him leave the kitchen just before dinner was served (he never enters the kitchen) and when I sat down with everyone to eat, my food tasted odd, so I had only a few bites. I was sick for several days after that, and realized that he had attempted to poison me, as Rockwell attempted to do to you.

I fear always to be alone with him and make to follow Elsie or Mother when they leave the room so I will have someone near to deter his attack. He nearly strangled me once when I forgot myself and found that I was alone for a moment in the house. Only the sound of approaching footsteps saved me that day, but his whispered, 'Next time' left me trembling.

I lock my door at night but can't sleep, and in my frightful watch I have several times seen the door handle turn quietly, then heard soft footsteps continue on. Mrs. Stowe has quit and no longer teaches me. I think she fears William, too. There is talk of sending me away to boarding school. I welcome such a change. I love Mother and Elsie, but if I remain, William will win somehow, I know it. He will finish me. I can't live with this kind of ever-present danger and fear. I must go. My trivial little concerns must seem quite silly compared to your situation. I'm so sorry.

I've tried so many times to visit you, Thomas, but have always been turned away. Mother keeps trying, too. She's so distraught over you. William says you're not allowed visitors because you attacked an inmate, but I know that's not true. He's trying to keep us away from you, but know this Thomas: I will never give up. I'll keep trying for as long as it takes, and eventually will see you. They can't keep up this ruse forever.

If I never see you again it can mean only one thing... that William has won somehow, and I am no more. He's agreed to send me to a boarding school, suggested it even, which makes me suspicious. I know he wouldn't allow me to escape his grasp, so I suspect a trap. I fear that when I am away from home, off the grounds of the estate, away from Elsie and Mother, he will find me easy prey.

I'm so sorry my love. This is all my fault. I miss you so.

With love,
Sophia"

I need not mention that I read the letter with a heavy, anxious heart, or that I feared for the safety of the author. Whatever delicate hope remained that Sophia was well, and that I would see her again one day, was torn from my heart at that moment, and its tattered remains were carried away by the cold, cheerless breeze that whisked through the rotting shack. How long I remained there staring mutely at the note in my hand I cannot say, but I saw at last that the faded ink was beginning to run on the yellowed page and realized with a shiver that it was raining lightly while I stood under the gaping hole in the crumbling roof.

Even in death he has struck at me. Will William's malice continue to reach out even from the grave to deliver heartache and misery? How I loathe the man. My pensive fingers trembled as they carefully refolded the letter and reverently slipped it into my torn shirt pocket. How depressing it was to look upon it all: the rain soaked sofa with its cushions on the floor, the kitchen counter bleeding wet rat dung, the moldering dining table with the remains of a newspaper melting into it, and upon everything the scattered pages of newspaper distributed by the wind that curled and twisted rhythmically in the breeze while the fluttering curtain waved goodbye, and in the air the scent of death and decay. Sighing heavily, regretting that I had ever made the hopeless journey, I turned again to leave and heard a sound within the festering shack, a tiny, feeble whimper somewhere inside. I might have attributed it to a cry of the wind, or a creak of the rotting floor as I shifted my weight, but it seemed to have a frail, pleading intent that caught my ear.

A few tentative steps through the scattered newspapers led me to the sofa where the cushions had fallen on the floor in a haphazard heap, and I moved them cautiously aside to find a hollowed space underneath. A mother dog lay on her side, her lifeless brown eyes staring vacantly ahead. The inside of her rear leg had a deep gouge where she had been sliced somehow, and she had bled tremendously. There was a dark stain on the wood floor beneath her. But even as she lay dying, she had offered herself to her pups, who had gathered around her to nurse. They were dead, too, all five of them, lying side by side with their little mouths at their mother's belly. Someone had whimpered, though. I heard it, I knew, so I gently poked each little pup with my finger, and finally one stirred. He lifted his little head weakly in the direction of my prodding touch and turned his closed eyes to me. What a blessing to find a new life in the midst of so much chaos and decay. I lifted him carefully (he fit in the palm of my hand) and studied him in the pale light. His eyes hadn't opened yet, he was that young, and I could feel his emaciated little body trembling from cold and hunger.

Later I would return with a shovel to bury the others, but at that moment I needed to hurry home and care for my new friend. In hurrying past the broken window I glimpsed a spot of blood on a jagged piece of the window frame, and the mother dog's fate was clear.

I now faced a dilemma. With my fragile cargo in hand, I could not take the gnarled, twisted, biting path in return. He would not survive the passage. I had to find another way. There must have been another way to the shack, I reasoned. A way that connected to the main road of the island. That would be the way Sophia's mother would take when she went to town. Cradling my helpless charge carefully in my hands, I walked along the fringe of the tall grass where it met the forest and discovered a road behind the dangling tree limbs that hung nearly to the ground. It too was forgotten and over grown, and while it may not accommodate a car, it would easily accommodate me. It was a flat, winding path, picturesquely covered in a carpet of short grass and fir needles and hemmed in on both sides by the thick forest that sprawled out over it in many places.

It was several hours before I reached home again. The path eventually connected with the main road that circles the island, and led me home. When at last I turned down the familiar drive lined with the naked trunks of our maples, I was footsore and weary, and the crunch of my footsteps upon the fallen maple leaves had a more melancholy and remote melody than ever before. Likewise, the distant call of the ocean surf reached my ears like a funeral dirge, and over the trees, the gulls that circled in the gray sky seemed to call out to me that Ravenswood was different and that Sophia was gone from it forever, never to return.

The damp, chill day was cloaked in a brooding fog that came on suddenly, bringing rags of mist over the land, and with it a tense shiver. I hurried along the lane, longing for the warmth and comfort of a fire, how much more so my little companion? He hadn't made a peep all the way home, but I felt him shift and twist from time to time, encouraged by the warmth of my hands. The coals were still glowing brightly when I entered the house and, with a little fuel added, they burst into flame. I slipped the shivering pup into one of my fur-lined slippers and placed it on the hearth near the crackling fire. He turned his little face to the heat and snuggled contently in his slipper bed, next to the bowl of milk I had placed there for him. Finally, I could rest, or could I? I fell back into my favorite seat near the fire thinking that the warmth, combined with the soft, melodic crackle, would soon have me dozing off to sleep. But my thoughts kept returning to her, always to her. I have spilled much ink in my silent musings over Sophia. I feel as though I'm standing at the edge of the ocean shouting over the swells and roaring surf and waiting in vain for a voice to shout back. She is gone. How much better it was to live with the hope, the illusion, that I might see her again one day.

Thomas Moore

November 10th 1929

I've busied myself with repairs to the estate. It wasn't as bad as it first seemed in the moonlight, viewed through the eyes of a broken heart after an absence of nine years. Deferred maintenance, mostly. Cluttered rain gutters, clogged drains, ivy-covered windows. I've removed all of the coverings from the furniture, washed and folded them, and put them away. All of the bedding has been cleaned and replaced, and I've swept, dusted, cleaned, and polished until I feel like a servant in my own home. I had no idea it could be so much work. It was windy and cold, but I opened all of the windows anyway and allowed the winter breeze to sweep through the house, removing the musty air and stale presence. William was one of the last to draw breath here, and I wished to be certain that no trace of his exhale or sign of his existence remained. The brave note from Sophia has revived my feelings of animosity for him and removed all thought of pardon or forgiveness that time's softening influence may have provided. This afternoon I favored myself with a pleasant pastime. I selected Dante's Inferno from the library, made a cup of tea, then built a fire in the main room. With my chair next to the hearth, I read while casually feeding William's clothes into the consuming flames, which seemed well pleased to have such excellent fodder. With the introduction of each garment, they flared up, licking greedily, and it was with malignant pleasure that I imagined their owner suffering a similar fate. His books were next, and then whatever other personal items I could find. The house is quite free of him now and feels better for it.

How odd, I mused pensively, watching the flames, that one man could so change the life and circumstances, the fate and destiny, of so many around him, for good or ill. The world is a better place without William Thomson.

Thomas Moore

November 11th 1929

What a joy Picasso has become to me. That is the name of the little puppy that has come to live with me here. As I was casting about for a name, it occurred to me that the surroundings in which I found him resembled a Picasso, inasmuch as everything had a surreal, chaotic, disorder to it, as if it were all bleeding together in a montage of weeping color. So, I have named him Picasso. It has been only a few days, but he has developed a ravenous appetite and is quite an active little fellow. As soon as his eyes opened, he stood on shaky little legs then began to walk and then to run, after a fashion. He stumbles, trips, falls, slips, and always with as much speed as he can muster. He's an impatient little fellow: energetic, intelligent, fearless. Oh how he makes me laugh. I've fashioned a bottle from an eyedropper and feed him constantly throughout the day. How he eats.

Thomas Moore

November 12th 1929

In the days that have passed since my interview with Mr. Goodfriend I have considered the identity of my benefactor at great length and have given the matter no small thought. Again and again, as I walk the grounds or trim the grass from the headstones in the cemetery or stir the fire or stare pensively from Mother's window, my thoughts turn inexorably to that generous soul who wishes to remain unnamed and unthanked. What could be their motivation in helping me, and why not reveal themself? My small circle of association was almost entirely restricted to the grounds of the estate, and I could think of no one with the means or motivation to aid me in this way.

Just before dusk, a south wind blew in over the water and began to gust heavily. I built a fire and then sat nearby reading a book by the light of it as the house grew dark and the windows began to rattle in their frames. Several minutes passed, and it occurred to me, as I looked down at the open book in my hand, that I hadn't been reading at all. I was so intrigued by this mysterious person who wanted no credit or recognition for their generous act that my thoughts constantly returned to them.

The wind continued to howl and gust, growing in its intensity. It was only a matter of time before a tree fell on a power line and the electricity failed. I had scarcely framed the thought before the lights flickered and were extinguished. All went dark. Setting the book on the hearth, I reached up to remove a candle from the mantle and lit it by the flame of the fire. Taking the candle in hand, I was on my way to the cellar for a bottle of wine when I heard a knock at the door. I don't really know anyone on the island and had received no visitors since my return. With guarded apprehension, I followed the candlelight through the dark hallway that led to the entryway. Who would come at such an hour, on such a night, I mused? It was with misgivings that I opened the door ever so slightly. In the doorway stood a large man who I vaguely recognized as I held the feeble light at my waist. Behind him at the fountain a car was parked and a driver sat at the wheel waiting. I lifted the candle to better see the face of the man in the doorway.

"Thomas Moore?" he asked, with an inquisitive frown, as he peered through the little opening in the door. There was something in his features that I recognized. His face was older, though mostly unchanged since I had seen it last, but I couldn't recall when that was.

"What is your business here?" I inquired.

"My business here? Ah yes, I'll explain that in a minute."

"Would you like to come in?" I asked, inhospitably enough. There was something in his familiarity of me that I resented, as if it required a familiarity on my part, and acceptance as well, which I was loath to give. I reluctantly opened the door wider and beckoned him inside. As he followed me, and I followed the candle through the dark hallway, I reflected on where I had seen that face before. It was familiar, I knew, but I couldn't place it.

"I thought we might talk a minute, ya see," said the voice behind me in the darkness as it followed along. "I know it's late, but I wanted ta have a word with ya, and I can't always move about as I like. This was the only time I could come." Then it came to me. It was the voice that I recalled. The voice and manner of speech. One that I knew from ten years ago. One that I knew from my little jail cell. It was the importer who had spent part of a night with me. If I had encountered him by chance while walking along the sidewalk of our little town, I would have welcomed him and been glad to see him for a few minutes on the street, but to find him on my doorstep like this in the night? There was no one among the men I met while I was away, the criminals, I mean to say, that I wished to see again in the free air outside that world, and he was not excepted. What did he want with me, I wondered?

I took his hat and heavy wool overcoat from him and motioned him to a seat before the fire where I could sit opposite him. While he looked about the room with an approving eye, I ran one of my own over him by the light of the fire. He was dressed well, in a pinstriped suit that spoke of his tailor's skill. The shoes were Italian if I wasn't mistaken and the tie hand spun silk like the handkerchief in his suit pocket. My importer was doing well.

"Nice digs," he said.

"Thank you," I answered. "How did you know I had returned? I had a much longer sentence."

"Ah that," he said, knowingly, with a nod of his gray head. "We have a mutual friend, ya see."

"A mutual friend?" I asked, much surprised.

"Well, not so much friend as acquaintance. We have a mutual acquaintance."

"I have so few associations out here in the country. I can't imagine who it might be," I said, puzzled.

"Can't ya now?" he asked, with a satisfied smile. "Can't ya really?" He studied my face keenly in the firelight. "Have ya seen anyone in town lately that might be known ta both of us? Someone in an official capacity?" He watched my face for a sign of recognition. "A lawyer perhaps?"

"Howard? Howard Goodfriend?" I asked, astonished.

"That's him," he said, slapping his leg. "That's him, sure enough."

"But..." I stopped myself, and took a moment to think. I received my first visit from Howard soon after meeting my importer friend (I couldn't recall his name), but why would he do this?

"Ya have a question or two that you'd like ta put ta me, I suppose?" he said, amused by my confused state.

"Well, yes," I said, with questions racing through my muddled head. "You're my mysterious benefactor?"

"Well," he said, "that's puttin' a fine point on it. It was me that paid Mr. Goodfriend ta be for ya, if that's what ya mean."

"But why?"

"Ah, now we come ta it. There's a bit of a story behind that, ya see. Do ya wanna give that fire a stir before I begin?" The fire had burned low and the light was failing, so I stirred it with the poker and added wood.

"Would you like something to drink? A glass of wine perhaps?" I asked, as I returned the poker to its stand on the hearth.

"No, thank you," he said. "I've got my own." And he produced a silver flask from his suit pocket, twisted the cap loose, and raised it to his lips in one smooth, practiced motion. He screwed his face up like he was giving birth, slapped his leg with his free hand, and lowered the flask with a satisfied scowl. "Kentucky Bourbon," he said. I rushed off with a candle to fetch a bottle from the cellar. When I returned I found him staring into the flames of the crackling fire thoughtfully. I opened the bottle, poured a glass, and settled into the chair to listen.

"Now then," he began, seeing that I was listening intently, "the question as I remember it, was why. Was that the question?"

"Yes."

"All right then, as ta the why, it goes something like this. I used ta work fer yer pa, ya see. I was a boatwright in his shop down there in Deer Harbor. Well," he said, scratching his gray head as he frowned behind bushy gray brows, "ta say that I was a boatwright might be stretchin' the term a bit. But I worked fer yer father, ya see. I got on pretty well there, too, I might say. Since I was a youngster, I was just crazy 'bout boats. Wanted ta build 'em an work on 'em all the time. What I lacked in skill I made up fer in enthusiasm. Now Daniel, that Daniel being yer pa, was no fool. When I came inta the shop lookin' fer work, he could tell straight away that I wasn't the most skilled fella that ever held a block plane or worked a wood chisel. Most a my experience came from hangin' around the docks an fishin' boats an takin' whatever little job might come up, an them fishermen ain't too particular about the finish a things. But he could see the fire in my eyes, yer father could, an he hired me. He never had cause ta regret it. I kept my eyes open, watchin' those around me an learnin' quick. In no time a'tall, I was as fast an skilled as any man in the shop." He took the flask from his lap, and repeated the ritual as before, unscrewing the cap, tipping the flask to his lips, screwing his face up to give birth, then slapping his leg with the exclamation: "Kentucky Bourbon."

"You probably knew Father better than I did. He passed away when I was only six."

"Ah, that was a sad day lad, a very sad day. Everyone to a man liked your pa. He was a good man," he said, thoughtfully, looking into the flames. "I lost my job after that."

"Why?"

"Well, yer pa. He made the shop work, ya see. Folks wanted a boat designed by him. With him gone the orders just dried up. I was the last one hired, so I was the first one ta go, ya see. Your pa now, he was keeping me on and findin' work for me at the shop. He knew a job was a difficult thing ta come by on the island, and he was lookin' out for me. But when he passed away the shop foreman let me go."

"Oh."

"I got nothin' against him fer that. He did the right thing. I got nothin' against him fer what he did."

"I'm sorry you lost your job," I said, sincerely.

"Sorry? Ha, not fer me I hope. It was the best thing that could a happened for me. That's when I started my import business. Never had so much fun in ma life."

"It seems to be treating you well."

"Mr. Moore," he said, drawing his chair closer and lowering his voice to an almost conspiratorial tone as he fixed his keen eyes upon me, "no one's ever given me a break in my life. I never asked for one, ya understand, but they was never showered down on me like some folks. Even my own family never seemed ta take much notice a me. Your pa, now, he was the first. He took a chance on me, and I proved him right. I worked it out so he was right. When my pockets was bulging with money, I wanted to do something ta pay him back, but a course he wasn't around no more. The sea had taken him. I couldn't help your ma any; she had everything she needed. But when I bunked with ya that night in lock up, an heard yer story, an learned who ya was, well, right then I knew that fate had stepped in and sent me ta ya."

"I'm very grateful. If not for you, I would be spending the rest of my life in prison," I said, with a shudder.

"I wanted ta help ya, and I did. That Mr. Goodfriend, he's a sharp one. I knew if anyone could work things ta yer advantage it was him. He's got me out of a tight spot or two." He paused to consult with his flask once again, and concluded his ritual as always, with a slap of his knee and an exclamation. With the flask once again in his pocket, he continued. "That Judge Thomson, now, I had reasons a my own for wantin' ta be a thorn in his side, so helping ya served me there."

"You have my thanks. I wish there were something I could do to repay you."

"Maybe there is," he said, squinting at me through a half open eye behind his bristling brow, his head cocked to one side. "Maybe there is at that."

"What do you have in mind?"

"Mr. Moore, I'm retirin'," he said, abruptly.

"From the import business?"

"From the import business," he replied, nodding his head. "I've got more money than King Solomon, and I'm too old fer this monkey business anymore. I'm quite particular about sleepin' in my own bed of a night, an those bunks, ya know the ones I mean, ain't any too comfortable on these old bones. I'm watched, followed, an spied on everywhere I go. Don't worry, I lost 'em before I came here," he said in response to my look of alarm, "An I can't use the phone without 'em listening in. I've just had enough. I don't need ta do it no more. Now, a mutual friend, excuse me, a mutual acquaintance, tells me that things could be a bit better with ya." He fixed me with his squinting eye, awaiting confirmation. I rose from my seat to stir the glowing embers of the fire, keeping my back to him while I worked the poker over the coals. What was he leading up to, I wondered. "There's no shame in it. Many a soul's fallen on hard times these days. There's no shame attached ta it," he said. I gave the poker a final flourish, sending a twirling mass of flaming sparks up the chimney, then returned it to the stand and sat down on the hearth.

"I can't accept money from you," I said. "I already owe you a debt that I'll find difficult to repay. I can't accept money from you as well." He sat back in the chair crossing his arms over his barrel chest, studying me by the light of the fire.

"I was right, then? About your circumstances I mean." The heavy sigh that escaped my lips was unmistakable. "I thought as much. How would ya like a job?"

"That's very generous of you," (I still couldn't recall his name, or I would have employed it here). "That's very generous of you, but I'm not a…"

"Smuggler?" he said, interrupting me.

"I was going to say, criminal." He fixed me once again with a squinting eye, leaning back in his chair, his arms crossed in front of him in the firelight. I wondered if I might have offended him. The fire popped, sending a flaming chunk of wood out onto the hearth. His face gave away nothing as I looked at him and he looked back at me. Then he smiled and it spread over his entire ruddy face, bringing forth a good-natured chuckle that shook his limbs.

"Not a criminal? You're already known ta everyone on the island as a murderer." He slapped his leg jovially. "And you're concerned about smuggling booze. That's rich." He laughed. There was a curious affability about the man that invited affection.

"I confessed to save someone else."

"Do you think anyone else knows that?" he asked, and then produced the flask again. His cheeks became rosier with each tip of the silver vessel and were verily glowing by now. With it tucked away in his pocket once more, he continued. "Mr. Moore, I'm retirin' as I said, an I need a good man ta take over fer me. Now these ole boys that I been workin' with have been with me fer years. They're a good bunch, all of 'em, but there ain't a leader among 'em. They need direction, ya see. Someone ta run things. You know how ta handle a boat an ya know the water around here, which can get pretty dicey with the rocks an the currents an the shoals. You've been sailin' this stretch a water all yer life. Ya know all the little places that a boat can squeeze inta an hide. My boys will like ya an do what ya say. You're a leader. I can show ya all ya need ta know, an this'll give ya a chance ta get yer feet back on the ground."

Everything he said made perfect sense. I had read enough stories in the newspaper about enterprising individuals who had made fortunes smuggling alcohol from Canada, that I knew this was a tremendous opportunity. What other options did I have? Even if I miraculously revived the boatyard, somehow, and raised the capital to hire a work force and get the machinery running again, there was no market for boats. He was right about that. Without Father's reputation to sustain it, the boatyard would be difficult to revive, especially in this economy. The Dearborn money would not last. The electricity would be turned off again. The table would be bare. But more than that, without the back property taxes paid, and soon, I would lose the family estate that had been handed down from father to son for seventy years. Lost on my watch.

This was the opportunity I needed and just when I needed it most. But my pride was stubbornly refusing to become a criminal to save my home. The Moore family had always been proud of our tradition and uncompromising standards. We built some of the finest yachts in the world and had a reputation for integrity. Somewhere there had to be money. In some bank account that I hadn't yet found, or some vault or safe deposit box, were bonds or stocks or investments of some sort. There had to be. I didn't want to be the Moore to tarnish the family name. My benefactor was correct; everyone on the island already thought of me as a criminal. But I knew the truth and it was a comfort to me, especially on the long, chill nights when I was alone in the house and had only my thoughts for company. When I lay down in my bed at night, and pull the covers up over myself, staring into the dark room with my conscience clear, knowing that I did a noble thing saving someone better than myself, then it didn't matter what everyone else thought.

"I'm very thankful to you for this opportunity," I said.

"You'll do it then?" he asked, eagerly, studying me with his squinting eye.

"I will not."

"You're a difficult man ta figure, Mr. Moore," he said, shaking his head with a puzzled frown. "A difficult man ta figure." He stood then, taking his hat and overcoat from the chair where I had placed them. "Good luck ta ya, lad," he said, mustering a disappointed smile. With the overcoat flung over his arm, he stood turning his hat round and round in his hands distractedly, clearly wishing to say something more, but then thought better of it. "Well then, that'll be the end of it," he added. Cupping the hat in his giant hand he set it precisely on his gray head. "Good night," he said, and departed.

Thomas Moore

November 17th 1929

Picasso continues to grow and entertain. He still fits in the palm of my hand and is so adorable. All white with a little black nose and puppy breath. I don't know who his father was, of course, but his mother appeared to be an American Eskimo. I suspect he'll grow up to be just like Tolstoy, only smaller.

Thomas Moore

November 19th 1929

Thanksgiving approaches. I have less to be thankful for than I expected, but, wishing to be of good cheer, I drove to town to buy a turkey and celebrate the day. The car needed gasoline. Since money is again becoming scarce, I allowed one dollar for gas (it is now ten cents per gallon - scandalous) and so have half a tank, which should last quite some time. Then I went to the market and purchased a turkey, potatoes, dressing, and cranberry sauce. That was just over a dollar, so I am left with twenty-three dollars to last until more is found. It was early afternoon when I finished my shopping, and the thought of returning to the empty house was an unpleasant one. I enjoy the little town, the people, the activity, the movement. It was a welcome change from the reclusive monotony of home. I walked around town casually, looking in storefronts, watching people, enjoying the bustle of the little community. Quite accidentally, I found myself outside the window of an antique store that looked as old and inviting as anything that could be found within. On display in the window was a collection of ancient bronze boat hardware, recovered from the wreck of an old whaling ship that sank years ago, blown up on the rocks in a storm. There were giant bronze winches wearing the green patina of seawater, a barnacle encrusted harpoon, a knife carved of whalebone, a huge, battered, broken ship's wheel. I found myself irresistibly drawn inside.

A little bell above the door announced my presence when I entered. All was quiet inside the shop when I shut the door behind me. No one was behind the counter at the back. I wandered around the little shop, which was overflowing with knick-knacks and antiques. For several minutes I walked from shelf to shelf, looking at old compasses, binnacles, cleats, chocks, wooden blocks.

"You don't look like a tourist," came a voice from the back of the shop. Looking up from the ship's bell in my hand, I found a woman about my own age at the counter. I say she was about my own age, but that is a mere speculation. Her face wore a youthful appearance, but her eyes seemed old, wise almost, and her hair was black with a wide gray streak. She was tall and thin, dressed in curious garments that reminded me of a witch or gypsy. Her eyes were dark and piercing. She watched me with amused intensity, like a cat watches a mouse.

"I've lived on the island all my life," I replied.

"Really?" she answered skeptically, then reached for a large deck of cards, which she shuffled and began to lay down on the counter. She studied me carefully as I continued to look around the shop. "Would you like to know your future?" she asked at last, wearing a thin smirk.

"And you can tell it from those?" I said, with a wry smile.

"You've recently returned to the island after a long absence," she said, looking up at me as she splayed her cards on the countertop. I toyed absently with a little brass telescope.

"How long of an absence?" I asked, to test her.

"Oh," she shrugged, casually, "eight or ten years." I set down the telescope, and approached the counter where I could see her better. The cards she held were unlike any I had seen before. Instead of numbers, they had pictures on them. "Things aren't what you expected. You're all alone." She smiled now, watching my face, knowing that she had my interest. "You're looking for someone."

"Do you know where she is?" I asked, eagerly.

"You'll see her again."

"When? How?"

"I'm sorry, it's closing time," she said, unconcerned as she gathered up her cards and returned them to a wooden box on the counter. Stepping around the counter then, she took my hand and led me to the door, which she opened with her free hand. "Soon," she said, and gestured for me to leave. When the door had closed and locked behind me, I stood on the sidewalk pondering the strange conversation. And when I looked through the storefront window, I saw no sign of her within. My thoughts raced. Could she be right? Can the cards tell the future? Will I see Sophia again?

Thomas Moore

November 21st 1929

Today I read the journal...I am at a loss for words. That William played some part in Mother's death seems clear, but how? What has become of the missing pages that tell of that? Who removed them? Why? Poor, poor, Mother. My heart is sickened by all the suffering and death, and yet my spirit cries out for justice and revenge. If William were here now I wonder if I would not kill him with my bare hands. I fancy I could peer into his malicious eyes while I choked the life out of him. That such evil should have resided under this roof is unconscionable.

There is kindness and tenderness in the journal as well. Lorelei was a kind and loving woman with a faith that never wavered, and always she believed in the goodness of mankind and the greatness of the human spirit. I am moved by her faith, and touched that she felt so kindly toward me, but all of those feelings are pushed aside by the grief I feel for Mother and the rage I would like to visit upon William.

So torn was I between those emotions, that I sat beside the fire trembling with impotent rage as I read. Little Picasso came bounding playfully into the room just then, and paused, searching for me. When he spotted me, he bolted in my direction with all possible speed and, tripping in his haste, crashed head first into my leg. He shook it off with the indifference of a puppy, then sank his teeth into my pants leg and began to pull with all the force his little body could muster. I laughed through my grieving tears. What a little devil he will be one day.

I am so sad about Mother. So very, very, sad.

Thomas Moore

November 22nd 1929

My thoughts keep returning to Mother, and I find that I must know more. I must know what is written on the missing pages of this book, and who removed them. To that end, I shut myself up in Father's study and considered the matter at length, tracing the path of the journal from Lorelei's hand to mine. Only one possibility, only one conclusion, could be reached. I didn't see how it could be so, but with that thought in mind, I drove to Robert's home. It was obvious at once that he was hosting an event of some sort there. Every light in the house was blazing. Valets rushed about, parking the cars that lined the drive. Music filled the air. I simply parked behind the car in front of me, and tossed my keys to the valet as I entered the house. Observing that I wasn't dressed in the formal wear that everyone else had employed for the occasion, the doorman took particular care to ask for my invitation. With the measured indifference of a fellow who would not be troubled by such trivial things, I brushed past him, and fell in with the crowd of laughing, chatting, drinking, dancing social climbers who smiled insincerely at all around them as they gauged the social value of each potential introduction. Pushing my way through the rabble, I made my way past the band to a quiet space at the north end of the house. Nowhere did I see Robert. Uncertain of the reception I could expect from him, and caring little, I left the crowd below and searched the rest of the house.

I found him eventually in a study on the second floor, sitting at a desk with a decanter of whiskey before him and a nearly empty glass in his hand. My presence in the doorway muted the soft tones of Mozart that reached his ears, and he glanced up to find the cause.

"What took you so long?" he asked, simply.

"I only just read the journal," I answered, and crossed the room to where he sat, "and then I had to deduce why a trusted family friend would do such a thing."

"Did you?"

"That part is still a mystery." I saw the missing pages on the desk before him, next to a burning candle, and a large ashtray. He made no effort to stop me, as I reached over the desk to pick them up. I was turning to go when he finally spoke.

"Thomas," he said. I turned. "I took my duty as executor very seriously. You should know that. I never would have read the journal." As proof that he was lying, I held the missing pages up for him to see, then turned to go once more. "Wait. Just wait a moment. Please." Sighing wearily, I turned back again, and waited. "Norman startled me when he announced that you had arrived that day. I was thinking about Charles and Lorelei and was startled when he entered the study suddenly. I knocked over a glass of water that was on the desk, and it spilled over the journal that was sitting there for you. I hastily attempted to dry it off, but could see that it had already soaked into some of the pages and the ink was running. I was frantically trying to dry the pages so the ink would not smear. That's when I saw...well, that's when I saw...that." He indicated the pages in my hand. "I only had a minute. You were waiting for me. I only had a minute to make a decision. Maybe it was wrong. I may have done the wrong thing."

"Did I hear you correctly? You're not even admitting that it was wrong?"

"Legally it was, of course. But there are other scales by which one could measure."

"Like what?"

"I have very little to gain by this, Thomas. It's not for myself that I did it."

"Are you protecting someone? Is that it?" Robert didn't answer, except to level his proud eyes upon me. "Who could you be protecting?" I asked. "Not William surely?"

"You can't be serious," he said, contemptuously.

"Then who?"

"I think it should become clear to you when you've read what's in your hand."

"We'll see about that."

"I didn't know if I could trust you. Is that any surprise? Look where you've been. Remember why you were there. I feared that you might exploit the situation for financial gain."

"What situation?"

"Read the pages."

"I will," I answered, turning to go once more.

"Read them now." But I didn't want to read them then. I wanted to read them in the comfort and solitude of my own home, where I could be alone with my thoughts, where I could grieve privately. "Please, Thomas, read them now." The concerned expression on Robert's weary grieving face won me over. With a reluctant sigh, I fell into a chair across the room and held the pages to the lamp nearby to better read.

Ten minutes later, I set them down on my lap with an unsteady hand and a lump in my throat.

"I see," I said, quietly, when I finally found my voice. "No harm will come to him through me, or anything written here. You have my word," I said, struggling to maintain my composure, then stood to leave. In a sort of preoccupied daze I shuffled across the room. As an afterthought, I stopped in the doorway a moment, then turned and walked back to Robert, who watched me approach with misgivings. "You're a good man, Robert," I said, and shook his hand respectfully. He seemed quite moved by the gesture.

Thomas Moore

November 28th 1929

It is Thanksgiving Day. I put the turkey in the oven early this morning and reclined before the burning fire with a book. In a short time, the delicious smell of cooking turkey filled the house, and for perhaps the first time since my return it began to feel like home. What would everyone be doing right now if they were here, I wondered? Mother would be reading at the window, Elsie would be bustling about the kitchen making certain everything was just right, and Sophia would be sitting in a chair before the fire with her feet folded under her as she sketched in her pad. If only they were here. I struggled to remain cheerful on this day of thanks, but, being all alone in this big house, my mood was turning to melancholy and the memory of Mother's passing was one I could not shake.

The radio was in a wooden cabinet that sat forgotten in the corner of the dining room. Father said there were programs on the radio: detective programs and comedy shows that he enjoyed, but our radio produced only static. There were no radio stations close enough. Pity. It was just the sort of distraction I needed.

The piano is a family heirloom, easily as old as the house. It sits across from the fireplace, nearer the windows on other side of the room, and in the polished wood the flames sparkled. Seeking a diversion, I sat down and played for several hours. The music was like a light in the darkness driving away the gloom and despair, but like a light, the darkness returned when it stopped. As the last note dissolved to silence, and all was quiet once more, I was alone again. It was no use. Try as I might, I could not be happy on this day, especially on this day. I sat at the piano looking out the window at the gray sea stretching on and on. I knew it was foolishness, but the shop girl had given me hope that I would see Sophia again, and my thoughts turned to her.

I heard a sound then and turned my head listening. Someone was knocking at the door. Intrigued that I should have a visitor, I rose from the bench and moved swiftly to the door where I paused. Who would visit on Thanksgiving Day? Sophia? Could the girl from the antique store be right? I threw the door open and found a woman standing on the doorstep, with her back turned, looking out over the grounds as she awaited a response to her tapping. At the sound of the door swinging open, she turned inquisitively, and I found myself looking into the beautiful, welcome eyes of my childhood nanny. Her surprise at seeing me was equal to my surprise at seeing her. We stood open-mouthed gaping at each other over the threshold, looking quite silly I'm sure. Then, as if responding to the shot of a starting gun, we rushed together at the same instant, throwing our arms around each other in the doorway. Shall I remark to you who read this how very welcome she was, or how I reveled in her touch, or how I closed my eyes and simply held her to me? At length we parted and stood tenderly regarding each other in the doorway. She ran an apprising eye over me from foot to crown.

"Thomas, my lord how you've changed. You're so much bigger, and so handsome. Why, I might have passed you by if I had seen you on the street," she said, much surprised.

"And you, Elsie, look just the same as when I saw you last. As beautiful as ever." Her shy smile was just as I remembered it. I took her hand and led her inside to the fire.

"Are you cooking a turkey?" she asked, smelling the pleasant aroma.

"I'm attempting to."

"You?" she asked, surprised.

"There was no one else."

"May I have a look?"

"Your look would be most welcome," I answered, and she whisked away to the kitchen she knew so well. I heard cupboard doors open and close and pans rattling. She returned a short time later.

"I made a few little changes," she said, and took a seat at the fire.

"What brings you here, Elsie? How did you know I was home?"

"I didn't," she said. "I come every June and January to visit the cemetery."

"That's very kind. Thank you."

"Did you know," she asked, her face becoming very serious, "did you know about your mother?"

"Not until I returned."

"But you know now?" she inquired.

"I found her headstone in the cemetery," I replied.

"I'm so sorry Thomas," she said, taking my hand. "What a terrible way to find out."

"Yes," I answered sadly, and changed the subject. "What brings you here today? Isn't it a bit early for your visit?"

"I've been staying at my parent's farm on San Juan Island, and yesterday as I was passing by on the evening ferry, I saw a light in the window here. I was so surprised and curious. I was awake all night wondering if you could be home by some miracle, or if someone had purchased the estate, or if Sophia had returned. I just had to come and see."

"I'm so glad you're here," I said warmly. "Can you stay for dinner?"

"My parents will be expecting me for dinner of course, but my brother and sister will be present, so they'll have company. It seems more fitting that I dine with you. I should think you would feel very lonely in this big, empty house."

"I never knew a place could be so lonely."

"Lonelier even," she paused, searching for the right words, "even than where you were before?"

"That was a stark, friendless place. I expected it to be lonely there.

234 | *Kevin Kincheloe*

The inmates were as hard and cold as the concrete and steel that restrained them. But coming home to find an empty house nearly swallowed up by the creeping ivy, the pools overrun with blackberries and thistles, and the garden gone to seed, and sitting here in the dark, unnerving quiet each night…"

"Was it not quiet there?" she asked, softly, taking my hand.

"There was always some little sound or other. The cells were stacked eight tiers high: three concrete walls with bars on the front. There was always the sound of a steel door sliding open or closed, or footsteps, or someone coughing, or hushed voices of men talking together. Every little sound carried throughout the place and bounced off the barren surface of the concrete."

"What did you do all day, Thomas? How did you employ yourself?"

"I can think of far more pleasant things to talk about," I said, "such as you, Elsie. You look well. Have you not married in all this time?"

"Who would I marry?" she asked, smiling. "Where would I find such a soul on this little island? But I know the question that you most wish to ask," she said, coyly, holding my eye. "Go on, Thomas, ask me if you wish."

"Very well," I said, with my eyes on the floor. "Have you heard anything about her? Do you know where she is, or why she is not here?"

"It broke her heart when you went away, Thomas. It crushed her spirit. I never thought to see her like that. She tried everything she could think of to free you, and when she failed she wanted to just give up. To lie down and die. She was that distraught. She confessed to Carolyn and I one evening, before this very fire and in these same seats, that it was she who killed Rockwell and not you. Your mother always wondered why you would do such a thing and never got to speak to you about it. She was so relieved to hear Sophia's account of the accident. I know that you sacrificed yourself to save her Thomas, but Sophia would have preferred a prison cell to the one she built for herself and carried with her always for you. She never knew a moment of peace after that night."

I listened to my visitor's description of Sophia's pain, and I am ashamed to say that I was encouraged, nay, thrilled, that she had suffered for me as I had suffered for her. My mean little spirit lapped greedily, insatiably, at the news. Not that I wished for her to be miserable, or even uncomfortable on my account, but because it demonstrated that she cared for me as I cared for her.

"But where is she, Elsie? Where did she go?"

"I don't know." She shrugged. "William wanted no one to know where she was going. She didn't know herself until she claimed her ticket at the train station. But Thomas," she said, uneasily, "I should tell you, there is a rumor on the island, that William, that William…" Elsie's voice trailed off.

"Killed her?" I said, softly. "Yes, I know."

"No on has seen her or heard from her since she left the house for boarding school."

The kitchen timer rang then, indicating that the turkey was ready. Where it came from I didn't know. I had not thought to employ it. Elsie dashed away to get the food, and I set the table (the dining table, not the little kitchen table that we often used) with china, crystal, silver, and two long, slender candles. When Elsie arrived with the turkey, potatoes, and gravy, and sat down across from me, and smiled sweetly as she reached across the table to take my hand, and uttered a prayer of thanks, it felt like home again. I lifted my head at the conclusion of her prayer and, looking past her to the sky beyond, saw the cotton white clouds part suddenly and a glowing ray of sunshine issue forth to illuminate the gray sea below. The gloom was departing, driven away by the light.

We dined together that afternoon, and I believe it was the best Thanksgiving dinner that any two people have ever enjoyed. Not an extravagant meal consumed through recognized tradition and affected by established ceremony, but an event of genuine thanks experienced by two souls who were grateful for their circumstances and companionship. We talked long into the afternoon, and the constant chill that had been present since my return was eclipsed by Elsie's smile. How much more so if it had been Sophia's.

It was nearly dusk. The candles on the table cast a soothing glow that was reflected in the silver and crystal.

"I should be getting back, Thomas. My family will be worried if I don't return tonight, and the last ferry will be leaving soon." We stood up from the table and walked to the door.

"Will you be coming back?" I asked, hopefully.

"Would you like me to?"

"I would like nothing better." At that she smiled, knowing that there was perhaps one thing I might like better, but Sophia would not be returning anytime soon.

"I'm not really needed at the farm. There's work enough when the time comes, but it's the off-season now, and my parents can always find someone to work when they need them. I can come back here, if you like." She paused in the doorway, her hand on the door, looking back at me.

"I would love that," I answered eagerly, then remembered my circumstances, "but I can't pay you. I have no money."

"Oh, Thomas." She laughed. "I'll see you in a day or two." And she skipped away merrily to a car parked near the fountain. It was an old delivery van wearing the faded symbol of her father's dairy farm on the side. I watched in the fading light as it passed between the hulking maples and the taillights disappeared from sight when it turned onto the road. I shut the door with a light heart and was of good cheer as I cleared the table and washed the dishes.

Thomas Moore

November 30th 1929

I slept well that night. I remember falling asleep in my chair before the soothing flames and comforting crackle of the fire, thinking about Elsie and how different things will be with her here. Though she is only ten years older than myself, she felt of a different generation because she had been my nanny, and Sophia's too. I awoke in my chair some time later, when the fire had burned low. The blanket I had wrapped myself in was bunched on the floor at my feet and a little chill had roused me from slumber. The house was dark and quiet, but pleasantly so. How different from before. Even the promise of a houseguest has made it feel less lonely. I pushed myself up out of the chair and made my way to bed.

The next day I bustled about cleaning and preparing for Elsie.

Thomas Moore

December 6th 1929

Met Elsie at the ferry terminal and drove her home. We were both as giddy as teenagers as we eagerly wound our way along the twisting country road that led home. My home and hers. She was such a big part of my life as a child that it was almost like having Mother back again, though no one can replace Mother. I miss her terribly.

Elsie moved back into her old room and resumed her old duties, though this time without pay. I must do something about that. She had been here only a few days when she took the car to town and returned with groceries that she purchased with her own money. I saw that she had paid the utilities as well, which were soon to be turned off again. Such a kind and generous gesture on her part, but I cannot allow it to continue. I wonder if she knew what she would find here when she arrived? I didn't think to tell her, and feel horrible about it. I can do without electricity or hot water, but can't ask her to.

I have searched, probed, and explored every possible avenue to locate the family assets, but found nothing. There is only one bank on the island, and Mother's checking account there was closed shortly after her death. William withdrew all of the money in the savings account, and removed the contents of the safe deposit box before closing that as well, according to bank records. That's all they could tell me. Dispirited, I wandered absently toward the door, wondering where to look next, and ran into Mr. Gabriel, the former bank president who had retired a few years earlier. He was a friend of the family and had some news for me. There were considerable assets, he said, in the form of bonds, stocks, and real estate, but William had liquidated everything a few days after Mother's funeral. What he did with the money no one knew, but it was rumored on the island that he had a penchant for gambling. Mr. Gabriel speculated that the money was gone.

It's bad enough that I can't pay Elsie for her service, but I can't have her supporting me as well. If the money is gone, then I have no choice. I exited the bank and walked across the street to Howard Goodfriend's office, where I asked him to arrange a meeting with Herbert Mayer.

Thomas Moore

December 16th 1929

Fisherman's shacks abound on the island, and range in scope and scale from little lean-tos to fully appointed homes. One such shack sits back in the woods and is reached by a winding little trail that turns from the main road and follows a twisting, turning footpath tread by many feet. From the outside, the shack appears to have been deserted many years ago and allowed to fall into disrepair. The shingle roof is almost entirely covered in thick, green moss, upon which tree limbs have fallen from the firs and cedars nearby. The weathered siding is gray, like the trees all around it, so that it is difficult to even see and could easily be overlooked if not for the beaten path that leads to the door.

This was the location of my meeting with Herbert Mayer. Why he chose this place was a mystery to me. I knew of the place. Everyone on the island knew of the place. But why he chose to meet with me there just mystified me. I thought about it when I reached home, and concluded that he wanted to illustrate the fickle nature of the human spirit, or to introduce me to the ridiculous hypocrisy of the law.

I heard the muted murmur of many voices as I wound along the well-worn footpath in the fading light, and followed the sound as much as the trail. Both led me to the shack, which was nearly invisible at dusk, so well did it blend in with the trees and brush around it. With my hand on the door, I paused. Entering this establishment on this night, with this purpose, would introduce me to a lifestyle that I did not wish and set me on a course that I may not be able to change. Standing there in the dark, with my hand on the door, the murmur of voices and the beat of the music pouring through the walls, I thought of Elsie. I thought of her almost as I would think of Mother. Would she approve? My dear Elsie, who was driven by her industrious spirit to sweep, polish, scrub, launder, cook, stock pantry shelves, and a hundred other things without a word of complaint, would never consent to what I was about to do. She was too good, too virtuous, too honorable. Is it possible to know how the actions of one honest, hard-working soul can fly out into the world and influence the thought and character of those around them? In my mind I saw her kind yet judgmental frown as she learned of my smuggling enterprise and pictured her turning sadly, reluctantly, away, to pack her things and leave my house forever.

I considered my options again, as I had done so many times. Elsie, I knew, would continue to slip away buying groceries and paying the utilities until her money was gone. It is a grand thing to have a friend who cares so deeply for you that they would sacrifice all for your benefit. It is grand, and troubling. Each time I sat down to a meal (which Elsie prepared), I was mindful that she had purchased the groceries with her own money, and felt awkward. There was nothing in her manner to suggest that anything was different. She served the meal with a smile as she had always done, but it left a bitter taste in my mouth that the wine would not wash away. Each time I turned the page of the book that I read by the light of the lamp beside my chair, I was aware that the light was provided by the generosity of Elsie's purse. I felt inadequate, like a beggar on the street. The only way to stop her was to send her home, and I could not suffer another day of solitude in that empty house.

Taking a deep breath, I pushed open the door and stepped into the glare of lights, music, laughter, dancing, cigarette smoke, and noise. The inside of the place was as lavish as the outside was barren. A band played on a stage at one end of the room. Several overworked bartenders hustled to keep up with drink orders at the bar in the center, and at the other end of the shack, as far from the stage as possible, Herbert sat at a table alone, a glass of whisky before him. He looked oddly out of place there, a tired old man staring thoughtfully into his whisky glass, wishing to be alone in a crowded room bustling with laughter and activity. I pushed my way through the crowd and took a reluctant seat across from him. If he was dogged and followed everywhere, as he claimed before, then there would almost certainly be spies in the crowd watching him at that moment, and my presence at his table would introduce me to them. It seemed unwise, but I dropped into the chair and cast a furtive eye about me. A weary frown was all he could muster as he glanced at his watch on the wrist of the hand that held his shot glass.

"Have trouble findin' the place?"

"I just...I was..."

"Havin' second thoughts about comin?" For all his plain speech and simple ways, Herbert was a clever man. He studied me at I sat across from him groping for words in that noisy, bustling room and read in my face and manner all that was in my heart. "All right, then," he said, at last, more to himself than to me, as he apparently reached a decision. He glanced around the room then, hoping to find a distraction of some sort, and finding none, grabbed his shot glass almost as an afterthought, and tossed it back. With his eyes clenched tightly shut, he tilted his head, grimacing, then his whole frame shuddered and he slapped his leg as he always did after a drink. When he opened his eyes again he was looking across the room at a table behind me. "See those fellas over there?" he said, in a hoarse voice still smarting from the whiskey, and jerked his head in the direction indicated. I propped my arm on the table and leaned my head on my hand as casually as I could before turning surreptitiously to glance in the most obviously un-casual manner at the table, where two clean-cut gentlemen were sharing a drink. There was nothing remarkable about them. I thought Herbert would tell me they were spies watching his every move and that they should be avoided at all costs, but they didn't appear to notice us at all. I turned back to the table, puzzled.

Amid all the noise and clamor, with the bartenders bustling frantically and patrons jostling at the bar to order, Herbert had scarcely returned his empty glass to the table before a smiling young server girl swept it away and replaced it with another. "Thanks Sally," he said, his eyes never leaving mine as he studied me steadily behind those bristling brows. "See those fellas over there?" he asked again, indicating a table behind me on the other side. "The three with their wives," he added. The table was across the room and in the space separating us people were walking and milling about, making it difficult to see around them. For some time I strained to see the group through the little gaps that presented as people walked and shifted about. Finally, for a few brief seconds, I caught an unobstructed view of them and saw three handsome, well-dressed men accompanied by three beautiful, well-dressed women. They were all laughing, smiling, drinking heavily, and obviously on intimate terms with each other.

"What about them?" I inquired, as I turned back to the table, but Herbert was gone, his seat empty. Overcoming my momentary surprise, I quickly scanned the room for him but saw his large frame nowhere in the bustling throng. Then I noticed the shot glass. It was still filled with whiskey, but had been pushed across the table to the space where I sat. The gesture was clear. It was for me, and he was gone.

I was still pondering his silent departure when I closed the great oak door behind me and entered the house. Sitting beside the fire, a blanket over her legs, Elsie read a book by the glowing light of the flames beside her, looking snug and content. But, feeling the rush of cold air that I carried in with me, I saw a shudder run through her, and as she shifted to pull the blanket tighter about her legs, she glimpsed me entering the room.

"Oh, Thomas, there you are. I didn't know you were gone until I tried to find you for dinner," she said, seeing me in my coat. "Why didn't you tell me you were going out?"

"I intended to be gone only a minute," I said, lying to her for the first time in my life.

"Where have you been?" she inquired, innocently. "Did you go to the shipyard to check on the boats?" I sometimes went to the boatyard to check that the mooring lines were secure when it was stormy.

"Yes. I went to the shipyard," I answered, lying to her again, then slinked away before she could wrench any more deceit from my skulking heart and shut myself in the study feeling quite wretched. It was only a little lie, but to deceive Elsie of all people, sweet, kind, always forgiving Elsie, weighed heavily upon me. I opened the window and looked out into the night at the trees swaying in the darkness under the light of the crescent moon piercing the clouds, and the rustling boughs seemed to speak furtively one to another that there was a liar present, watching from the open window.

With a restless sort of indecision, I closed the window and wandered about the study, eventually dropping into a chair at the desk. With my arms on the desk and my head on my arms, I sat in my father's chair wondering how I would ever face Elsie again. To my awakened conscience, even the silence of the room cried out that I was a deceitful villain.

When I lifted my head at last, my eye fell upon Grandfather glaring down at me with a disappointed scowl. I studied his portrait, occupying a prominent place over the fire, and saw a kind of magnificence in his proud eyes, a confidence in his bearing, an independence in his stern face, that spoke of a time when men had manners and honor and truth. Those proud eyes were watching me now in a fixed stare that pierced my soul, challenging my character, questioning my integrity. They were asking what I was going to do, prodding me to find a solution that would not compromise all he had achieved and passed down to me from father to son.

There was a soft knock at the door then, and Elsie entered tentatively with two cups in her hands.

"I thought you might like a little tea. You must be quite chilled after knocking around down there among the boats. It's been raining all afternoon," she said, setting a cup on the desk before me. "Aren't you cold, Thomas?" she added frowning, seeing the water that had dripped from my coat to form a pool below my chair.

"Elsie," I said, standing suddenly to remove my heavy overcoat, looking up at her kind, honest face. "I...I wasn't at the boatyard."

"No?"

"I was at a business meeting," I said, lowering my eyes to the teacup before me and keeping them there.

"Why did you say..."

"I didn't want you to worry," I interrupted.

"Why would I worry? That's wonderful," she added enthusiastically. "Why would I worry?" I kept my head down and my eyes on the teacup. After a long, silent pause, I cast a sidelong glance in her direction, and she perceived in my manner that something was amiss. "What sort of business?" she asked, frowning.

"The kind that'll keep the lights on and food on the table."

"I have money enough for that, Thomas, you needn't worry about that."

"Elsie," I said, taking her hands in mine, "you should be receiving wages from me, not paying my bills."

"I don't mind. Daniel and Carolyn were quite good to me. I want to help."

"I know you do." I took her slender hand and pressed it to my cheek, as I looked into her kind, questioning eyes. "But surely you see that I can't allow it to continue. I'm so thankful for your help, Elsie, but it can't continue." She hung her head, knowing that it was true. The expense of maintaining the estate would soon exhaust her meager resources, but more than that it was a matter of honor. I simply couldn't live at her expense.

"What will you do?" she asked, quietly, her eyes on the floor. "What can you do, Thomas?" Elsie lifted her head, studying my face. "What sort of business meeting was this?" she asked, with a hint of suspicion. I scratched my head nervously, and glanced about the study, looking anywhere but at her. "You're not thinking of selling the estate?" she asked, horrified.

"Of course not."

"Well, what then?"

"I'm thinking of getting into the import business," I responded flatly. Elsie raised a finger to her chin and regarded me sternly, the way Mother would when scolding me.

"And what will you be importing?" she asked, her gaze boring into me.

"Commodities in Canada that are not available here," I added, in my best business voice.

"Ah, commodities in Canada that are not available here," she repeated, under her breath, and held my eye by the flickering light of the blazing fire. A wry smile played on her lips and she laughed out loud as she turned, and began across the study. "Thomas, you're so silly."

"What?" I answered, somewhat put off by her cavalier attitude. "What do you mean?"

"That's what this is all about?" She had paused at the door and turned to face me. "That's why you've been staring thoughtfully into the fire, and gazing out over the sea, and sighing, and moping about the house?" She watched me inquisitively, waiting for an answer. "I thought it was about Sophia. I felt so sorry for you thinking you were missing her. I never dreamed you were thinking of becoming a 'Businessman'," she added, with a smirk. "So, what's the problem? Are you afraid of getting caught and going back to jail?"

"Of course not," I answered, offended that she would think me a coward.

"Well, what then?" she asked, sounding very much like Mother. "Come, tell me."

"All right. I don't want to dishonor the family name." My

confession took her by surprise, and she paused with a meditative frown.

"That's very noble of you," she said at last, "but I think…" She was groping for the right words.

"Think what?"

"Well, I think," she said, cautiously, "that your sentiment may be misplaced."

"What do you mean by that?" I asked, somewhat mystified.

Elsie walked back to the study, taking a seat on the hearth, and patted the space next to her in an invitation to join her there. We sat together in the soothing warmth of the fire, the only sounds the rain pelting the windows and the gusting wind.

"You didn't know your grandfather, or even your father, that well, did you?"

"No."

"Thomas," she said, uncertain of how to proceed, "I think you may be a little naive." And when she saw me bristle, added quickly, "In a good way. You're naive, and charming, and noble, and chivalrous. It's one of the reasons Carolyn wanted you to spend time with Sophia. We thought that a well-traveled tomboy was just what you needed to expand your worldview."

"But why, Elsie? I asked, hurt. "Am I that simple? Have I been that sheltered?"

"No. No, of course not," she added, quickly. "You're honest, and virtuous, and brave. What you did for Sophia," the tears were welling in Elsie's gentle eyes, "that was the most noble, precious thing. I adore you for that." She paused a moment to wipe her eyes, then regarded me steadily. "But you see, your worldview has been shaped almost entirely by the books you read. You had never really been beyond the borders of the estate, so you didn't know what the world was like outside. Even if you had explored the whole island, it wouldn't have helped. It's different here. The world isn't like in your books, Thomas. People aren't that honest and noble. I thought you might have learned that when you went away. I feared that you would return angry and bitter at what you found and suffered." I took a deep breath and thought about her words.

"I'm not angry, Elsie," I said. "And I'm not bitter."

"No," she said, watching me closely, "and you're not naive

anymore, either. Not as you were before. If you get into this import business you're talking about, you won't be doing anything your grandfather wouldn't do."

"Really?" I asked doubtfully.

"He was above all a businessman. As soon as this foolish prohibition passed, he would have begun organizing a fleet of boats to start importing from Canada. He wouldn't have required financial pressure to motivate him."

"But," I began, rather confused, "Mother always said what an honest, hard working man he was. He built the shipyard himself, with his own hands, and worked two jobs to get money enough to begin. He was a fine man."

"Yes, he was all of those things," she said earnestly. "He would never steal or cheat anyone; he was an honest man. But this is different. It's just alcohol. You're not robbing banks. You're not cheating widows out of their life savings."

"And if I got caught?"

"It wouldn't be an embarrassment to the family name. No one on the island would think any less of you," she said, with her sweet nanny smile. "Always so noble." Then she kissed me on the cheek and whisked away, leaving me alone on the hearth to ponder her words. I turned again to grandfather's portrait on the wall overhead. He seemed different somehow. Less rigid and inflexible. Less stern. Did I detect a certain playfulness in those proud eyes that I hadn't noticed before? Perhaps the suggestion of a smile on those stern lips? When viewed from one perspective it appeared to be a frown, but from another it could have been a smile. Maybe one sees whatever one expects to see in it. Why had I not seen a smile in that face before? Maybe, for the first time in a considerable period, fate is smiling down upon me.

Thomas Moore

December 18th 1929

It would seem that a second meeting with Herbert is much more difficult to orchestrate than the first. I left word with Howard that I would like to meet with him again and, after a wait of several days, was told that there would be no meeting. I don't blame Herbert for changing his mind and rescinding his offer. I'm certain he sensed the hesitancy and lack of commitment on my part. The offer he made to me was quite generous, and he may have been offended by my lack of interest. He's a good man. I find no fault in him.

Can I do it without Herbert? I already have a boat that I can use to transport the goods, and I can legally purchase all I want of alcohol in Canada. The problems: I haven't any money to purchase the goods and I have no network to sell to on the island. Big problems, these. I've gone through the house in an effort to locate anything that I could sell for investment capital, but it's all gone. All of the valuable artwork, the paintings and sculptures that once adorned the halls and living spaces, are missing. All of Mother's jewels are missing as well. It seems William had sufficient time to thoroughly plunder the estate and squander all of the proceeds. The only thing of any real value at this time is the machinery and equipment at the boatyard. There is no market for it, however, since no one is building boats at present, and, anyway, I would like to one day revive the yard and build boats again, so I will require it. What can I do?

I spoke to Mark Peterson, the owner of The Shack, about selling to him, but he was adamant. He already has an exclusive deal with someone else he said. I don't see how I can make this happen.

Thomas Moore

December 22nd 1929

Yesterday afternoon, I had gone upstairs to the library for a book and was passing through the main room where we would often gather before the cracking fire. There was always a sunset to be witnessed from that room. Regardless of the weather or patches of cloud that clung to the afternoon sky, the sun would fall below the clouds on the horizon before sinking into the sea and there were a few brief moments of glowing color before it vanished. As I passed Mother's seat, I paused with a hand on the chair back, watching that brief moment of sunset. Mother should be here, would be here, if not for William, I mused. Sophia too. Life is made up of so many partings woven together by time and fate, or torn asunder by destiny. I have lost Father, and Mother, and Sophia. I would not loose Elsie. I must find an income. I was thinking about her when I heard her voice behind.

"Thomas," came the soft inquiry. The house was quiet, with a peaceful serenity that came each sunset, and her soft voice was like a ray of fading sunlight. I turned to find that she was sitting next to the fire with her legs folded under her as she worked at her knitting. "I was hoping to have a word with you."

"What is it, Elsie?" I asked, and slipped into the seat opposite her at the fire.

"I find that I'm making beds all over the house," she said, with a playful smile. "How many people are sleeping here each night?"

"I'm sorry," I answered. I couldn't sleep in my old room, and hadn't been able to settle into any particular place. I would just sleep wherever it seemed best each night. Often in one of the guest rooms, but sometimes a sofa or chair. "I'll make my own bed."

"Dear boy," she looked up from her knitting and smiled, "I don't mind the work. I'm only concerned about you. Is there something wrong with your old room?" Perhaps it was the uncomfortable shifting in my seat, or the way I suddenly grabbed the poker to stir the fire, but I felt that she read my thought as clearly as if I had spoken, and I was embarrassed by it. There was something wrong with my old room. I could no longer enter it without becoming painfully aware of how foolish and naive I had once been, or how simple and trusting I once was. All of the furnishings, from the sailboat model on my desk to the book I was reading when I went away (Treasure Island), reminded me of what a silly little boy I was then. It was that boy that allowed all of this to happen. It was his fault that this misfortune was visited upon us, and each time I passed my old room it was a glaring reminder of how inadequate I had been in defending my family.

I gave the fire a final angry stir with the poker, then returned it to the stand on the hearth and remained with my back to her so she could not see my face. Elsie always knew me so well. When I turned at last, she was knitting again, and I saw in the hesitant action of her fingers when she saw my face, as plainly as if she had told me with her lips, that I was not to blame for what had happened. But I knew better. As if perceiving my thought, she added gently:

"It's not your fault, Thomas. Really it's not."

"Yes," I answered, firmly, "it is." And I left the room.

Thomas Moore

December 24th 1929

It is Christmas Eve, a bittersweet, nostalgic day for me. Thinking to bring warmth and good cheer to the house, Elsie decorated while I was at the boatyard a few days ago. I returned to find candles in the windows, a wreath on the door, and a decorated Christmas tree near the fire. She greeted me with hot buttered rum, and we settled into chairs beside the fireplace. It was cozy and warm, especially with the rain drumming on the windows and the wind gusting outside, but something was missing. Neither of us spoke. We were both lost in our own thoughts, missing Mother and Father and Sophia. Elsie at least has family on San Juan Island, and tomorrow leaves to be with them on Christmas day. She asked if she might not stay with me, but I insisted that she go. Why ruin Christmas for her?

Thomas Moore

January 12th 1930

Elsie, my dear, sweet Elsie, has made the empty house so much more comfortable. I treasure and adore her, but today I needed to get away from the estate for a time. The little town here on the island is no thriving metropolis teeming with people and activity, but it felt good to walk along the street and gaze into the storefronts. Quite accidentally, I found myself at the little antique store and stepped inside. I wanted to have a word with the girl there, anyway. A question had been weighing on my mind which only she could answer, but when I entered I noticed a different woman behind the counter. She was much older. A stout Scandinavian woman with wild gray hair that hadn't seen a brush in quite some time. It fell about her face randomly, wherever it liked, and reminded me of a bird's nest. Her cheeks had a rosy, pleasant glow, her eyes were keen, her hands twisted and arthritic.

"May I help you find something?" she asked.

"I was hoping for a word with the young girl who sometimes works here."

"What's your interest in her?" she inquired, lowering her head to look at me over her reading glasses.

"She told me some things last time I was here. I have a few questions for her."

"What sort of things?"

"Personal things."

"I see," she said, and there was an amused smile in her lively old eyes. She reached into a drawer under the counter and produced a deck of cards, which she slapped down on the countertop. "Was she using these?"

"Yes," I answered, a little surprised. The woman shook her head, smiling.

"That girl has a playful side," she said, "I'll give her that."

"What do you mean?" I asked, curiously.

"She's just a young girl with a very active imagination."

"I don't understand."

"She's no fortune teller. That's my granddaughter, Deanna. She played a Gypsy fortune-teller in a school play once, and she's been hoodwinking honest folks like yourself ever since. It's good sport, I guess."

"Are you quite sure?"

"Known her all of her young life. Quite sure."

"But how could she know…" I paused, thinking. How could she have known those things about me?

"What did she tell ya?"

"First she said I didn't look like a tourist."

"Yeah, no mystery there. Then what?"

"Then I said I had lived on the island all my life."

"Lived on the island all your life, eh?" She studied me closely from behind the counter, her keen eyes boring into mine while she rubbed her twisted hands together. "Guess that would make you Thomas Moore, then, recently returned from prison for killin' the judge's boy."

"But, how could you know that?" I asked, astonished.

"Son," she said patiently, "I've never laid eyes on you in my life. If you grew up on this island you could only be Thomas Moore, stuck out there in that mansion where no one ever goes. Folks knew your mother and father some, we'd see 'em around town now and then, and everyone knows Elsie. But no one's ever really seen you. If you grew up on this island, you could only be Thomas Moore." And while I stood open mouthed, staring at her, she added, "If I had used these," she indicated the tarot cards, "to tell you the same thing, you'd be thinking I was a fortune teller. That's all Deanna did." I still couldn't believe I had been so gullible and lowered my head, embarrassed. "Did you give her any money?" I shook my head. "Well then, no harm done."

"Thank you for your time," I said, shamefaced, and quietly departed.

It was cold and wet, of course. December days are always cold, wet, and short. I pulled my coat collar up against the wind and rain and walked along the sidewalk in the direction of my car a few blocks away off the main street. Whatever interest I had in seeing the town was lost. I huddled deeper in my coat as I walked along the sidewalk, with my eyes on the ground. The rain fell quietly and the wind blew in little flurries, finding the seams of my coat. Feeling every inch the fool, I stepped off the main street and made my way to a little alley behind the row of stores. I was reaching for my car key when my arms were suddenly pinned down and a bag was pulled rudely over my head. Without a word, I was pulled roughly along the street and shoved into the back seat of a car.

"Who is this? What are you doing? You've got the wrong person," I said, struggling wildly to free myself. I felt someone slide onto the seat beside me and heard the car doors close. "Let me go!" I said, struggling to remove the hood over my head. But just then I felt the sharp edge of a blade pressed to my throat.

"Hold on there, mate. I wouldn't want ta spill yer blood. It's bloody difficult ta get the stain out a this upholstery." I relaxed back into the seat and the blade was removed. I heard the engine start and felt the car lurch ahead. We drove on through the little town, and then into the country. All the time I was aware of the man beside me. His leg was pressed against mine and I imagined him holding the knife in his hand. In fifteen minutes or so the car stopped, and the engine was shut off. I heard two car doors open and felt the man next to me slide over and get out.

"All right mate, come along now," he said, and I felt his hand on my arm pulling me across the seat toward him. I got out of the car and was led along a smooth path, down a slight hill, and through a door into a building. I could hear my two captors speaking quietly together as they led me along and caught an occasional word here and there... "Tie him up...beat him...shovel..." and the like. Eventually I was pushed roughly into a wooden chair and my arms were secured to the sides. Then the hood was removed from my face, but I could see nothing. The room was dark but for a blinding light that glared into my face.

"Who are you? What are you doing with me? Do you even know who I am?" I asked the darkness.

"We'll ask the questions here, Mr. Moore. Tell us what we wanna know and ya might walk outta here with both legs," came a voice behind the light, speaking with a heavy accent.

"What do you want to know?"

"What do ya know about Herbert Mayer?"

"Who?"

"What are ya, an owl? Herbert Mayer."

"I don't know anyone by that name."

"We happen ta know that ya do mate."

"You're mistaken."

"Mr. Moore, my companion here likes a baseball bat fer this sort of thing, but I prefer a rubber hose. I just don't care fer the sound a breakin' bone. That smart little crack that the hose makes when it slaps yer skin, now that's music ta my ears." A long, silent pause followed. Finally he began again. "Well?" he asked.

"Well, what?" I answered.

"Am I gonna need the hose?" he asked. I was tied to the chair, squinting into the glaring light, trying to make out the two vague shapes that stood behind it threatening to beat me, but I wasn't frightened. I wasn't frightened in the least. I was angry. I was furious that I had served nine years in prison for a girl I would never see again. That I had returned to a cold, empty house. That Mother was dead. That William had squandered all of the family fortune.

That my faith in the goodness of God had been misplaced. That I was so naive a teenage girl could make a fool of me. And now this. I was frustrated, annoyed, and angry. Everyone on the island seemed to know of me.

"If you know who I am, then you know what I've done, and what I'm capable of," I said, with a quiet calmness that was easily heard in the silence of the dark room. "Touch me with a hose or bat and I'll beat you to death with it."

Nothing was said after that. I sensed surprise, and an uneasy shuffling of the two men and then I heard the door open and close. They were gone. I sat alone in the room with the light beating down upon me. Thirty or forty minutes passed. In the absolute stillness that followed, I thought I heard the faint rush of the ocean and the distant call of a seagull. Eventually I caught the first vague ring of voices that grew clearer and more distinct as they approached. Unless I was mistaken, there was a new voice.

"...you bringing me down here? What's this all about?" asked the new man.

"...little surprise."

I heard the latch turn and saw a dim sliver of light that gradually grew as the door opened. Three men were silhouetted in the opening. A brief silence followed as the new man took in the scene, and then he rushed forward.

"Good God, Jack, what have ya done?" he said, as he rushed to me and began untying the rope that bound me to the chair. "I'm so sorry Thomas. Ya have ta forgive 'em. I hope no harm was done. Are ya all right lad?" he said, and took my hand, pulling me up out of the chair. "Are ya all right?" The light had been at his back, but when he turned to help me up, I saw that it was Herbert, and he looked so concerned.

"Yes, I'm fine. I'm unhurt."

"Thank God," he said, and took me by the arm to lead me away. Passing through the doorway, I felt the rush of salty night air and looked ahead to see the beach nearby, and the top of the sun setting into the ocean in a feeble little burst of color. The rain had stopped. Herbert led me to a blazing fire on the sandy beach, around which driftwood logs had been cut into blocks and used as seats. The other two men followed sheepishly behind, and we all took seats around the fire. I saw then that I had been held in a good-sized beach shed and that beyond it, further back from the surf, was a large home with light issuing from the many windows.

"What the blazes were ya thinking, Jack?" Hebert asked, looking roughly at the man beside me. He was a thin fellow, with sunken cheeks and a long face. His hands, I noticed, were rough, and he slouched on the stump seat as if bent from hard work. He wasn't much older than me, but looked a great deal older.

"Ya said ta bring him out here," Jack answered, with a thick Australian accent. He removed the gnawed stub of a wet cigar from his mouth and pointed it at Herbert. "He's in good nick."

"We're not gangsters. We'll never be gangsters. We don't do things like that." Then he turned to me and added kindly, "I'm so sorry about this, Thomas. I asked the fellas to bring ya out here, ya see. I guess somethin' got last in translation."

"There wasn't nothing lost nowhere, mate," Jack said crossly. "I wanted ta have some fun with the bloke and see what he was made of." He turned his defiant eyes upon Herbert and continued, "If I'm gonna be taking orders from this silver spoon dandy and puttin' myself in harm's way, I wanna know what he's made of and if he's gonna peach on us." He shoved the cigar back in his mouth then turned his angry eyes upon me.

"Silver spoon?" I asked.

"What would ya call it, then? Born in that big old mansion, surrounded by servants, never worked a day in yer life."

"I was imprisoned before I was old enough to work."

"Too good ta go ta public school."

"Did ya find out what he was made of, Jack?" asked Herbert. "Cause my money's on Thomas, there. Did ya find out what ya wanted ta know?"

"He's a stand up guy," answered the other man, whom I later learned was Martin. He was a big, soft-spoken, quiet man, with kind eyes and a gentle manner. "Jack threatened him with everything he could think of, and Thomas wouldn't talk. He wouldn't even acknowledge knowing you, Herbert."

"That right, Jack?" asked a smug Herbert. Martin slipped away and returned a moment later with cold beer for everyone. For hours we sat on the beach feeding driftwood into the fire as we drank and talked by the light of the flames. A gentle breeze blew in over the water as the surf washed rhythmically over the wet sand, nearly reaching us at times. I came to know Herbert, Martin, and even Jack as our campfire talk stretched late into the night and the drinks continued. I had never had beer before, and liked it. For the others, it was probably a routine event that they had experienced many times in the course of their alliance, but for me it was a cherished camaraderie with the promise of budding friendship. For perhaps the first time in my life, I felt as though I was not alone, that these men could become my friends. And, as ridiculous as it sounds, I had never had a friend before outside of Sophia. In all of my sequestered young life at the estate, there had been no boys my age to play with, or talk to, or confide in. I had grown up alone.

I looked around the circle at everyone's face while Herbert told us about how he met his wife on his way home from the dock one afternoon, at the tender young age of twenty-three. They all looked into the flickering flames, listening respectfully, with warm interest as he recounted how he came upon her beside the road, pondering how to get home on her bike, which had a flat tire. He walked her home that day, and the next, and the day after that as well, and two months later they were married.

Everyone was quiet when Herbert finished. The bottles were empty and had been for quite some time. It was late and we were all tired, but it seemed that everyone enjoyed the peaceful serenity of the warm fire and the soothing roar of the surf as it broke on the beach. At length Herbert broke the silence.

"Give Thomas a ride back to his car, Jack," he said, standing stiffly. Then he turned to me and extended his hand. "And thank you for joinin' us."

"Why did you want me here tonight, Herbert?"

"We never really got round ta that, did we?" he said, attempting to straighten his stiff limbs. "I heard ya made an effort ta establish yerself as an importer after I failed ta meet with ya the second time. It sounded like ya had overcome those moral objections or legal considerations that gave ya pause before. It sounded like ya was ready. Did I read that right?"

"You did, yes."

"Come back over in a few days, an we'll talk about patic'lars."

"Okay," I said, and turned to follow Jack who was starting for the car. "Herbert?" I added, as an afterthought.

"Yeah."

"Those two men that you pointed out at The Shack that night. Who were they?"

"A couple a prohibition officers."

"Prohibition officers?" I asked, in my naivety. "Really?" Herbert nodded, with a smirk. "And the three men with their wives?"

"Judge Norman, Judge Jones, and Jerry Daniels, our new District Attorney."

I'm certain Herbert found amusement in the confused furrow of my brow and the puzzled wonder in my eyes. With a smile and a shake of his head, he turned once more and began up the path to his home.

Jack drove me back to my car. It was a silent trip as we wound along the dark country road, through the tall timber that sometimes offered a view of the ocean. He chewed on his cigar, not once looking my way or acknowledging my presence, and I saw in his stoic face, illuminated by the muted glow of the instrument lights, that he probably still longed for a chance to use that rubber hose. When we reached my car, he sat motionless with his hands on the wheel. Chewing on his cigar while the engine ran, he looked silently ahead, waiting for me to get out. I did. And when I bent down to the open car window to thank him, the car shot forward before I could utter a word.

The house was dark when I arrived. I entered quietly and found Elsie asleep in her chair before the fire, which had burned down to a few faintly glowing embers. Picasso was curled into a ball, sleeping at her feet. I draped a blanket over her and continued upstairs to Sophia's room. It was the one bed in the house that always seemed to fit me, but it carried with it a bittersweet remembrance that I didn't always wish to entertain. I could not but smile when I recalled how I first saw her in that giant canopy bed. A little ten-year-old girl squirming and twisting under the covers, rubbing the soft sheets upon her delicate face, smiling delightedly as the luxury of the moment washed over her. But my joy would invariably fade with the knowledge that I would never see her smile from that bed again. So many times had I wondered how she met her fate and what William had done with her. If only she had a grave in the family cemetery. If only I could visit her there, but I was not afforded even that simple consideration. I would never know what became of my dear Sophia, I mused as I crawled under the covers and, with a heavy heart, switched off the lamp.

Thomas Moore

January 14th 1930

Small wonder that I awoke in Sophia's bed exhausted, after a restless night of unpleasant dreams that left me thinking about her. Perhaps it was her portrait on the easel across the room. I could just see her face watching me from the shadows, and it was as if her spirit were calling silently to me from the grave, asking why I had failed to protect her. Where is she? What did William do with her?

So many terrible dreams troubled my sleep that I rose from her bed at last and went downstairs to the fire in the main room. Elsie was gone to bed by then, so I fell into her seat, still warm from her presence, and eventually drifted off to sleep with Picasso at my feet. If anyone could inspire sweet dreams it is he. It is almost as if little Picasso is the incarnation of young Sophia, so bright and playful is he. I awoke refreshed late in the morning to the sound of Elsie making breakfast, and as I turned in the chair my eye fell upon the rain-spattered window that offered the familiar view of the cemetery. Much as I loathed to admit it, what was needed was a headstone for Sophia. She needed her place there with the rest of the family where I could see her and visit her and speak with her. I could finally acknowledge her death then, and we could find closure, Elsie and I. For she still entertained a false hope that Sophia would return to us one day. She didn't speak of it, but I could see it in her manner and in the way she sat knitting or reading, always listening for a knock at the door. Whenever there was one she would immediately stop what she was doing and rush excitedly to see who it might be. It was never anything more than a wandering vagabond looking for work, yet I knew she hoped each time to find Sophia on the doorstep with a portmanteau in her hand and a smile on her face. But she has not seen the letter that I found on the mantle, and I will not tell her of it.

I drove into town after breakfast and ordered a headstone from the stonemason's shop. When I returned, Elsie and I changed clothes and had a service for Sophia. We stood somberly among the headstones, I in a black suit, she in a black dress, huddled together under a black umbrella as the rain fell quietly about us. I could not begin and neither could she. We could not find the words. So many graves have opened in the path of my life. I thought of the words that Sophia spoke at the fishpond so many years ago when she named the estate Ravenswood and said it was a magical place where nothing bad ever happened. How terribly mistaken she had been.

Elsie's hand was cold and trembling when she slipped it into mine, and her troubled eyes fell upon the wet ground where Sophia's headstone would eventually be. I had never seen her face so drawn and sad. Her lip quivered, I felt her body tremble, and then she turned suddenly, burying her face in my chest as she burst into tears. The service concluded without a word spoken, and we returned somberly to the house. Elsie threw herself into the chair near the fire and picked up Picasso. I saw her pet him tenderly, taking comfort in his cute little puppy face as he lapped the salty tears streaming over her sad cheeks.

I went upstairs to Sophia's room for one last look, then locked the door. I will not enter it again.

Thomas Moore

March 30th 1930

Months have passed since my last entry. I wished to forget about love and death and the pain that accompanies each, so I threw myself into my new enterprise. My first trip to Canada in *Mary Adda* was a casual adventure that began a few days after Sophia's funeral. I drove the car to the boatyard, which offered a neglected, melancholy appearance, and parked near the shop. Baked by the summer sun and pounded by winter rain, the white paint was flaking off in patches, littering the ground below, while the grimy windowpanes were broken out in many places, affording access to the swallows that flew in and out. There was a sort of rustic charm to the place, with its peeling paint and broken windows and rusty old machinery entangled in blackberry vines and tall grass. It looked so picturesque in its abandon and neglect. It broke my heart.

I tossed the mooring lines on the dock, started the engine, and motored away without looking back. *Mary Adda* handled well. We headed west, taking the wind on our nose and bobbing ever so gently with the little swells that broke on her plumb bow. I smiled. It was delicious to be on the water again. To feel the motion of the boat as it worked with the swells, to taste the salt air and drink in the lovely blue sea. It was a beautiful, cloudless day, early in the spring, and I felt the thrill of adventure and the rush of life that I hadn't know since Sophia and I sailed together on *Diva* all those years ago. My heart has always been with the ocean and returning to it that day was like embracing an old friend. I passed Jones Island where Sophia and I had often anchored in a quiet bay, and then rounded the north end of San Juan Island. In three hours or so I was pulling into a quiet harbor at Sidney, and tied up where I could find space on the crowded dock as the last rays of the sun were sinking into the ocean. Herbert said the Prohibition Officers had men on all of the major docks nearby, and they were constantly alert for visiting boats that were taking on illegal cargo. They could do nothing in Canada, of course, but they would note the boat, and the course it took when it departed, and their men would be waiting for it when it returned to the islands. It was best, Herbert said, to arrive after dark.

I had only just tied the boat to the mooring cleats and was rising to have a look about me when two men suddenly appeared.

"You'll be Mr. Moore then?" one of them asked, "Mr. Thomas Moore?"

"That's right."

"Herbert said to expect you," he added, all business. "Where do ya want it?"

"Um…in the salon."

"Right," he said, then he and his companion took opposite ends of a canvas tarp that had been covering a lump of goods on the dock, and pulled it away. Beneath it was a formidable collection of wooden crates, neatly stacked next to the boat. They had undoubtedly kept this slip open for me on the busy dock after carrying the crates there. With an efficiency that told of long practice, they had the cargo stowed below in the salon of the yacht within minutes, and the leader, the one who had done the talking, paused after stepping off the boat one last time. He was breathing hard and sweating when he extended a hand.

"That's a damned fine boat," he said, with an admiring eye. "Be careful headin' back. I saw a few unfamiliar faces earlier. I'd turn my nav lights on and head north for a ways if I was you. Then turn 'em off, and turn back east toward the island."

"Thank you," I said, shaking his hand, and then he and his friend departed. It couldn't have been more than thirty minutes from the time I reached the dock until the time I started the engine and began back home. With my navigation lights on, I headed north for twenty minutes, until it was quite dark, then switched them off and turned east toward Orcas Island.

Only a sliver of crescent moon was visible in the clear night sky, and by that faint light *Mary Adda* would be hard to spot on the dark water. I enjoyed a pleasant trip back. There was the faintest breeze whisking over the dark water and the tiniest little waves that lapped at the elegant hull with a music that I found soothing. The boat rocked with a gentle rhythm that nearly lulled me to sleep. I passed Jones Island again, then on to Deer Harbor and the boatyard. Martin and Jack were waiting when I arrived. They were lying on the dock using their jackets as pillows as they kept a watch and awaited my return. Martin sprang up to catch the boat and tie her to the dock. Jack just watched indifferently. When the boat was secure, and the engine off, he rose at last, making his cross way to the vessel where he sullenly began offloading the cargo without a word.

Elsie was waiting anxiously when I returned just before midnight, and listened excitedly when I told her of my adventure. It was an uneventful but profitable journey, and we toasted my success with a glass of sherry while sitting at the blazing fire in the main room. She was proud of me, she said, with a look that I had often seen in Mother's eyes, then kissed me on the cheek and went off to bed with Picasso following close behind. When I climbed the stairs toward bed some time later, it was to the master bedroom that my feet carried me, to the room that belonged to my parents. I was master of the house now and, for perhaps the first time in my life, felt like a man. I would take charge of the family estate. I would restore the family fortune. I would revive the family business and return the family honor. When I pulled back the covers and slipped between the sheets of the bed that had belonged to my father, and my grandfather before him, I felt as though I were carving my own place in the Moore history.

Herbert had an exclusive arrangement with Mark Peterson, and it called for him to provide enough inventory that The Shack would be fully stocked at all times. I found that I was often at the helm of *Mary Adda*, but avoided a regular routine or schedule so that no one could predict my movements. I varied my departures, changed my course, and altered the locations where I made my purchases. I might take cargo at Victoria, Sidney, Vancouver, or a number of other ports, and I offloaded it at different places on the island. Rarely did I return to the boatyard with cargo.

The importing business was lucrative. I returned all of the money that Elsie had contributed to the estate for utilities and groceries and gave her a retroactive salary with a considerable raise in pay. Then I quietly hired a few immigrant workers who would sometimes stop at the house looking for work. They quickly returned the grounds of the estate to their former glory and gave special attention to the family cemetery which was so dear to me. These workers seldom spoke English and kept to themselves. They would remain for only a few weeks before continuing on again, so that I need not be concerned about gossip of my affairs spreading over the island. They pruned the trees, cut the grass, trimmed the ivy scaling the walls of the house, repaired the chimneys, cleaned the roof, tended to the hundreds of budding flowers in the gardens, and last of all, to my infinite pleasure, cleaned the stagnant pool of the fountain, repaired the broken arm of poor Aristotle, and revived the flow of water. The fountain bubbled with a symphony that spoke of affluence and success. It was the music of its falling water that signaled the return of Ravenswood at last.

One thing only did I forbid any change or alteration to: the little caretaker's cottage had a rustic charm of its own with the ivy climbing the red brick walls, the white paint peeling from the windows and door, and the maple leaves heaped upon the dormered roof. I adored it as it was, and recalled with a nostalgic smile how Sophia and I would play in the little attic there as children.

Herbert shared his experience with me, and his mentorship

proved invaluable. I knew the water and shoreline of the island far better even than he, but he knew the legal system and the people involved on both sides of the smuggling business. He even had informants on the police force. One of them told him about some hotshot on their way from the east coast to work with the District Attorney's office and finally put a stop to this illegal alcohol business on the island. And he told me that the officers rarely took their boats out in a storm, for example, and that they preferred not to take them out at night. "Low hangin' fruit, Thomas. They like the low hangin' fruit," he said. "For many of 'em, it's just a job, ya see. But there's the fanatics too, and them ya have ta steer clear of. They believe they're thwartin' Satan and doin' God's work. Just plain squirrelly." But most important, he intimated that friendship of the low hanging pickers could be purchased at a price, and that he had done so. The problem, he said, was that they changed boats often, and one never knew what boat a "friendly" was on until they boarded you.

I had been running the boat for nearly three months without incident, nearly always under cover of darkness, and was beginning to think that all of my precautions were nothing more than silly inconveniences. I hadn't seen any vessels that looked like police boats, but that didn't mean they weren't around. They could have doused their running lights as I did, and would have been nearly impossible to see in the darkness. I was growing weary of the dull monotony; skippering the boat through the long, dark passages, picking my slow way along the narrow channels, standing alone at the wheel for hours at a time.

It was a cold, dark night late in June, with a strong north wind that blew over the port beam. The outgoing tide coming up against the wind from the opposite direction created a choppy, confused sea that rocked the boat in a harsh, unpleasant manner. I was returning from Victoria with fresh cargo. Since all of the smuggling occurred in Canada to the north, I would usually skirt the west side of San Juan Island, heading south, then turn north toward Orcas Island so it would appear that I had come from the south if anyone should see me. But that night I was restless. I was bored. It was quite late in the evening, and I wanted off the tumultuous, rocking vessel with all haste. So I abandoned my usual precautions and made directly for my destination, slipping under Spieden Island and making straight for Deer Harbor.

Suddenly, from the utter darkness that surrounded me, a spotlight swept over the bow and came to rest upon the wheelhouse, shining in my eyes with a crippling intensity. I lifted a hand to shade my eyes from the glare, but could see nothing in the darkness except the blinding beam bearing down upon me.

"Heave to," came a voice over the gusting wind. "Lay by," it demanded. I was taken off guard, completely by surprise. Eluding them was clearly impossible, so I hove to and waited. Eventually, I could make out the vague outline of a tallish prow as the spotlight approached and drew up alongside. Over the biting cold of the howling wind I heard the hurried voices of what appeared to be three or four men rushing to make fast their lines. "What boat?" a voice shouted over the wind. "What boat is this?"

"*Mary Adda*," I shouted in response.

A moment later, I felt *Mary* dip to port as someone climbed aboard. The wheelhouse door swung open suddenly, delivering a rush of cold air, and just as quickly closed again. Still the spotlight poured through the windows of the wheelhouse, illuminating my visitor in its harsh glare. Squinting, he raised a hand against the glaring light, and brushed past me impatiently before I could see much of him. Into the salon he went.

I followed and found him there looking down at the neatly stacked cases of whiskey with the stern, grave face of a middle-aged fanatic. The spotlight only seeped through the little portholes in the salon, providing a soft, muted glow that lit everything perfectly, and by that soft, perfect light, I witnessed a tall man with gaunt, sallow features, and short hair, who clearly denied himself basic pleasures of life so that he might better serve a higher master. This man was discipline and sacrifice: one of the fanatics that Herbert spoke of. I could expect no quarter from him. With all of the authority that the uniform afforded him, he stood with his arms crossed, regarding the cargo as if it were the root and source of every sin suffered by weak, corruptible mankind. The righteous flame in his godly eyes said that he would like to smash the sinful cargo and set fire to the spilled contents.

The wait was unnerving. While the muffled howl of the gusting wind sang in the rigging, and the boat rocked with the storm, and dipped with the waves, I wedged myself in the doorway and waited. Finally, he lifted his eyes from the distasteful cargo and turned his wrathful face to me, as if expecting me to wither under the weight of his judgment. But I would not surrender, not to that uniform, not if it were worn by the Almighty Himself. I had seen such uniforms while I was away and had only contempt for them and the cruel hypocrites who wore them. If he thought to intimidate me with his bearing and position he was sorely mistaken. I would go with him quietly, like a gentleman, but I would not cower or ask for anything. I stood taller in response to his silent challenge, and met his judgmental stare with a defiant one of my own.

He studied me by the subdued light pouring through the portholes, a light that constantly shifted and changed as the spotlight bounced with the waves. While the wind howled and the boat rocked with the storm, he studied me in the shifting light, grasping the galley table to keep his balance. He seemed to make up his mind then and brushed past me briskly, stepping up into the wheelhouse. With his hand on the door, he turned, and I saw a little smile in his stoic eyes.

"Tell Herbert I send my regards," he said, and departed. Of all the events I had witnessed since the spotlight appeared, that was the most shocking. "It's nothing." I heard him tell his crew over the gusting wind, then he added in a louder voice that I was certain was for me. "He said he lost his nav lights. Fuse went out or something." A moment later the spotlight was switched off, and the vessel vanished in the darkness.

I was free. After I had collected my wits and realized my good fortune, I started the engine and continued on without my navigation lights. When I reached the dock at the boatyard, Martin and Jack were waiting anxiously. They caught Mary, threw a couple of quick cleat hitches in the mooring lines, and rushed to the wheelhouse where I waited for them to board the boat and off load the cargo. But they remained on the dock, tense and alert, peering tentatively into the unlit wheelhouse where I was invisible in the darkness. When they made no move to enter, I opened the door and waved them aboard.

"Are you going to stand there staring all night," I shouted over the gusting wind, "or are you going to do your job?"

"We ain't liftin' a finger until ya tell us what just happened out there mate," said Jack firmly, hands on his hips. They had seen it all Jack said. The key to the shop was hidden under a rock near the door, and they sometimes used it to let themselves into the building where we would occasionally store the crates. With the storm coming on suddenly, and the wind sweeping over the water with a bitter chill, they retreated to the comfort of the vacant shop to await my arrival. In Father's office, they watched from a second floor window, scanning the dark water with an old bronze telescope that had been set up there years earlier when the shop was still in use. I remember using it as a child when I was waiting for Father to finish a drawing. It was large and shiny, on a wooden tripod, beautiful in its antiquated simplicity and heavy with the weight of its seafaring quality. Martin stood at the window while Jack was bent over the telescope searching the darkness for any sign of *Mary Adda*. When they suddenly saw the light switch on in the blackness of the night they knew it meant trouble. There was no mistaking it or its purpose. In all of the dark night there was no light present anywhere. At that hour all of the island homes had extinguished their lights, and in the heavily clouded sky not so much as a star was visible. The glaring spotlight that bore down on *Mary Adda* with arresting intensity drew their immediate attention.

Martin and Jack watched with bated breath, expecting to see *Mary Adda* follow the police boat away, and were discussing what to do. When the spotlight shut off, they could see neither boat in the darkness, and their hearts sank, certain I had been arrested. Martin told me they were debating who would wake Herbert in the middle of the night to tell him what had transpired when they peered out the office window and saw *Mary* approaching the dock. They knew I was returning with cargo, of course, and couldn't imagine that the police boat wouldn't easily discover it, so they were puzzled when they saw the boat approach the dock. They speculated that I had told the police about them to save myself, and expected a trap. When *Mary* reached the dock, they anticipated a boat filled with officers. It was quite a shock to see me alone on the vessel. They suspected me of colluding with the police. My simple explanation that the police found nothing, and let me go, was received with skepticism and suspicion, especially when Jack boarded the boat and found the cargo in the salon as always, uncovered and unhidden, in plain sight for all to see.

But could I tell them the truth? I recalled the conversation Herbert and I had in jail the night we met. I remembered what he said about running out of fuel and being arrested when he stopped at the fuel dock for more. The only person who knew he would be stopping there was the man who didn't fuel Herbert's boat properly. I never thought to ask Herbert who that was. It was one of the duties of my crew (Jack and Martin) to fuel my boat. Could one of them be the same man who betrayed Herbert that day, or could it have been a simple oversight?

The cargo was offloaded silently, without a word. Gone was the usual bantering chatter that always existed between Martin and Jack when they were transferring the whiskey crates from the boat. It was done quietly, suspiciously, and even in the darkness with the wind blowing wickedly over the water and the boat tossing and bouncing at the dock, I could feel the wary weight of their mistrust. I could see it in their tense, tentative movements. I could feel it in their guarded silence. When the last crate was loaded in the panel truck nearby, they shut the doors, climbed in, and drove away without a word of goodbye or a glance back.

Elsie was in bed when I returned home, and most of the lights were off in the house. My import business, which at first had kept her up many a night out of concern for me (she worried about me like Mother, and could not sleep until I was home and she knew I was safe), had eventually assumed the droll monotony of every day life, and she stopped waiting up. I never had anything exciting to report to her when I returned, so the whole affair had gradually assumed the plain routine of a regular job. I slept in rather late, had breakfast with Elsie, and then drove to Herbert's house for a talk. It was difficult for the police to watch his home because of the way it was nestled in the woods, so they monitored the entrance of the long driveway that led to his property. I would simply park a half-mile away on the road, then take a little footpath that had been cut into the forest and led to his home.

I peeked in at the window before ringing the bell and saw Herbert seated at the fire, with both hands on his walking stick and his chin on his hands, peering into the flames with thoughtful contemplation. At the sound of my knock, he turned suddenly and, seeing that it was me, motioned for me to enter.

"Been expectin' ya," he said, with his eyes on the fire as I took a seat next to him.

"You've already heard about last night?"

"Heard about it last night." He turned to me, and I saw the tired lines on his concerned face. "Jack's always eager ta deliver bad news," he replied, grimly, "especially when it concerns you."

I told Herbert what happened, or that is to say, began to tell him what happened. I had only just begun to tell of the officer boarding the boat when he interrupted me suddenly, as if he could keep still no longer. "That's enough, Thomas. You've done enough," he said, firmly. "It's time fer ya ta get out."

"Get out?" I asked, incredulous.

"It was selfish a me ta drag ya inta this." His hands, bent and twisted by age, shook as they held the walking stick, and I realized for the first time how old he appeared. "I thought ta do a good thing fer ya, and help myself at the same time, but it's too dangerous. I want ya ta give it up."

"But Herbert…"

"I worry about ya. Every time ya go out, I worry somethin's gonna happen," he said, turning his kind, honest eyes upon me. "I wanted ta help ya, ya see. Yer pa was the only person in my life that ever took a chance on me. It ate at me every day that I couldn't repay him. When I got the chance ta help ya, I took it, and it seemed good fer everyone."

"It is good."

"No it ain't. Yer gonna get killed or arrested. What would yer pa think a me then?"

"But I like it, Herbert," I said, adamantly. "It's great sport. I was getting bored before because nothing ever happened, but now that I know they're out there and they're looking for me, it adds a whole new element to the business. Before it was like checkers, now it's like chess."

"I can't fault ya there," he replied, with a smug grin. "Outwittin' them fellas is the most fun I've ever had. Things have been kinda boring round here since I retired. Got nothin' ta do."

I told Herbert of the police boarding, and he leaned close, listening with keen interest, his gray eyes alive and alert. When I recounted the experience of the officer examining the vessel, and his departing words to Herbert, he broke into a wide grin and his gray eyes sparkled.

"It's got ta be Father Keith."

"Father, did you say? He's an actual Father? A man of the cloth?" Herbert nodded.

"Not anymore a course, but he still likes playin' the part now and again. The good Father has quite a flare fer the theatrical. Gives him a chuckle. Must a had ya thinkin' ya had a one-way ticket ta jail," he laughed. "The good Father had a problem with one or two a his vows, ya see. That vow a chastity fer example. That was more than any man could endure. He wrestled, and fought, and grappled with it every day. Just ain't right ta expect a grown man ta abstain fer the rest a his natural life. Father Keith did a tolerable good job of it until Jenny walked in ta his confessional one day and he was just smitten with her. Left the church three days later, an as soon as they could get the weddin' invitations in the mail an arrange a service, they was married."

"He's one of the friendlys?"

"He is," Herbert replied, with a grin, then turned back to the fire. I watched him there by the firelight, as his jovial grin gradually faded and his meditative frown returned. "I worry about ya, lad. You're not like Jack or Martin. You're more like a...well...I just worry about ya."

What was he going to say, I wondered, as I made my way through the woods to my car? More like a what?

Thomas Moore

May 6th 1930

Moonless nights were best for this enterprise. Without the unwelcome light of a revealing moon I would be all but invisible, even to someone watching from the beach. Sophia and I had discovered the little bay one afternoon when we were sailing together as children. We were looking for a place to beach the dinghy and have lunch when we happened upon a secluded bay that was rarely visited by anyone. With the dinghy pulled up on the beach, we explored it on foot and found a tiny fisherman's shack in the woods not far from the water. We remarked at the time that it would be a great place for smugglers or pirates, little thinking that I would ever use it as such. Herbert had found it too and had used it on occasion, but rarely. The tide and moon had to be just right, and that occurred only a few times per month.

I made several more journeys after my encounter with Father Keith, always planning every aspect with meticulous detail and taking every precaution. But it was this little cove, neatly tucked away and hidden by all but the most experienced eyes, that I wanted to master. Very secure, but very difficult to approach. It was used by Herbert only when circumstances required the greatest caution. I suppose I wanted to impress upon Jack that I could skipper the boat as well as anyone and that I was no silver spoon dandy without courage. The entrance was quite narrow, just wide enough for a single boat, with rocks on both sides that were covered at high tide, just enough to hide them. Rocks that would easily smash a hull to bits, and the current was often strong in the narrow opening, making it difficult to navigate. Everyone avoided it.

Without the moon to give me away it was nearly impossible for unwelcome eyes to see the boat approaching the island. As I entered the tiny opening, I felt the current grab the boat, pulling her to one side of the channel then the other. I kept a steady hand on the ship's wheel, quickly correcting course to bear to the middle of the way that was so difficult to find in the darkness. The wheel shook in my hand with the turbulence of the current tugging at the rudder. But the treacherous little passage was thankfully short and swiftly negotiated. I passed suddenly into a wide bay. Scanning the shoreline for the white rock placed there as a marker, I throttled back the engine, slowly cruising alongside the sandy beach. The water was shallow there (too shallow to get close) and the night was so very dark. I passed back and forth along the shore, rocking gently in the surf, getting a little closer each time, and fearing to feel the sickening thud of the boat striking the bottom. Again and again I passed, searching for a marker that was impossible to see in the darkness. I was considering what course of action to take when

I saw the glowing butt of Jack's cigar on the shoreline. It presented only for an instant then was extinguished, but in the absolute darkness of the night it was like a lighthouse guiding me to safety. I mentally noted the position and bumped the throttle forward. As I approached, I saw the faint glow of the white rock on the beach and made directly for it.

There was at this location the broken stub of an old piling that rose up out of the water about twenty feet from shore on a low tide. On the beach, mixing with the driftwood tossed haphazardly at the furthest reach of the high tide, was a narrow little float bleached by the sun to resemble the driftwood piled all around it. At my approach, Jack was to drag the float to the water and secure it to the piling so I could tie up next to it and offload the cargo. The piling was only a short distance above the water at low tide, and we had to move fast or the incoming tide would carry the float above the piling and away. Jack was tying the float in place when I pulled up alongside.

"It's about bloody time, mate. You looked like a bloomin' tourist out there drivin' up an down the shore. Doin' a little sight seein' were ya?"

"I might never have found it if not for your help. I could barely see that rock. We need to use something else next time."

"Herbert never had any trouble findin' it," he grumbled.

Biting my tongue, I went below to study the charts for the return leg of the journey. With the curtains closely drawn, I unrolled the chart and spread it out upon the table, where I examined it by the dim light of a candle while Jack and Martin offloaded the cargo. I heard them grunting as they lifted each case, and their mumbled curses were music to my ears. Their destination was the rundown little fishing shack not far from the beach, but to reach it they had to carry wooden crates of whiskey over the tipsy float, across the sandy beach, and up a bank to the shack in the woods. It was hard work. After about twenty minutes of their grunting and mumbling, I decided to lend a hand. Grabbing a case, I fell in step with them and made my way along the path they had beaten into the sand. We were all breathing hard when we set our cases of whiskey on the floor of the dark shack, and paused to rest a bit before starting back for another load.

"Thanks for the help," Jack said, sardonically.

"Don't be too generous in your thanks, Jack. Every case I carry is coming out of your share," I joked.

"I don't doubt it," he growled.

"What took ya so long to get here?" Martin panted, catching his breath.

"He couldn't find the bloody place," Jack snorted.

"Herbert never had any trouble findin' it," answered Martin.

"That rock is impossible to see on a night like this. I'd still be looking for it if Jack hadn't lit his cigar."

"What are you talkin' 'bout mate?" he said, frowning at me over the dim light, "I didn't light any cigar." It was silent after that. No one made a sound. We were gathered around a candle on the floor that was covered by a coffee can someone had used for target practice. The feeble light scarcely leaked out of the little bullet holes at all, grudgingly illuminating the dusty old planks so we could see a little when stacking the whiskey cases. It was too weak even to be seen from outside the shack. By its meager glow we huddled close, looking from face to face in the darkness. Jack's cigar was unlit, I noticed. He was simply chewing on the mauled stub.

"What are we gonna do?" whispered Martin, turning his frightened eyes from me to Jack.

"They've probably surrounded the shack," Jack whispered.

"What are they waitin' for?"

"They're waiting for us to unload the boat so they won't have to," I answered, quietly. "This is all evidence that'll need to be transported to town. Listen," I said, moving even closer into the little circle, "I'll head back to the boat and carry another case of whiskey up here so they won't know we're on to them," I whispered. "That'll give you guys enough time to escape. Take one of the trails and go quietly as you can through the woods. On my next trip to the boat I'll untie it and motor away before they can stop me. It's so dark tonight they'll never know until they hear me start the engine, and by then it'll be too late."

"That's awful fine of ya, Thomas," Martin whispered, reaching over the coffee can to shake my hand, "givin' us time to get away and all." When my hand met his over the candle, I felt a tremor of fear in his cold fingers.

"It's the least he can do," Jack whispered, with a grin.

"I'll see you both tomorrow," I said, with more confidence then I felt, and started for the door. Jack caught me my arm as I passed.

"Good luck, mate," he said. I smiled, and stepped into the darkness, leaving the shack behind me. Through the woods I made my way, taking little care to be quiet, mumbling as I went as if talking quietly to the others. With each step I expected to feel the grasp of an arresting hand reaching out from the darkness to take me, but I saw no one and heard nothing. Emerging from the trees, I crossed the sandy beach to the boat and paused. Should I motor away now? Did my crew have enough time to get away? I told them I would make another trip, and they may need the time. I hefted another case of whiskey from the hold and retraced my steps across the beach, through the woods, to the shack. The coffee can cast its feeble light about the little room, illuminating the whiskey cases in a shadowy corner. All was quiet. Jack and Martin were gone. I stacked the case on top of the others and left the shack, this time creeping quietly along the path through the woods. After only a few steps I heard a voice call out far behind me.

"Stop. You there. Stop, I say." They must have happened upon Martin and Jack. I ran then, stumbling along the uneven ground of the trail as best I could in the dark and haste, breaking through tree limbs and branches. Suddenly, in the heavy salt air of the sea that drifted up from the beach, I caught a scent in the darkness that struck a familiar cord, and a moment later, before I could give it a thought, had tumbled into the grasp of someone awaiting me on the trail.

They threw their arms around me in a firm, arresting embrace, but the pinioning arms were thin and lacked the strength I expected to find in them. There was, too, a frailty in the body pressed to mine that seemed peculiar. And there was that scent again. It came rushing back to me, so familiar. Could it be?

"Sophia?"

"Thomas?" came the shocked reply. We stood there in the night holding each other in the darkness, unable to see a thing. With her arms around me, I felt the press of her cheek upon my chest. "Is it really you?" she asked.

"What are you doing here?" I stammered.

272 | *Kevin Kincheloe*

"What are you doing here?" she asked. Behind me I could hear the approaching thud of feet rushing along the trail. Many feet, if my ears didn't deceive me. Reluctantly, I took a step down the path, expecting her to release her hold of me, but instead she held me tighter.

"Sophia, we must go," I uttered, quickly. "Come with me to my boat. It's just down the trail on the beach." She held me tighter still, with her head upon my chest, gripping me with all the loving strength she could summon, her arms trembling from the effort. "Sophia." And then it was too late. Men were rushing around me, surrounding me. Pulling me away from her. I couldn't tell how many. Five or six I think. I heard more in the woods.

"Good work," someone said.

"What about the other two?" asked someone else.

"Got away," was the answer.

I was cuffed and led away through the woods, away from Sophia once again. With several men in front of me, and several more behind, I was pushed and pulled along the dark trail that eventually opened in a clearing where a car was parked. I was ushered into the back, with a man on each side of me, and we drove the shoreline road that led to town. I was going to jail. For how long I didn't know, but I didn't care. I had found Sophia.

This jail was unlike the other. Orcas Island rarely experienced the crime and intrigue of the big city, and the jail was built long ago to simply house drunken fishermen who were a bit too fresh with the barmaids. There were two cells, with red brick walls on three sides and black bars on the front. A comfortable looking bed was attached to one wall and was made up nicely with a down pillow and heavy woven blankets probably from someone's home. On a little table beside the bed were a few books and a lamp. I almost expected to see a mint on the pillow, it looked so cozy and comfortable. It reminded me of a stage play I once saw where the protagonist was in a jail cell. It had a charming sort of theatrical flavor about it, even if my circumstances did not. I sat on the bed looking through the bars at a desk across the room, upon which a lamp burned, casting its soft rays dramatically for effect. I had been deposited there hastily by my escorts who hurried away, eager to be home and in their own beds.

Sophia. My thoughts had never left her since our surprise meeting. My mind ran through a hundred scenarios to explain her presence there in the darkness, but lit upon none. Where was she now? I dozed off thinking about her, and when I awoke some time later, a woman was standing outside my cell in the faint light, looking through the bars at me.

"Hello," I said, and yawned. She seemed amused as she stood at the bars studying my face.

"You don't recognize me," she replied, smiling. In truth, she was correct; I didn't recognize her in the poor light of the little room. It was her voice that I recognized, and her eyes, still the bluest I have ever seen.

"Sophia?" I asked, wiping the sleep from my eyes.

"Hello, Thomas," she smiled. She was so very different. So much more beautiful than I remembered. She had matured into a breathtaking woman. How very much she had gained where I had not. Hopelessly I slipped back into a modest little boy, eclipsed by her beauty, poise, and charm.

"Am I dreaming? Is this a dream?"

"Do you dream about jail?"

"No, I dream about you."

"Then maybe this is a dream," she said, with a laugh. I pushed myself up out of bed and rushed to her, reaching through the bars separating us, taking her hands in mine. When I saw her last she was only a teenage girl, but now she was a woman, and even more striking than I remembered. With her hair pulled back in a ponytail, she stood across from me wearing a dark, smartly tailored pinstripe suit that gave her a professional appearance I didn't expect.

"I looked for you everywhere, Thomas, every day, every place I could think of," she said, pressing my hand to her cheek. She closed her eyes, savoring my touch, and the tears began to flow. "Oh, I'm so happy."

"I tried to find you, too, but…"

"I know," she interrupted, "William was cunning. When were you released? How did you get out so soon?"

"It didn't seem soon to me."

"Oh, Thomas," she reached through the bars to run her palm

tenderly over my cheek, "I'm so sorry about that. Can you forgive me?"

"There's nothing to forgive."

"So noble. So gallant." She fixed her lovely eyes upon me, the most beautiful, piercing blue eyes I had ever seen, and her sentiment was clear. If the touch of her gentle hand upon my face didn't say it clearly enough, the expression in her searching eyes did. They held me spellbound. "Look how handsome you've become. You were always a handsome boy, but now you're a handsome man."

"Look at you. You're so..." I faltered, at a loss for words.

"Yes?" she smiled, studying my face.

"So beautiful."

We stood there in the dim light of the distant desk lamp, I on one side of the steel barrier that had for so long kept us apart, she on the other, reaching through to caress my cheek. Closing her eyes, she moved toward me for a kiss, and started suddenly when the wind shook the door in the frame. She glanced over her shoulder at the entrance.

"I'm so sorry, Thomas. I have to go. If someone should catch us together...they can't find out about us knowing each other. It's a big deal," she said, earnestly.

"I don't understand," I replied. "How did you even get in here?"

"I have a key," she smiled, holding it up for me to see. Moving quickly, she hurried to the door and turned, with her hand on the handle. "Don't worry about your boat. I returned her to the boatyard. She's moored right behind *Diva*." With a hurried wave, she slipped out the door, and as the bolt clicked shut after her I stood alone once more in the quiet, dimly lit little jail, gripping the cold steel in my hands, with only the blustery wind for company. It gusted in little bursts, rattling the windows, shaking the door, and I felt oddly relaxed and at peace when I slipped under the warm covers of the tiny bed. Can sleep come easily to a fellow taken in the dead of night and tossed into a jail cell with only judgment and incarceration to wake to? I slept free and untroubled, without a care for the first time in years. A passerby would have wondered at the smile on my slumbering lips. I had found Sophia at last.

The afternoon sun, an hour or so from setting, poured through the majestic treetops and fell upon Lauren in broken shadows that swayed with the breeze. The elegant wrought iron gate, which had always been open when he arrived, was closed, and he sat on the Harley looking through the bars at the house beyond. Twilight was settling upon the narrow point, and lights were just coming on in the houses there. The rustic timberframe home with its huge unpainted beams, intricate joinery, and soft light glowing from the many windows, looked so comfortable and inviting in the cool, quiet moments before dusk. Lauren found himself staring almost wistfully, drawn to the peace and serenity. When the smell of cooking penne reached him, he was instantly taken home and smiled at the memory.

Next to the main entrance was a smaller gate in the wrought iron fence that allowed for foot traffic. Lauren found it to be open, and leaving the Harley at the gate, walked across the courtyard to the home. He was raising his hand to knock at the carved door when a voice caught his ear and he paused, listening. Nina was talking to someone inside. He couldn't understand what was being said, but he could tell that she was talking to someone. When he knocked at the door the conversation stopped abruptly. A moment later the door opened.

"Mr. Lauren," she said, much surprised, "I thought you were coming tomorrow."

"I thought we agreed on today," he replied, casually looking past her to see who else was there.

"Well, you're here now," she answered, after a moment of thought. "It would be silly to have you come back tomorrow. Come in. I'll get your check." Lauren followed her into the house and looked around for her guest. "Have you eaten? I was just making a little dinner."

"No. I intended to stop on the way home," he said, as they entered the dining room. Curiously, the table was set for two and looked quite intimate with burning candles, china, folded white napkins, wine. Lauren was puzzled. "I don't want to impose."

"You're not imposing."

"But..." he began, and his eye went to the cozy table. Nina lowered her head with an embarrassed blush and stepped into the kitchen.

"I need to give the penne a stir," she said. "Make yourself at *home. I'll just be a moment.*

A grand piano near the windows caught his eye and he stepped over, admiring the craftsmanship in the soft light of the room. Standing at the piano Lauren tested it, giving the keys a little tap.

"This wasn't here last time. Did you just get it?"

"I just had it moved here," she called out from the kitchen. "It's been in storage for years."

Lauren took a seat at the piano, and finding several sheets of hand written music lying there with a pencil on top, took them in hand a studied them with an intrigued, curious, eye. A moment later the rich tone of a complex composition filled the quiet night. Nina stepped from the kitchen to watch in wonder, and her interest in him grew as he performed. Her guest seemed very much in his element and played with a level of skill that astonished her. The music ended abruptly when he turned the page, and found there was no more. Responding to the applause that followed he stood and bowed.

"Where is the rest?"

"I haven't finished it yet," she replied.

"You wrote this?" he asked, greatly impressed.

"I started it years ago," she replied, and motioned him to the table with the spoon in her hand. "Take a seat," she added, and stepped back into the kitchen.

The table, set for two, whispered that he was not welcome there. Flickering candlelight reflected in the sparkling wine glasses revealed an intimate, romantic intent that suggested he leave. Moreover, there was an odd chill in the warm, otherwise inviting room, that drifted through the house like a draft, and seemed to come from the fireplace where no fire was laid. Lauren felt welcome, and yet not so.

"I think I'll just..." he called out, just as she stepped out of the kitchen with the penne in hand.

"Have a seat," she said, interrupting him.

"Well...Where?"

"There, of course," she answered, indicating one of the set places.

Feeling very much like he was interrupting, he nevertheless took a seat at one of the set places, and waited uncomfortably. Would she set another place, he wondered? Would they not be joined by her husband?

The food was wonderful, the wine perfect, the conversation intriguing. And so the evening slipped away without notice.

They were opening their third bottle of wine when the subject turned to past lovers. Smiling, partly from the wine, and partly from the memory, Lauren began.

"Tami Chapel," he said, removing the cork from a fresh bottle.

"Was she pretty?"

"The prettiest girl in all of New York City," he answered, pouring them each a new glass.

"Oh, New York?"

"Her father was...well...an undertaker."

"Oh," she replied with a sour face.

"My parents didn't approve of her, so they wouldn't let me use their car for dates," said Lauren, with a curious smile.

"Well?" prompted Nina, curious to hear more.

"Her father let us use one of his hearses."

"Dear God," she frowned. "Really?"

"There was plenty of room in the back, and it was always immaculately clean," he laughed. "I lost my virginity in the back of a hearse."

They shared a good laugh and sipped of their wine.

"What about you, Nina? Who was your first love?"

"My first love, my only love, was Nikolas."

"Really?" said Lauren, moved by the warm smile that appeared on her face at the mention of her husband's name.

"He was such an adorable boy. We were sixteen when we met," Nina said, and took a sip of wine. "I went to an all girls school, so we didn't see each other much during the day, but when school was over we would always meet somewhere. He was so kind and so clever. He just doted on me. It was difficult for him when I went to college. He was so afraid I would meet someone else, but I only had eyes for him. He was my best friend."

Her eyes drifted to the fireplace as they always seemed to do when she spoke of her husband, and she smiled, a sweet, sad smile, that Lauren wondered about.

"Well?" he prompted.

"Well, we were married of course. Quite young. While I was still in college. My father wanted me to wait. He liked Nikolas, but he wanted me to wait. Nicky came from a poor family, and never really felt like he was good enough for me. He worked very hard to provide for us. To prove to my father that he could take care of me." Nina

stared pensively into her wine glass. "I didn't care about any of that, Mr. Lauren. I just wanted for us to be happy. But Nikolas couldn't be happy without the financial success. And with each victory came a subtle change. By the time we moved into this house he was a different person. He was working long hours, spending very little time at home, traveling. There were phone calls. They would hang up when I answered."

"I'm sorry Nina," said Lauren sympathetically.

"Nikolas didn't like me leaving the house. He didn't like me doing a lot of things that I use to take pleasure in," she said, glancing at her music.

"Like playing the piano?"

"He didn't play. It made him feel stupid when I composed and played. I would do it when he wasn't home, but eventually the sight of the piano was too much for him. I had it removed."

Lauren took an especially large gulp of wine, and shook his head, frustrated by Nina's plight.

"You probably think I'm a fool," she muttered.

"No," he said, compassionately, "I think you're remarkable."

"I remembered," she began, nearly moved to tears, "how sweet, and kind, and tender he was as a boy. I knew that person was still there. He did all of this for me. Because he didn't feel good enough for me."

"Where is he, Nina?" Lauren inquired, posing a question that he very intentionally avoided until that night, but the alcohol was having an effect. "Where is your husband?" As if in answer to his own question his eye was drawn to the fireplace mantle that he had seen so many times before. There was a skillfully scrolled silver vessel upon the mantle that looked so much like the silver items taken from Mary Adda, that he never gave it a thought. It wasn't until that very moment that he realized what it was. Nina saw his eye travel to it.

"He died when his plane crashed in the mountains," she said, suddenly somber. "He was a pilot."

"I'm so sorry," he said, sincerely. "I had no idea. Why didn't you tell me?" She held his eye over the space of the table that separated them, over the candlelight between, seemingly at a loss for words.

"Why would I do that?" she said, at last.

"Why wouldn't you?" he asked, puzzled by her remark, then his eye returned to the vessel on the mantle. He seemed to recall seeing

it there the first time he was at the house. "When was that? How long ago?"

"July eleventh," she said, and added, "four years ago."

"Four years ago?" he asked, incredulous.

"It was the day of our twenty year anniversary."

"He was flying on your anniversary?" he asked, his head spinning.

"He was flying," she said, flatly, "into the arms of his mistress." She stood suddenly at the table. "If you'll excuse me, it's getting late."

"Yes...of course," he answered, when he could find his voice.

And just that quickly their pleasant evening ended. At the door Lauren paused, stunned by the abrupt manner of his host, and ran his eye over the coat and shoes in the entryway. They were different each time he visited. Why would she do that, he wondered? Was she still so in love with the man? To think that her husband had been with them all the time, watching from his place on the mantle. Lauren glanced back over his shoulder. With her back to him Nina stood at the window silently looking out over the dark lake.

She was roused suddenly at the sound of the Harley rumbling away. When Lauren left, the house became so very quiet with a silence that she wished to fill somehow. There were voices in the house, the very, very quiet house, echoed voices of whispered infidelity that shouted to her in the still night. She could still see her husband bent over the phone, speaking in a hushed voice so early in the morning before the sunrise. She could still see him sitting next to the window as the first few faint rays of sunlight dimly lit the room. She could still hear the whispered excitement in his voice, though she couldn't make out the words. It was that excitement that broke her heart.

She fell lethargically into a chair at the table and drank deeply of the lie that she had poured for Lauren and herself. A lie that began innocently with the ring that never left her finger and served as a shield to ward off or deflect approaches.

Lauren was preoccupied the next day, and went about his work on Mary Adda *in a distracted, musing sort of way. He would work for a while, and his hands would slow, then stop altogether. His eyes would be fixed on something in the distance, and he would start suddenly as if realizing where he was, and return to work. But his enthusiasm for the lovely* Mary Adda *waned, and as the days passed and his thoughts of Nina became an irreconcilable puzzle, his enthusiasm for the old boat expired. The very city itself, a city that he fled to and sought sanctuary in, seemed suddenly stifling and unwholesome.*

He was in the act of varnishing Mary Adda *one afternoon. As he dipped the brush into the can he was struck with a thought, and smiled. Of course. He dropped the brush into a coffee can of paint thinner, tapped the lid back on the can of varnish, and stepped off the boat. The high pitched whine of the starter always brought a smile to his face, and the throaty rumble promised a much need adventure. He pondered the possibilities for just a moment, then toed it into gear. There was no need to go home first. He had spare clothes and a sleeping bag. A campfire next to a creek. A sandy beach near the ocean. An open road in the country. It didn't matter. He just needed time to think.*

I awoke the next day to the sound of jingling keys, and the heavy squeak of my cell door swinging open. Opening one sleepy eye, I found a smiling jailor stepping into my cell with a plate of food. He was a chubby fellow, around twenty-five years of age I should say, and the buttons of his police uniform were straining under the weight of their confining task. His smooth, rosy-red cheeks had never seen a razor, and an affable smile played in his simple blue eyes. He stood beside the bunk, the plate held before him in both hands, his mouth open, regarding me with curious interest as if I were some novelty washed up on the beach.

Nina read by the light of the afternoon sun that streamed through the window blinds. It was several months since her dinner with Lauren. They hadn't spoken, but she assumed he was still working on Mary Adda. *She wondered, with an embarrassed blush, if she would ever see him again. The house felt even emptier and colder than before. She sat in the warm sun at the window thinking about Lauren, and remembered the journal. It was just the distraction she needed. She rushed to her bedroom, grabbed the journal from under her pillow, and settled in at the window to finish it.*

"Oh, uh, good morning," he said, when he saw that I was awake. "Breakfast-time." He moved a book aside and set the plate on the table beside the bed. The smell was delicious. I rose up on an elbow and glanced to the plate beside me, finding hash browns, eggs, and toast. There were three sausage links, but the sauce of a fourth was clearly visible on the plate where it had been. Seeing my eye travel to the vacant spot on the plate, he shifted nervously. "I dropped one on the floor," he explained, but I was pretty sure it had been dropped elsewhere, somewhere closer to his mouth.

"Where did this come from?" I asked.

"The diner across the street. They make all our meals for us. There hasn't been anyone in this jail in months," he said, "and we've never had a murderer before," he added, growing excited. I threw back the blankets and twisted around, sitting on the bed.

"How do you know about that?" I asked, as I reached for the plate and began to eat.

"Everyone knows about you, Mr. Moore. You killed the judge's son," he said, with something approaching hero worship.

"That was a long time ago." The food was delicious. I would have to visit that diner sometime.

"I wouldn't worry about it. No one liked Rockwell much, nor the judge neither."

"Do you have a phone I can use?" I asked between bites.

"I don't know," he said, hesitantly. "We have one, but I don't know if you're supposed to use it or not. I'll ask when we're in court."

"Court?"

"Yeah. Soon as ya finish eatin' I'm supposed to take ya to court. Come on out when you're done," he said, and walked out of the cell, leaving the door open. He went to the desk, shuffled through a few drawers, and found a dusty pair of handcuffs. Then he searched the rest of the desk looking for something else. "Shucks," he said. "I wonder where that key got to. Handcuffs ain't no good without a key." I slipped on my jacket and shoes and let myself out of the cell, joining him at the desk. "Would ya mind holdin' your hands together in front of ya, so ya look like you're handcuffed? I don't wanna get in trouble."

"I can do that," I answered, hesitantly, wondering if it were a joke.

"Okay, then, if you're ready lets go."

The town was only about a half-mile long, with buildings on either side of the street that ran along the water a short distance from the surf. We walked along the sidewalk under the gray morning sky, suffering the bite of a cool sea breeze that blew in over the water as we passed the storefronts and shops on our way to the courthouse. I held my hands together before me as if I were his prisoner, and he whistled proudly along beside me as if he was escorting Al Capone to the gallows. We climbed the steps to the courthouse (they always seem to have steps, as if the judgment within is of a lofty and divine nature) and made our way to the courtroom where I spotted Howard Goodfriend at the defense table beyond the first pew. He had apparently been waiting for me, for he was turned around in his seat watching the door and motioned for me to join him directly. I turned to my escort.

"Will you remove the cuffs?" I asked, holding my hands out before me.

"Sure thing," he answered, and made as if reaching into his pocket for the key then unlocking the restraints.

"Thank you," I winked, and joined Howard at the table. "How did you know to find me here?" I asked, leaning close and speaking quietly.

"Elsie. When you didn't come home last night, she called me." Head to head, we spoke quietly together at the defense table until a voice rang out in the courtroom singing the usual ceremony about the Honorable so-and-so. We all rose and then resumed our seats. Charges were read; a not guilty plea was entered. The matter of bail was raised. Howard expressed his opinion that I should be released on my own merit without the formality of bail. The question was then put to the people.

"The people have no objection, your Honor," came a familiar voice from the prosecution table beside me. It was a voice I knew, a voice I would know anywhere. The rich, beautiful tenor of a voice I knew from my youth. I had not offered so much as a glance beside me since the proceedings had begun; my attention had been on the judge. But I turned to look then, and saw Sophia standing at the table dressed as an attorney with a briefcase open on the table before her. Her eyes were on the judge. Not once did she look beside her. The request was granted. A trial date was set a few months distant, and I was ordered to appear at that time. A gavel struck the bench. People in the courtroom stood and began to wander away or mill about. Sophia gathered up the documents on the table, arranging them in her briefcase, then closed it, snatched it up, and left the room without a glance in my direction. I hadn't taken my eyes off her since I heard her speak.

"Quite pretty, isn't she?" Howard said, noting my stunned expression. "That's our new ADA." My chubby escort was suddenly at my side, waiting to take me back to jail. "Call me in a few days," Howard said. "It'll take a while to get the police report and figure out what's happening with this."

The return journey was uneventful. The pretense of carrying my hands as if they were bound was dispensed with since I would be released when we arrived at the jail anyway. My escort whistled and prattled on cheerfully, but I heard little. My thoughts were on the new Assistant District Attorney.

It was late afternoon when I finally turned down the familiar tree-lined lane and made my weary way to the house. I had stopped at the jail long enough to sign the release forms and then began the long walk home, but long country walks can be soothing and I had much to consider. Lives take strange turns. Somehow, among the infinite possibilities that weighed in my mind, I had chosen the one course that would lead me to a fresh young assistant district attorney who unwittingly awaited me in the bushes of a dark beach.

I opened the door and smelled dinner coming from the kitchen. At the sound of my entry, Elsie rushed out to greet me, throwing her arms around my neck and scolding me in a motherly fashion.

"I told you it meant trouble," she said, as if I had broken the neighbor's window with a baseball. "What happened, Thomas? I was so worried about you." I took a seat at the kitchen table and Elsie returned to her dinner preparations, stirring the pots that were cooking on the stove. Often she would turn to ask for greater detail, or clarification of some little event, as I narrated my adventure of the previous night. "Why have you stopped, Thomas? You have me on pin and needles," she said, brushing her hair back from her flushed face, and waving a wooden spoon in her other hand. "What happened next?"

"This is where I am apprehended, Elsie. Are you sure you're up to it?" I asked innocently.

"Yes, yes. Hurry. I can't bear the delay," she answered, excitedly.

"All right. Jack and Martin slipped away from the shack into the night. I was hurrying along the dark path. All I had to do is reach the boat."

"Yes?" said she, impatiently. "What then? Why are you smiling?"

"I ran straight into the arms of the law."

"Couldn't you get away? Couldn't you throw those arms off and bolt into the darkness?"

"I didn't wish to."

"Didn't wish to?" she said, surprised. "Good lord, Thomas, why not?"

"Because Elsie," I said standing and walking to her, "the long arm of the law had suddenly taken a very attractive turn."

"What?" she asked, exasperated.

"Having those legal arms around me was divine."

"You're not making any sense," she said, but before I could continue there was a knock at the door, and she rushed away, wiping her hands on her apron, to answer it. I remained at the little kitchen table resting my weary feet, so very sore after my long walk. Moments later, I heard a shriek that rang throughout the house and may have carried through the hills and valleys of the island. I rushed out of the kitchen and, as I stepped into the hallway, saw Elsie. She stood motionless in the half open doorway as a gentle breeze rustled her dress and blew little wisps of her blonde hair behind her. I approached tentatively, unsure of what I might find, and as I drew closer I heard her crying softly. It was not without apprehension that I came up quietly behind the door and peeked around. There stood Sophia. She held Elsie's hand, and the two friends were crying in the joy of their unexpected reunion.

Minutes later, we were all seated before the soothing fire as a warm spring rain pelted the windows and a weak wind blew through the trees.

"It looks just the same," Sophia said, turning to look behind her at the sun setting into the ocean. "Just as I remembered it."

"It didn't feel the same. Not without you here," I said. She smiled, tenderly.

"I would have come before now if I had known. I've only been in town a few weeks, but I would have come before now if I had known you were here. I wanted to visit Carolyn's grave, but feared that William was still here." She looked concerned. "He's not, is he?" Elsie shook her head gravely. "Where is he, then?"

"He's believed to be dead," I answered.

"How?" she asked, surprised.

"No one knows, and I don't believe anyone cares," I answered.

"Where have you been, child? Where did you go, and what did you do, and when did you come back?" Elsie asked.

"She's an attorney now," I said, proudly.

"How do you know that?" Elsie inquired.

"I found out this morning when we met in court. It seems she is the new Assistant District Attorney and is prosecuting me for my harmless little adventure last night."

"That's right, Thomas, and I shouldn't even be here right now. I should have recused myself for even knowing you. If anyone finds out, my career is over before it gets started," she said, concerned, and stood to leave. "I'm sorry, but I should go."

"Sophia," I answered, hurt that she would leave so soon.

"I can come back when your case is settled, Thomas."

Is there anything as intimidating as a poised, beautiful woman with a manner of casual indifference? I wanted to stop Sophia, to tell her how I cared for her and missed her, but I imagined her dismissing me with a smile and a careless toss of her pretty head as she flittered away. Words failed me, but not Elsie.

"Sit down, Sophia. You kids haven't seen each other in ten years. You owe Thomas that much. Sit down." Her tone was kind, but insistent.

"I'm trying to save him, Elsie."

"It sounds like you're trying to save yourself."

"It's the same thing," she said desperately, then walked to me and took my hand. "I tried to find you Thomas. I know you suffered for me, but I suffered too," she said, and I felt her hand tremble.

"Why? What happened to you?" I asked. She checked her watch, and then looked toward the door. Her eyes met mine in a moment of indecision, but when they fell on Elsie and our nanny nodded her head insistently, she sighed and dropped into the seat she occupied a moment earlier. "Things got much worse here after you left, Thomas. Much worse. William followed me constantly, and I feared to be alone with him. It wasn't overt, but he would just sort of happen to be wherever I was, as if by accident, and I felt that he wanted to harm me. I was always mindful to be in a part of the house where Mother or Elsie were, but my thoughts often turned to you. One afternoon I wandered to the north end of the house and stood looking distractedly at the window, out over the sea, wondering where you were and how you might be. It was a winter day. A dark cloud nearly black with rain approached, but before it the sun shone down through an opening in the clouds, illuminating the rainfall in a brilliant shower that fell to the gray sea. I was fascinated by it and lost track of time as I watched. How long I was there I don't know, but I suddenly felt a chill as I realized I was alone, and, perceiving my danger, thought to leave. When I turned, I found William standing silently behind me."

Without realizing it, Sophia was squeezing my hand as she thought back to that day. She paused a moment, then continued.

"The look in his eyes…the look in his eyes was just blank, and cold, almost as if he was looking right through me, but I saw malice there, too. Smiling ever so slightly, he stepped forward and raised a hand to cover my mouth so I couldn't cry out, but just then he heard footsteps approaching from the other end of the hallway, and lowered his hand again.

'Next time', he said quietly, then walked away back down the hall. I kept my bedroom door locked after that whenever I was inside, and a few times when the hall light was on I saw a shadow stop at the bottom of my door, then the handle would turn softly and the shadow would move on. I was just terrified when I was at home, Thomas," she said. "I never knew when he might attack me."

"Didn't you have lessons during the day?" I asked.

"Mrs. Stowe left," Sophia answered. "She said she had other obligations and couldn't continue here."

"William scared her away," Elsie said. "I saw him talking to her one night, and I could tell she was frightened. The next day she quit."

"Is that why you were sent away to school?" I asked.

"What else was there for me to do? I needed to finish school, and William said he knew of a good one. You don't know what it was like here, Thomas. Your mother was so depressed. She thought about you and worried about you every waking moment. So did Elsie. So did I. She sat at the window for hours looking out over the sea without moving. And she roamed about the house. I would see her sometimes at night when everyone was in bed, wandering through the dark house in her white nightgown as if lost. It was so depressing. I felt so sorry for her." Her eyes fell to the floor, and she stared a moment. "Maybe I was wrong, but when she asked if I would like to go away to school, I went. I stopped to see you on my way, then went to the train station and claimed my ticket. I had no idea where I was going until I saw the destination on the boarding pass, but I didn't care."

"It was much better after you left," Elsie said. "William wasn't as hostile after you left."

"I almost missed the train, but hurried aboard just as it was pulling away from the station and took a seat. It was late at night, and there were few passengers, maybe five or six in the car I was on. Everyone seemed quietly pensive, as if they were all going on some reluctant errand to a destination they dreaded. No one even looked up when I stepped aboard. I just took a seat next to the window and stared out at the city lights slipping past, wondering when I would see them again and how I could ever come back to a house that William was in. I missed Mother and Elsie already, and you most of all.

"I dozed off eventually. When I awoke, the sun was in my eyes and the train was descending from a high mountain pass with patches of snow all around. Then we began across a long, flat plain. I don't know how long I was on the train; it just went on and on. We would stop at a station, often little more than a shack beside the tracks, and take on passengers or let them off, then continue on again. Sometimes I had time to get off and stretch my legs and sometimes I didn't, and then the train would be moving again. Eventually cities began cropping up in the distance, and I knew we were reaching the East Coast. I think I was on the train for three or four days when it finally reached its last stop at Vermont and I wearily got off. I wandered around the train station wondering where to go next, carrying my portmanteau with me. No one had told me the name of the school, or even the name of the town it was in, and I was quite lost. All the passengers on the train wandered off with friends or family that met them, so that I was the only one remaining. With nothing else to do, I sat down on a long bench near the wall and waited. There was a giant clock at the train station, and I sat on the wooden bench watching the minutes tick past as an old gentleman bent with age approached slowly, pushing a broom methodically over the station floor.

'Excuse me, sir,' I asked when he came close. 'Do you know of a school nearby? A boarding school?'

'Eh?' he answered, holding a cupped hand to his ear.

'Do you know of a school near here?' I asked, in a louder voice.

'There's no pool near here.' He smiled, and continued sweeping. I fell back to the bench tiredly and considered what to do. Maybe this was a trick by William, I mused. Maybe he just sent me off to nowhere thinking I wouldn't come back. Watching the hands on the big station clock, I saw half an hour pass, then an hour. I was getting hungry but had only enough money for one or two little meals, and there was no place at the train station to get food. Where would I spend the night? How would I get home? Could I even go home? Overwhelmed by everything that had happened, I hung my head and began to cry quietly. It was all just too much for me. With you going away to prison, Thomas, and your mother roaming around the house like a ghost, and William wishing to hurt me... Then finding myself abandoned at a train station three thousand miles away, with no way to get home. I hung my head and cried. I was still crying when I heard a shuffle and opened my eyes to see a pair of shoes. As my gaze traveled up from the shoes, to trousers and then shirt and finally a pale, freckled face framed by short red hair, I perceived a slender boy a few years older than myself.

'I'm so sorry,' he said, apologetically, attempting to catch his breath. 'I had a flat tire on the way and it took some time to fix,' he added, panting for air. 'I'm not the most mechanical fellow, you understand, and there were no instructions, though the process was rather intuitive: lift vehicle, replace flat tire with new one, lower vehicle again. I drove as fast as I could and ran from the car. I assume,' he said looking around the deserted train station, still catching his breath, 'that you are Sophia Nagel. You could hardly be anyone else.'

"It is a silly consequence of my troubled childhood perhaps, but I have always kept the flannel shirt that I wore when we first met, Thomas. I didn't have a blanket like some children, and that flannel shirt was a comfort to me. I would take it out and rub it on my cheek, or pull the soft flannel through my fingers when I was troubled, and it would ease my mind. I had been dragging it through my fingers as I cried at the train station. When the young man approached, I dried my eyes on the flannel and stood.

'I am Sophia,' I said, with a sniffle, 'and you are?'

'Amadeus,' he replied, and extended a hand. But I was so relieved that I threw my arms around him in a thankful embrace and held him close, feeling his body tense. 'It's just a nickname, you understand,' he confessed, nervously, into my shoulder. 'I'm quite a Mozart aficionado,' he added.

"I released him at last and looked into his embarrassed brown eyes. They were darting shyly all around the station, looking everywhere but at me.

'I'm very pleased to meet you, Amadeus,' I said.

'I'm very pleased to meet you, Miss Nagel,' he answered. 'May I get that for you?' He indicated the portmanteau at my feet.

'Thank you,' I replied. So, struggling under the weight of the luggage that even I had born without burden, he began over the station floor to the double doors across the way, with me close behind. When he reached the car, parked a considerable distance from the station, Amadeus opened the rear door and, with both hands on the portmanteau, attempted to lift it up on the seat, but the task was beyond the capacity of his weary arms. He made the attempt again, and again, but the result was always the same. He raised it but half way, and it fell back to the ground. He was breathing hard, and sweating, when he finally paused.

'I only need a moment to rest,' he said.

'That's quite understandable after changing the tire, then carrying the luggage all the way out here,' I said. 'You must be fatigued. But I've been sitting for ever so long and could use some exercise. Shall I try?'

'Be my guest,' he replied, with a smile that said he clearly doubted I would succeed where he had failed. I lifted the little portmanteau lightly, with one hand, and set it on the car seat. The surprised look on his face was precious. Without a word, he climbed behind the wheel, I climbed in beside him, and we began away.

"It was a narrow country road that wound through the snow covered hills and valleys, climbing gently for miles. Amadeus was quiet as he drove along with both hands gripping the wheel tightly, his chin thrust forward, and his eyes peering intently ahead.

'Have you driven much, Amadeus?'

'Not much, Miss Nagel. Not much,' he said, without taking his eyes off the road for even an instant.

'But you know how?' I asked, with some apprehension.

'Oh yes,' he replied, confidently, 'I've read all about it.'

'You've read about it?' was my incredulous reply.

'Oh yes, there's quite an informative manual on the subject.'

'But this isn't your first time driving, surely?'

'Oh, goodness no. I thought it best to practice alone. I've driven twice before today.'

'Oh, well, I suppose you're quite seasoned then.'

'Yes, quite.'

"It was a lovely drive. All was quiet, still, unmoving, without a breath of wind, like a postcard. We had been driving through the snow for about twenty minutes when we crested a little hill, and in the distance I saw a large home in a clearing surrounded by snow covered trees. It sat on the crown of a hilltop overlooking the valley below and was impressive in size.

'Nearly there now,' he said. 'That's the Porter Mansion.'

'We're not going to the school?' I inquired.

'That is the school,' he answered, his eyes never leaving the road. 'It was abandoned many years ago and finally converted to a school.'

'Abandoned, did you say?'

'Mrs. Porter was a widow with three sons. They were all killed in the Great War, and she just quietly passed away shortly after, without an heir.'

'Poor dear. It must have been terrible for her in that big house all alone.'

'Yes. It feels big and empty sometimes, even with all the students there. It has a certain lonely quality about it that will probably always remain.'

"Excuse me," Elsie said, "I need to check on dinner before everything is burnt. I'll set a place for you, Sophia." She meant to protest, but Elsie was gone in an instant, so she settled back in her seat and turned to me.

"Remember when we were in the attic, and I asked if you had ever kissed a girl?"

"I remember it well," I answered, with a pleasant grin. Sophia reached forward, with a hand on my neck, and pulled me to her in a long, passionate kiss.

"Welcome home, Thomas," she said, with a serene smile. "I've waited a long time to do that." I was still reeling from her sensual embrace when Elsie returned.

"All right," she said, "what happened then?"

"I started school," Sophia said. "The headmaster had been warned about me by William and was quite severe to me. The institution was very structured and inflexible. The girls were awakened by bell every morning. The bed had to be perfectly made, then inspected. If it passed, we were all marched to the cafeteria for a measured breakfast. Then classes began."

"Did you have any friends?" I asked.

"I had two. On my second day there, I met Ellen. She was in my Geography class and was seated in the front row, at one end. The only open seat in the classroom was next to her, so I took it. The instructor, Mrs. Spoon, was going around the room calling on each girl to answer a question, then moving on to the next. Finally she reached Ellen.

'What is the capital of Greece, Miss Reed?'

'Athens,' she answered tensely, her eyes straight ahead.

'And Belgium?'

'Brussels.'

'And Nepal?'

'Kathmandu,' she replied, growing uneasy as the questions continued.

'And Portugal?'

'Lisbon.'

'What about Greenland, Miss Reed?' she asked, stopping before Ellen's desk and glaring down at her with a wicked smile. 'Sit up straight. Now, what is the capital of Greenland?'

'I don't know, Mrs. Spoon,' Ellen answered, simply, with her eyes forward and her hands folded on her desk. All of the other girls had been asked only one question, I remarked silently to myself.

'Your hands, please,' Mrs. Spoon demanded. Ellen held her pale hands out before her, and Mrs. Spoon struck them several times with a wooden ruler that she had been holding under her arm the entire time. All of the other girls simply read along in their books, taking no notice, as if this was a matter of course, and Ellen bore her punishment without a word of protest. I dreaded my turn, but it didn't come that day.

"When classes were over and dinner had been served, I was walking through the old mansion exploring and found Ellen wrapped in a blanket, reading a book by the fire in the common room. The other girls seemed to avoid her, I noticed. She was a small girl, thin and frail, with dirty blonde hair and freckles.

'What are you reading?' I asked, taking a seat beside her.

'My geography book. My knowledge of geography is so poor.'

'I thought your knowledge was exceptional.'

'Mrs. Spoon didn't find it to be so.'

'Mrs. Spoon is a bully. I don't care for her.'

'She is stern, that's true, but it is for my own benefit. You judge her too harshly.'

'Too harshly? How can you believe that?'

'I need a stern hand. She is only trying to help me.'

'By abusing you?'

'By pointing out my deficiencies.'

'You should stand up for yourself. You can't allow her to treat you that way. I wouldn't.'

'You would be expelled. You would be sent home and would embarrass your family.'

'What about your family?'

'I'm already an embarrassment to them,' she said, quietly, looking away.

'Wouldn't they help you if they knew how you were treated here?' I asked.

'They sent me here to learn structure and discipline,' she said. 'I'm very lucky. Many of the girls here are orphans.'

'Who pays their tuition?'

'Wealthy donors who support the school.'

'Will you be returning to your family when you are finished with school?' But Ellen began to cough just then, a muted little cough that had a nasty, throaty sound to it.

'I must continue reading,' she said, when she had recovered. 'It will be lights out soon, and I must finish before then. Goodnight.'

"I continued on to my room. There was a dormitory, but there were also private rooms, or I should say semi-private rooms. These were bedrooms in the old mansion that had four to six beds in them and were much more comfortable than the big dormitory. I wondered at the division, and then it occurred to me that the orphan girls were assigned to the dormitory, while the paid girls enjoyed the privacy of the bedrooms. The house was always a little cooler than was comfortable, and I climbed into my semi-private bed in the hope of getting warmer, then lay on my side between the cool sheets looking at the vacant bed across from me. That there was someone assigned to it was obvious by the photographs, books, and clothes all neatly placed near it. I thought to ask the other two girls in the room, but they were lying on their side across from each other, whispering and giggling back and forth. I wondered if they were talking about me. Then I heard the call, 'Lights out,' and all went dark.

"As before, we were awakened early the next day while it was still dark outside. Our beds and uniforms were inspected and found to be satisfactory, and we were allowed to go to the cafeteria for breakfast. We read the bible for an hour, and then our classes began. I feared Geography class, as much for myself as for Ellen. Mrs. Spoon's eye had rested on me the previous day, and I found it to be quite unnerving. My fear, I discovered, was not unfounded. Ellen was picked on first and soundly abused by Mrs. Spoon who found fault with her uniform, her posture, her tone of voice. It was all I could do to keep my tongue, but the poor girl bore it as before, without retort or comment. Then it was my turn. I was asked to read a paragraph from the book, but had hardly uttered a few nervous words before she told me to begin again. Again I began, and again she stopped me and insisted that I start over. She told me to read louder. She told me to read with more passion. She said to sit straight. To hold my head up. To keep my shoulders back. And each order was delivered with condescending malice. I was so flustered that I was near tears.

'Are you going to cry, Miss Nagel?' she asked, with wicked delight, as she approached my seat. 'Won't you cry a bit for us?' I bit my lip to fight back the tears as she drew close, eagerly studying my face. 'What? No tears today? Pity,' she said, and returned to her place at the head of the class. Why had she chosen to target me, I wondered? I felt it was because she saw the angry, defiant look in my eye when she abused Ellen.

"I dreaded her class after that. I knew that nothing I did would be good enough to avoid her ridicule and scorn and that I had no recourse. What if I spoke up and was expelled? How could I return here with William stalking me? That the school would portray me as a lazy, obstinate girl, I knew, and I couldn't face your mother like that, Thomas. I wouldn't have her think of me that way. It was three days after the first incident. Mrs. Spoon warmed up by abusing Ellen, but I could tell that she was growing weary of that passive target and wished for greater sport. She turned her attention to me once more, and asked that I read. I knew it wouldn't be good enough, that she would find fault with all I did, but I had no choice, so I began nervously and, as predicted, she corrected me at every turn. She maligned, abused, and vilified me before the entire class until I was on the brink of tears, but I saw the amusement in her evil face and swallowed it all back. I sat up straight and met her eye with a fierce, determined glare.

'What, no tears Miss Nagel?' she mocked.

'You'll never make me cry,' I said stubbornly.

'Class,' she said, addressing the girls assembled in the classroom, 'we received word of Miss Nagel before she arrived. Her stepfather, who showed her every kindness, reports that she is an unconscionable liar. Beware of her. Avoid her, all of you.'

'That's a lie,' I shouted.

'Are you calling me a liar?' said Mrs. Spoon, approaching

my seat with her eyes boring into me. 'I'll see you expelled. Are you calling me a liar Miss Nagel?' she asked, hovering over me contemptuously and glaring down at me

'She doesn't know you well enough to call you a liar, Mrs. Spoon,' said a calm voice behind me. 'I, however, do. And I have found you to be a malicious, bold-faced liar on many occasions.'

'Miss DePaul!' said Mrs. Spoon, in horror. I turned round in my seat and saw a beautiful girl at the desk behind, which had always been vacant. She had long black hair, blacker than I had ever seen before, tapered black brows, and black eyes, exotic and beautiful. Her skin was slightly dark, and she sat with a sort of natural elegance, as if born to it. I imagined her sitting on a throne.

'This girl is my friend, and I don't suffer my friends to be treated in this manner,' she continued, then said something in French. I saw Mrs. Spoon's face change from shock to fear, and she returned to the front of the room. A moment later, the bell rang, and class was dismissed. I gathered up my books and turned to thank my beautiful benefactress, but she was gone. Through the rest of my classes, and then dinner as well, I thought about her and wondered who she might be but didn't catch so much as a glimpse of her in the cafeteria or anywhere else. After dinner, I stood in the hallway at a second story window, looking out over the snow-covered grounds, thinking about you and home. It all seemed so very far away. I couldn't imagine ever seeing any of it again. How could I ever come home to a house where William resided? Hearing the call of lights out, I returned to my room to find the formerly vacant bed across from me occupied by the beautiful girl from class. She was sitting on her bed reading The Confessions of Saint Augustine.

'Hello,' I said, enthusiastically.

'Hello,' was her measured response as she looked up from her book, regarding me with reserve.

'Thank you for your help today,' I said. She shrugged indifferently.

'It was good sport,' she replied, and her eye fell on the portmanteau under my bed. 'May I see your luggage?'

'Of course.' I removed it from under the bed, and set it in the space between us. Without getting up she turned her head slightly, looking down at it on the floor.

'Hum. You may put it away now,' said she. I put it back under the bed. 'Where did you get it?'

'It was a Christmas present from my mother...' I corrected myself, 'my guardian.'

'Really?' she answered, regarding me curiously. 'It's European you know? Made in Florence Italy by Guccio Gucci.'

'Oh,' I replied, genuinely surprised. She got up from her bed, then pulled the covers back.

'It's worth more than these impoverished teachers here earn in a year,' she added, casually. As she climbed under the blankets and they lifted slightly, I saw that she had two such portmanteaus under her bed, and then the lights went out.

"I learned in the course of time that my roommate's name was Camille. Camille DePaul. Her father was the French Ambassador to the United States, and not only paid for her tuition but also that of several other students. Camille didn't really have any friends at the school, but everyone adored her and idolized her. She kept them all at arm's length.

"Mrs. Spoon never dared be unkind to me after that day, but I fear Ellen suffered all the more because of it. The animosity that she felt for the poor girl increased, and the wrath that she couldn't visit upon me found its way to the silent, ever-patient Ellen. I turned away and covered my ears when she was called upon; Mrs. Spoon was that cruel. One afternoon, a few days before Christmas break, she delivered an especially severe criticism of poor Ellen and followed it up with another beating. Mrs. Spoon always kept a thin ruler in her desk drawer, and applied it without restraint to Ellen's poor knuckles. Always, Ellen bore it silently, without comment or reproach. One night, just before lights out, I returned to my room after visiting Ellen in the dormitory, and found Camille going through her closet.

'Camille?'

'Yes, Miss Nagel,' she answered, without turning, as she perused her closet.

'Why don't you ever help Ellen the way you helped me?'

'You defended yourself. She does not,' she replied, casually.

'She doesn't feel that it's right.'

'She is wrong.'

'She believes that God would have her act as she does.'

'Then let God help her.'

'God uses people to do his work.'

'Well, he doesn't use me. I'll not be his pawn,' she said, firmly.

'But Mrs. Spoon is so ill tempered.'

'Yes, I'll probably see to it that she is replaced next term. A woman like that has no business teaching.'

"I looked for Ellen in class the following day, but her seat was vacant and I didn't see her in the cafeteria either. After dinner I looked for her at the fire in the common room, but she was absent from there as well. I went to the dormitory, but she wasn't at her bed.

'Does anyone know where Ellen Reed might be?' I asked the girls there.

'She's in the infirmary,' someone said.

'Where is that?' I inquired.

'Upstairs at the south side of the building.'

"The mansion was quite large, and I had not explored all of it. I didn't know that there was an infirmary, but I made my way there and, among the ten or so beds in the white, antiseptic-smelling room, saw its only occupant in the middle bed, looking even thinner and more frail than usual in the soft light of the lamp beside her.

'Ellen?' I said softly as I approached.

'Who's there?' she answered, weakly, lifting her tired head from the pillow. 'Is that you Sophia?' she asked, trying to focus her bleary eyes upon me.

'Yes, I've come to see how you are. Why are you here Ellen? Are you ill?' I asked, finding that a chair had been placed next to her bed for visitors. Who would occupy that chair, I wondered? She had no friends that I had seen, but it felt warm to the touch when I sat upon it, as though recently used. Beside each bed was a little table, upon which was a lamp. Ellen's also held a bible, a glass of water, and a white cloth with little flecks of blood staining it.

'I'm glad you've come. I wondered if someone might miss me.'

'I missed you all day. I looked for you everywhere.'

'I'm so glad you're here.' She started coughing then. I saw her reach out to the white cloth on the table and hold it to her mouth as she coughed. Then she returned it to the table, and her head fell back to the pillow. The effort left her exhausted. She closed her eyes and lay without moving on the old hospital bed as her chest rose and fell slowly. I took her hand, which seemed to comfort her, and a short time later she drifted off to sleep. I must have dozed off as well. I awoke in the chair sometime later to the sound of whispered voices beside me, and I remained still. With my eyes closed, I listened but could hear only a soft word or two spoken quietly.

"When I lifted my head to see who was speaking, I found a doctor and nurse standing over Ellen's bed, looking gravely at her sleeping face. They stopped talking abruptly when they saw that I was awake and wandered away together.

"A few days later, Ellen was released from the infirmary and resumed her studies. Over the next few weeks, she seemed to have changed her habits and wasn't in her usual haunts. She had always been thin and frail, but since the infirmary she looked healthy and happy, with a cute little smile that she kept to herself. Her eyes sparkled when I saw her in class or in the hallway, and she seemed to go about with a happy secret that she never spoke of. No one noticed but me (I don't believe anyone else cared), and I found after a few days of her smiling eyes that I had to know what her secret was. We were very close. She told me everything, or so I thought. I decided to ask and went in search of Ellen. She would normally be found beside the fire in the great room, with a blanket over her legs while she read, but she wasn't there. I didn't find her in her dorm, either, but even her Spartan little space there seemed unusually bare. All of the other girls in the dorm had photographs of people who were important to them on the table next to their beds, and little personal items that they took comfort in. Ellen never did, and it always struck me as odd. It was almost as if she intended to punish herself or devote herself entirely to some higher cause or purpose. Though her space was always bare and free of comfort or distraction, it seemed somehow different to me that day, and I stood next to her bed puzzling over the change that I couldn't define. One of the girls a few beds down passed by then and saw my perplexed frown. Knowing Ellen and I were friends, she explained in passing.

'She's gone,' the girl said.

'Gone? Ellen?' I asked. 'When? Where did she go?' The girl shrugged.

'I saw her packing a few little things from her drawer, then she hurried away. I'm not certain, but I think she may have gone into the woods,' the girl said, and led me across the room to a second story window that looked out over the grounds. There was a vast clearing of gently rolling hills covered in a smooth blanket of snow, at the distant edge of which was a dense forest. In the perfect, unbroken snow, a little trail of footsteps led from the school across the clearing to the forest.

'Why would she leave?' I asked in a panic. 'Where would she go?'

'I don't know.'

'Was she upset?'

'No. She seemed happy.'

'When did she leave?'

'A few hours ago, I think.'

'Oh dear,' I replied, rushing away. I was wearing a thin sweater over my school uniform because it was always a bit chill in the drafty house, but my coat was upstairs in my room and I didn't dare fetch it. The last class of the day would start in a few minutes, and if I were seen in the hallway I would be forced to attend. So I rushed down the stairs, pushed through the big double doors, and followed the path in the snow that led across the field to the woods. It was easy to follow, or that is to say, easy to find. The snow was several feet deep, and I sank almost to my waist as I plowed along. The brisk air was so cold I could see every breath I exhaled. It must have taken me an hour or so to reach the forest, and I was exhausted when I finally fell at the trunk of the first tree I came to. But I thought of frail little Ellen out there in the cold and pushed myself back up. The snow wasn't as thick under the dense tree limbs, so I made a better pace. The footprints were still easy to follow in the clear snow, but it was already getting dark and becoming so much colder. I continued on in the fading light, rushing along after the footfalls in the snow, until they ended abruptly. They had simply stopped. How could that be? I looked about me, and saw what I had missed before in my haste. Ellen was sitting in the snow a few paces off the trail, with her back against a tree. Some snow had fallen since she fell there, and she was covered in a sparse layer of white powder. I rushed to her.

'Ellen. Ellen. Are you all right? What are you doing here?' Her eyes fluttered open at the sound of my voice.

'Sophia?' she asked, as her eyes finally came to focus on me. Little snowflakes clung to her eyelashes. 'Angel. Have you come to take me home?'

'Why did you leave the school, Ellen? What are you doing out here?' I took her hands in mine and attempted to warm them, but her little fingers were stiff and frozen by the cold. It was only about seven degrees, and the temperature was falling. 'Ellen. Ellen. What are you doing? I don't understand.' Wearing a serene smile, she sat back against the tree with her eyes closed. When I shook her, she looked up at me through sleepy eyes that didn't focus. 'Get up, Ellen. We have to get you back.'

'Oh, it's so peaceful here,' she replied softly, with her eyes still closed. Then the snow began to fall again heavily, silently, covering us both. It was too late for her, I knew. She couldn't get up and I couldn't carry her back. So I held her hand and spoke with her as she drifted in and out of sleep and her life ebbed away. 'Must get home...must...go home Sophia,' she muttered, opening her eyes ever so slightly. '... See Mother and Father one more time,' she mumbled, and closed her eyes in sleep once more.

'Why?' I asked. 'What is so important?' I rubbed her frozen cheeks vigorously with my chilled hands, and she revived a little, opening her eyes at last. 'Why are you doing this, Ellen?'

'I must...show...them I'm...normal,' she said, drifting in and out of sleep.

'Why would they think otherwise?' I asked, and returned to rubbing her bare little hands.

'Laura... kissing Laura,' she answered, barely able to find the strength for a few words. '...had the loveliest...lips. Perfectly... innocent...only friends...'

'And they sent you away because of that?' I asked.

'...Must tell them...that I'm normal...Sophia,' she smiled. 'In love...with...a boy.'

'You're in love with a boy?' I asked, surprised. 'Who? What boy?'

'Amadeus,' she said, dreamily. 'Tell Father that I'm not sick. Tell him...'

'How can I find him?'

'Father is pastor of...' her voice trailed off. 'Such...a...good... friend,' were the last words she uttered. She died that evening, sitting in the snow with her back against the cedar tree while the snowflakes fell softly all around her. I loathed myself for leaving her there, but I was trembling from the cold and would perish too if I remained. I kissed her cold cheek and..."

Sophia covered her face with her hands as the memory of that wretched event moved her nearly to tears, but she was stronger than when I left her, or perhaps it was something else. She had survived a conflict of her own, and none emerge from such trials unscathed or unblemished. What part of my childhood friend was left behind in the snow that day so that she might survive? She took a deep breath, and continued.

"I was able to follow the path that I had already plowed through the snow, or I never would have made it back. Even so, when I reached the school, I found that my frozen hands wouldn't work the door and I couldn't get inside. Amadeus heard me bumping at the door and opened it for me. He had been looking for Ellen. I was trembling violently when he threw an arm around me and led me to the fire, which he stoked to a roaring blaze while I sat on the hearth with my hands extended to the warmth.

'Not too close, Miss Nagel,' he said, observing that I had my fingers nearly in the flames. 'Not too close or you'll burn them. They're numb you know. You've got frostbite.'

'You...' I stammered through chattering teeth, noting that he wore a lab coat. I had not seen him since the day he drove me to the school. 'You work in the infirmary?'

"He nodded. I told him..." Sophia choked on her words, growing emotional again, "I told him about finding Ellen in the snow, and..." Elsie interceded.

"There, there, love," she said, taking Sophia's hand. "We don't need to talk about that right now. Are you all right?" Sophia nodded as she fought back the tears. "Would you like something to drink?" Again Sophia nodded. Elsie shifted to rise from her seat, but it was easier for me, and I thought it best if the two of them were alone for a while.

"I'll get it, Elsie." I said, stepping quickly into the kitchen.

Pouring iced tea reminded me of the many times Sophia and I had played in this big old house and ran into the kitchen to have Elsie pour us tea or make us a snack. I grabbed the drinks and returned to the other room to find Sophia nodding off in the chair with her eyes closed. She awoke when she heard me approach.

"I'm sorry," she said, tiredly. "I didn't get any sleep last night," she smiled, "thanks to this outlaw."

"He was just telling me the story when you arrived," said Elsie. "How did you catch him?"

"Yes, how did you catch me?"

"Well," Sophia smiled, "you might say you caught yourself. You were too sneaky for your own good."

"How's that?" Elsie asked.

"Well, Elsie, when Thomas and I were young, we discovered a tiny shack in a secluded little bay that we had sailed past a number of times and never noticed the entrance to. It was that hidden. I was hired specifically to stop the flow of alcohol to the island, so the first thing I did when I arrived was rent a boat and circumnavigate the island, looking for the places where smugglers could offload their cargo. But there were just too many. We didn't have enough men to watch all of them. Even with agents in Canada reporting when the smugglers were leaving the docks, we couldn't catch them. There is too much open water between here and there, and we couldn't find them. What I needed was a location where I knew they would come on a certain day, at a certain time. The little shack in the hidden bay was just such a place. I knew it would be used only when there was no moon to reveal the boat, and I knew it had to be between a one-foot negative tide and a three-foot negative tide. Any less, and the water would be too shallow for a boat. Any more, and the piling would be covered, so they couldn't use the float. That narrowed it enough that it made a perfect trap."

"So you found the float?" I asked. "That's what tipped you off?"

"I checked the shack first, but it looked abandoned, so I walked back down to the beach where I noticed the driftwood had washed up and was tossed haphazardly along the shore at the furthest reach of the tide. I sat down on a smooth chunk of wood to think, and I watched the water. The current was pretty strong there, and the wind was from the north, making it difficult to beach a boat of any size. I was almost convinced that the location was a wild goose chase, but as I glanced up and down the beach one last time my eye fell on a little float among the driftwood. It was so weathered that it looked just like the driftwood surrounding it and blended in perfectly. I would have missed it if I hadn't been nearly sitting on it. But there was nothing unusual in that, really. I wondered that it would wash up right there, though, and as I glanced at it in passing, I saw a rope that led from it to a stake in the sand. It was tethered to keep it from drifting away at high tide. That seemed odd since there was no way to use it without a piling of some sort to attach it to. I sat down once again to consider how that float could be used, and was there for quite some time, but nothing came to mind. I was walking back up to the trail and was already thinking about some of the other locations when I spotted the top of a broken off piling that just became visible with the out going tide. Just at the surface of the water, I could see the jagged top of the piling as the water lapped at it. Intrigued, I sat back down on a smooth piece of driftwood and waited. Soon I could see ten or twelve inches of the piling sticking up out of the water, and then another piling appeared fifteen feet further out. When I examined them, I could see fresh grooves in the wood where a rope had rubbed. So I looked more closely at the shack. At first glance I missed it, but looking closer I saw scratches on the wood floor where it looked like wooden cases had been dragged. And there was a shaded little stub of a candle. The pieces were starting to come together, and I was convinced that I had discovered a site that smugglers were using. And they were careful smugglers, too. Rarely had they ever taken such care to hide their lair or cover their tracks before. When I returned to the beach and thought the process through, I realized that certain conditions had to exist for this location to be used. So I researched when those conditions would next occur and set up a trap. Since the lair was only available three or four times per month because of the tide and moon, I was pretty certain it would be used when it could be."

"A brilliant bit of observation," I said, quite impressed.

"Thank you." There was a pause in the conversation as we all sat beside the fire enjoying the company of our little group. The circle was nearly complete, and the house felt like a home again. "It feels so good to be home. To see you all again," Sophia said, and then stood. "I really must go now. I have court in the morning and so much work to do."

Elsie stood and threw her arms around our guest in a heart-felt embrace. "Come back as soon as you can," she said.

"I won't be able to return until this case is over. I shouldn't even be here now. But I'll be back after that."

"Come back to stay, Sophia. Come back for good," Elsie added.

"I will, Elsie. I will."

I walked Sophia to the door, and she turned to me there. In the stillness of the late night, I heard the fire crackle softly in the other room and the persistent tick of the grandfather clock in the hallway. The searching was over for both of us. She took my hands in hers and pressed her head to mine, reveling in the touch. Still holding my hands, she pulled back and looked into my eyes.

"I can't believe I found you here. After looking for you everywhere, I find you right here where it all started. I'm so happy, Thomas."

"I didn't even know where to start looking for you," I said.

"I'll come back when this is all over. I'll come back for good," she said, shyly, "If you want me to."

"If I want you to?" I said. "You can be so silly." I wanted so desperately to tell her how I felt about her, how I thought of her constantly, but as always the words failed me. She bit her lip as her eyes began to tear, and regarded me bashfully.

"Guess I'll see you in court."

"Are you going to put me in jail?" I said, with a wry smile.

"Oh Thomas," she said, quickly, "I would never do that. I'll do everything I can to keep you out of jail."

"I was only jesting. Goodbye, Sophia." We shared a long, lingering kiss, and she left. I watched from the open doorway as her car traveled down the tree-lined drive, and the taillights disappeared around the corner as she pulled into the street. When I turned at last and closed the door behind me, I felt as though I was beginning a new chapter of my life. I had found Sophia at last, and she would be returning soon for good.

Thomas Moore

May 21st 1930

Elsie and I have been all smiles and grins since our visitor left. Having my childhood nanny back has driven away the shadow of emptiness and loneliness that clung to this old house and given us both hope, but to have Sophia back here again is more than we could have ever hoped for. Finally it will feel like home again. We all hope for a speedy resolution to my court case so that she may return for good. To that end, I called Howard. The news was not especially good. That he had secured Herbert's release on several occasions I was well aware, but there was no foundation for such technicalities here, he said after studying the police reports. There was obviously someone new involved, and they did things in strict observance of the law. I felt a certain rush of pride for Sophia, even if it was at my own expense.

Thomas Moore

June 16th 1930

Howard has spoken to the Assistant District Attorney (he's unaware that I know her) and has been told that she will recommend probation since this is my first offense. All we need to do is appear in court, enter a guilty plea, and receive my slap on the wrist. Then Sophia can come home. I'm so happy. Court is in three days. I can hardly wait.

Thomas Moore

June 21st 1930

There are complications. It seems my case has somehow landed on the desk of the District Attorney, a Mr. Jerry Daniels, who wishes to review it. He has asked for, and received, a continuance. My court date has been moved back a month. This does not bode well. No word from Sophia.

Thomas Moore

June 26th 1930

It was nearly dusk. I was watching the sunset from the window of the library while searching for a good book to pass the evening, when I heard a knock at the door and turned to find Elsie.

"Sorry to disturb you, Thomas, but you have visitors."

"Visitors?"

"Jack and Martin."

"Oh. I'll see them here in the library, Elsie. Thank you." She left with a nod of the head and returned a short time later with my guests, leaving us alone. I poured them both a drink, and we fell into chairs to talk.

"I take it this isn't a social call."

"We wanted to thank ya, mate. Ya did right by us, letting us get away like that, especially when ya got caught," said Jack.

"That's right," added Martin.

"I'm sure Herbert would have done the same thing," I answered.

"Yep, he would," said Martin. "Did they ask ya about us? They knew there were three of us there. They heard us runnin' through the woods."

"I haven't spoken to them at all. I don't think I will," I said, certain that Sophia would not probe into the matter any more than necessary.

"That's peculiar," said Jack.

"Damned peculiar," added Martin. "They knew ya had help. Why wouldn't they want ta know who was with ya?"

"I don't know." The room was quiet as we all thought about that. Martin stirred his drink nervously with his finger and seemed focused on his glass.

"We need ta go out again, Thomas," he said, at last.

"What?"

"We need the money mate," Jack added.

"But Jack, it's too risky. They know the boat now."

"I need the money."

"How can you need the money after all the shipments we've made?"

"It's my mum," he said, with his downcast eyes on the floor. "She's in bad nick. Doesn't know who I am most a the time. I can't leave her alone at all. Got a private nurse that looks after her all the time. It's bloody expensive."

"I can give you some money," I said.

"I don't want your money, Thomas. Thanks, but I don't want your money. I just want to make another run."

"I don't see how we can. It's just to risky right now," I said. "And to be honest, I was thinking of retiring from the business."

"What?" said Martin.

"Retiring?" added Jack. "Does Herbert know about this?"

"I haven't mentioned it to him yet."

"Well, someone's got ta keep The Shack supplied. That's the deal. We got an exclusive contract, but we have ta keep 'em supplied. If you don't do it, then Herbert'll have ta. Think about that, mate."

"Look Jack, I don't want to keep doing this. I want to…"

"What happened, ya get cold feet?" he interrupted, growing angry. "Ya get pinched one time, and ya go soft on us. That little jail cell too harsh for ya? Herbert got caught three times and never complained. I knew I was right about you."

"How quickly you've forgotten that I was caught helping you get away."

"Think about someone else for once in yer life. A lot of people depend on this for their living. If you quit Herbert'll step in and take over again. He'll have to. Ya want that?"

Martin had fixed me with a quiet, meditative frown throughout most of this conversation, as he held his drink in hand. He finished it in a gulp then, set the glass on a nearby table, and began toward the door without a word. Jack raised his glass to his lips to finish it as well, but changing his mind, hurled it into the fire where the glass shattered upon the brick and the flames flared with the whiskey like Jack's volatile temper.

And then they were gone. I turned off the lights and then fell into a chair near the fire where I sat in the dark, pondering what to do by the flickering firelight. Like Sophia, I always took comfort in the fire. The warmth, combined with the hypnotic effect of the flickering flames, soon had me dozing off, and I awoke sometime later as I felt a blanket draped over me.

"Oh…Elsie," I said, rubbing the sleep from my eyes.

"I'm sorry, Thomas, I didn't mean to wake you."

"It's all right." I stretched and sat up. Only coals remained of the fire, and the room was dark. "But what are you still doing up at this hour?"

"I was waiting for you to come downstairs. I thought you may want to talk."

"About what?"

"It's a big house," she said, adding more wood to the glowing coals before taking a seat beside me, "but angry voices carry."

"Oh, that."

"What are you going to do?" she asked by the dim glow of the coals. "I'm sorry I got you into this, Thomas. Maybe it wasn't the best thing after all."

"You got me into nothing," I said, taking her hand in mine, "and to be honest with you, I've enjoyed it. There's a certain intrigue to outwitting the police and working under cover of darkness. I was a little bored by the whole thing until I had a close call and realized they were everywhere, actively searching for importers like myself. Then it became fun."

"Are you thinking of continuing?"

"I don't know yet. It's complicated."

"Yes, I heard. But Thomas, if you ever want to be with Sophia again you can't continue with this. You can't expect her to help you, knowing that you will continue. I'm certain her expectation is that you'll stop."

"I don't need to continue. We have enough money that I could stop now."

"Really? Already?" she asked, incredulous.

"Yes, but others depend on me to continue with this."

"What about Sophia? Don't you want her to return? How could she come back here to live knowing that you're still in that business? She believes in what she's doing, Thomas. It would never work. Don't you want her back?"

"Of course I want her back. It's all I thought about for years."

"Then find someone else to take your place," she said, eagerly, and I saw at last what I failed to perceive in my selfishness.

"You want her back, too, don't you Elsie. You want her back as much as I."

"Is that such a bad thing?"

"I'm just surprised I didn't think of you, that's all. I'm sorry."

"I missed you both when you went away. You kids were such a joy. This house can feel so empty, even with two here."

"I'll talk to Herbert tomorrow."

"Thank you," she said, and her face was as happy as I have ever seen.

Skipping breakfast, I left the house early the next day, hoping to reach Herbert before Jack got there. I parked in the usual place and began down the little trail that led to his house. I was just emerging from the brush when I saw him across the clearing. He exited the house in his robe and sat down at a table on the rear patio to read a newspaper. His movements were slow and stiff, like those of an old man, and when he lifted the newspaper from the table I witnessed something I had not noticed before. His left hand shook uncontrollably. Whenever I had seen him before he had always held his left hand in his right, and I had assumed it was a peculiar quirk that was habitual to him, but now I saw why he did so. It was to keep his hand from shaking. He wanted no one to see.

His trembling hand held the newspaper while the other reached into the pocket of his robe for his reading glasses, which he slipped over his nose and began to read. But a moment later he set the paper down on the table, removed his glasses, and looked out over the blue ocean. It was not the gaze of a man who enjoys what he sees. The cloudless blue sky reflected in the rippling blue water was dotted by tree-covered islands in the distance. It was a stunning, inviting sight, but he took no pleasure in its beauty. It was then that I knew what Herbert was thinking and that Jack had been there before me.

I walked across the yard and took a seat at the table beside Herbert.

"Ah, there ya are lad," he said, mustering a smile. "Been expectin' ya."

"That can only mean that Jack has been here already this morning."

"This morning?" Herbert said, tiredly. "Ya mean last night. He came directly here when he left yer house." An uncomfortable silence followed then. I saw Herbert covertly grab his hand to keep it from shaking.

"I'm sorry, Herbert."

"It's all right Thomas," he said, tightening his grip on the palsy hand. "It's all right."

"Things have changed," I said.

"I know."

"You do?" He nodded. "Are we talking about the same thing?" I inquired.

"I'm talkin' about a girl. What are you talkin' about?"

"You know about her?" I asked, surprised, which drew a grin from Herbert. "But how?"

"There ain't much happens on this here island but what I know about it."

"Does anyone else know?" I inquired, with some alarm.

"Don't think so."

"But how do you?"

"Well," he said, "there's a bit of a story to that. Remember that night we was in stir together? You was pretty talkative that night. Told me all about yer circumstances, remember?" I thought back to that day in jail with Herbert. We spoke for many long hours in the lonely solitude of the little cell. I was so glad for his company. "There was that little shaver of a tomboy that ya met while ya was playin' that day. The two a ya became best friends, ya said. And then her ma up and left her one day, and she went ta live with ya out there in yer house. Sophia, ya said her name was. Yer beautiful little Sophia, with the lovely blue eyes." I looked at him in awe, wondering how could he remember all of this. "Them was yer words not mine," he said, smiling, and then continued.

"I was makin' deliveries out at The Shack even back in them days, and I used ta sometimes see a little tomboy there in the afternoon when no one else was around. She would just come in sometimes an sit up on a bar stool so she could see her ma, who worked there tendin' bar. Always wore boy's clothes. I think it was all she had. Sophia was her name. I heard her ma call her by it a time or two. Had the prettiest blue eyes.

"Well, Peterson, that being Mark Peterson, the owner of the

place, was always on her ma ta get back ta work. She was a flirt, was Sophia's ma. A pretty thing, too. Looked jus' like her daughter. Quite young. Anyways, she was always chattin' with the fellas there, and Mark would say, 'Back to work Nagel,' and she would roll her eyes in her flirtatious way and coyly polish the bar or some such thing.

"So, when I heard we got us a new prosecutor from out of town and her name was Sophia Nagel, I was naturally curious, ya see. And I pops inta court one day and takes a seat there ever so quietly and get a good look at her tryin' a case. She's a lovely creature, Thomas," he said, moved by the memory of her that day. "A lovely creature. The spit and image of her ma."

"Do you know what became of her mother?" I asked, after a moment of reflection.

"Jus' ran off with some fella from the bar. Some drifter who was jus' passin' through." I heard the whistle of a teapot from the kitchen, and Herbert pushed himself up from the table, but his palsied hand upon the tabletop failed him and he collapsed back into his chair holding his leg painfully.

"Are you all right, Herbert? I asked, and helped to right him in the seat, which he had fallen into awkwardly. His robe had fallen open, and I glimpsed the leg that he had clutched at. It wore an ugly brown bruise on the thigh that looked painful. "How did this happen?" I asked.

"I took a little tumble while I was fueling the boat up the other day."

"Why were you fueling up the boat?"

"Well," he said, stalling for time to think, "It's always good ta keep her fueled up. Never know when you'll want ta use her."

"Were you planning on making another run?" The teapot was whistling with an angry whine by then.

"Excuse me, Thomas, I can't abide that noise," he said, and he made to rise from his chair again.

"I'll get it," I said, quickly darting away. I turned the burner off and set the whistling teapot on the counter where it quickly calmed down. Then I opened a few cupboards looking for tea fixings. What caught my eye was the unmistakable fact that Herbert had far too much time on his hands. Everything in the cupboards was neatly, precisely arranged on the shelves, and nothing was out of place. The kitchen towels were folded perfectly and meticulously arranged for effect on the countertop. There wasn't so much as a water spot on the kitchen sink or a speck on the window. Nothing in the entire house was out of place, I noticed. The poor fellow must have been dreadfully bored.

I returned with the tea fixings, and we sipped a cup together.

"You were about to tell me, when we were interrupted by the teapot, why you were fueling the boat. Were you expecting to make a run to Canada?"

"Maybe I was."

"Isn't that my job?"

"I've been expectin' ya to retire from the business since ya was arrested. It's what ya should do."

"Why do you say that?"

"Ya have a chance at a good life, Thomas. Take it. Marry that girl. Raise a family. Bring some life back inta that big house." There was nothing, absolutely nothing, that I wanted to do more than that very thing. I wanted to marry Sophia, to fill the house with the ring of children's laughter, to continue the family line. But there was Herbert sitting before me. "Ya can't do both, Thomas."

"What do you mean?"

"There's two kinds a people involved in this Volstead business. Ya got yer opportunists and yer fanatics. We're opportunists, me and you. Yer girl now, she's a fanatic. I seen her in court. She's got the fire in her eye. There's somethin' drivin' that girl. Somethin' deep. Somethin' strong. She believes in what she's doin' an' won't back down."

I sipped my tea as I pondered Herbert's words. For all his simple speech and backward ways, he was a brilliant man. How very keenly he observed people; how cleverly he divined their character; how precisely he deduced their actions. The affable smile that was so much a part of him returned, but it was summoned with great effort, I could tell. He was attempting to put me at ease. To make me feel good about my decision to abandon him. The morning sun at my back shined upon him with an intensity that highlighted every furrow and wrinkle in his haggard, smiling face. His palsied hand shook in spite of the insistent grip of his good hand, and he slumped in his seat, though he tried to sit up straight. He was simply getting old.

"Where is Susan, Herbert? I've never seen her in any of my visits here."

"Passed away two years ago," he said, sadly. "Had the cancer. Just wasted away. Nothing anyone could do."

"I'm sorry. I didn't know," I said. "You're all alone out here, then? Do you have any children?" He didn't answer immediately. Herbert thought about it for a moment, and then shook his head.

I recall that my tender conscience received several sharp blows that day, in regard to my capricious nature. That it would suffer on Sophia's account I knew quite well, but it also had to answer to Elsie. It was much upon my mind (especially when I saw her eagerly going about the house dusting and polishing with a light heart in expectation of Sophia's imminent arrival) that I ought to tell her the entire truth. Yet I was hesitant to do so because she seemed so very happy at the thought of Sophia's return and for the reason that I mistrusted her response to my unwelcome news. Would she not think less of me? The thought of losing Elsie's confidence, of sitting before the fire in the evening staring drearily at her vacant chair, tied up my tongue. I knew that I would suffer no reproach from her forgiving lips and that she would quietly accept the burden of my news, but that was no motivation to tell her. Quite the contrary. Her kind, good-natured soul would seal her lips, just as my faint heart sealed mine. And so I went about the house in a sort of nagging dread, knowing that it must some day come out, and fearing that day and the consequences of it.

But I could not abandon Herbert and retreat to the comfort of my home and the ease of my chair while he resumed the clandestine trade from which he had retired. He was too old, and his broken body would not bear the strain. He would perish at sea, unable to react properly to the sudden changes of the ocean, or be arrested and suffer the hardship of jail. But more than that, I owed the man my life. If not for him, I would have spent my life in prison. If not for him, I would have lost the estate to back taxes. And all this he did for me because my father once gave him a job when no one else would. Abandoning him to facilitate Sophia's return was no way to repay Herbert for his kindness toward me.

"Elsie?" I asked, seeing her washing windows, after my return from Herbert's house.

"Yes, Thomas."

"Do you know Herbert Mayer?"

"I know of him," she said, as she continued scrubbing the glass. "I've seen him a few times in town."

"What do you know of him?"

"Only that his wife died a few years ago of cancer, and he lost his son in the war."

"Oh, he had a son?"

"His name was John. He would have been your age, I think. Yes, about your age."

"How is it that everyone on this island seems to know everything about everybody?"

"Everyone except you, you mean?" she asked, smiling, as she pushed the hair back behind her ear.

"Yes. I know nothing about anyone."

"You don't get out much."

"Would you mind doing me a little favor?"

"That depends," she said, and her polish rag paused as she peered through the glass with an appraising eye.

"On what?"

"On what the little favor is, of course."

"Unless I'm mistaken, you appear to have a little time available from day to day."

"I don't know that I like the sound of this," she said, with a playful smile.

"Herbert is quite old and has no one. He's just alone all day out there at his home. I thought perhaps you could go out there and have lunch with him now and then. There's nothing like a pretty girl to lift a man's spirits."

"Aren't you the charmer?" she replied coyly, and gave the glass a final flourish with her rag. "Sure. I'll go have lunch with Herbert. He's a sweetheart."

"Thank you," I said, and remained, watching her move to the next window and continue her work.

"Is there something else?" she inquired, seeing that I hovered nearby.

"Yes. I told Herbert that I would continue smuggling alcohol to the island, so don't expect Sophia to return any time soon," were the words that died unspoken on my sealed lips. "No." I muttered. "Nothing else." And I retreated to my study where I began preparations for my next venture to Canada.

Thomas Moore

July 1st 1930

Received word from Howard today. He has spoken to the District Attorney's office, and they will recommend probation if I allocute and name everyone else involved. I told him I would not name anyone else. That would probably mean a little jail time, he said. I'm not concerned. The first offense is always dealt with in a lenient fashion, and I would be very surprised if I served more then a few months in their comfortable jail.

Elsie and I have been readying the house for Sophia's return. She's washed the blankets and sheets on her bed, dusted and cleaned the windows in her room, and put fresh flowers on her nightstand every day. I've hired a few more gardeners so the grounds will be perfect. We're both so excited to have her back. If all goes as planned, I will have found a replacement by then and will be free of my importing duties. That's my solution to this. I can't imagine slipping out of the house at night without Elsie taking notice, so I may have to tell her that I am still making deliveries, but if I can tell her it is only until I can find someone to replace me, I'm certain she'll understand.

Thomas Moore

July 14th 1930

Howard has left a number of messages with Elsie asking that I speak with him, but frankly I prefer not to think about that ridiculous smuggling case. I'm focused on Sophia's return and have been readying the house in preparation of her arrival, but this morning I was in town and walked past his office, so I stopped. He was deep in thought, pondering a law book that was open on the desk before him, when I entered his office. With his head bent over the book, his eyes lifted at the sound of my entrance and looked none too friendly.

"To what do I owe this honor?" he asked.

"I was in town," I answered casually. "Walking past your office actually."

"None too concerned about your current case, I take it?"

"Why should I be?"

"Because you could go to jail."

"Ah." I dismissed the notion with a careless wave of my hand. "You worry too much, Howard."

"I see," he said, quietly, and leaned back in his chair, studying me with those keen eyes. A moment later he smiled and shook his head.

"What's so funny?" I asked.

"You've fallen victim to the island lifestyle."

"Island lifestyle?"

"Unless I am greatly mistaken, you awoke in the comfortable little jail to the smell of hash browns, eggs, and toast, which was presented to you by the smiling, good-natured face of Billy, who left the cell door open while you dined." I nodded. "I noticed that you held your hands before you when you entered the courtroom, as if cuffed, but there were no cuffs on your wrists, which means that Billy misplaced the key again." Again I nodded. "At first I thought that it was all a ruse to lull suspects into dropping their guard and taking things too lightly, but I've seen it again and again. It's just the way they do things here. The island is small. They can always find you if you run."

"I know how things work, Howard, I've been through this before, remember?"

"I don't think you do, Thomas. Something about you has changed. Your focus has shifted. You're so carefree."

"Nonsense," I said, with a blush.

"Take a seat." Howard said. I sat down across from him at his desk. He closed the book that he had been studying, and regarded me with piercing eyes. "I first came to this island twenty years ago by boat," he said. "I was on my way to Alaska and pulled in to the dock at Olga for breakfast. I'm sure you've been there before.

There's just that one little street, with eight or ten houses on each side, a country store at one end and a restaurant at the other. It's so quaint it could be a postcard. I stopped on my way to the restaurant to pick an apple from a tree beside the road. I had one in my hand and was reaching for another, when I felt something tugging at the apple in my hand and turned to find a deer eating it. Right out of my hand. It was a beautiful little fawn, on standing shaky legs, eating that apple without the slightest concern. I was a city boy and had never even seen a real deer before, so I was quite shocked and enamored.

"I had the best breakfast of my life at that little restaurant up the street, and afterward I was telling the waitress that I would like to see more of the island but that I had arrived by boat. Know what she said?" I shook my head. "She asked if I would like to borrow her horse. Can you believe that? I had just met her, and she was asking if I would like to use her horse. Everyone's like that here. This little island hasn't been touched by the pessimism and indifference of the big city.

"Fresh out of law school, I had been practicing law for four years, winning a lot of cases, building a reputation as a criminal defense attorney. But what they don't tell you in law school is that you have to live with the victories as well as the losses. It's a terrible burden to see your client, who you believe to be innocent, led away in chains to serve a prison sentence because you failed to do your job. That'll keep you awake at night. Know what's worse?" I sat silently, watching Howard. He seemed to need this, to get this off his chest. "Seeing your guilty client go free. When all the courtroom rhetoric is over, the verdict is in, and you're sitting in your office at night, your unnervingly quiet office, reflecting on the fact that you did your job so well that thanks to you an unconscionable killer has gone free. In a cold cemetery somewhere a dead body lies covered in dirt, silently crying out for justice."

"It wasn't your fault the jury reached that verdict."

"Oh? And who persuaded them to do so? Who worked so diligently and effectively to persuade them? You didn't see the grief on the faces of the victim's family. You didn't feel the weight of their judgment and grief and anger. When my client came to my office the next day and handed me a check with a wicked little smirk, I felt like Judas collecting his thirty pieces of silver. I may as well have been an accomplice to murder. I had received other acquittals of course but never knew if they were guilty or not. It was never clear. I believed they were innocent but didn't know for sure. This fellow I knew was guilty. I had my doubts when I heard the evidence against him, but when he handed me the check, his smug grin and smirking eyes said it all. How would you deal with that, Thomas? What would you do? The victim was a beautiful young girl, seventeen years old, so innocent and full of life, until she was strangled to death by the wealthy socialite she rejected."

"I don't know how I would deal with that, Howard," I answered, quietly. Without a word he rose from his seat, and walked to the bookcase where the law books were all perfectly arranged on the shelf. With a melancholy smile he traced his finger over the leather cover.

"So young and so naive," he said, as his finger continued over the book. "I was going to change the world."

"Why did you take my case, Howard? How did you know you weren't helping another killer to go free?" He smiled then, and such a smile. It was joy and gratitude, inspiration and mirth, all at once.

"Thomas my boy, gentlemen like you, and situations like yours, are the reason I got into law. I could tell at a glance that you were no killer. And when you confessed, I knew I was right about you and that you were protecting someone. I desperately needed a case like yours to restore my faith in the system, my faith in humanity, my faith in myself." He crossed the room to where I sat and extended a hand. The gesture took me off guard, and I hesitated, but stood and clasped his hand in mine. Looking me in the eye, he shook my hand firmly, with respect. "I didn't save you; you saved me," he said.

Thomas Moore

August 6th 1930

Another phone call from Howard indicated that he needed to see me, so I went to his office today. There was something in his tone that rang of trouble, but as I walked along the sidewalk toward his office and saw a few little sailboats glide silently over the blue water in the bright sun, trouble seemed so far away and unlikely. I entered to find him at his desk as always, but his chair was turned around toward the window, and he sat looking out at the sailboats gliding past with a thoughtful, meditative expression. I was surprised by that. With Howard's quick manner and busy schedule, I wonder if he had ever looked out of that window before that day.

Hearing me enter he turned, and I saw fatigue in his face, or concern.

"Thomas, good to see you," he said, with a weary smile. "Take a seat."

"What's wrong, Howard?" I said, as I took a seat before his desk.

"Is it that obvious?" he answered, trying to be cheerful. "I'll get right to it. When you refused to tell the DA's office who you were working with, they reexamined all of the evidence and interviewed all of the prohibition agents who were involved in the arrest. One of them said he heard a man speaking in an Australian accent that night. Apparently there is only one Australian man on the island, and he is known to work for Herbert."

"So?"

"So they believe that you are working for Herbert or are directly involved with him."

"So? I can't see where that's an issue."

"They want Herbert," he said flatly.

"Why?"

"I don't know, but they're adamant. They want him, and they're not backing off."

"Who have you been talking to?"

"The new ADA, Sophia Nagel."

"And this is what she's telling you?"

"Yes, but it's coming directly from Jerry Daniels, the District Attorney. It's all very unusual. A DA would never sully his hands with a little smuggling case like this. He has bigger fish to fry."

"What are you saying?"

"Why would Daniels take a personal interest in you?"

"I don't know. I've never heard of the man."

"Well," said Howard tiredly, "you've got some tough decisions to make."

"Like what?" I said, uneasily.

"Thomas, they want you to give them Herbert. If you don't,

they'll seek the maximum sentence."

"Can they do that?"

"Yeah, they can. They can make a pretty good case for it actually, since you've only just returned from prison on a murder charge. Especially with your reduced sentence and all. That got some attention. I'm guessing Daniels will be looking into that to see how you got out so early."

"I have no intention of delivering Herbert to them. I won't do it."

"I knew you would say that," he answered, with a weak smile. "I've gone over this police report a dozen times looking for procedural anomalies, or any little loophole, but Miss Nagel is by the book. All we can do is try the case in court and take our chances with a jury, but they got you red handed. It's not looking good."

I thought about that on my drive home; in fact, it so occupied my thoughts that I was home before I realized it and was surprised to see a car parked near the fountain when I pulled up. As I entered the house I heard voices and followed them to find Elsie and Sophia sitting together near the fireplace. There was a small fire on this warm summer day, probably more for effect then anything. They sat close together, speaking quietly, and their faces were grave. My heart leapt when I saw Sophia. It always did.

"Sophia. What are you doing here? I thought you weren't coming back until after the case was settled. Have you seen your room? Elsie has been putting fresh flowers there every day."

"I needed to speak to you, Thomas," she said, earnestly.

"I'll leave you kids alone to talk," Elsie said, and left the room. I took her seat beside Sophia.

"I'm glad you came," I said.

"It's difficult to stay away. This is the only home I've ever known."

"Oh," I smiled, "is that why you came back?"

"What other reason could I have?" she answered, demurely, twirling her hair. "None that I can think of," I answered, innocently. An uncomfortable silence followed. She was hesitant to begin, and I was reluctant to hear what she had to say, primarily because her visit was an official one. Her smartly pressed suit and handsomely tooled briefcase told me that. As always, we found comfort in the dancing flames of the fire as we sat together silently watching it burn. I was reminded of our first time together.

"Remember the first night you spent here at our house? Mother found us sitting here at the fire and invited you to stay so you wouldn't have to walk home in the storm."

"That was one of the best days of my life Thomas. I remember it like it was yesterday. I've never felt so warm and safe in my life."

"You were so adorable when you came downstairs wearing my white dress shirt and white socks. It was so cute the way your hair fell over the collar of my shirt and your little arms extended through the rolled up shirt sleeves."

"My, what a memory you have."

"You made quite an impression."

"That was seventeen years ago. Things were so much simpler then."

"Excuse me a moment," I said, as I stood, "I haven't had anything to drink all day. I'll be right back." I found Elsie in the kitchen making iced tea. She poured two glasses for me, and when I returned to the fire with them, Sophia was gone. I didn't hear her leave, but she wouldn't have left without a word of farewell, so I assumed she would return. I sat down at the fire to wait. A moment later she arrived, and took a seat beside me on the floor. She was wearing a white dress shirt, and white socks from my closet. Just as before, it hung to her knees and her thin arms extended through the rolled up sleeves. Her black hair was lovely, the way it fell over the shirt collar. She motioned for me to join her, and just as before I sat behind her on the floor and wrapped my arms around her. She leaned back into me, squirming gently like a child in my arms. The fire burned quietly, its light growing brighter as the sun sank into the ocean at our back and the shadows began to fall about us. Sophia wrapped her arms around mine and wiggled into me.

"It feels just as good as before," she said.

"Better, if that's possible."

"If only your mother were here."

"Yes," I replied, quietly, as I looked into the flames, and thought about Mother. "There's something that I've always been curious about, Sophia."

"Yes, Thomas."

"You always call her my mother. Rarely did you ever call her your mother."

"We talked about that, Carolyn and I. My second year here she asked if I would like to be adopted and become Sophia Moore."

"I didn't know that."

"I was touched and honored."

"Yet you didn't do it."

"Of course not."

"But why?"

"Have you no idea?"

"None."

"Well then," she said, and turned around between my legs to face me, "it's because that would make me your sister, and sisters can't very well do this," she leaned close, closed her eyes, and pressed her lovely red lips to mine in a long, tender kiss, then pulled back and studied my face. "Now, can they?"

"Not in most states," I stuttered, finally finding my voice. As I considered her lovely face by the amber light of the glowing flames, it was as if all of my dreams had come true. There she was in my arms again before the fire, just as before. I didn't want her to go. I believe she found the intensity of my adoring gaze to be slightly embarrassing, for she turned away shyly, with a blush, and her eyes drifted over the family cemetery visible through the window behind me.

"Can you stay the night?" I asked.

"I would love to. But I'm only here because my boss came up with a deal, and I offered to present it to you tonight. He wants an answer right away."

"What is it?"

"You just need to tell who you're working with and testify. The charges against you will be dropped."

"Is that all?"

"That's all," she said, with a delighted smile.

"I can't do it."

"What?"

"I can't sacrifice my friends to save myself. You know that. What kind of man do you think I am?"

"But Thomas, this is a good deal. I worked hard to get you this deal. Daniels didn't want to do this at all. He wanted you in jail."

"Sorry. I can't do it."

"You'll go to prison."

"I can't do it, Sophia. I'm surprised you would even ask."

"They're breaking the law, Thomas. You're all breaking the law."

"It's a ridiculous law."

"You can't pick and choose which laws to obey; it doesn't work that way."

"Yes, it does."

"No, it doesn't."

"Yes, it does."

"You're incorrigible."

"I won't turn on my friends. You of all people should appreciate that."

"I tried to do the right thing, Thomas. I was frightened, but I confessed to save you. I was willing to go to jail to save you."

"And I was willing to go to jail to save you." I reached out, as we both sat on the floor in the glow of the fire, with darkness falling all around us. I reached out and ran my hand tenderly over her flawless cheek, her beautiful, perfect cheek. It was the moment I had dreamed of so many times in my little prison cell. "The nature of chivalry is facing danger bravely, smiling as the noose is dropped over your head. I smiled each day, knowing that I had saved someone better than myself from the fate I was suffering."

"Oh Thomas," she said, taking my hands in hers, "this time your noble spirit is misplaced. If you don't take this deal I'll have to prosecute you. You'll make me the instrument of your destruction."

"I'm not too concerned."

"But you don't understand. We have an airtight case against you. Even Howard Goodfriend can't get you out of this. I'll win, and you'll go to prison." I smiled. "Why are you doing that?" she asked.

"You would never send me to prison."

"I'll have to. If I don't prosecute the case Daniels will, and he's utterly ruthless in the courtroom."

"I won't turn on my friends, Sophia."

"But Thomas…"

"Judas," I said, interrupting her, "betrayed Christ for thirty pieces of silver. Brutus betrayed Caesar for the betterment of the Republic. They're both despised by the entire world. You want me to betray my friends simply to save myself. That's the worst form of treachery."

"Alcohol is ruining lives and destroying our nation. It has to stop."

"Did you hear that at some rally?" There was no answer to that, and I believe we both thought it best to change the subject. "How did you become an attorney Sophia? We're so proud of you."

"Oh Thomas, do you really want to know that now?"

"Yes, I really do." Heaving a frustrated sigh, she leaned back into my arms as she peered into the fire.

"Things were never the same after Ellen died," she said. "I had always disliked the school, but after that I loathed it, I despised it. They buried Ellen without a service of any kind, in the Orphan's Acre. It was a little plot where all the orphan girls were buried, and there were so many. Only a little wooden cross marked her place there. It didn't even bear her name. Soon after that was Spring Break. Camille went to her father's house in DC to visit, and I was left without a friend. Even with all the other girls there, I felt so isolated and alone. But I soon had other things to occupy my thoughts and time. The headmaster called me to her office to tell me that William had not sent that month's payment and that I must move out of my private room and into the dorm." Sophia paused, and while I couldn't see her face, I sensed that she was growing emotional. "They gave me Ellen's bed," she said. "Ellen's bed. And they had me work in the laundry to pay for my room and board. They were twelve-hour workdays, with a twenty-minute lunch. I had Sundays off. That continued for two weeks, until school started again, then I was to work in the laundry after class.

"Camille returned from her father's house the day before class was to resume and saw that my things were gone. She was hurt, thinking that I had gone home without speaking to her or leaving word. The two girls sharing our room knew nothing of my fate, but Camille always had adoring followers who were willing to do whatever she asked, and it didn't take long for one of them to carry news of my new residence to her. Minutes later she was standing beside my bed while I prepared for class the next day.

'What is the meaning of this, Sophia? Why have you moved from our room?' I turned to see Camille with her hands on her hips, and fire in her eyes.

'The headmaster asked me to,' I answered, demurely.

'Why?' was her terse response. I couldn't tell her that my expenses hadn't been paid, but she saw the embarrassment in my eyes and the blush on my cheek. She also saw that my hands were dry and cracked.

'Have you been working in the laundry?' she asked in disbelief, but I didn't answer. 'Collect your things,' she said, firmly.

'But I was instructed to…'

'Collect your things,' she said kindly, taking my hand, 'and return to our room. I'll straighten this out.' She left then, and there was an unmistakable purpose in her stride as she made her way among the dormitory bunks, that did not require interpretation. I did as she instructed, collecting my possessions and returning to our former room. There was little doubt that Camille would have her way. I had scarcely begun to arrange my things in our old room before she appeared again. She stood beside me as I unpacked my portmanteau, which was open on the bed, and seemed a little unsure of herself, which was so unlike her. I was reaching for a dress from my luggage when she suddenly took my hand.

'I'm sorry about Ellen,' she said, peering into my eyes. 'I know you were very close.' Then she added under her breath, as if to herself. 'That they should put you in her old bed…' And she shook her head sadly. She had taken my hands in hers and held them distractedly as she spoke, but suddenly the texture captured her attention and she looked down at my dry, cracked fingers. 'And had you working in the laundry. My God. I'm sorry, Sophia.'

"I'm not certain what she said to the headmaster that day. I think she had her father pay my expenses at the school. He was paying for several other girls already, out of a sense of charity for them, and I think she asked him to pay for me as well. It was the first time I had seen the softer side of Camille, and I adored her for it. I had not shared much of my life with her, but felt so very close to her at that moment that I wanted to explain my circumstances and tell her of my life. I wanted her to know more about me. So I took her hand and led her along the hallway to the top floor of the house. We were climbing the stairs when I heard the call of lights out and the house went dark. We weren't supposed to be out of our rooms after lights out, but of course Camille could do as she wished and I knew that I could too if she was with me. I took her to the infirmary. It was always the warmest room of the house, and I knew we could be alone there. No patients were there just then, only two long rows of hospital beds in the center of the long room. I sat upon one while she sat across from me on another. A little light from the hallway leaked into the room, giving us just enough to see by as I told my story.

"I told her everything, Thomas. How we met while you were chasing pirates and how I attended school with you, and about Mother abandoning me and Carolyn taking me into your family. And I told her about Elsie, and William, and Rockwell, and what you did for me that night. She sat on the bed, wide-eyed, listening in wonder when I told her how you sacrificed yourself for me. I finished by telling how William had stalked me in the house and finally sent me away without even telling me where I was going. I hadn't learned of Carolyn's death at that point, so there was no mention of that, and I was at a loss to explain why my school expenses had not been paid. I thanked her again for her help that day, and she just smiled.

'You're a tower of hope and inspiration, Sophia. I wish I were half as strong as you,' she said, hugging me close, then pulled back and looked into my eyes intensely. 'And Thomas, mon Dieu, I've never known anyone as brave and courteous. Is he handsome?'

'Very,' I answered.

'You must see him,' she said, eagerly. 'Have you gone to see him since he went away?'

'I don't know where he is. I can't find him.'

'I shall ask my father to help. I'll do it first thing in the morning,' she said, her French eyes dancing with excitement.

"She telephoned her father early the next morning, and he said he would call back later that day with the information she requested. I was so excited to think that I would finally get to write you and see you again. It was all I could think about in class all day long. But there was no call that day, or the next. Camille said her father was very busy and called him on the third day. But there was no news. His secretary worked for weeks calling the courthouse and different prisons, but there was no record of you anywhere. My heart sank when I heard the news, and I knew that William had hidden you away somehow. Ambassador DePaul called some friends in the State Department, and even they couldn't help. He told me it was hopeless.

"School was over soon, and while I very much wanted to be far away from there, I had nowhere to go. I couldn't come back to a house that William was in. That much was certain. Camille knew my circumstances, of course, and again came to my rescue. We stayed with her father in DC for a week or so and then traveled by steamship to her home in France. They lived in Marseille, in a large chateau with servants. But Camille didn't want to stay home; she wanted to travel. She had been looking for a traveling companion for some time and found the perfect partner in me. We began at once, going to Spain, Portugal, Morocco, and then Italy, Switzerland, Austria, Germany, and Belgium. Camille was so happy and I loved being with her, but I couldn't enjoy myself. I thought always of you and your little prison cell. Was it little?" Sophia asked. I nodded.

"I'm so sorry, Thomas. We saw remarkable things, but I was always distracted, thinking about you. I had to find you somehow. I told Camille I needed to return to America. She understood. She returned with me to Marseille, and I boarded a ship for New York without any clear plan of what I would do or how I would find you when so many powerful people had failed. Mr. DePaul had a car waiting for me when I arrived, and it took me to his residence, where I remained for several weeks while I spoke to attorneys and politicians and combed the libraries for information. I thought about returning to the island. I wanted very much to return to the island because I felt that much closer to you, but my entire network was there at the capital. I had met a number of influential people who knew the legal system and could guide me and advise me. I spent so much time searching the law library and talking to lawyers, that Jean, that's Camille's father, suggested I become an attorney.

I hadn't thought about that before, but it made sense. I needed a career of some sort, and Mr. DePaul offered to pay for my college tuition and expenses. He had always hoped that Camille would follow after him and become an attorney or politician, but of course she had no interest in that. So he took great interest in my career and helped me where he could. I resided at his house, near the capital, and attended Georgetown University."

"You really did try to find me."

"Of course I did," she said, sincerely, "It was nearly all I thought about."

"Isn't Georgetown difficult to get into?"

"Very. But I had an Ambassador in my corner. Mr. DePaul wrote a letter, and I was admitted on his recommendation."

"How did you find employment in the District Attorney's Office?"

"That was much easier than Law School. The Ambassador was constantly entertaining at his home, and I would frequently meet his guests. It wasn't unusual for him to entertain businessmen, attorneys, congressmen, even senators, and I met them all. He would often ask me to join him at the dinner parties. I became well known to that circle. Everyone knew that I was pursuing a law degree. They were all eager to help me when I got it. I'm sure some of it was the novelty of seeing a woman with an interest in law. There aren't many of us. But I distinguished myself with my knowledge and ability too. There were many job offers. I wanted something in the criminal justice system so I could learn the intricacies of the law, and thus find you and help you. I took a job as an Assistant District Attorney in DC and had a short but distinguished career there. When an opening came up for an ADA here, I jumped at it, and look what happened. It led me right to you."

"Visiting the house would have led you right to me as well," I said, with a playful smile.

"I desperately wanted to come home, but I thought William was still here," she said, "and, of course, I had no idea that you were here. How did you get released?"

"The judge wrote to the parole board on my behalf. You got me out after all. I'm certain it was your conversation with him that convinced him to write."

"I'm glad I was able to do something helpful. But where were you all this time, Thomas? Where were you incarcerated? Why could I not find you?"

"William was as cunning as he was cruel. He thought of everything." I said, with a chill as I thought of my lonely prison cell. "He booked me in under another name."

"That's highly irregular, Thomas," Sophia said. "It's done only under extreme duress."

"I don't know for certain, but I believe he told the warden that he feared for my life. He had sentenced a number of men to the prison I was in, and I suspect he told the warden that they would harm me if they knew I was related to him."

"He made it sound as though he was concerned about your safety," Sophia said, "when he really only wanted to make it impossible for us to find you."

"He intended to send me to Texas and make me work on a chain gang. He died before he could do it."

"Is he really dead? You said he was presumed dead. Does anyone really know?"

"One person knows," I said quietly, as I peered into the soothing flames. "One person knows for certain."

"Who?" she asked, studying my face tensely. "What happened? Was he killed?"

Sophia perceived the wicked smile that I could not restrain as I recalled the details of William's death, a smile that grew as I pictured myself twisting the garotte that choked the life out of him. Studying my face, she perceived something of my thought.

"Was it you? Was he here when you returned from prison, Thomas? Did you kill him?" she asked, with some apprehension, moving away slightly as if she feared me.

"I wish I had killed him," I said, quietly. "I wish I could take credit for it. I wish I had strangled him to death with my bare hands." With her fear assuaged, she slipped back beside me on the floor and moved close, studying me inquisitively by the light of the fire.

"Have you changed that much? Did prison change you that much? Could you really do that now?"

She was the same Sophia that I had treasured and adored since my youth, but there was a difference in her too. Her convictions had moved her to a confidence that allowed for no opinion but her own, no option but the law. In her study of the law she had grown to respect and revere it, and with that reverence she had become so serious, where she had always been carefree, inquisitive, and playful before. She peered into my eyes there before the fire, reading the anger, the pain, the hostility, which was never present when she knew me before.

"My God, you really could do that now," she said, covering her face with her hands. "I'm so sorry I did this to you." And she stood suddenly, looking down at me with sympathy and remorse in her judgmental eyes, as if I were to be pitied for what I had become. As if I were broken or wounded, or somehow less than what I had been. I found it offensive.

"I was bound to grow up sometime, Sophia," I said, tersely, "I wasn't going to be that naive, gullible boy forever."

"This isn't growing up, Thomas. Becoming angry and cynical doesn't make you mature."

"No, it's just a happy consequence of being locked up for nearly a decade and treated like an animal." Heaving a frustrated sigh, she moved back to the hearth and sat peering into the flames. "He's a murderer, Sophia. William murdered Mother."

"The official cause of death was natural causes," she said, sympathetically. "I checked."

"Natural causes," I repeated, through clenched teeth. "You could say that. Another way to put it would be murder." I left the room for a moment. When I returned, I had Lorelei's journal in hand, open to the pages Robert had torn out. They were not fixed in the journal but were returned to their proper place.

"What is this?" she inquired.

"Just read it," I answered, and passed the journal to her. She accepted it reluctantly, finding no alternative in my insistent face, and moved closer to the fire to read by the light of the flames. But her hesitant manner quickly yielded, and I saw her focus entirely on the words in her hands as she read....

"Caroline Moore was beauty, poise, and elegance," Robert said, reverently, as he gazed out over the bay. "Everyone on the island loved and adored her. How she ended up with that William Thomson is anyone's guess. He was attractive and charming, I'll give him that. But there was a dark side to him as well, and he was able to keep that well hidden. I didn't see much of her after Daniel's death. She kept herself sequestered at their home and rarely left. But after Thomas went away, I began to see her more often. I think she wanted to get away from William. She would sometimes come here for little events I had, dinner parties or book club meetings or the like. But her smile wasn't as I remembered it when Daniel was here. I suspect she was thinking about Thomas. I took her by the arm to escort her through the room one afternoon, and she winced ever so slightly. My movement was gentle, but I knew I felt her wince. When my eyes met hers, she was smiling as if nothing had happened, but we both knew better. She began talking of something to distract me, and that's when I knew. If she had said she had fallen or injured herself somehow, I would have given it no more thought, but there was an obfuscation in her manner that was so unlike her. I stood at the window of my study later that day thinking about the incident, and saw Patrick O'Leary open the big garage door of the shop below.

"Grandfather?" said Nina, alertly, and continued reading with even greater interest.

"Patrick was on the Olympic crew team when he was younger and was building crew shells in the shop there, renting space from me. He was a strapping fellow, about six feet, four inches, and all muscle. Like everyone on the island, he loved Carolyn, but his affection went deeper than most. He had had a romance with her once, and she would have married him if not for Daniel. But there was no animosity between them. He and Daniel were best of friends, and Patrick was a frequent guest at their home. I needed to talk to him about some things anyway, so I walked to the shop and caught him sanding a shell. We exchanged greetings and he asked about Carolyn, as he always did. I told him what I suspected and saw fire in his gray, Irish eyes. His jaw was firm and his teeth clenched when I left the shop that day.

"The next morning, when William arrived to borrow a law book from my library, he found the only place to park was in front of the shop. My clerk gave him the book, and when he returned to his car, Patrick was waiting. I watched expectantly from the upstairs window of the house, which commanded a perfect view. Patrick threw a jovial arm around him and led him inside. I waited impatiently, pacing back and forth at the window, watching alertly, but didn't have long to suffer. Minutes later, William emerged from the shop, limping heavily as he dragged one leg behind. His clothes were torn, his face battered and bloody. Slowly, he struggled to pull the car door open and climb inside. As the car drove away, Patrick stepped to the open garage door, leaning casually upon the doorway, observing with a grin. He caught sight of me at the window and nodded pleasantly, grinning from ear to ear. I returned his smile, and that was that." Robert said, quite pleased with himself.

"I'd like to meet this Patrick O'Leary," Charles said, grinning.

"But what became of her, Robert?" I asked, anxiously. "Did William…kill her?"

"In a manner of speaking, yes," he answered, grimly. "It was after Thomas went away. She complained of abdominal pain and went to bed mid-afternoon. Elsie was concerned and wanted to send for a doctor at once, but Carolyn thought it was nothing. The next day she had a fever but still didn't think there was much wrong. Doctors are difficult to come by on the island, you see. One must often send word to Anacortes, and they travel over by boat. It can be quite a process. You don't do it for a cold. But by evening she was nauseous and vomiting. Then she wanted a doctor, but William wouldn't send for one. She was in tremendous pain and pleading for a doctor, but William wouldn't allow it. He said it was nothing. Elsie wanted to fetch a doctor herself, but still William said no. So she sneaked out at night and rode all the way here on a bicycle. I was playing bridge with several friends when she arrived, one of whom was a doctor, and when he heard Elsie's description of the symptoms, he grabbed his medical bag and urged us on with all possible haste. Doctor Tobias Rice was a friend of mine visiting from New York. We had known each other for many years. Elsie, Tobias, and I all climbed into my car and raced to the Moore house. Thankfully the giant oak door was unlocked. I don't think William even knew that Elsie had fled from the house and warned us. We followed Elsie upstairs to Carolyn's room. She was in a bad way when we found her," Robert paused, recalling the painful memory. "I at least expected to find William at her bedside, but he was downstairs playing billiards. Carolyn was lying in bed, feverish and sweating, her damp hair matted upon her still beautiful face, which was contorted in pain. Tobias studied her face a moment, then pressed gently on the right side of her abdomen.

'Does this hurt?' he asked, and Carolyn winced suddenly in pain. He turned grimly and questioned Elsie about the symptoms again. 'Nausea and vomiting, did you say?' Elsie nodded. 'Fever, and abdominal pain on the right.' He was silent a moment, then his eyes met mine, and he reluctantly announced his diagnosis. 'Appendicitis.'

'Can you perform an appendectomy?' I asked. Tobias drew us away from the sickbed, out of earshot.

'I could have a few hours ago,' he replied.

'What are you saying?' I asked.

'It's ruptured,' Tobias answered.

'What does that mean?' Elsie asked, frantically.

'All I can do now is give her something for the pain,' he said, quietly, his voice breaking.

'Doctor please,' Elsie pleaded.

'It's out of my hands, Elsie. There's nothing I can do. There's nothing anyone could do.' Elsie burst into tears, and buried her face in my chest.

'This husband of hers should be brought up on charges of manslaughter. He killed her by withholding medical treatment,' Tobias said, quietly, the anger clear in his grieving voice.

'We'll cross that bridge later, Tobias. Can you give her something for the pain?'

"He administered a shot of morphine, and her face relaxed almost instantly. She looked peaceful, serene almost, as she lay there dying. Elsie sat beside the bed, holding Carolyn's hand and weeping uncontrollably. Suddenly William entered the room.

'There you are, love. How is she, Doctor?' he asked, playing the part of the good husband. Tobias still had his stethoscope around his neck and medical bag on the bed. Carolyn's eyes fluttered open at the sound of William's voice, and she motioned to Elsie who leaned down close, listening. Elsie rose up.

'She doesn't want him here,' she said, in a clear, firm voice.

'She must be delirious,' William said. 'What did you give her, Doctor?'

'She's not delirious. She wants you out of here, now,' Elsie said, firmly.

'I'm inclined to agree, William,' I said.

'I won't be ordered about in my own house.'

'Get out, or I'll throw you out myself,' I said.

Sensing that no one in the room was fooled by his improvised kindness, William dropped the façade of concern for his wife, and smiled maliciously.

'My work here is done,' he said, smugly, and left the room.

Sophia had read the journal breathlessly, huddled near the fire with a hand over her aching heart, her wide, alert eyes darting rapidly over the pages. Here she paused and turned to me with tears streaming over her flushed cheeks.

"Oh my God, Thomas. I'm so sorry. So sorry for Mother. So sorry for you." She wiped her tears away with the back of her hand, and her eyes fell to the journal once more. Taking a deep breath, she reached a trembling hand to turn the page, and my arresting hand fell upon hers.

"If you read further, Sophia, it is as my friend, not as an officer of the court." Her weeping eyes met mine over the journal. After a moment of indecision, she nodded. I removed my hand, and she turned the page...

"Carolyn died peacefully, under the effect of the morphine, a short time later, without her children by her side. Thomas was in prison; Sophia had been sent away. Elsie was still crying at her bedside when Tobias and I solemnly departed. I didn't see William on my way out. I don't know what I would have done if I had seen him." Robert lowered his head, and covered his eyes with his hand. "She was such a lovely woman," he said, in a faint voice, as he struggled with his emotions. Charles and I waited, concerned for him. A moment later he continued.

"The funeral was held two days later, on a Wednesday. It was expected to be a small gathering of only twenty-five or thirty people, just close friends of the family. But word of her death, and the circumstances surrounding it, spread rapidly over the island. Carolyn was loved, and even those who didn't know her personally loved her by reputation. Everyone, to a man, loathed William for his part in her death. On the day of the funeral, all of the shops, businesses, restaurants, hotels, every business in town, closed for the day, and everyone attended the service. People began arriving early in the morning, and by afternoon at the start of the service, close to four hundred people were crowded into the cemetery. William played the role of grieving husband admirably, but everyone knew the truth. Many tears were shed, but there was also an undercurrent of anger and hostility that is rarely seen at a funeral where people gather to mourn the loss of a loved one. Tempers were kept in check out of respect for Carolyn, but there were many dark looks directed at the murderer, or so they called him. In the front row, arriving earliest of all was Patrick O'Leary. He stood next to Elsie with his hands at his side, clenched in fists, staring straight ahead. A few times during the eulogy, when the pastor spoke of Carolyn's kindness and compassion, or a particular way that she carried herself, or something she used to do, the tears ran freely down his proud cheeks, and he didn't care who saw them.

"After the service, people sort of milled around and formed little groups. There was a lot of talk among the men about making William pay, about lynching and hanging, but I knew it was just talk. They were angry, certainly, but there were no killers among them. The one man who might take action was silent, and made no threats, but that was even more telling. There was a firm resolution in the set of his jaw, a silent determination in his gray eyes that didn't bode well. He had reached a decision of some sort; time would tell what it was. Everyone felt that he had the greatest claim to vengeance because of his romance with Carolyn and knew that he was just the man for the job. William heard the rumors, of course, there are few secrets on the island, and took measures to protect himself. He carried a revolver with him everywhere he went and nearly had occasion to use it a time or two when he came into town and was seen by workers from the Moore boatyard. There may not have been many folks who were willing to commit murder, but there were plenty who were eager to administer a sound beating, and William would have received a number of them if not for that revolver. He produced it on more than one occasion to keep his attackers at bay.

"Everyone was surprised when a week passed and William was still alive. Then two, then three, then four. Patrick went about his work in the shop as if nothing had happened. He grieved of course, like everyone, but seemed more sad and pensive than angry. He occupied the same seat at The Shack, but where before he would joke and laugh and people would always gather to him, he now sat quietly, staring into his beer mug, morose and withdrawn.

"Six weeks after Carolyn's funeral, he announced to everyone's surprise that he was going to Vancouver, BC for a week. Patrick hated to leave the island and did so only in the greatest need, so everyone wondered at his leaving. William seemed to relax a little when he heard about his rival leaving town. I loathed his company, but needed the law book back that he had borrowed from me earlier and was passing the driveway to the Moore house, so I turned in."

Here a uniformed gentleman from the household staff approached and leaned down, speaking quietly into Robert's ear. The man straightened then, waiting attentively.

"If you'll excuse me a moment, I need to take this call," Robert said to us, and stood to leave.

"Robert?"

"Yes, Lorelei."

"If you attempt to leave before finishing this account, I'll not be responsible for my actions." Robert smiled.

"I'll call them back," he said, to the attendant who gave a quick nod and rushed back to the house. Robert resumed his seat and continued. "Quite spirited when the mood is upon you. Where was I?"

"You had just turned into the driveway of the Moore estate," I answered.

"Right," he said, then leaned forward and lowered his voice, looking first at Charles, then at me. "What I've told you so far is common knowledge on the island. Only I know the rest. Understood?" Charles and I nodded eagerly and waited for him to continue.

Winter Dance | 337

"The front door was open wide, and moved slightly with the breeze that blew through the opening. I had a vague feeling something wasn't right. I knocked and called out, but there was no answer from the house, so I walked around the outside, half-expecting to find a body behind every bush I passed. At the north end of the estate, I saw movement in the cemetery that I couldn't distinguish too well without my glasses, but it looked as though someone was bent over one of the graves. This was the only person I had seen on the grounds, and it called for a look. So, following the paved path, I entered through the rusty, wrought iron gate and picked my way around the headstones, coming up behind a fellow that I took to be a gardener. As he had his back to me, I still hadn't seen who it was, but he was kneeling at a grave, arranging flowers that he had just placed there." Robert paused for effect, and smiled. "Who do you suppose it was?" Charles and I shrugged impatiently. Robert leaned even closer and lowered his voice to a whisper. "Patrick O'Leary."

"No," I said, astonished. "Really?" Robert nodded. He paused a moment, letting the significance sink in. Then he glanced around to confirm that no one else was listening.

"He didn't seem terribly concerned when he saw me. He just stood slowly, as if stiff from having been on his knees for so long, and rubbed his hands together, knocking the loose dirt from them. I asked what he was doing there.

'Roses were always her favorite,' he said. 'I used to give her fresh ones every day.'

'They're beautiful,' I answered, noting that there were dozens and dozens of roses in every possible color, arranged carefully about her grave. Patrick must have purchased every rose on the island. 'I'm sure Carolyn would appreciate it.'

'I'm sure she would,' he nodded, somberly.

'They may not last long in this heat, though. Do you intend to replace them in a few days?' I answered, a little surprised at my own casual acceptance of the situation.

'I probably won't be back for a while. I expect there will be a lot of people around here soon enough,' he said, matter-of-factly.

'I'll try to come out and replace them when the time comes,' I said. 'If there are any left on the island.'

'Thank you Robert. That's very kind.'

'Has anyone else been around here today? Did anyone else see you here?'

'No,' he said casually, 'not that I know of.'

'Was the…' I began, and paused, uncertain of how to ask, or that I even wanted to know the answer, 'was the door open like that when you arrived?' He leveled his gray eyes upon me and gave me a slow, deliberate look that said volumes. I swallowed hard, and stumbled for words.

'Say,' he said, wiping his dirty hands on his pants leg, 'would you like to have lunch today? I wanted to talk to you about some improvements I wanted to make to the shop.'

'Sure…come over to the house when you're ready,' I replied, still somewhat shaken by the circumstances.

'All right. I'll see you this afternoon.'

"As I walked back through the cemetery, passing the graves of all the Moore family, I reflected on my friend's felonious indiscretion. Where was William? What had become of him, I wondered, as I walked back to the house to find my law book. It was lying open on the desk in the study where it had apparently been recently consulted. The study brought back so many pleasant memories of an earlier time when I was a cherished guest at the Moore house, but I hadn't been there since William called it home. I wondered how he might have met his end as I reached for the book and noticed the desk chair lying on its side, a leg broken, and a short length of rope on the floor next to it. It was a rope I recognized. I had seen Patrick fussing with that short piece of rope a few times when I entered the shop to talk to him. It was a two-foot long halyard that he had added a stopper knot to each end of. What he would want with such an apparatus was beyond me, but I observed him several times as I glanced through the open shop door in passing. He was holding one end of the rope while he pulled it slowly through the closed fist of his other hand, again and again, wearing a far away, almost wicked smile.

"I grabbed my book and left the house. As I drove away, I saw Patrick was still in the cemetery, kneeling at Carolyn's grave. Would anyone blame him for what he did? Would you?" asked Robert, regarding us steadily. "For the first time since Carolyn's death, he was at peace. Nothing could bring that generous, beautiful woman back, but he did what he could; he delivered justice. There's not a soul on this island that mourned the loss of William Thomson, and you would be hard pressed to find anyone who doesn't think Patrick O'Leary was responsible for it. You'd be equally hard pressed to find anyone who doesn't endorse the act. It was quite some time before the jovial smile returned to his Irish face, but he couldn't enter The Shack without someone buying him a drink as a sort of unspoken gesture of thanks. Still can't."

Robert sipped his iced tea, absently. His thoughts seemed to be elsewhere. Sharing his story with us seemed to revive his feeling of loss for Carolyn. I almost wished I hadn't asked about her. Eventually he rose from the table.

"May I be excused now?" he asked. I just nodded numbly, and he walked back up the hill to the house...

Sophia wiped her eyes with her delicate, artist fingers and tenderly lowered the journal to her lap, then set it carefully upon the hearth. There was a bond between she and Mother from the very first. An affection that grew and flourished with the knowledge that Mother chose her and took her into our home because she cared for her and cherished her, not because she was bound to her by maternity or obligation. Sophia respected and adored her. Mother was just the gentle, elegant, beautiful woman that Sophia had always wanted in a parent, and wished to be herself. I know she felt the loss as deeply as I.

We sat together that summer evening, she with her face in her hands, I watching silently as the fire burned down and out. I sensed that she wished to be undisturbed, so I said nothing and simply waited. The sun had fallen low enough in the afternoon sky to burst through the window in blaze of color, and while I had seen the sunset from that window thousands of times, I never grew weary of it. I rose from my place on the floor before the fire and walked to Mother's seat. With my hand on the chair back, I watched the end of that beautiful day. Sophia joined me there a moment later. I felt her slip an arm around me and lay her head on my shoulder as she watched too. We were finally together again as I had imagined so many times in my hopeless prison cell.

"I've never been to visit Mother's grave," she said quietly, and I turned to see that she was looking out at the family cemetery. "Is there another grave there, Thomas?" she asked, concerned. "Is there a second new headstone?"

"What?" I asked.

"Who is it?" she inquired, straining to read the name in fading light of the setting sun. "Not William?"

"As if I would put him there," I snorted.

"Who then?" Leaning forward Sophia attempted to read the name on the headstone and, finding that she could not, made as if to move to another window that offered a better view of the cemetery. But I could not have that. How it escaped my notice, I could not answer. I should have removed it the day I discovered her, but so much had happened. There had been so many distractions. Sophia had so occupied my every thought since I rediscovered her that I had not given any thought to the cemetery. I held her close, preventing her from moving, and shut my eyes as my mind raced and I frantically considered how I might tell her. When I opened them after a moment of pause, she was looking at me with curious concern.

"What is it? What are you so desperate that I not see?"

"I didn't know if I would ever see you again, Sophia."

"I didn't know if I would ever see you again, Thomas. I looked so hard for so long. I'm so happy you're back."

"I...we...thought you were dead," I stammered. A puzzled sort of wondering frown clouded her eyes. Then her face changed suddenly, as the realization washed over her, and she moved away in spite of my efforts to hold her. She threw my arms off, not in an angry manner, but rather an insistent one that allowed for no negotiation, and walked to the other window. A summer breeze sang through the trees. I saw the shadows of the maple leaves skipping over her face as she peered through the glass. I saw, too, that her lips were pursed and her eyes open wide in a curious sort of amusement as she read the name on the headstone.

"Oh," she said, turning to face me, "it's for me."

"Yes, well..."

"How did it happen?" she asked, smiling playfully. "Was it a nice service? How did I die?"

"William killed you, of course."

"Of course." She walked back and stood beside me at the window. "Did I suffer? I hope I didn't suffer."

"It was a quick and painless death."

"Well, that's something. I'm so glad I didn't suffer." She slugged me playfully, as she had sometimes done in her tomboy days here, and added, "What possessed you to do that. Why did you bury me in the family cemetery?"

"Because you're family, of course."

"The last thing I did before leaving DC was order a headstone for Ellen. I would have had her buried somewhere else, but I could think of no other place. She spoke of her home only that one time, and I couldn't find it, so I had to be content with simply supplying a marker for her grave."

"That was kind of you."

"But why is there a headstone bearing my name?"

"Sophia," I began, "when you returned a few weeks ago everything was much as you left it."

"Except that Mother's gone," she added, quietly.

"And I didn't even know of that until I saw her grave. I expected to come home after my nine-year absence to find everyone in their usual place. In my fantasy, I would quietly enter the house and would simply take a seat on the hearth, as if I had just returned from a short walk. I would revel in everyone's surprised face, and you would all rush to greet me."

"That's how you should have been welcomed home," she said, taking my hand.

"When I arrived it was dark, and the house was a shambles. Everything was overgrown and crumbling in decay. It had been abandoned for nearly a decade."

"I hadn't thought of that. I'm so sorry, Thomas."

"William had plundered the estate and spent all of the money. I had nothing. I never knew a home could be so quiet, or empty, or cold, or that I could be so hungry." Sophia hung her head. "Thankfully, Elsie saw a light one night and came to investigate. She's been here since."

"Where did you find the money to restore everything? It looks just as it once did." The awkward shuffling of my feet answered for me. "Oh, yes. Of course." She was silent a moment as she considered all I had said. "That doesn't account for my headstone. How did I come to have a headstone?"

"It broke my heart to see how excitedly Elsie hurried to the door each time there was a knock, thinking it might be you. Then she would return solemnly and resume whatever she was doing before. I couldn't stop thinking about you. I knew you were dead, so it seemed best to have a funeral and get closure."

"How did you know I was dead?"

"I found your note," I said.

"My note?" she asked, puzzled.

"The one you placed in the book before you left the island."

"But...how?" She frowned. "How could you have found that?"

"I knew about your little house in the woods. I followed you home one night."

"You what?" she asked, shocked.

"I knew how terrified you were to walk home after dark, so I followed you one night to make sure you made it home all right."

"But Thomas," she said, with an embarrassed blush, "I was clear that I didn't want you to do that."

"I was just trying to help. I never told anyone."

"Why would I care who you told?" she asked, with an intensity that I had not seen in her eyes before.

"I...I...don't...know," I stammered.

"You're the one I didn't want to know about it. You're the one who I didn't want to see how we lived."

"But why? It didn't matter to me."

"It mattered to me. Do you understand? It mattered to me." She pushed herself away from me and sat down upon the hearth with her eyes on the glowing coals.

"I'm sorry, Sophia. I was just trying to help."

"It mattered to me a great deal," she said, firmly. "I didn't ever want you to see that."

"But..." I faltered, at a loss for words. "We didn't care that you had a little house. Or that you were a tomboy."

"I wasn't embarrassed to be a tomboy," she said fiercely, turning to face me. "I was never embarrassed to be a tomboy." Then she turned back to the fire, and her voice grew faint. "I was ashamed to wear those clothes because my mother was a drunk. She spent what little money she had on whiskey. It ruined her life. It ruined my life. Someone gave those cast away clothes to her out of pity. It was all I had to wear. I wasn't embarrassed to have a little house. I was humiliated because Mother found that abandoned shack one day and just moved in. Someone's rundown abandoned hovel became our home. And the shack…the clothes…everything I did or possessed shouted out how coarse and common and uncouth we were." Sophia covered her face with her hands. "And I never knew it. I never knew it until I met you. Until I came here and saw all of this."

In her distress, her downcast eyes fell upon the dress shirt from my closet, that gleaming white, perfectly pressed shirt without wrinkle or imperfection, that didn't fit her or belong to her. It was as if it became at that moment, in her eyes, an unstained, unblemished symbol of a life that was never meant for a wandering little tomboy. I saw the inequality in her troubled face. Never had she felt the disparity between her youth and mine as acutely as she did at that moment, while looking down at the borrowed shirt that she had slipped into just as she had slipped into our perfectly ordered and unblemished lives.

Hanging her head in shame, she ran from the room pulling wildly at the buttons. I could hear her footsteps climbing the stairs. For a moment I was too stunned to act but instinctively made a few tentative steps to follow, and Elsie was suddenly at my side with fresh iced tea.

"No, Thomas," she said, gently, and put a hand on my arm to prevent me from following.

"But, what did I do? I was only trying to help when I followed after her," I explained.

"She's just embarrassed. It's not your fault. I'll go talk to her." And Elsie left the room. I remained at the fire, waiting, for what seemed an eternity. I hoped that Sophia would return to me, but it was Elsie that I saw entering the room sometime later.

"She'll be all right, Thomas," Elsie said, gently. "Everyone has their secrets. Things they don't want anyone else to know about. You stumbled right into hers," she said, and continued on to the kitchen. Moments later, Sophia entered. The change in her was dramatic. She was once again wearing her business attire and assumed her role as agent of the court. With short, curt movements, she opened her briefcase, removed several pages of documents, and placed them on the table near me.

"I've been instructed by the District Attorney's Office," she said without looking at me (she couldn't look at me), "to offer you a deal. In exchange for your testimony against Herbert Mayer, my office will offer immunity from prosecution and drop your pending charges." She shut her briefcase and took it in hand. "This deal is good until five tomorrow afternoon," she said, and, with briefcase in hand, started for the door.

"Sophia?" I ventured, with an injured air as I followed after her. "Sophia. Wait." With her hand on the open door, she paused and turned at last, but her embarrassed eyes were on the floor. "I'm sorry," I said. "Must you go?" She said nothing but looked up from the floor, and for an instant her eyes met mine. There were words in those beautiful blue eyes that I had not seen before, words like anger and mistrust and betrayal. Words that didn't belong to the Sophia I knew as a child. But so many years had passed since then. Had we both changed so very much? Who was this Sophia? Her eyes weren't as blue or as beautiful as I remembered them. They were clouded with cataracts of ambition and success and judgment. Without a word, she turned and walked away into the night.

Several days passed. I went about the house in a sort of moping stupor. So much of my life had been wrapped up in Sophia. Since I first met her at the Pimpernel Tree, our lives had been inexorably bound. We had studied together, played together, cried and laughed together, exchanged gifts, and kisses, and intimacies. I thought there was nothing I would not do for her, and she for me. No sacrifice I would not make. Who was this Sophia? I still loved her to distraction, but she was different.

With my arms on the windowsill, and my chin upon my arms, I sat in Mother's chair gazing absently at the blue sky and blue ocean.

"Don't judge her too harshly, Thomas," came Elsie's voice behind me. "She takes her job seriously."

"I know she worked hard to get where she is, but how can she expect me to do as she asks?"

"She can only do so much. She's doing all she can," Elsie added.

"She's changed, Elsie," I said after a moment of reflection. "She's not as she once was."

"Neither are you. Did you think she would remain a little girl forever? You're not the same as when you went away, either."

"Am I better, or worse?"

"Both," she said, after a moment of reflection, and then continued through the room.

"Both?" I muttered. "How could I be both?"

Thomas Moore

August 21, 1930

Took *Mary Adda* to Sidney. Summer was in full bloom, and the days were long and beautiful. I departed early, before sunrise, so that I was far beyond the reach of prying eyes before the sun revealed my presence. From the darkness the dawn came creeping slowly on and with it little patches of cloud and mist that hovered low over the cool water. The first rays of the morning sun dispersed them, revealing a blue sky unbroken by clouds over a blue sea that was crisscrossed by the white hulls of fishing boats passing slowly across. By noon I reached Sidney Harbor and had a casual lunch while the cargo was loaded aboard the vessel. Jack and Martin received news of my return to the business with good cheer, and I had made three journeys before that day. Each time the cargo was hidden away in secret locations on the island. I was hoping to store as much inventory as possible so that I could take time off if needed and have a suitable quantity to supply The Shack. Storing cargo at the boatyard was risky, but it would only be there overnight, then Jack and Martin would move it. To do so that night would have invited suspicion. Cars traveling late at night on the island always caught the eye of the police.

I read a book while waiting for the sun to sink a bit lower in the summer sky, and departed at sunset so that darkness would cloak my return to the island. When I reached the boatyard I found Martin and Jack sitting cross-legged on the dock playing cards by the faint light of a candle between them, which flickered with the gentle evening breeze. They jumped up at my appearance (that is to say Martin jumped up at my appearance, Jack was always slow and insolent to me) and tied the boat up.

When I threw the doors open they immediately stepped aboard to begin off-loading the wooden crates, heavy with whiskey. I simply watched from the wheelhouse. No longer did I help them. It was their job, and they were paid well for their time, but Jack always took offense.

"Have a nice trip?" he asked mockingly, as he passed by me, struggling under the weight of the crate.

"Quite nice, yes. Thank you for asking." Muttering something under his breath, he stepped off the boat and struck off into the darkness, stumbling over the loose, uneven planks of the pier. It took very little time, twenty minutes or so, and their work was finished whereupon they piled into their car, and without a word of thanks or goodbye, drove away hastily, leaving the shop door open for me to lock.

It was a warm night, just as it had been a warm day. I sat on the stern deck of *Mary Adda* with my legs dangling over the transom, peering up at the twinkling stars and a thin crescent of moon in the night sky. Chirruping crickets performed a symphony while the boat rocked ever so slightly with the swells lapping upon the hull. That crescent moon so bright and perfect hanging just over the dark treetops captured my attention, and I admired it as only a lonely lover can. Was she still angry with me, I wondered?

I rose with a sigh and stepped onto the pier intending to lock the shop before driving home. Having crossed the open space to the shop, I was reaching for the door when the crickets stopped suddenly. That vast multitude of singing chirruping voices stopped as one, and silence filled the night. I paused, listening curiously. In the stillness I heard the distant whine of a car engine growing louder as it approached, and saw headlights moving through the trees. Moments later it appeared in the clearing, and then pulled to a stop next to the shop with its headlights fixed upon me in a blinding glare. The engine was shut off, but still the glaring lights bore down on me as I raised a hand to shade my eyes against the intensity. I heard the click of a car door, and the crunch of footsteps in the gravel as someone moved toward me.

"What are you doing here, Thomas?" she said, in an angry voice, as she stepped into the beam of the headlights.

"This is my boatyard," I answered, one hand shading my eyes from the glare, the other on the open shop door. "What are you doing here?"

"I went to the house to speak with you but Elsie said you weren't home, so I headed back. I was almost to town when it occurred to me that you might be here. What are you doing here?" I saw her eye travel to *Mary Adda* rocking gently at the dock in the moonlight, the door of which was still open. Then she looked to the open shop door still in my grasp, caught in the beam of the headlights. "What are you doing Thomas?" she asked, angrily. "What are you doing?" And she struck off at once toward the shop that she knew so well from our youth. I grabbed her arm, but she jerked away and stepped past me insistently. Even in the darkness I could see her hands clench in angry fists and her body tense as she stood in the doorway peering silently inside. A single crate could have been overlooked perhaps, but there were dozens, all smartly stacked upon the walls. She closed her eyes a long, searching moment, then looked up at the twinkling stars overhead as if they would shed some light upon her hopeless dilemma.

The crickets, one by one, began to chirp again. Their voices, building to a chorus, provided a welcome distraction in the uncomfortable silence of the night. Sophia turned to me at last. It was a look I had seen on her face before once, in the courtroom as I was being led away to serve my sentence.

"How could you do this?" she asked, quietly, and hung her head. "I spent so many years looking for you. Wasted so many years looking for you."

"Wasted, did you say?" I replied, growing angry. "Attending college? Touring Europe? I can tell you something about wasting time. I can tell you a great deal about wasting time."

"We're even," she said, softly. "After tonight we're even." The vision of my enterprising vice repulsed her. She swung the shop door closed with all bitter strength her unforgiving arm could summon. I wondered if she were not shutting me out of her life forever. There were angry tears in her blue eyes as she brushed past me to her car where the headlights continued to glare blindly into the night, and the crescent moon hung over the treetops.

"Goodbye, Thomas," she said, with a finality that gave me pause, and then climbed into the car and started the engine. But the car didn't move. The headlights shined on indifferently, the engine ticked at idle, but the car remained. I didn't wish to part like that and took a step toward the headlights, but the car sped away suddenly then, back the way it came, up the winding drive and into the woods. Sophia was gone.

I kicked my frustration into the shop door, and received a sore toe for my effort. At length, I looked about me in the darkness, under the twinkling stars and crescent moon, at the vague shapes of the shop, and the dock, and the boats *Diva*, and *Mary Adda* still rocking gently in the water.

The boatyard looked just as it did when I returned to the island after so many years away. It seemed to best serve my purpose that way, so I did nothing to alter it. The grass and weeds that grew up the sides of the weathered shop, the broken windowpanes through which the Barn Swallows darted, the peeling paint that lay in strips on the ground, the 'To Let' 'To Let' 'To Let' signs perched crookedly in the dirty windows, all spoke of something that had passed out of time and memory, forgotten and neglected. Weathered planks of the crippled pier stood in the low tide mud on festering stilts and leaning crutches covered in barnacles. There were slippery stakes in the mud. And slippery rocks on top of the mud. And a decaying boathouse sinking into the mud. And old boats nestled tiredly in the mud. And chains leading from them to rusty anchors that still bit into the muck and silt. The stagnant air smelled of salt and mud. It all looked so deserted, neglected, abandoned, that no one would suspect it of being used for anything.

I always found comfort in the shop. Among the heavy iron machinery I would wander. Among the old woodworking tools of my grandfather's time worn smooth in the skilled hands of the boat wrights that wielded them, I was at home. The soft cooing of pigeons nesting in the high timbers above, was like a bedtime story that lulled me to a gentle mind and reflecting mood. By the small light of the crescent moon streaming through the dirty windows, I wandered about the place trailing my hand over the hulls of the unfinished boats. Sophia and I had played there so often as children, that it was impossible to disassociate her from the dreams and aspirations I had formed for that place, and for my life. I thought that she would be always at my side, and share in all that was mine, but I had the perfectly pressed white shirt, and everything that came with my family name. What did she have but what she could earn for herself?

With my hand on the transom of an unfinished fishing boat I paused. The smell of oiled machinery, undisturbed air, and age, was a comforting scent that transported me to a simpler time when I was a child. A little shaft of moonlight streamed in through a broken windowpane, falling upon a dusty longboat tossed into the corner that had been built for a whaling company. But they had departed suddenly before it was finished, and never returned for their craft. Sophia and I used to play in it, pretending we were chasing after those giants of the sea. She would stand in the bow directing me which way to go as I pretended to row and steer. I could still see her in the bow of that little longboat, wearing her tomboy clothes and pointing to port or starboard with her slender arm extending beyond the rolled up sleeves, and a hand shading her eyes from a make-believe sun.

And then it struck me, like the moonbeam shining upon the longboat. Alcohol was her white whale, and prohibition her avenging harpoon. In her eyes it had crippled her just as surely as the whale had crippled Captain Ahab, and like him, she was determined to kill it, to stamp it out, to erase its existence. With all the fervor of Ahab she would pursue her cause until it was extinct. Whiskey ruined her life, she said, and I never until that moment understood the impact it had on her, or the animosity that she felt for it. Great enough even, to supplant her feelings for me?

It was quite late when I finally reached home. Elsie was in a chair near the burned out fire where she had fallen asleep waiting for me with Picasso in her lap. At the first sound of my entry she sprang up cradling Picasso in her arms.

"Did she find you, Thomas?" she asked, worried. "She came here looking for you, and I didn't know what to say. It took me off guard to find her there on the doorstep." My face said it all. "Oh," she said, and her eyes fell.

"It's not your fault, Elsie, it's hers. She needs to grow up."

"She came here to apologize for the other night, Thomas. She realized that you were only trying to help when you followed her home, and she meant to apologize."

I didn't know what to say to that. Heaving a frustrated sigh, I went upstairs to bed, leaving Elsie with a long face as she fell back into her seat at the fire.

Thomas Moore

August 21st, 1930

Experienced a bit of a surprise today, which I am still pondering. It was a beautiful summer morning. The sun shined brightly in the blue sky, pouring in through my bedroom window and warming my face as I lay in bed. A warm breeze smelling sweetly of garden flowers carried the song of the finch through the open window. After a quick breakfast at the kitchen table, I thought to get some country air and, telling Elsie that I would be returning for lunch, I drove to the boatyard. It was still a favorite playground of mine. I could while away an afternoon spieling a plank or caulking a seam or simply wandering about the place. There was a nostalgic ring in the tone of my caulking hammer that carried through the shop and transported me to a time when such hammers rang for days or weeks and the shop bustled with activity. Father could nearly always be found there in those days, huddled over the drafting table in his office above the shop floor. A high tide covered the muddy bay, lapping at the sandy shoreline and lifting the homeless boats from the foul mud. The blue water rippled with a gentle breeze as I stepped aboard Mary, and walked up on to the deck. Sitting on the foredeck in the warm sun while the gentle sea rocked me, I mused on my favorite subject. Where was she, I wondered? How was it all going to turn out? I couldn't see the end. I was occupied with thoughts of Sophia as I stepped off the boat, and walked about the boatyard, reminiscing about a time when it buzzed with commerce, and men supported their families through their employment there. My own family had made their name and fortune there. What had I become but a lawless criminal? Motivated by the greatest need, I embarked upon my import business with eyes wide open, and the promise of adventure, intrigue, and financial reward. There was an inviting sense of excitement in my late night adventures that urged me on. It was, as Herbert said, great sport eluding the police, but there is a feeling one gets from hard work and honest achievement, that was missing from my import trade. I wanted to walk away from the drafting table at the end of the day knowing that I had contributed something significant to the world. I wanted a career. I wanted to continue the family legacy, and build yachts again.

Noting that several hours had passed, I grabbed a bottle of Bourbon from the shop (intending to deliver it to Herbert) and started back to have lunch. When I pulled into the lane, I saw a strange car parked near the bubbling fountain. Visitors were quite rare, and I wasn't expecting anyone, so my interest was piqued when I pulled up behind the car and parked. I was still looking it over when I stepped to the oak door, and gave the handle a turn. Scarcely had I touched it before it was pulled open by Elsie, who had apparently been watching for me. She quickly ushered me inside, and spoke rapidly, quietly, in the entryway.

"I didn't know what to do, Thomas, I thought it was you," she said.

"What are you talking about?" I whispered, in response to her hushed voice.

"I was making sandwiches a little while ago, and thought I heard a key turning in the door. I assumed it was you."

"But I never lock the door. I don't believe I've ever locked the door."

"I know. That's why I thought it was odd. I came to check, and when I opened the door, he was standing there."

"Who?" I asked. Elsie jerked her head silently toward the other side of the house, and I followed her gesture to find a man standing at the window next to Mother's chair, looking out over the sea. He stood straight and tall, with his hands clasped behind him, and turned at the sound of our hushed voices.

"Ah, at last," he said, seeing me there. "Quite a view, Mister Moore," he added, turning back to the window.

"We're fond of it," I answered, as I left Elsie at the door and approached the visitor. He turned again and faced me.

"And that door," he added, looking beyond me to the door

through which I had just entered. "What a work of art. Where would one find something like that?"

"It was a gift from Albert Edward, the Prince of Wales," I replied. "Grandfather built a yacht for him, and the prince had that door removed from his wine cellar and shipped here as a gift to signify that his door was always open to grandfather."

"Well, the Moore family keeps some interesting company," he said, with a smile, then his eye fell upon a painting near the piano. It was the self-portrait that Sophia began in my absence. I had the painting, and the easel upon which it rested, moved from her bedroom after her return, and placed near the piano where I could see it each day. "Who is this lovely creature?" he asked. Though he was smiling and pleasant, I felt a growing apprehension for the man and his questions. A vague notion of his identity was beginning to form, and if he was the man I suspected him of being, it would be a disaster for him to find a portrait of Sophia in my house. But the painting was ten years old, and she had changed so very much. There were similarities, certainly, but would he see them?

"I think it would be more appropriate if you told me who you were," I answered.

"Oh, forgive me," he said, feigning embarrassment, "I assumed your housekeeper told you. Jerry Daniels," he added, and extended a hand.

"I don't suppose you drove all the way out here to talk about architecture or art. What can I do for you?" I answered, ignoring his gesture.

"Right to the point. I like that. What you can do for me is cooperate with my investigation and testify against Herbert Mayer," he said, crossing his arms before him, as he waited for my response. I simply smiled. "Well, I had to give it a shot," he added, grabbing his hat from Mother's chair where he had placed it. "I thought I might succeed where Miss Nagel failed."

"She was much more convincing than you."

"She does have a winning way about her, doesn't she?" he replied, smiling, and turned to go.

"Sorry I couldn't be of more help," said I. With his hand on the door he turned, and a thin smile spread over his lips as his fox-like eyes fell to my hand.

"Don't get caught with that," he said, and shut the door behind him as he left. I had not noticed until then that I still held the forgotten bourbon bottle in my left hand. I walked to the window, where I watched him slide into his car and start the engine. Daniels was a young man, perhaps five and thirty, with long black hair that fell to his shirt collar and shrewd dark eyes that moved constantly. His thin, dark brows and high, delicate cheekbones gave him a polished, almost feminine quality, and he was quite popular with the women if the local rumors were to be trusted.

As the car rounded the fountain and began down the long, tree-lined drive, I felt certain that I would be seeing him again, perhaps often again, and didn't relish the thought.

"Inconceivable," Howard said, when I related the experience to him the following day. "It's inconceivable, Thomas," he repeated, as he sat at his desk with his fingertips pressed together, thinking. "Daniels is a busy, ambitious man. He wouldn't take time out of his day to drive out there and have a brief, ham-handed conversation about you cooperating with his investigation. He would have known your answer in any case. Something else drew him out there," he reflected. "That was just a cover to disguise his intent. What was his real motive?" he muttered, with a concentrated frown. "Why would he even bother with this case at all?"

Several days later, I was roaming about the boatyard on a lazy summer afternoon searching for something to do, but nothing really appealed to me as I shuffled about my childhood playground reminiscing. I entered the shop, dragging my hand along the hulls of the unfinished boats that were abandoned so many years ago. It was Father who made the shop work. When he sailed away from the boatyard that blustery October afternoon and *Diva* was towed back without him, the island was shocked and life changed for so many. Orders for new boats stopped almost immediately, and even those who had already commissioned a yacht lost interest in completing it. Their unfinished vessels looked sad to me somehow, and lonely, gathering dust in their aborted infancy, within a shop that once rang of prosperity and success. Once was the time when one could hear the clang of hammers, the buzz of saws, the ring of caulking irons, for miles as men went about their work.

The melancholy silence was broken by the persistent advance

and retreat of the surf upon the muddy shoreline. It drifted through the broken windowpanes where I stood, while the soft cooing of Pigeons reached my ears from the timbers above. Nothing was as I expected. The new Moore industry, which was making me a criminal and driving a wedge between Sophia and I, was stacked in felonious columns against the backdrop of the old Moore industry.

Wiping the dirt from the grimy window, I looked out at the blue water sparkling under the summer sun. There was *Diva*, rocking gently at the dock. She too had been abandoned. For nearly a decade the sun and rain had beaten down upon her in my absence, but her grace and elegance could not be so easily marred. Barnacles infested her hull. Seaweed trailed from her keel in long wavy strips that followed the current. Her meticulously applied varnish had all worn away in time. Her deck and hull were gray, like bleached and tumbled driftwood. But there was a dignified refinement in her beauty that would always remain. Perhaps she was too pretty, too perfect before. If anything, she looked more handsome to me now. More approachable. There was no disguising her elegance, but there was a comfort in her now that had been absent before. With her perfection came a sense of care and careful movements, careful actions, like a Steinway that one wouldn't dare scratch. Now she was beauty with a feeling of casualness. I was even more enamored with her.

As I studied her there by the imperfect agency of the grimy window where I had wiped a clean spot, it occurred to me that I had not sailed her in ten years, and the thought was like seeing an old friend again. I grabbed the sails from the sail loft in the shop and ran with childlike enthusiasm to my old girl, who greeted me with a welcome dip as I stepped aboard. A half hour later we were sailing in the bright sun. She was just as I remembered her; perfectly tuned to glide effortlessly over the rippling water. For hours I sailed with the warm sun on my face, the gentle breeze in my hair, and the exhilarating salt air in my nose. I found a soothing, peaceful tranquility in the movement of the yacht over the water. All that was lacking was someone to share it with. Someone with the same appreciation for it as I, but would she ever sail with me again? The sun was low in the orange sky when I turned *Diva* east, and began headed back. The air was cooling quickly with the sunset. I noticed little pockets of fog forming in the narrow passages between the islands, and thought of Charles and Lorelei. The fog could move quickly, very quickly, and surround a boat. But I knew the water well. By the time I reached Deer Harbor it was shrouded in a thick mist. I could see the hazy silhouette of boats at anchor, and picked my careful way through them, reaching the boatyard at last. I pulled slowly to the dock behind *Mary Adda*, and stepped off with the mooring line in hand. As I bent down to throw a hitch over the cleat, my eye caught movement, and I saw through the mist that *Mary's* wheelhouse doors were open, and swinging softly with the gentle motion of the water. I finished tying *Diva*, and walked to the other boat for a closer look. Her doors had been forced, pried open somehow, and the wood was splintered. Before I could give it much thought, I heard sounds behind me, up toward the shop. There were muffled voices in the fog. Voices of many men. I heard heavy crates tossed down. The clink of bottles clanging together. Footfalls. Banter. Puzzled, I peered into the white mist, but saw only dark shadows of figures moving back and forth along a path they had made.

Rushing through the heavy fog I reached the shop, and paused in stunned silence, disbelieving my eyes. Men were carrying crates of alcohol, and loading it into a police panel truck.

"There he is." Came a voice from somewhere in the stagnant mist, and a moment later I was tackled from behind and wrestled to the ground. Without thinking, I threw an elbow into the face of the man behind me, and scrambled to my feet, making my way toward the shop, but several more men rushed upon me at once, roughly pinning me to the ground. Someone cuffed my hands behind me, and then I was pulled up to my feet once more. My clothes were torn, my nose bleeding. The officer in charge approached just then, and stood looking me over with a stern face as he slapped his hand with his nightstick. Behind him the men loading the crates had not even paused in their work.

"Get him outta here," he said.

Officers took me by each arm and pulled me through the fog to a police car parked nearby, but the greatest shock of the evening was still to come. It occurred when we passed the open doors of the shop. The fog was much too thick to see inside. We were not close enough that I could see into the shop, but her scent lingered there in the still, heavy air. It reached my nose like a treacherous knife through my heart. I was still reeling from it when an officer opened the car door, and shoved me inside.

I saw nothing during the drive into town. My eyes were on the floorboards of the car, my thoughts miles, or years, away. How could she do this? Had she changed so very much? Could it be that I didn't know her anymore. It seemed like no time at all before we were pulling up outside the little jail, and I was escorted inside. My cuffs were removed. I was shown to the same cell as before, and the barred door clanged shut behind me with a familiarity that brought a chill.

Sitting on the edge of the bed, I looked about me. It was exactly the same as last time. The bed had the same thick blankets and comfortable down pillow. Beside it was a little table with a lamp that cast a soothing glow. But it wasn't nearly as quaint or charming as I remembered it.

Across the room an officer sat at a desk typing a report. He and I were the only ones there. It must have been about a half hour after I arrived, that I heard the phone ring, and he picked it up.

"Hello," he said, "yeah, he's here…Okay." The phone was returned to the cradle. The officer glanced up at me over his typewriter. "Someone from the DA's office is coming' over to see ya."

But no one came. The officer finished his report an hour later, grabbed his jacket from a hook on the wall, and left without a word, locking the door behind him. I wasn't surprised that she didn't come. What could she say? How could she justify what she had done? I drifted off to sleep at last, and was awakened sometime later to the sound of a door clicking shut, and a little rush of cold air that carried across the wood floor. In the soft light of the quiet room, I saw a man approaching my cell.

"The view has changed since we spoke last," he said.

"What do you want now?" I replied, tiredly.

"The same as before," he answered, with a smug little smile. "Cooperate with my investigation, and testify against Herbert Mayer."

"My answer hasn't changed," I replied, lying back down on the bed, and pulling the covers up to my chin.

"Then you should get used to the view. You'll be seeing a lot of it," he said, grasping the steel bars as if to illustrate his words.

"Why are you so intent on arresting Herbert? What's he done to you?" I asked, as I huddled deeper in the covers. "Howard said no District Attorney would bother with a simple case like this. Why are you?"

"I'm giving you a chance to help yourself," he answered. "Are you going to take it or not?"

"I would like to get some sleep, if you don't mind," I said, closing my eyes and turning away.

"Whatever you say, Mr. Moore," he said, casually. "I'll see you in the morning." He turned away then, and began toward the door with his briefcase in hand. "I wonder how well you'll sleep though, knowing that you could be seeing Judge Barron tomorrow," he added. I could not think of that man with his black robe, pale skin, and bloodless lips, without shuddering. Daniels observed my reaction, and smiled. "Ah, you remember him I see. Hanging judge Barron they call him, though that's a bit harsh I think. He's only sentenced two men to actually hang. Still, he does tend to impose the more severe penalties. Built quite a reputation for it," Daniels added, as he returned to my cell and stood at the bars once more, studying me by the dim light. "The rumor in my office is that he's taken a personal interest in you. Seems Judge Gillespie attempted to have him disbarred. Know anything about that?"

"That was a long time ago," I said, with much more conviction than I felt.

"You're right," he added, with a sinister smile that chilled my blood. "I'm certain he wouldn't hold a grudge over a little thing like that." My thoughts raced. What if I was appearing before Judge Barron? What was the worst he could do? It was only a smuggling case. "The charges against you are growing Mr. Moore. I can always add resisting arrest and assaulting an officer."

"Assaulting an officer?"

"I have a man with a broken nose. He said you did it."

"He tackled me from behind. I didn't know he was a policeman."

"You're facing another fifteen years."

Heaving a frustrated sigh I threw the covers back, swung my legs around, and sat on the edge of the bed with my head in my hands, thinking. It was just the gesture Daniels was waiting for. He moved closer, watching eagerly through the bars and wearing a look of triumph in his shrewd, cunning eyes: eyes that were so different from the kind, gentle eyes of my friend. I thought of Herbert sitting on his boat, watching the sunset pensively as he prepared to go away to jail to save me once more.

"Mr. Daniels," I said, moving from the bed to stand before him at the bars of my cell. "I wouldn't help you to incarcerate that kind old man if it meant my immortal soul would suffer in hell for all of eternity." He studied me there in my quiet little jail cell, I on one side of the bars, he on the other, and I saw a puzzled sort of confusion in his face.

"I've dealt with a number of criminals in my day. They've always been quite willing, eager even, to make a deal that would save themselves."

"You should be dealing with a better class of criminal," I answered, to the amusement of my adversary.

"All right, it would seem that you're forcing my hand. I didn't want to do this just yet, but..." He opened the briefcase that he had been holding the entire time, reached inside, and stepped close to the bars. "Recognize this?" he asked, holding a key up to the bars for me to see. It was pointless for me to deny it. My face reacted before my presence of mind. I was looking at the sterling silver skeleton key that fit the great oak door of my home.

"So that's why you were at my house. You wanted to see if it fit the lock." His only response was a smug grin. "Where did you get it?"

"I think you know where I got it, Mr. Moore. It was in the pocket of an escaped convict who washed up on the beach."

"If that's all you have..." I answered. He once more reached into the briefcase. This time he produced a photograph, which he pressed to the bars for me to see.

"It has your fingerprints all over it." I was looking at a photograph of the gaff from Robert's car. "You can't tell from the photograph," he said, holding it to the dim light of the lamp across the room, "but there's a good deal of blood on it."

"Of course there is. It's a fishing gaff."

"It's not fish blood," he replied, with a condescending smile. "You must have a thousand questions. How much do I know? How did I know the key fit your house? How did I find out about the gaff?" he said, his shrewd eyes studying me through the bars of the jail cell. "Play ball, or go to prison for the rest of your life Mr. Moore. You'll never see the outside of a prison cell again." Daniels returned the evidence to his briefcase, and snapped it shut. "I'll give you a few days to think it over. The next time I arrest you it will be for murder. Four counts. And there won't be any bail. You'll be in jail until your trial, then off to prison."

I opened my mouth to speak, but nothing came out. What could I say? What could I do? I simply stood at the steel bars in dismay, my thoughts a jumble. He had me. "Come to my office in two days with your answer. If I don't hear from you, I'll have you arrested." With his briefcase in hand he walked to the door. When he reached it, he turned. "Prisons are full of stupid people, Mr. Moore. Don't be one of them." And he was gone. I fell listlessly onto the bed, and pondered. What could I do?

It was far into the morning before my thoughts slowed enough that I could sleep. It seemed as though I had only just closed my eyes, when I was awakened by the smell of hash browns and eggs, and turned sleepily to find Billy watching me expectantly, as if I were a hero. Breakfast was on the table next to the bed, just as last time. But I was in no mood for breakfast, or jail, or Billy. He told me that we were expected in court as soon as I had finished breakfast, and I rose at once, and started for the door. He cast a hungry eye at the food on my plate, but I insisted that we leave and pushed him toward the door, ignoring his pleas that I carry my hands before me as if cuffed. We entered the courtroom as before, and I found Howard waiting for me. Leaving a frustrated Billy at the back of the courtroom, I joined Howard at the defense table.

"How did you know I was...?

"Miss Nagel called me this morning," he answered, before I could finish. Sophia was at the table beside us, shuffling through documents in her briefcase. The judge arrived (not Judge Barron) bail was set, Howard said something about meeting him at his office to discuss my case, and I departed with Billy struggling to keep up with me as I wordlessly left the courtroom, and returned to the jail to post bail and get my things. Not once did Sophia even glance in my direction. Not once did she acknowledge my presence.

Just as well. My thoughts toward her were not kind. That black-hearted ingrate discharged her duties with the cold, detached, precision of a machine; a machine that had been reared, grown, and flourished, under my roof. That she should organize and oversee a raid of my shop, a shop that we had played together in as children, was unconscionable. It was the darkest form of treachery, and she the worst form of traitor. I loved her and despised her.

The walk home in the bright sunshine along the tree lined country road, was a long one, clouded by angry thoughts of betrayal. My dark mood was softened at once when I was greeted by Elsie. She had no doubt been watching for me from the window and ran down the drive at the first sight of me.

"Oh Thomas. I've been so worried," she said, throwing her arms around me at the fountain. "Were you arrested again? What happened? Where have you been? Why are you walking?"

She had to know that I had continued with my "importing" business. It was not spoken of between us, but I continued to slip away in the afternoon to "go for a drive," and she continued to nod her assent, as if she believed that was all I was doing. And never a word of reproach or censure. When I returned late in the night, or early the next morning, there would always be a light on, and she would be seated beside the fire with Picasso at her feet knitting or reading. (Since my first arrest, she had taken to waiting up for me whenever I went out on business) When I returned, she would kiss my cheek, gather Picasso in her arms, and quietly go to bed. Never did we speak of my late night activities. I pretended nothing was amiss, and she pretended not to see. It was our own silly little deception, and no one was deceived by it.

Elsie took a step back, and looked me over with the eye of a concerned mother, noting my wrinkled, disheveled clothes, and wild, uncombed hair.

"Are you all right, Thomas?" Her concerned face brought a smile to my lips. "What?" she asked, seeing my grin.

"I'm not a little boy with a skinned knee," I said, smiling.

"Maybe not," she replied, playfully stern, "but it's pretty clear you still need looking after," she said, and walked back into the house.

There is a freedom of movement, and pleasure of motion, in simply walking about and going where one will. It is something that few people know or understand. It is something that caged people know all too well. In a normal world, normal people get a small taste of that freedom of movement through injury or illness. Limping along in a cast for example is a vexing inconvenience, and when the leg is mended and the cast removed, how wonderful it is to have use of both legs once more. Finally free of my tiny prison cell, I take pleasure in the most mundane of things. I enjoy simply walking about the house. Peering through the great leaded windows that look out over the blue sea. Wearing my own clothes. Eating what I wish. But most of all it is the freedom of movement. Going where I will. I cannot go back to prison. I cannot spend years of my life in a concrete box, thirsting to feel the sun on my face and the wind in my hair. Neither can I betray Herbert.

Thomas Moore

July 16th 1933

My life is consumed by legal battles, motions, statements, and all manner of legal jargon that is tedious and prosaic. How Howard has made a life of this, and does it daily, is quite beyond me.

I was sitting outside with an iced tea, thinking about my legal troubles as I pondered a lovely old sailboat that slipped slowly past. She was heeled heavily on a starboard tack, making her way over the blue water toward Jones Island in the distance. I could just make out her bow rising and falling with the ocean swells that broke so gently on her slicing prow, and pictured myself at the helm, rocking with the soothing motion of the vessel, the sun on my face, the wind in my hair. It was one of the few untroubled moments that I had enjoyed since my jailhouse conversation with Daniels. His threat rang constantly in my ears, and in my heart.

All day I roamed restlessly about the house pondering what I would do if charged with murdering the escaped convicts. I threw myself into the chair, I threw myself onto the sofa, I paced before the window with my eyes on the ocean, I roamed about the grounds with my hands in my pockets and my head bowed in thought. And each of my restive, fidgety movements seemed to be accompanied by a heavy sigh that spoke of my frustration.

"Good lord, Thomas," Elsie blurted one day, looking up from her book, "you're making me dizzy. What's on your mind?"

So the sailboat in the distance was a welcome distraction that lifted my spirit ever so briefly, and took my mind away from the constant threat of judges, and courtrooms, and jails, and attorneys, and motions, and laws. My thoughts were miles away. I didn't realize that someone had taken a seat beside me, until I heard her voice.

"Paperwork crossed my desk this morning, Thomas," she said, urgently. "Daniels is preparing to charge you with four counts of first degree murder. He's preparing an indictment."

The yacht sailed on in the distance, leaving me behind. I was no longer at her helm, but instead had been torn from her tiller and thrown into a hostile courtroom where I had nothing to gain but the freedom that every citizen enjoys from birth. I continued looking out over the water.

"It should only be three counts," I replied, with my eyes on the sailboat.

"What?" she asked, incredulously.

"There were only three of them," I said, casually, taking a sip of my iced tea. "I don't know what became of the fourth, if there was a fourth."

"Do you mean to say that you did it? You're guilty? You beat those men to death?"

"Well, Miss Nagel," I said, turning to face her for the first time since her arrival, "it wouldn't be very prudent of me to comment on that without my attorney present, now would it?"

Utterly shocked and horrified, she stared at me open-mouthed. It may be that in the darker recesses of my soul I was searching for a way to harm her as she had harmed me in her betrayal, and for perhaps that reason a wicked little smile played on my lips as I observed her reaction.

"Oh my God. Oh…my…God," she said, standing suddenly and looking down at me in horror.

The noble, chivalrous boy who adored her and sacrificed so much for her had been slain, and in his place, occupying his seat, was a ruthless killer. It was as if the tie that bound us together broke in that instant, on that uneventful sunny afternoon while the sailboat glided away across the water, the sun shined down upon us, and the birds sang their song in the nearby maples. Our studies together in our little school room, our meals together with Elsie and Mother, the gifts that we had exchanged, the laughter and tears that we had traded, the secrets we had told, all of the shared experiences of our youth that bound us together in a spiritual tie that I thought would never end, were severed at that moment. I fancied that I could almost hear it break over the soft roar of the distant ocean. For the first time in my life, I saw Sophia not as the helpless little orphan girl that Mother had rescued from a nomadic life of poverty and ignorance. Not as the dirty-faced, illiterate, Tomboy, raised on a barstool, who we took into our family and accepted as one of us. I saw her simply as an agent of the court. An ambitious, inflexible, unforgiving attorney, not unlike her mentor Jerry Daniels. And she saw me as a killer.

"Go," I said, with my eyes on the blue sea in the distance. I didn't trust myself to look at her. Sophia stepped back hesitantly, stumbling in the shocked chaos of her troubled thoughts. "Go away," I added, still looking out over the water, summoning all of the cold reserve that I could find in my bitter, unforgiving heart. "I prefer to remember you as you were."

I sensed the pain, the shock, the heartache that she felt at that moment. She paused for just an instant as if to reconsider, then stumbled away. I heard her shoes clicking on the stone floor, and considered running after her. A second later the oak door creaked open, and closed. She was gone.

Elsie arrived a moment later carrying a tray with iced tea.

"Where's Sophia?" she asked, looking around.

"She's gone."

"Is she coming back?"

"No," I answered, barely able to find my voice, "she's not coming back."

Thomas Moore

"Oh Thomas," Nina said, closing the journal and setting it down, "how could you be so foolish?" Wearing a thoughtful frown, she walked to the window and looked out over the blue water of the little cove sparkling in the afternoon sunshine. But the image of sunlight and sparkling water was only a vague impression in her mind, like looking through a dirty window. Her thoughts were far away, of another time and place. A time nearly a century earlier. A place where fate determined that a boy and girl would collide in friendship under the branches of an old tree.

Lost in thought she remained at the window under the soothing warmth of the afternoon sun. When she turned at last, her pensive eyes fell upon the mantle. The silver vessel, so prominently displayed over the fireplace, filled the room with its cold, oppressive presence. She studied it curiously, becoming aware for perhaps the first time, of the authority and control it wielded. And like an observer who sees through a magician's trick, she smiled. How could she have not seen that before, she wondered?

The vessel, comfortable and secure in its honored place, asserted itself, confident that the epiphany in Nina's awakened eyes would be carried away by the force of its will. But her unwavering eyes held it in unprecedented disobedience, and it was taken off guard by the boldness of the coup. Secure in its power it nevertheless held firm, believing that a show of strength would end the defiance and quell the budding insurrection.

Her persistent gaze, so steady and true, would not be intimidated, however. Those gray eyes, so resolute and firm, began to realize their strength and power. For the first time ever doubt entered into the heart of the vessel. It began to waver, to diminish and fail, even as she grew stronger. But it would not go quietly. Too long had it been in control for that. It waged one last, great, impotent volley...and surrendered.

It felt strangely light in her delicate hand. She carried it outside, into the light of the afternoon sun, and set it on the paving stones that led across the yard. A cleansing breeze blew across the water carrying pardon up over the grassy hill. Nina closed her eyes in a painful moment of indecision. When she opened them at last, she reached a trembling hand to the vessel and removed the lid. Like a thief, the absolving breeze whisked over it, stealing away little by little the contents of the container, and scattering them forever in the wind.

"Goodbye, husband," she said, wiping the tears from her eyes. And to herself she added; "You're forgiven." With the burden of her husband's guilt lifted from her shoulders, she stepped back into the house wearing a relaxed, serene smile that she never thought possible after such a simple gesture. Too long had she blamed herself for her husband's infidelity. Too long had she borne the guilt.

Again her thoughts turned to Thomas and Sophia. The journal was on the chair where she set it.

May 22nd, 1933

Much time has passed since I last wrote in this journal. It's been years since Sophia walked out of my life. When she left that day some part of me went with her. The better part of me. My soul perhaps…or one of them.

I remember the events as though they were yesterday.

The house was empty once again. Elsie was gone. I sent her away. I never told her of my last conversation with Sophia, but that in itself was cause enough for her to suspect something was terribly wrong. She didn't question me about it; she wouldn't, of course. Instead, she went about the house in a small, quiet, way, being helpful where she could and watching me with a look of growing concern, as if I were ill or otherwise needed attention. It was that look, that expression, which began to weigh heavily upon me. I would see her at various times throughout the day, just watching me with a sort of puzzled frown mixed with concern. I thought it best that I have some time to myself, and she had not seen her parents since Christmas, so I sent her off to San Juan Island to visit them.

If I were restless before, I was even more so without my dear Elsie to speak with. The house felt so empty. I needed a distraction. Howard cautioned me in the strongest possible way not to resume my importing trade. Pity. It was just the sort of diversion I need. I went to the boat yard, started *Mary*, tossed the lines on the dock, and motored northwest to the back of Jones Island where no one could see me. In a little cove on the west side of the island, I dropped anchor and took a seat out on the foredeck in the bright summer sun. I napped for a while, rocked to sleep by the soothing waves, then swam to shore and walked along the sandy beach. About an hour before sunset, I swam back to the boat, weighed anchor, then motored back to the boatyard. It was dusk when I arrived. The gentle breeze that had been present all afternoon fled at dusk, and the boatyard was quiet, subdued. A setting sun at my back painted the dock, the pilings, the shop, everything in a tangerine glow. It was always quiet and still at dusk, but it seemed uncommonly so just then.

I pulled slowly to the dock, inching up behind *Diva*, and stepped off with a stern line to secure *Mary*. Scarcely had my foot touched the weathered planks when men suddenly sprang from behind trees, buildings, even my own parked car, and rushed toward the dock. Unconcerned, I moved to the bow of the boat and secured the bowline. Seconds later, I was shoved roughly up against *Mary* by the first few men to reach the dock. My hands were pulled around behind me and cuffed. Several others rushed through the open wheelhouse doors and boarded the vessel. I heard a commotion inside as a quick, frustrated search was performed. Moments later, they stomped out onto the stern deck.

"Nothing," one of them shouted to the agent on the dock as he stepped off the boat. The handcuffs were removed when the agent gestured to the officer who stood by.

"I think I've got some milk onboard," I said, rubbing my already sore wrists, "if you fellas want a drink. I can even warm it up if you like."

"Come on boys," the agent in charge, laughed. "Let this be a lesson to ya," he said, to me, and turned to follow the dozen or so officers who were heading back.

"Let it be a lesson to you," I said, with a smile. He nodded without turning and continued on.

I really didn't wish to go home after that. The house would be empty and dark. I had grown weary of reading and sitting and thinking about legal battles. I decided to drive out to Herbert's house. There wasn't much point to hiding our liaison, so I drove up to the front door and gave a knock. He was a bit surprised, given the late hour and unexpected nature of my call, and feared the worst when he saw me on his doorstep. He was wiping the sleep from his eyes when he opened the door, and I could see that he had fallen asleep in his chair next to the fire, which had burned out some time ago.

"Everythin' all right?" he asked, pulling his robe tight around him. "Jack hasn't been by," he added, dryly.

"I'm sorry, Herbert. I didn't mean to wake you," I answered, turning to go.

"No, no," he added. "Come in. I just dozed off. Had nothin' ta do."

Minutes later, we were seated before the faintly glowing embers of the dying fire. A little coffee table was between us, upon which he added a second teacup. Mine had tea, his something a bit stronger.

"Elsie won't be coming by this week," I said, searching for something to say. "She's gone to San Juan Island to visit her parents."

"That girl is a delight Thomas. Pleasant as a peach."

"You'll get no argument from me."

"Just lights up a room."

I looked about the room then. It was tastefully, elegantly furnished. There were overstuffed leather chairs, colorful throw rugs, and interesting works of art on the walls. There were also beautifully framed photographs of a lovely woman, stylishly arranged about the room in such a way that she was present whatever direction one looked. But it wasn't an overpowering presence. She just sort of happened to be wherever one's eye would naturally go.

"Is that Susan?" I inquired.

"A more lovely creature never drew breath on God's green earth." he answered, solemnly.

"She's beautiful, Herbert." I replied, as I continued to look about the room for other photographs. "Elsie mentioned you had a son."

"That'd be John," he said quietly, after a moment of reflection. "Yer probably wonderin' why there ain't any photographs."

I was wondering why there were no photographs of his son, but the pain that seemed suddenly etched upon his face said that I should mind my own business. I was wondering how I might change the subject when Herbert came to my rescue.

"It's all right, Thomas. It ain't what ya think. It's just, well…" Herbert produced the flask that he seemed always to have with him, unscrewed the cap, and topped off his tea with a generous pour. Then he replaced the cap and returned the flask to his robe pocket. "Ya see, when Susan passed, it was a slow, lingerin' illness. We both had plenty a time ta prepare. I held her hand many a night, and we had many a conversation. We said our goodbyes. So I can bear to see her beautiful face. It's pleasant." Herbert lifted the teacup and took a hefty pull on it. His face screwed up as always, and he put it down again on the table. "It wasn't like that with John. He was always a headstrong boy. Respectful, but willful, too. Island life didn't agree with him much. Too quiet. He wanted ta travel. See the world. We didn't have much money then. He figured he could see the world on Uncle Sam's dime, so he joined the Army. Got hisself killed in some farmer's field in France."

"I'm sorry Herbert."

"I never got ta say goodbye to 'im before he shipped out. Money was tight, ya see. I was takin' whatever odd jobs I could find. A fishin' boat was lookin' fer crew, so I signed up. Gone fer months at a time, ya know. When I got home, Mary said he had just shipped out. Never got ta say goodbye. I always felt like a bad father fer that. Never got ta see him again." Herbert finished the contents of his teacup, which of course was mostly bourbon, and I looked about the room, feeling ill at ease.

"I didn't know, Herbert. I'm sorry."

"Are the police still watching you?" he asked, returning to a subject that we were both more comfortable with.

"Oh, a little here and there. Not so much really," I replied, and my eyes drifted to the window. I could see the dock in the darkness, and Herbert's boat moored there, rocking with the gentle swells.

"She's fueled up," he said, following my eye.

"It's kind of late," I said, though I was intrigued.

"It always is," he answered, smiling.

"All right. Where to?"

"Well, I expect the Shack'll be needin' some booze pretty soon, an I hear yer a bit low on inventory. I say we go ta Sidney," he said, grinning ear to ear.

"I'll warm up the engine while you get dressed," I answered.

It was a warm summer night, dry and clear. The stars twinkling above seemed close enough to touch, and the waning gibbous moon glowed in the night sky. I had the cabin warm and comfortable when Herbert reached the boat. I saw him hurry eagerly along, leaning heavily on his walking stick as he negotiated the rough planks of his swaying dock that rocked with the sea. I tossed the mooring lines on the dock while Herbert settled in behind the wheel. His movements were slow, stiff, arthritic, and his palsied hand shook terribly as he reached for the throttle. But his excited eyes were alive and alert with the promise of intrigue and the mystery of what lay ahead. It warmed my heart to see the joy in his face. I had scarcely stepped aboard before he throttled forward in his eagerness, and we were underway. It didn't matter how many times I made the trip, there was always something fresh and exciting about it. I loved the salt air. The rocking of the boat. The ding of the navigation buoys. I couldn't get enough of the water. We motored along in silence, not feeling the need to fill the moment with conversation. The half moon lit the way well, and we were content to enjoy the journey quietly, alone with our thoughts in the darkness. In a few hours I recognized the gleaming lights of Sydney far ahead. Hearing the steady drone of the engine suddenly change pitch, I glanced beside me to find Herbert with one hand on the wheel, and the other pulling the throttle back. He allowed the engine to idle a moment, then shut it down. We were still an hour away. I wondered at the delay.

The boat rocked ever so slightly from side to side. Water lapped the wooden hull with a soothing cadence. Growing accustomed to the sudden quiet, I heard faint and far away the clang of a navigation buoy that sounded like a church bell carrying over the water. Herbert simply stood at the wheel, his eyes closed, rocking gently with the boat and wearing a serene smile as he savored the moment. We drifted with the current while nature went about its business, caring little for the boat that bobbed along in the dark water on that dark night, under the twinkling stars and shy moon. A little fog began to gather around us, little pockets of thin mist. I heard a blow like a sudden exhale of water and air and followed the sound to the port bow where the moonlight rippled on the dark water as the thin wisps of fog drifted along. A pod of orca whales passed through that moonlit patch, lunging and diving effortlessly through the thin veil of mist. The power and grace of movement was thrilling to behold. We watched for several minutes until they disappeared in the fog and darkness. Herbert bowed his head, as if silently thanking some higher power for the scene just witnessed, then started the engine once more and continued our journey. An hour later we were pulling up to the dock at Sidney Harbor. He edged the boat up in between two others at the dock, like an old pro, and I secured the mooring lines. We weren't expected of course, and the warehouse was closed, so we fell into the quarter berths and got some sleep.

I woke the next day to the thud of a crate hitting the floor and opened my eyes to blinding sunshine pouring through the cabin. Herbert had already been to the warehouse, and they were loading our shipment while he supervised from the dock, leaning heavily on his walking stick with his good hand and the other in his coat pocket where no one could see it. The cases were stored efficiently below deck by a couple of warehousemen who knew their business well, and we were ready to return. But it wasn't time to go back. Not just yet. Every officer and prohibition agent in the county knew Herbert's vessel, and it would mean certain arrest if we attempted to return before darkness. Even then, it would difficult with the gibbous moon revealing our presence. We dined at an outdoor table overlooking the pier and talked together for hours in the summer sunshine, with the sparlking blue water beside us and the gulls circling nearby. Herbert checked his watch several times as we spoke. In the early afternoon, I followed my mentor back to the pier. The more I was with him, the more difficult it was for him to disguise his infirmities. His palsied hand nearly always trembled if not arrested by the other, and his walking stick was employed everywhere except the boat, where he was always within easy reach of something to support him. But the defective hand still had grip. I saw that when he reached out, taking a grab rail in each hand, and pulled himself stiffly aboard the vessel. I considered helping a number of times when I saw him struggling, but to do so would have prompted acceptance on his part and acknowledgement of his need. So we took our time, and I pretended that I didn't notice his growing frailty.

I was surprised, and somewhat puzzled, when Herbert started the engine after I stepped aboard the vessel. It was my expectation that we would relax and converse until sunset and then begin our clandestine return under the cover of darkness, but Herbert seemed almost to have a schedule of some sort. It was with reluctant hands that I released the mooring lines and stepped hesitantly aboard, wondering if age were not diminishing my friend's mental capacity as it was his body. While we motored back over the blue sea, I considered where we might offload the cargo. There were several locations available, but all would require an approach that was hidden under the cloak of darkness, and with a gibbous moon in the night sky, there wouldn't be much cover. But Herbert simply motored on, making directly for the island as if there were no need for caution or concern.

An eagle joined us as we crossed, and captured my attention. He fell in next to us on our port beam, gliding along effortlessly, riding the breeze that held him aloft. He was at eye level, so close I could touch him, his sharp, keen eyes peering ahead. He would rise and fall ever so slightly with the changing breeze, but held his course following along beside. I was close enough to see the trailing edge of his black feathers flutter lightly as the wind passed over them. I turned beside me to see if Herbert noticed, and when I looked back the eagle was gone. Simply vanished. There was no sign of him in the blue sky above or anywhere around the boat. I was still pondering that when I glanced up to find that in my distraction the island had drawn quite near. We were only three or four miles away, and Herbert showed no sign of changing course or waiting for the cover of darkness. He was making directly for the dock outside the Shack. The building was at the top of a high bank and was reached by a little trail perhaps a quarter mile long that wound through the woods. It could not be seen from the water. But every officer in the county knew its precise location, and the approach to it was always watched.

With growing anxiety I looked beside me to find that Herbert maintained a fixed, determined, demeanor as he steered a course that could only result in our arrest. I snatched the binoculars that were always on the helm and turned them to port, where I saw a boat in the distance. It was far enough away that I could see little of it, but it looked as though there was a man in a dark uniform watching me with his own binoculars. Looking to starboard, I saw another boat about the same distance away. Upon it too was a man in a dark uniform, looking at me as I looked at him, through a pair of binoculars. Both boats were too far away for me to identify, but I was certain I knew their purpose. When I saw a puff of smoke rising from the starboard boat, indicating that he had started his engine, I knew what to expect. I had been looking at his port beam, but he had turned north, and was coming directly at us. So was the other boat on our port side. As both boats converged on us, I saw Herbert glance at his watch casually and bump the throttle forward a touch more. But his boat, like mine, was a displacement hull, and eight knots was the top speed. The boats pursuing us had planing hulls, and were skipping along on top of the water at a far greater pace than ours. I didn't see any way that we could reach the dock before we were intercepted. Even if we did, we would not be able to offload the cargo and escape. What was Herbert thinking? Was it his way of allowing Daniels to catch him without me turning on him? He stood at the wheel, a little bent with age, gripping it firmly with both hands as much to support himself as to guide the boat. The afternoon wind had built to seven or eight knots off our port quarter and the little swells rocked us about. I finally saw Herbert glance to starboard where he perceived the approaching vessel, then to port, where he also observed that danger, but still he seemed unconcerned by it all. If anything, there was a little touch of excitement in his otherwise unconcerned eyes. He was smiling and happy.

"How far do ya make her?" he asked, gesturing to the police boat on our starboard.

"Three…maybe three and a half miles," I answered, studying the boat as it bore down on us.

"About right," he replied, "and the other?" I turned to look at the other police boat.

"I'd say four."

"Good eye. She's gonna be a close one," he added, maintaining his course for the dock that was now about half a mile away. But I didn't see anything close about it. The police boats would reach the dock about the same time we did, and it was impossible to offload the cargo. We would be caught. There was no other way. They were probably marveling at our folly and their own good fortune.

Herbert seemed to shake off for a time the weary fatigue of his years, and stood a little taller at the wheel. He was enjoying himself. He was enjoying the game. A game we couldn't win. It was as if the excitement and danger were restoring his youth and vigor in some measure. He held fast the course, the slow, anxiously slow course, while the police boats sped toward us from both sides. They were close enough that I could see the badge glistening on the chest of the officer at the stern of the boat that approached from our starboard side. The other boat wasn't far behind. They were about a quarter mile away when I saw the starboard boat throttle back suddenly and the stern wave wash up under it, lifting it as it passed. The port side boat slowed too, not as abruptly, more reluctantly it seemed, and both boats idled in the water. Never had I been so relieved, or puzzled. I looked to Herbert, who seemed to expect that very reaction from the pursuing boats, but he simply smiled in response to my confused frown and pulled smartly to the dock where I saw Judge Jones and Mayor Barnes awaiting us, each with a drink in their hand.

"Cutting it a bit close, aren't you?" said Judge Jones, casually lifting his glass for a drink.

"Maybe just a bit," Herbert replied, "but I figured you'd be enjoying a sip about now."

I stepped off the boat and secured it to the dock. Herbert shut down the engines. The police boats, I noticed, were watching a short distance away. With the thrill of the chase over, Herbert was stooped and arthritic again. He hobbled stiffly from the boat, relying heavily on the handrails to support him, and joined his friends on the dock. Only then did I realize the cleverness of Herbert's strategy. Over half of the officers on the island could be found at The Shack when their shift was over. Nearly all of the attorneys went there. So did the judges. And the prosecutors. And the Mayor. By reaching the dock outside The Shack before the police boats could catch us they would think twice about arresting us, knowing their boss was probably inside having a drink just as they would be when they got off work. We could never do it again, but it worked that day. Herbert was brilliant. I grabbed a case and carried it up. It was mid-week and early afternoon, but the bar was always busy and Peterson was always happy to see me. He sent a few of his men down to carry the crates up, and I noticed that Judge Jones fell in step with them, and trailed along to the dock where he remained sipping his drink and watching as the cases were transferred from the boat to the dock, and then up the hill. With the judge close by, no one would think to bother us.

It was late afternoon when we returned to the dock at Herbert's house. I made fast the mooring lines, and he shut down the engine. He had been quiet for most of the trip after offloading the cargo, and I wondered what was on his mind. Mustering a smile, he thanked me for the best day he had experienced in years and shook my hand, but there was something he wasn't telling me. I noticed him at the dock when the crates were removed from the boat and he ran his hand (not the palsied one) over the perfectly varnished helm tenderly, as if saying goodbye. I saw it from the corner of my eye. It gave me pause. Was he simply getting old? Was he coming to terms with his age and health, realizing that he would soon be too old to use his boat? Or was it something else?

It was still sunny and warm. The sun was turning blood red, but hovered high over the horizon. It wouldn't be dark for hours yet. There was something he wanted to tell me. There was something I wanted to tell him. Neither of us knew how. We shook hands somewhat awkwardly, and shuffled our feet as I prepared to leave.

"I expected ya a few days ago, Thomas," he said, at last. "I thought ya might come out the other day."

"I thought about it, but didn't know what to say."

"I figured it must a been somethin' like that," he said. "Don't ya worry none. I'll be all right."

"You've heard about my situation? You know what Daniels wants?" I asked.

"I heard," he answered, grimly.

"But how? How do you know everything that happens on this island?"

"It's my job. How'd ya think I got away with it all those years?"

"I'm not helping them Herbert. I won't be the instrument of your destruction."

"You've got ta,Thomas. They've got ya dead ta rights. You'll go fer life if ya loose."

"Why does he want you so badly? What did you do to him?"

"I've never met the fella."

"Then why is he so determined to jail you?"

"Did ya notice he's runnin' fer Attorney General?"

"No."

"Well, ya really aught ta pay more attention."

"Why?"

"I don't suppose ya know who he's runnin' against?"

"No."

"Paul Burgett. That name ring any bells?"

"Maybe…" I answered vaguely. It had been years since I heard that name, and I never knew what became of the man.

"Ya really aught ta pay more attention. Burgett pinched me three times when he was District Attorney here. Beat 'em all, thanks ta Howard."

"How does that help us?"

"Daniels is after Paul Burgett's job, ya see. He figures if he can pull it off where Burgett failed three times, it'll make him look like a more competent attorney. It could be just the edge he needs ta win the election."

"That's it? That's all it is?"

"That's all there is ta it. Nothin' more."

"You astonish me Herbert. I have a notion that you could tell me which dogs on this island have fleas. You seem to know everything that happens here. I wonder," I said, thinking out loud, "how Daniels found out about the gaff?"

"Do ya now? Have ya no idea?"

"None whatsoever."

"Ya really aught ta pay more attention."

"But how could I know?"

"I've give ya the clues. Think a bit," he added, seeing that I was still stumped. "No? All right then. Moran just had a big fundraiser out there at the mansion ta bolster the Daniels campaign coffers. Now ole Moran likes ta show off his fancy new Franklin, so toward the end a the night when everyone's a bit giddy an feelin' no pain, he tells Daniels ta take the Franklin home for the night, which he does. And the next day when Daniels gets up and figures ta drive the car back out ta Moran, he's lookin' her over at his house, jus' sort a admirin' her an appreciatin' her, an finds a gaff inside which he takes particular notice of, and then a jack, too..."

"But how could you know all of this Herbert? How could you possibly know this? You speak as though you saw it."

"I have him followed," he answered with a grin that spread over his entire good-natured face.

"You have the District Attorney followed?" I asked, incredulously. "And he doesn't know?"

"I do a much better job a followin' him than he does a followin' me."

"Astonishing," I said, regarding Herbert with an even greater respect than I had for him before. "What happened then?"

"Well, back up a bit. There was a story in the paper sometime ago 'bout some escaped convicts that was found on the island." he said, studying my blank face. "They found two bodies on the rocks at the bottom a the cliff, an speculated that the other two was carried away by the sea. Well, Daniels was thinkin' a runnin' against Paul Burgett even back then, ya see, and wanted his face spread around as much as he could, so he rushes out there when he hears about the reporters and all the fuss they're makin' and gets in the middle of it. He gets his picture taken at the scene and says he'll personally oversee the investigation. They found tire tracks off a the side a the road, and all sorts of footprints and things in the soft ground, and they noticed a square depression that no one could make anythin' of.

"Now then, skippin' forward agin' ole Daniels drives out ta Moran's place ta return the car excited as the devil, and has lunch with Moran. And while they're sittin' together eatin', he asks Robert real casual like if he has allowed anyone else ta drive the Franklin. Well, Robert's so focused on his split pea soup, he loves split pea soup and his new chef makes the best around, he's so focused on his split pea soup that he doesn't even look up from it. He tells Daniels about Charles and Lorelei takin' the car one afternoon an not coming back until the next day because they had a flat tire and spent the night at yer house. Daniels was grinnin' like a canary-fed cat. He finished his lunch with Robert, and as he was leavin' he stopped at the Franklin and just sort of slipped that gaff up his sleeve, and measured the bottom of the jack. Then he drove up ta the turn out near the bluff, and measured the depression in the ground."

It was quiet after that. We sat in the boat rocking with the waves, thinking our own thoughts.

"What are ya thinkin' son? What are ya gonna do?"

"I don't know, Herbert."

"Well," he said, at last, "I got ya inta this, I can get ya out."

"How would you do that?" He seemed reluctant to answer. "You're not thinking of turning yourself in, are you?"

"Considered it, my boy, considered it. But that wouldn't work ya see. Fer Daniels ta get the recognition he's after, he needs ta catch me. He needs ta show that he beat me."

"Were you expecting to go to jail?" I asked, recalling how nostalgic Herbert was with the boat that day. "Is that why you wanted to take the boat out? Were you thinking you would be going to jail?"

"There's just no other way, lad. They've got too much against ya. If ya take it ta trial you'll lose."

"But Herbert, I can't..."

"Better me in jail fer six months," he said, interrupting me, "than you in prison fer life."

It was pointless for me to debate the virtues of his argument, so I did not. Instead, I simply shook his hand with a somber severity that allowed him to believe he had won. And as I walked up the beach to where my car was parked outside his house, I reflected on what a kind and generous spirit Herbert Mayer possessed. How old was his soul, I wondered? How wise was the man? But sacrificing that man (however brief it may be) to save myself was contrary to my own nature. It was abhorrent to my own spirit, my own soul. One may as well ask a Dalmatian to change his spots or a zebra his stripes. I looked back over my shoulder as I struggled through the soft beach sand and saw Herbert sitting on his boat, swaying ever so slightly with the little waves that rocked it. He was looking at the fiery ball of blood red sun that hung over the water, still an hour or so from touching the horizon. His back was bent with age, his head fell forward, his arthritic hands gripped the gunwales of the boat to keep his balance. He looked so old and fragile to me there and then, as he contemplated the next six months of his life in a prison cell.

Whether I had been born with a noble spirit or whether it had developed within me and was coaxed along by Mother and Father, I do not know, but it was as much a part of me as my heart and lungs and without it I could not draw breath. I was embarrassed, nay, ashamed, to think that I had for a time considered betraying my mentor, however briefly it may have been. How I would extricate myself from my vexing situation was still a mystery to me, but I knew with absolute certainty that it would not be by sacrificing Herbert Mayer. I started the engine, put the car in gear, and looked one last time over the sandy beach to where Herbert sat on his yacht, watching the lovely close of that beautiful day.

"You'll see many more," I said, to myself. "You'll see many more Herbert." And I drove away, feeling better about myself than I had in a good long time.

That Elsie was still away was a blessing to me. I could never deceive her or hide anything from her for long, and I dreaded the explanation that must follow when she saw the troubled, determined cast of my face. I went about my grandfather's house saying a silent goodbye to each treasured room that I had for so many years taken for granted. Daniels would take me into custody that very night, or at best, the following day. Stopping last of all at Mother's seat, I stood with a hand on the chair back watching the sun set into the blue ocean. I had seen that sunset so many times before, but it was never as precious to me as at that moment, when I thought to never see it again. Was Herbert still watching that sunset? Was Sophia?

Firm in my resolve and proud in my decision, I locked the door of the Moore estate for the first time in my life and climbed into the car.

It was late when I reached the courthouse building. The main entrance was still lit. So was a room on the second floor where I imagined Daniels' office to be, but all other lights had been extinguished. The building was closed by then and everyone had left for the day except for a janitor who was still mopping floors and cleaning windows. He glanced up casually from his mop, lifting his bald head and tired eyes, and continued working when he saw that he didn't recognize me. Daniels was seated at his desk running an eye over a document in one hand while pouring a stiff shot of scotch with the other. Hearing me at the door, he glanced up and then looked at his watch.

"Cutting it awfully close, Mr. Moore. I was just about to issue a warrant for your arrest."

"I wasn't looking forward to this," I answered, grimly.

"I can't tell you how many times I've heard that," he said, laughing. I could see that it wasn't his first scotch. The bottle was half gone, and so was he. There was a cold glimmer in his smirking eyes that said he held all of the cards and the game belonged to him. His suit jacket was on the chair behind him, his shirt collar was open, and his tie was knotted loosely at his neck.

"Care for a drink?" he asked, extending the bottle.

"No. Thank you."

He shrugged indifferently, then swirled the ice around in his glass and brought it to his lips, finishing it in a single gulp. He set the glass down on the desk, took a deep breath, exhaled.

"So, what's it going to be?"

"I think you know my answer," I replied, firmly.

"I do." He nodded. "I surely do. That's why I prepared a counter offer. But I have to tell you, Mr. Moore, this whole loyalty, nobility, chivalry thing, whatever you want to call it, isn't working out too well for you. You could spend all of your adult life in prison for murders you didn't commit. Why would you do that?"

"You know I didn't kill those men?" I asked.

"Oh sure," he said, pouring himself another drink. "The medical examiner said the gaff wounds were all superficial. It was the fall that killed them, and I seriously doubt that you could have thrown all four of those hardened criminals over that bluff. My guess is that they ran off the end of the trail in the darkness."

"That's right," I said. "That's what they did."

"What I figured."

"But you're still charging me?"

"Uh-huh," he said, nonchalantly, taking another sip of his drink.

"But the medical examiner..."

"Oh, he's moved to the east coast," he said, swirling the ice around his glass, "and I can't seem to find that report anywhere."

"It doesn't change anything," I said, after a moment of reflection. "I didn't know about that report, so it doesn't change anything. I'll take my chances in court."

"I was hoping you would be smarter than that," he said, cheerfully, and took another drink, "but I didn't think you would be. So here's what we'll do…"

"I know why you want Herbert," I said. "You believe a conviction will get you elected."

"That's exactly right. My campaign manager tells me it's just the little push we need."

"Well, I won't help you. You can't make Herbert's life a political chess piece. I won't allow it."

"I think you will."

"I won't."

"You know," he said, pouring himself another drink, "I've recently developed an interest in art. That painting at your house for example; you know the one, on the easel near the piano."

"What about it?" I answered, growing uneasy.

"Just captivating, wouldn't you say? Those blue eyes, for instance. Have you ever seen such blue eyes? It occurred to me as I was having lunch with Miss Nagel the other day where I had seen those blue eyes before." He watched me closely, looking for a reaction. I offered none. "I was always curious about your early parole. Even though the mandatory minimum was abolished after your sentence was imposed, it's rare for anyone to be released after only nine years on a murder charge like yours. So I did a little checking around. Seems the judge in your case was quite fond of you. Wrote a few letters to the parole board on your behalf. They're right here." He gestured to several pages inside his open briefcase on the desk. "They just arrived yesterday. Would you like to see?" He took another sip of his drink. "I also took a peek at your court transcript. Seems a young girl burst into the courtroom and confessed to killing the victim in your case.

"Here's the deal Mr. Moore. You give me Herbert Mayer, or I take Sophia Nagel. Either way I win. If I charge Miss Nagel with murder, I look like a hero for exonerating an innocent man and bringing the real killer to justice. If I prosecute Herbert Mayer, I'm the District Attorney who got a conviction where my predecessor failed three times. Your case was tried by Paul Burgett, so I look good, and he looks bad. I would rather have Mr. Mayer, but I'll settle for Miss Nagel."

I said nothing. When I entered Daniels' office that night it was with no clear purpose or intention of what I would do. My hope was that some course of action would present itself. That somehow Daniels would expose a weakness, or reveal a flaw in his plan. But his plan had no flaws. I could not save both of my friends, and had to choose which of them would go to prison. Daniels leaned back in his chair watching with amused delight.

"Oh, I should probably mention that Miss Nagel knew nothing about the raid at your boatyard. She learned about it only minutes beforehand, and insisted on going along. Mr. Moore...Mr. Moore..."

I still had not moved, or uttered a word. I was that dismayed, wounded, troubled, distraught, all of which must have shown clearly on my distressed face. Daniels found pleasure in my pain, and laughed heartily. With a callous smirk he swirled his scotch again, and lifted it to his lips for another drink. I thought about Herbert, that kind, generous old man who had lost his wife and son, and wanted only to enjoy his final years in peace at his own, lonely home. And Sophia. She had not betrayed me after all. I should have known that my childhood friend would never stoop to such a thing. Elsie knew, why did I not? And there was Daniels lifting the glass of scotch to his lips, his hypocritical, smirking lips, while I stared dumbly, confused and defeated. The look of gloating triumph in his shrewd, callous eyes was insufferable. It was a look I had seen in William. Rockwell, too. A look of cruel, pitiless, mirth. A look I could not bear.

I can't say for certain what happened next. I have no memory of crossing the room, or moving in the slightest. But when I came to my senses moments later, I was standing over Daniels with my hands locked around his throat while he struggled frantically to free himself. His manicured nails tore at my clutching hands, but I held him in a firm, unrelenting, grip. He was still sitting in the chair, his legs flailing wildly about kicking at the desk, kicking at me, while he looked up at me with wide, terror stricken eyes. At that moment, I was Smyth, burying my blade in the cruel heart of my drunken father. I was an injured child striking back at my abuser. I had a new understanding of Smyth and the chain of events that led to retribution and violence. I pitied him. I pitied myself for what I had become. But I did not release my hold.

The clawing fingers convulsed weakly, and fell lifeless to his side. His legs sagged. His terrified eyes closed. His body slumped in the chair. In a stunned sort of stupor I realized that I should remove my hands from his throat, and stepped back. He was dead. I had killed Jerry Daniels.

The janitor was gone when I exited the building. He had seen me, of course, and could identify me, but I cared little of that. I entered my home with a strange sense of peace that I never would have thought possible under the circumstances. It was still summer and quite warm, but a storm had arrived suddenly in the night, bringing wind and rain with it. I made a fire simply to watch it, and sat close, watching the flames flicker in the dark room, taking comfort in the dancing firelight while the wind gusted and the rain fell musically upon the rooftop. Not since I was a child had I felt so warm and comfortable, or so safe and trouble free. There was a tranquil calm in the stillness of the quiet night and the certainty of what would happen next. I almost imagined Mother reading beside me by the light of the fire as my ten-year-old eyes peered through the rain spattered window at Father's storm beaten headstone. I could almost feel her slender fingers in my hair.

When the fire burned out, I roused myself and went to bed, knowing to an absolute certainty that it would be my last night at Ravenswood. I slept well, free of any troublesome dreams, and woke the next day refreshed. A modest breakfast of hash browns and eggs followed, then I slipped into my best suit, left a brief, heartfelt note for Elsie on the dining table, and paused at the doorway for one last look at my home. Carved into the stone walls of the old house was the story of my life, and the lives of those before me. Never had I imagined leaving it in such a manner. Never had I imagined the Moore line ending in such an infamous way. I locked the door for the second time in my life, climbed into the car, and drove away without looking back.

Howard was sitting at his desk, holding the phone over the cradle as if he had just finished a conversation, and forgot to hang up. The expression on his face was one of surprise or wonder. Seeing me in the doorway of his office he realized the phone in his hand, and set it in the cradle.

"Thomas," he said. "I just spoke to the District Attorney's office."

"Yes?" I answered, with bated breath.

"Well, they're," he began, disbelieving his own words, "they're dropping all charges except the two counts of smuggling."

"What?" I said, disbelieving my ears.

"Apparently Sophia Nagel is handling the case now, entirely, and is recommending probation for both offenses."

"What about Daniels?"

"He authorized it. He said she could handle the case as she liked."

"When?" I asked, still unable to believe my ears. "When did he say that?"

"This morning."

"Are you sure?"

"Quite sure."

I never saw Daniels again. I never unraveled how he survived the attack that night. Perhaps he simply passed out. Perhaps that's what happened. I've thought about it hundreds of times and always shudder with the somber realization that my own life, my own future, hung in the balance. For my part, I cannot think about the men I witnessed in my incarceration who were serving a life sentence or marching to the gallows for a murderous act committed in a moment of passion; I cannot think of such men without sympathy and an understanding of their pain.

Daniels too, may have paused to reflect. I imagine him waking slowly in his quiet office sometime after I departed, slumped in his chair, unable to speak, his neck and throat twisted and sore. Would he not think about his own actions? Would he not consider how very close he came to death? Would he not reconsider his own life?

I saw Sophia only once more. She appeared in court at the table beside me just long enough to recommend probation for my offenses, and quickly departed when the sentence was pronounced. Not once did she look my way or acknowledge my presence. Elsie told me one day, months later, as we sat eating lunch one afternoon, that Sophia had moved back to the east coast. Boston or DC or some such place, she heard. The news was delivered quietly, sadly, as she sat beside me at the dining table, peering out over that great lonely sea that seemed to stretch on forever. Perhaps it was the vastness of that ocean view that invited lonely, melancholy thoughts. I could not look upon it without a gentle sadness, but that could be said of the house, too. It was lonely, even with Elsie there, and we were both restless.

She remarked to me one day after lunch that it was the sixth of May. I made no answer, wondering what was significant about that day, but she offered no explanation. The rain, which had fallen unceasingly for days, cleared away that morning, and the sun shined down upon the blossoming flowers and budding trees with the promise of new beginnings and new life, as only spring can do. I had been waiting for just such a day to escape the stale air of the house, and slipped out after lunch. Wandering ever further on the grounds, I found myself on the overgrown little path that led over the rushing creek to the bluff. I discovered a broken tree limb on the ground, which I used to clear away the grass and brambles that encroached upon the trail, and came at last upon the Pimpernel Tree. Then it struck me. May sixth was the day that I first met the little tomboy who had so changed our lives. The tree was so much bigger. Five feet across at the bottom and tall enough that I couldn't see the top. Fir needles on the ground cushioned my approach. The tree limb in my hand hung at my side. I stood with my hand on the rough bark of the old fir looking out over the bluff at the blue sea, thinking about a blue-eyed tomboy that I had met in that place so very long ago.

And then something strange. Among the birds singing in the tall timber, and the calling squirrels darting about the trees, and the buzzing bees floating lazily past, I heard my name whispered softly in the breeze. Looking around me I saw no one, but I was certain I heard the soft, wistful call of "Thomas." Stepping in front of the tree, I saw her. She was sitting in the broken old winter dance canoe. With one leg bent and her arm upon it, she chewed on a piece of grass while looking out despondently over the water. Hearing a twig break under my foot she whirled around suddenly, and I saw panic on her frightened face. I may have looked just like little Captain Moore pursuing pirates, with the tree limb in my hand again serving as a make believe sword. She was barefoot, wearing her tomboy pants and flannel shirt, just like my little Sophia. Tilting her head, she looked up at me with a tentative, uncertain smile, until she saw the expression on my face. Then she relaxed into a relieved grin. I sat down beside her in the canoe. She bit her lip shyly, took my hand in her own, and looked back over the blue water with tears in her blue eyes…

In the stillness of the quiet evening Nina heard a soft, distant rumble, and lifted her eyes from the journal to find a magnificent vessel turn the point and enter the cove. The blue water broke gracefully on her plum bow as her elegant hull cleaved the lake like a knife. Nina watched Mary Adda *glide across the cove so beautifully, and pull up to the dock below her house. The handsome* Mary Adda, *so rich in history, so ripe with intrigue. How many secrets did she keep in her silent timbers? She felt as though* Mary *were an old friend.*

There were more pages in the journal, many more pages. Whether they were filled or blank, she didn't know, but she shut the broken old book, and set it down, eager to begin her own chapter.

Mary Adda has returned to Seattle's Lake Union, and now resides within sight of the shop where she was launched so many
years ago. After nearly ninety years of cruising Lake Washington, Lake Union, and the San Juan Islands, she's mostly at
rest these days, but when she's feeling social she makes herself
available to admiring guests. DreamBoatSeattle.Com

KEVIN KINCHELOE

To my dear friend Ray

Made in the USA
San Bernardino, CA
09 August 2017